P9-DXN-375

CARTOON NETWORK

OVER THE GARDEN WALL

HOLLOW TOWN

kaboom!

OVER THE GARDEN WALL: HOLLOW TOWN, July 2019.
Published by KaBOOM!, a division of Boom Entertainment,
Inc. OVER THE GARDEN WALL, CARTOON NETWORK,
the logos, and all related characters and elements are trademarks
of and © Cartoon Network. A WarnerMedia Company. All
rights reserved. (S19) Originally published in single magazine
form as OVER THE GARDEN WALL: HOLLOW TOWN
No. 1-5 © Cartoon Network. A WarnerMedia Company. All
rights reserved. (S19) KaBOOM!™ and the KaBOOM! Logo
are trademarks of Boom Entertainment, Inc., registered in
various countries and categories. All characters, events, and/
or institutions depicted herein are fictional. Any similarity
between any of the names, characters, persons, events, and/or
institutions in this publication to actual names, characters, and
persons, whether living or dead, events and/or institutions is
unintended and purely coincidental. KaBOOM! Does not read
or accept unsolicited submissions of ideas, stories, or artwork.

For information regarding the CPSIA on the printed material,
call: (203) 595-3636 and provide reference #RICH - 844878.

BOOM! Studios, 5670 Wilshire Boulevard, Suite 400, Los
angeles, CA 90036-5679. Printed in USA. First Printing.

ISBN: 978-1-68415-383-1, eISBN: 978-1-64144-366-1

CN
CARTOON NETWORK

Over the Garden Wall

Hollow Town

CREATED BY PAT MCHALE

WRITTEN BY CELIA LOWENTHAL

ILLUSTRATED BY JORGE MONLONGO
WITH COLOR ASSISTANCE BY KIKE J. DÍAZ

LETTERS BY MIKE FIORENTINO

COVER BY MIGUEL MERCADO

DESIGNER
MARIE KRUPINA

SERIES EDITOR
WHITNEY LEOPARD

ASSISTANT EDITOR
MICHAEL MOCCIO

COLLECTION EDITOR
MATTHEW LEVINE

WITH SPECIAL THANKS TO JIM CAMPBELL AND VERY SPECIAL THANKS TO MARISA MARIONAKIS, JANET NO, BECKY M. YANG, PERNELLE HAYES AND THE WONDERFUL FOLKS AT CARTOON NETWORK.

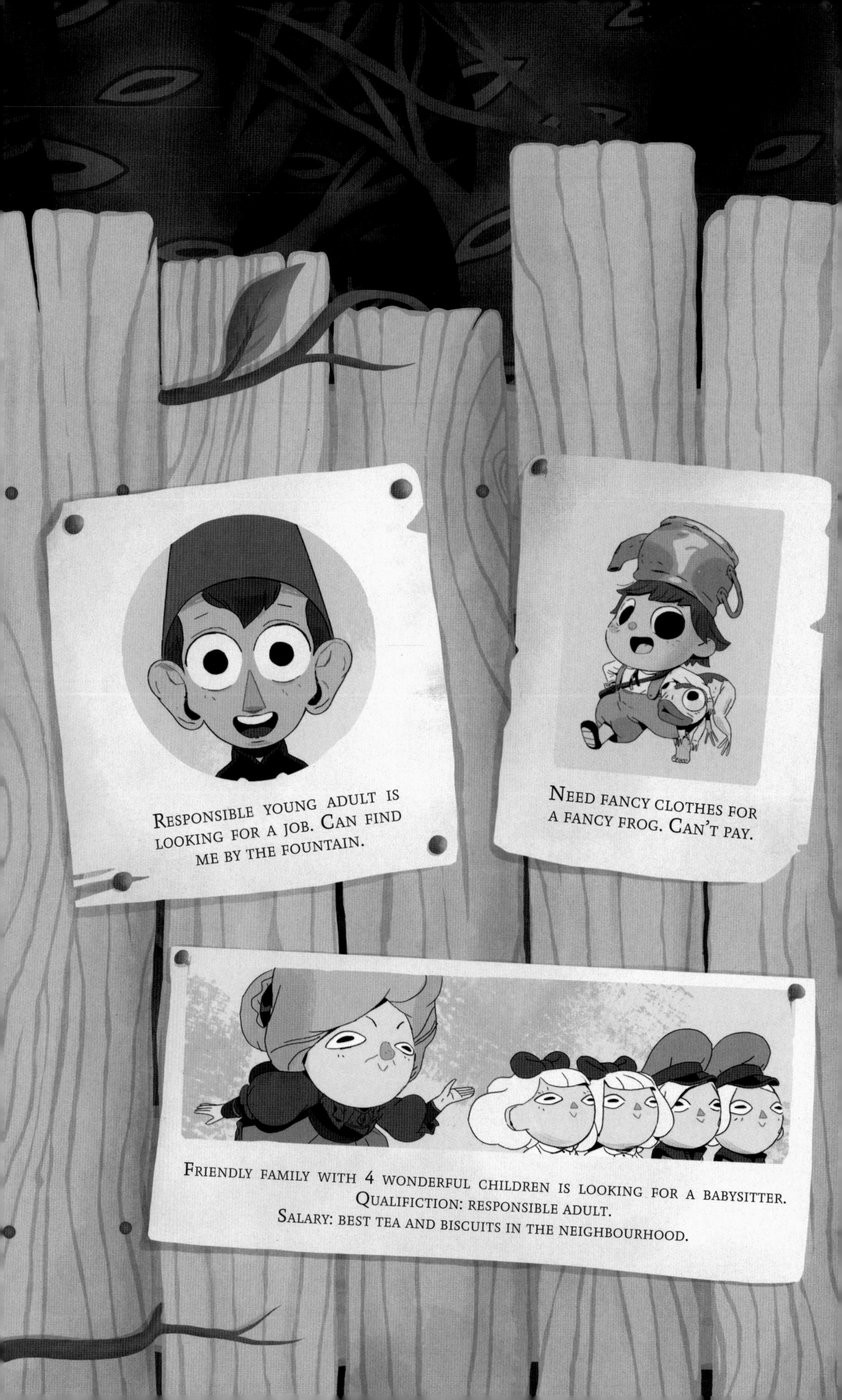
RESPONSIBLE YOUNG ADULT IS LOOKING FOR A JOB. CAN FIND ME BY THE FOUNTAIN.
NEED FANCY CLOTHES FOR A FANCY FROG. CAN'T PAY.
FRIENDLY FAMILY WITH 4 WONDERFUL CHILDREN IS LOOKING FOR A BABYSITTER.
QUALIFICTION: RESPONSIBLE ADULT.
SALARY: BEST TEA AND BISCUITS IN THE NEIGHBOURHOOD.

MEMORY IS A STRANGE THING, YOU SEE. SO FLEETING FOR
US MORTALS: YOU MIGHT NOT NOW REMEMBER WHAT YOU
ATE FOR YESTERNIGHT'S SUPPER OR THE NAME OF YOUR
CHILDHOOD BABYSITTER. BUT THE PLACES WE'VE BEEN,
THE PATHS WE'VE WALKED, THE THINGS WE'VE SEEN—
THEY NEVER TRULY FORGET US!

YOU MAY NOT LIKE IT, LITTLE ONE, BUT YOUR FOOTPRINTS
STILL LIE WHERE YOU SAW THEM LAST, AND THE TREE'S
BARK STILL SMARTS WHERE YOU CHOPPED AT IT. TIME IS OF
NO MATTER TO THE WOODS, YOU KNOW, AND THEY DON'T
FORGIVE EASILY.

SO, IF YOU EVER FEEL THAT YOU LEFT A PIECE OF YOURSELF
BEHIND SOMEWHERE—WONDER WHY NO LONGER. SOME
ORPHANED HALF OF YOUR SOUL IS STILL WANDERING
HERE, IN THE IMPENETRABLE PAST. BE GLAD YOU LEFT IT
BEHIND—YOU OUTGREW IT, AFTER ALL!

CHAPTER 1

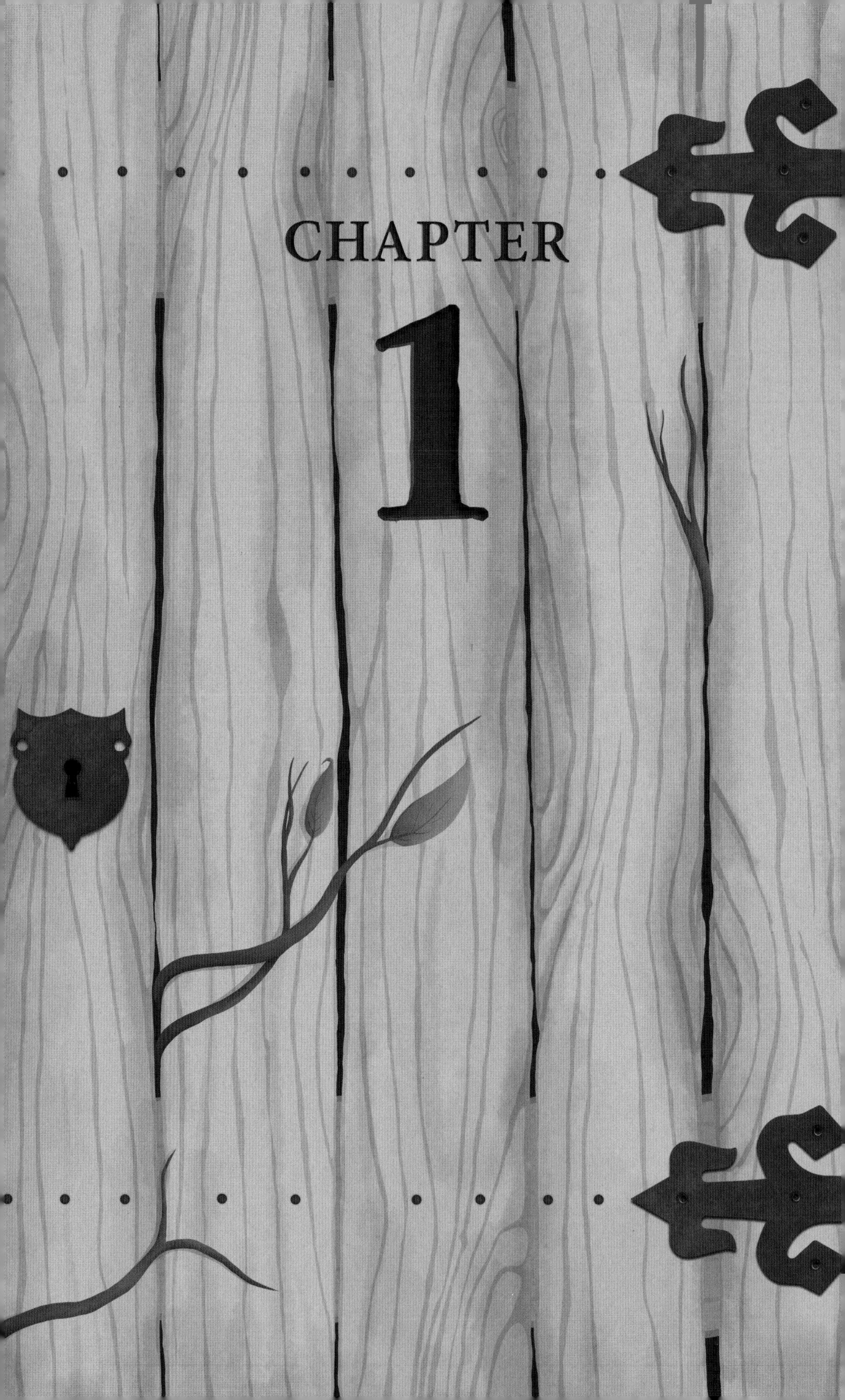

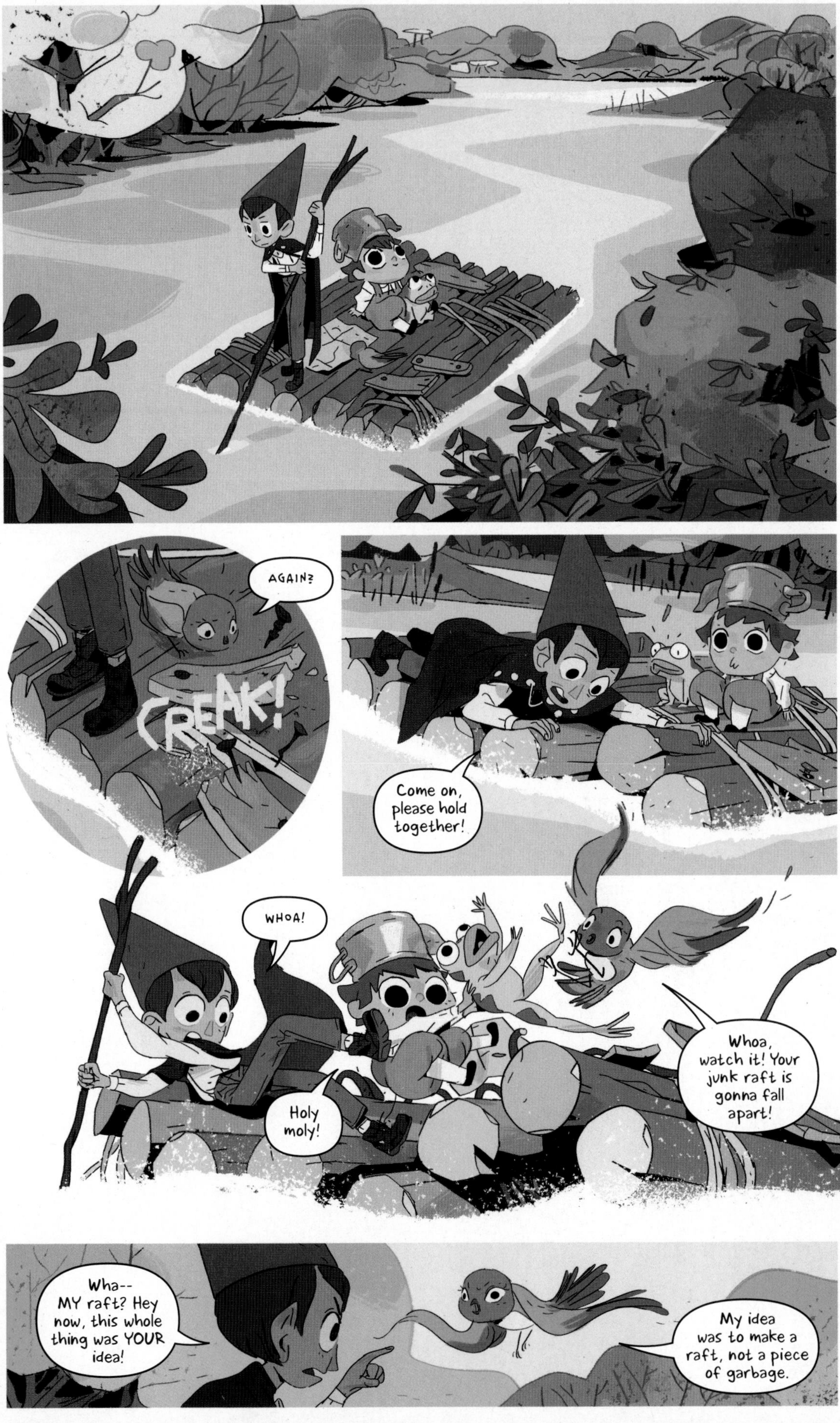
AGAIN?
CREAK!
Come on, please hold together!
WHOA!
Holy moly!
Whoa, watch it! Your junk raft is gonna fall apart!
Wha-- MY raft? Hey now, this whole thing was YOUR idea!
My idea was to make a raft, not a piece of garbage.

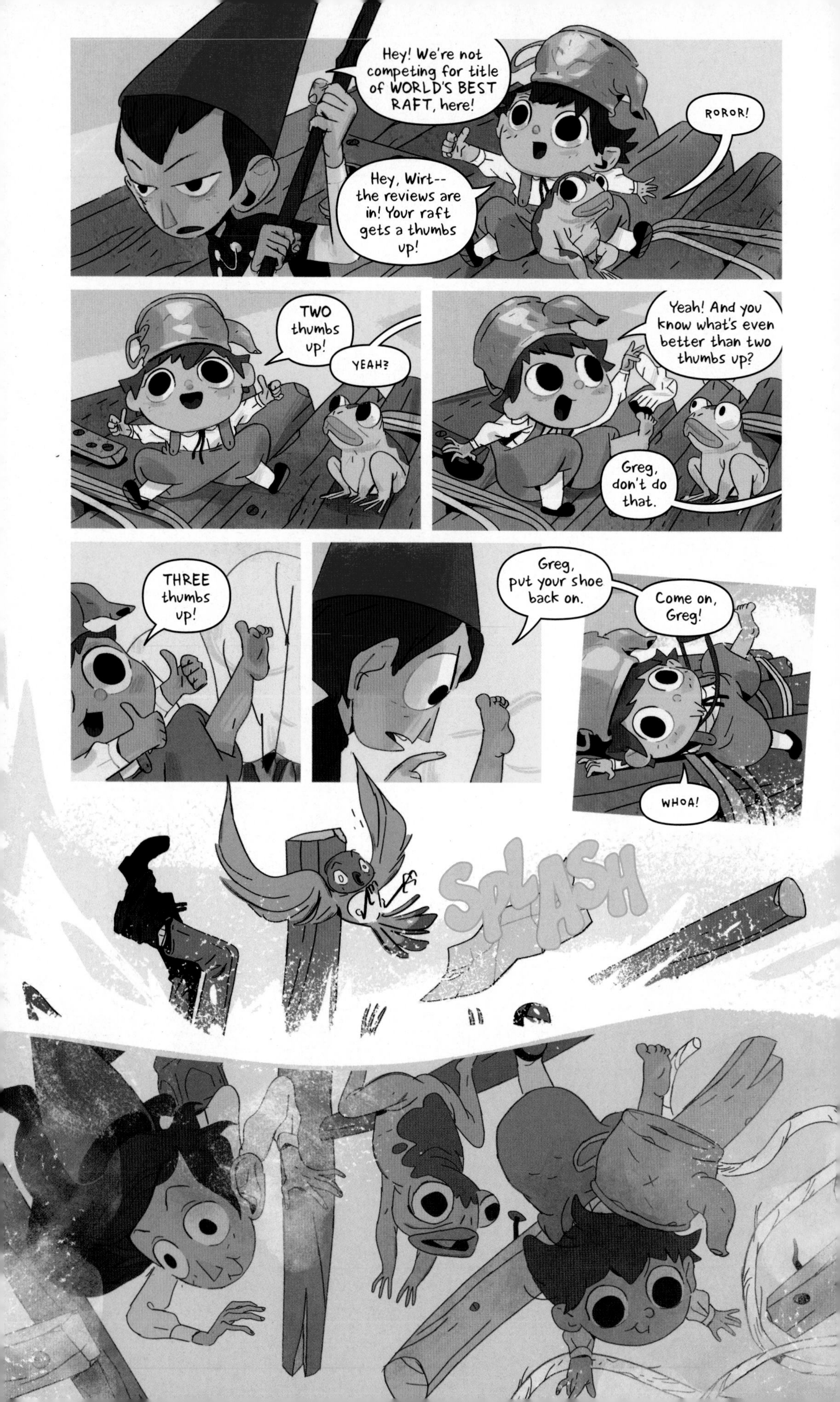

Hey! We're not competing for title of WORLD'S BEST RAFT, here!
RORОR!
Hey, Wirt-- the reviews are in! Your raft gets a thumbs up!
TWO thumbs up!
YEAH?
Yeah! And you know what's even better than two thumbs up?
Greg, don't do that.
THREE thumbs up!
Greg, put your shoe back on.
Come on, Greg!
WHOA!
SPLASH

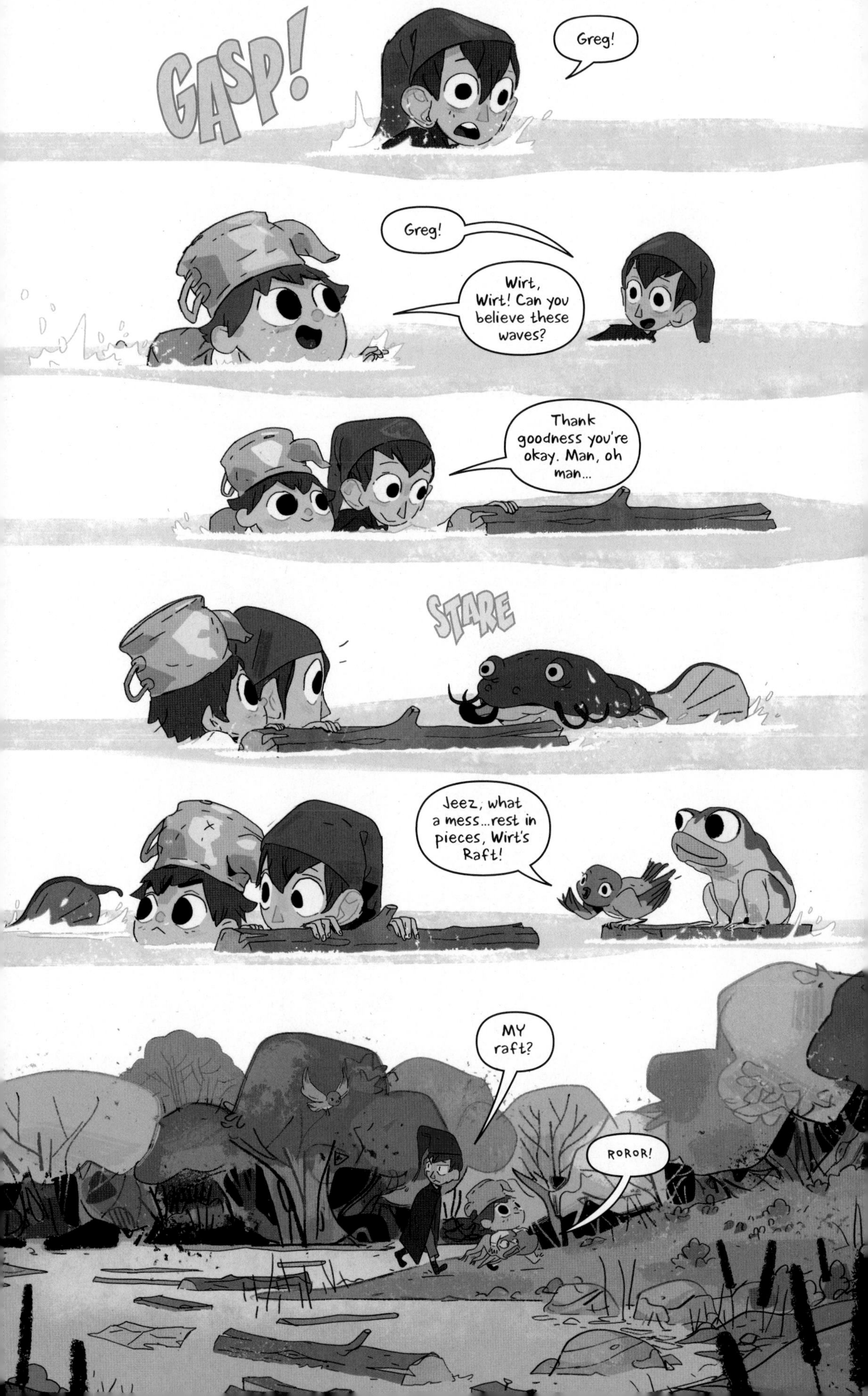
GASP!
Greg!
Greg!
Wirt, Wirt! Can you believe these waves?
Thank goodness you're okay. Man, oh man...
STARE
Jeez, what a mess...rest in pieces, Wirt's Raft!
MY raft?
ROROR!

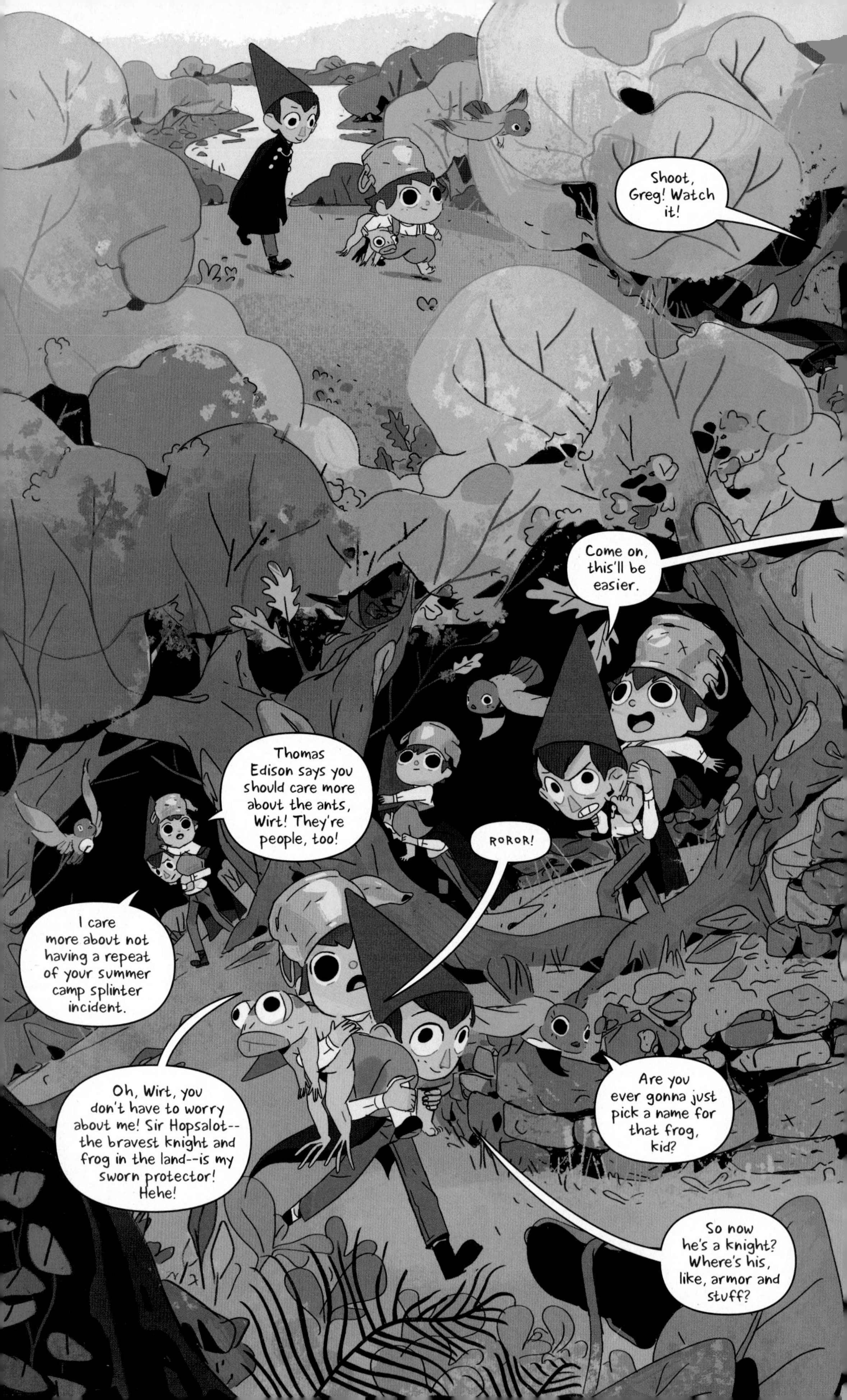

Shoot, Greg! Watch it!
Come on, this'll be easier.
Thomas Edison says you should care more about the ants, Wirt! They're people, too!
RORОR!
I care more about not having a repeat of your summer camp splinter incident.
Oh, Wirt, you don't have to worry about me! Sir Hopsalot--the bravest knight and frog in the land--is my sworn protector! Hehe!
Are you ever gonna just pick a name for that frog, kid?
So now he's a knight? Where's his, like, armor and stuff?

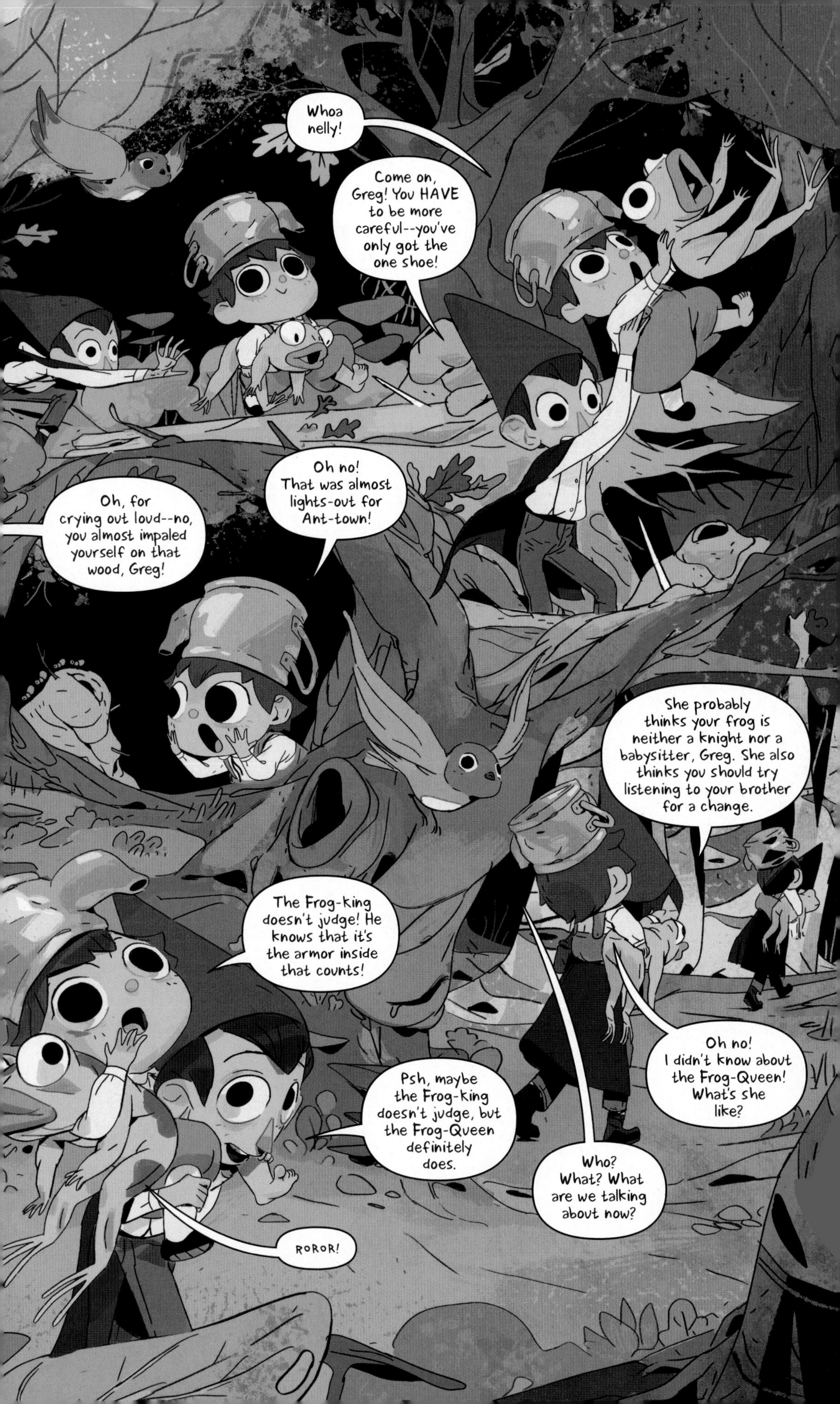
Whoa nelly!
Come on, Greg! You HAVE to be more careful--you've only got the one shoe!
Oh, for crying out loud--no, you almost impaled yourself on that wood, Greg!
Oh no! That was almost lights-out for Ant-town!
She probably thinks your frog is neither a knight nor a babysitter, Greg. She also thinks you should try listening to your brother for a change.
The Frog-king doesn't judge! He knows that it's the armor inside that counts!
Oh no! I didn't know about the Frog-Queen! What's she like?
Psh, maybe the Frog-king doesn't judge, but the Frog-Queen definitely does.
Who? What? What are we talking about now?
ROROR!

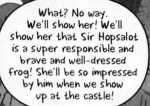

What? No way. We'll show her! We'll show her that Sir Hopsalot is a super responsible and brave and well-dressed frog! She'll be so impressed by him when we show up at the castle!

No, no, we're not doing that! We're just trying to find the road. Come on, chop chop!

Don't look at me, I didn't start this Frog-Queen business.

You LITERALLY did, though!

Man, it's like a funeral procession with you guys. Can't we pick up the pace a little?

Hff, I'm trying my best here, okay!

Hey, Wirt--are these trees creepy, or what? They all have eyes! They're TOTALLY judging you--don't you wanna skedaddle out of here?

Oh, for-- they're just trees, Beatrice. They're not, like, alive. And I'm not STUPID.

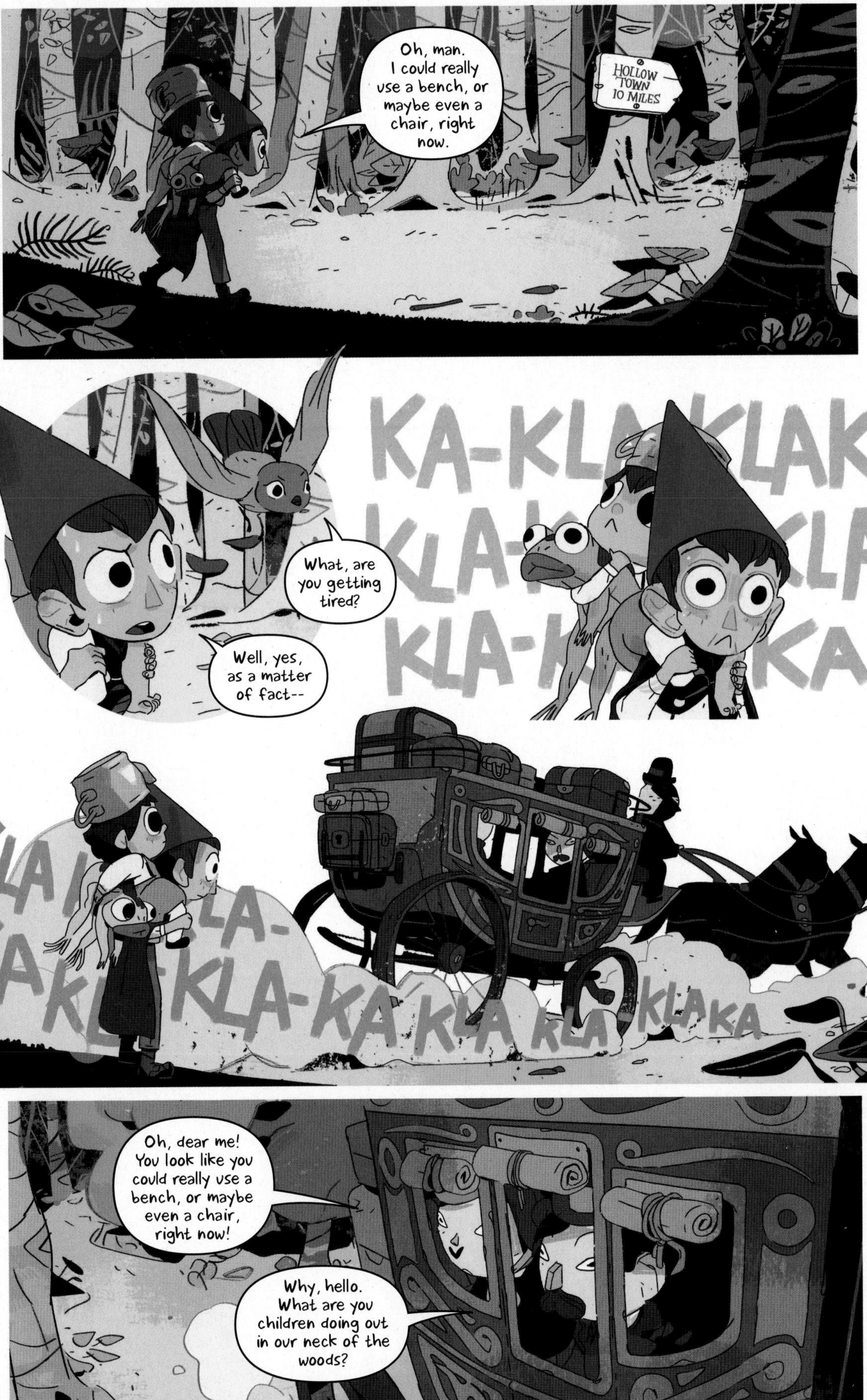
Oh, man. I could really use a bench, or maybe even a chair, right now.
HOLLOW TOWN 10 MILES
What, are you getting tired?
Well, yes, as a matter of fact--
KA-KLA KLAK-
KLA-K KLA
KLA-K KA
KLA-KA KLA KLA KLA KA
Oh, dear me! You look like you could really use a bench, or maybe even a chair, right now!
Why, hello. What are you children doing out in our neck of the woods?

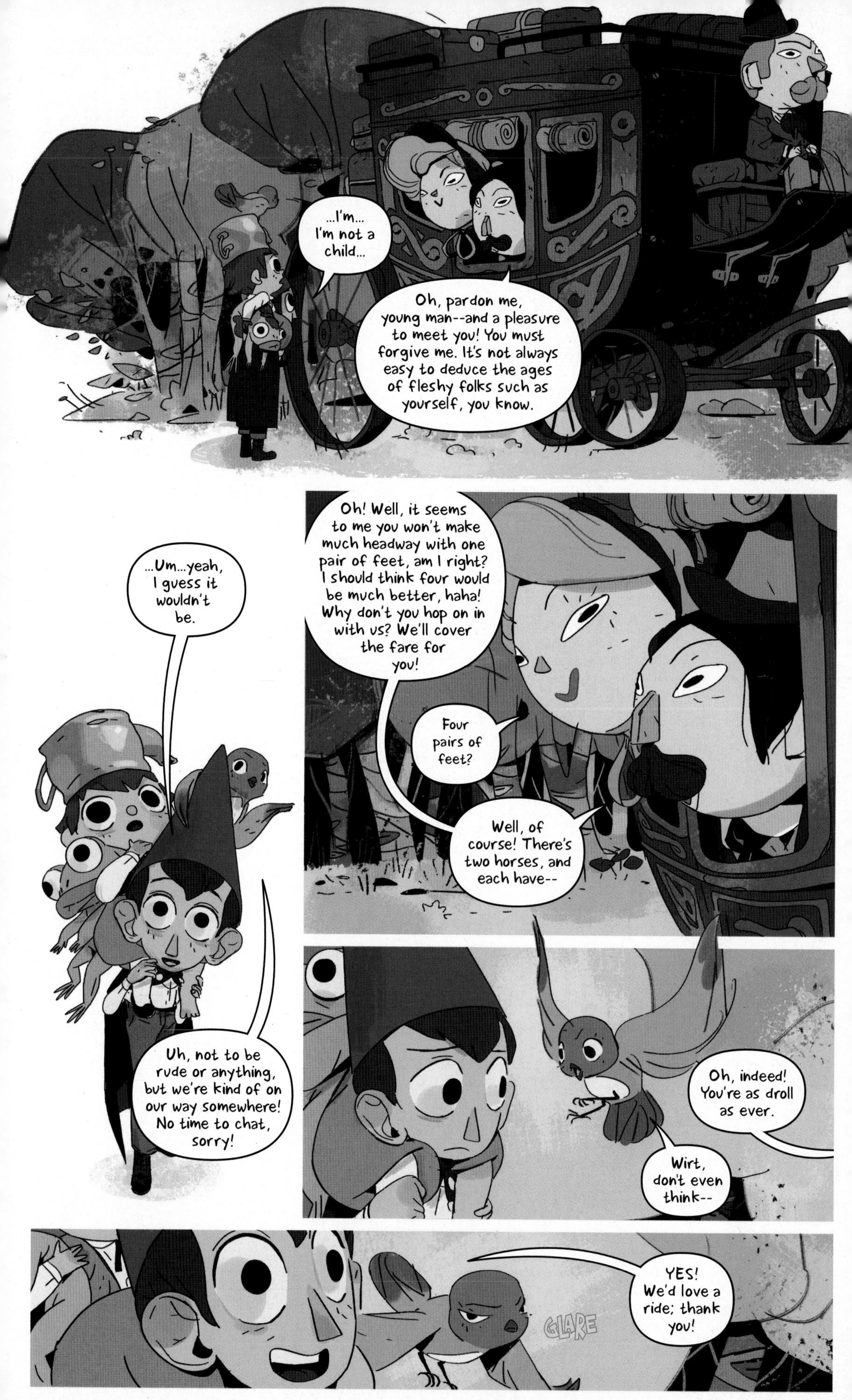
...I'm... I'm not a child...
Oh, pardon me, young man--and a pleasure to meet you! You must forgive me. It's not always easy to deduce the ages of fleshy folks such as yourself, you know.
...Um...yeah, I guess it wouldn't be.
Uh, not to be rude or anything, but we're kind of on our way somewhere! No time to chat, sorry!
Oh! Well, it seems to me you won't make much headway with one pair of feet, am I right? I should think four would be much better, haha! Why don't you hop on in with us? We'll cover the fare for you!
Four pairs of feet?
Well, of course! There's two horses, and each have--
Oh, indeed! You're as droll as ever.
Wirt, don't even think--
GLARE
YES! We'd love a ride; thank you!

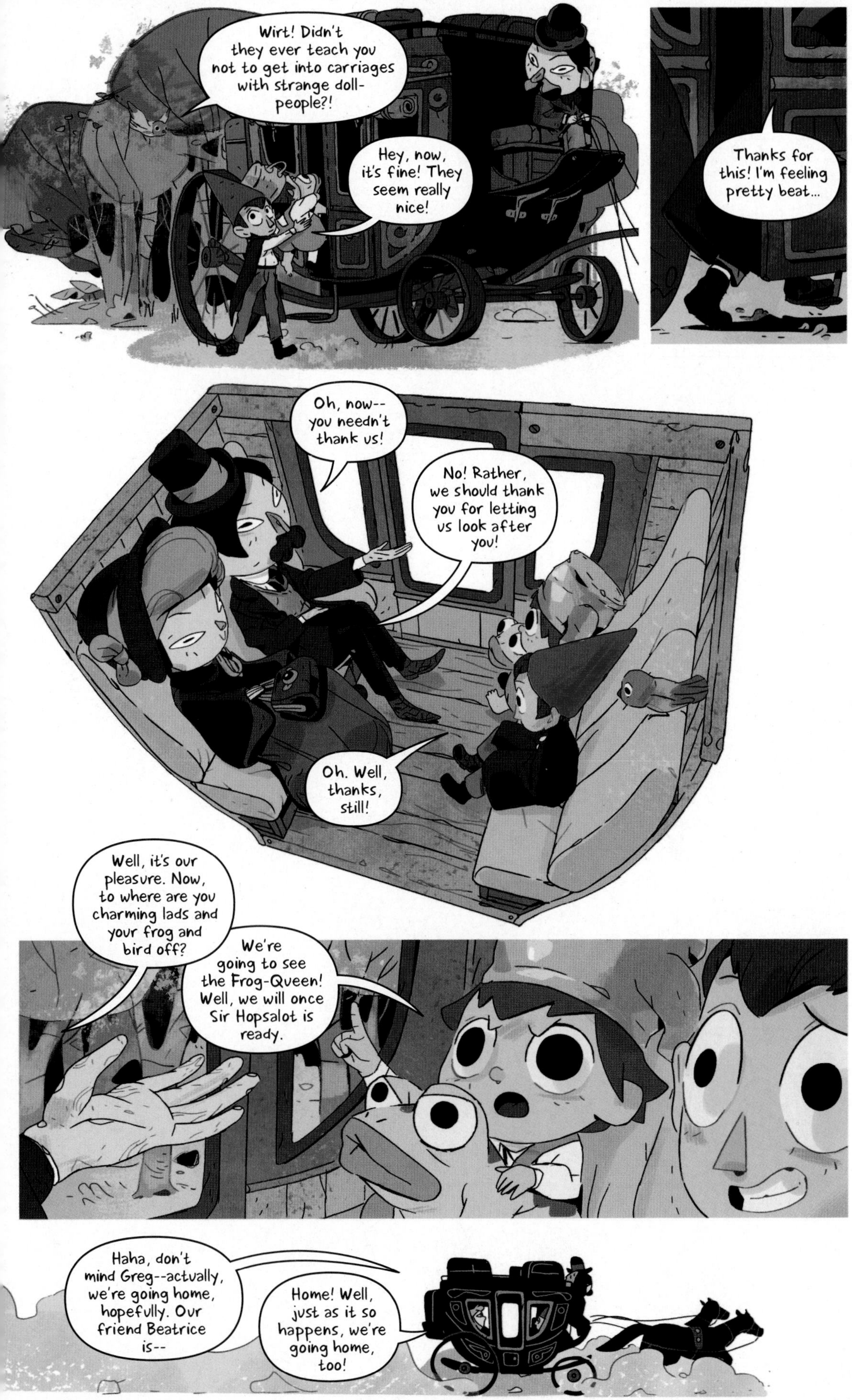
Wirt! Didn't they ever teach you not to get into carriages with strange doll-people?!
Hey, now, it's fine! They seem really nice!
Thanks for this! I'm feeling pretty beat...
Oh, now-- you needn't thank us!
No! Rather, we should thank you for letting us look after you!
Oh. Well, thanks, still!
Well, it's our pleasure. Now, to where are you charming lads and your frog and bird off?
We're going to see the Frog-Queen! Well, we will once Sir Hopsalot is ready.
Haha, don't mind Greg--actually, we're going home, hopefully. Our friend Beatrice is--
Home! Well, just as it so happens, we're going home, too!

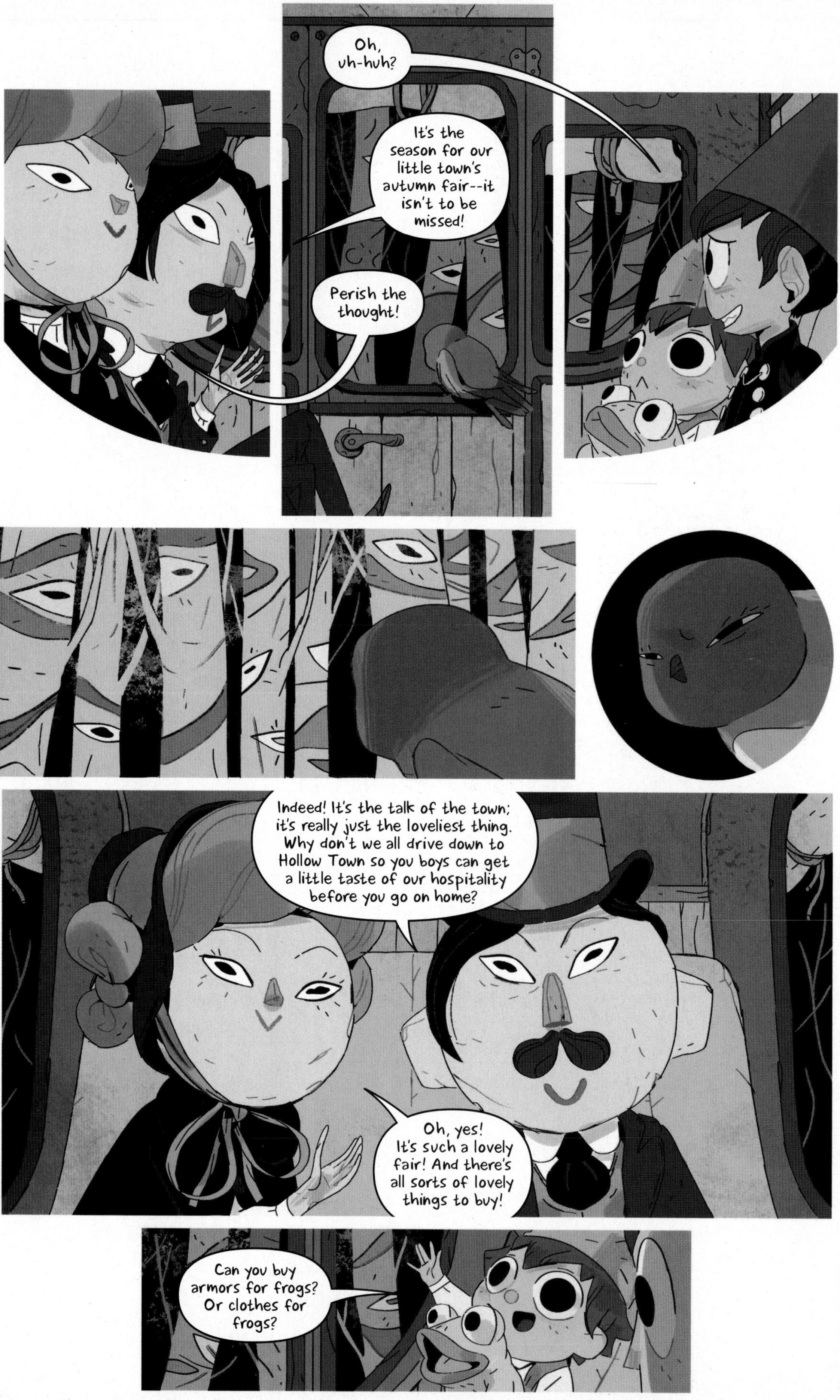
Oh, uh-huh?
It's the season for our little town's autumn fair--it isn't to be missed!
Perish the thought!
Indeed! It's the talk of the town; it's really just the loveliest thing. Why don't we all drive down to Hollow Town so you boys can get a little taste of our hospitality before you go on home?
Oh, yes! It's such a lovely fair! And there's all sorts of lovely things to buy!
Can you buy armors for frogs? Or clothes for frogs?

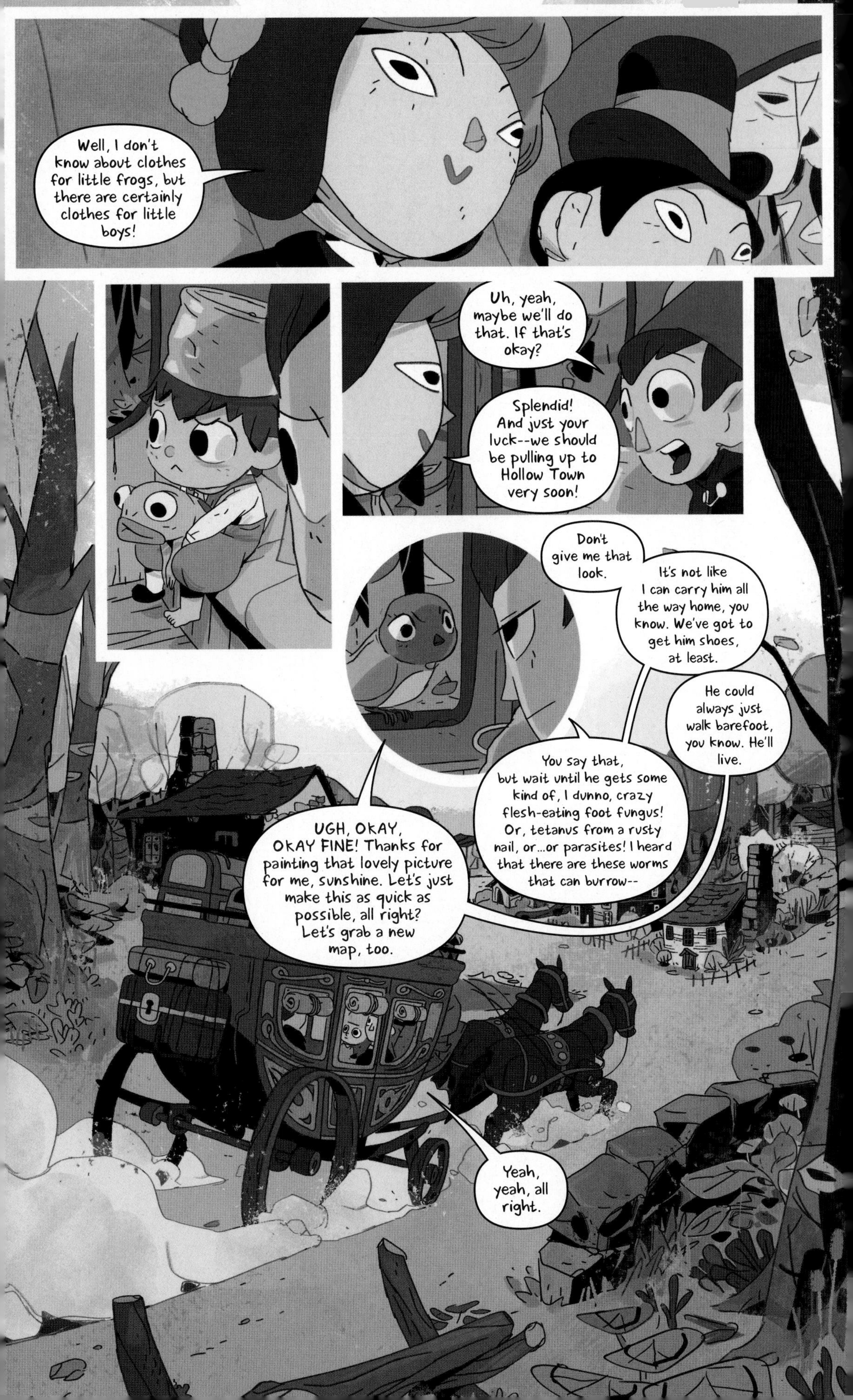

Well, I don't know about clothes for little frogs, but there are certainly clothes for little boys!
Uh, yeah, maybe we'll do that. If that's okay?
Splendid! And just your luck--we should be pulling up to Hollow Town very soon!
Don't give me that look.
It's not like I can carry him all the way home, you know. We've got to get him shoes, at least.
He could always just walk barefoot, you know. He'll live.
You say that, but wait until he gets some kind of, I dunno, crazy flesh-eating foot fungus! Or, tetanus from a rusty nail, or...or parasites! I heard that there are these worms that can burrow--
UGH, OKAY, OKAY FINE! Thanks for painting that lovely picture for me, sunshine. Let's just make this as quick as possible, all right? Let's grab a new map, too.
Yeah, yeah, all right.

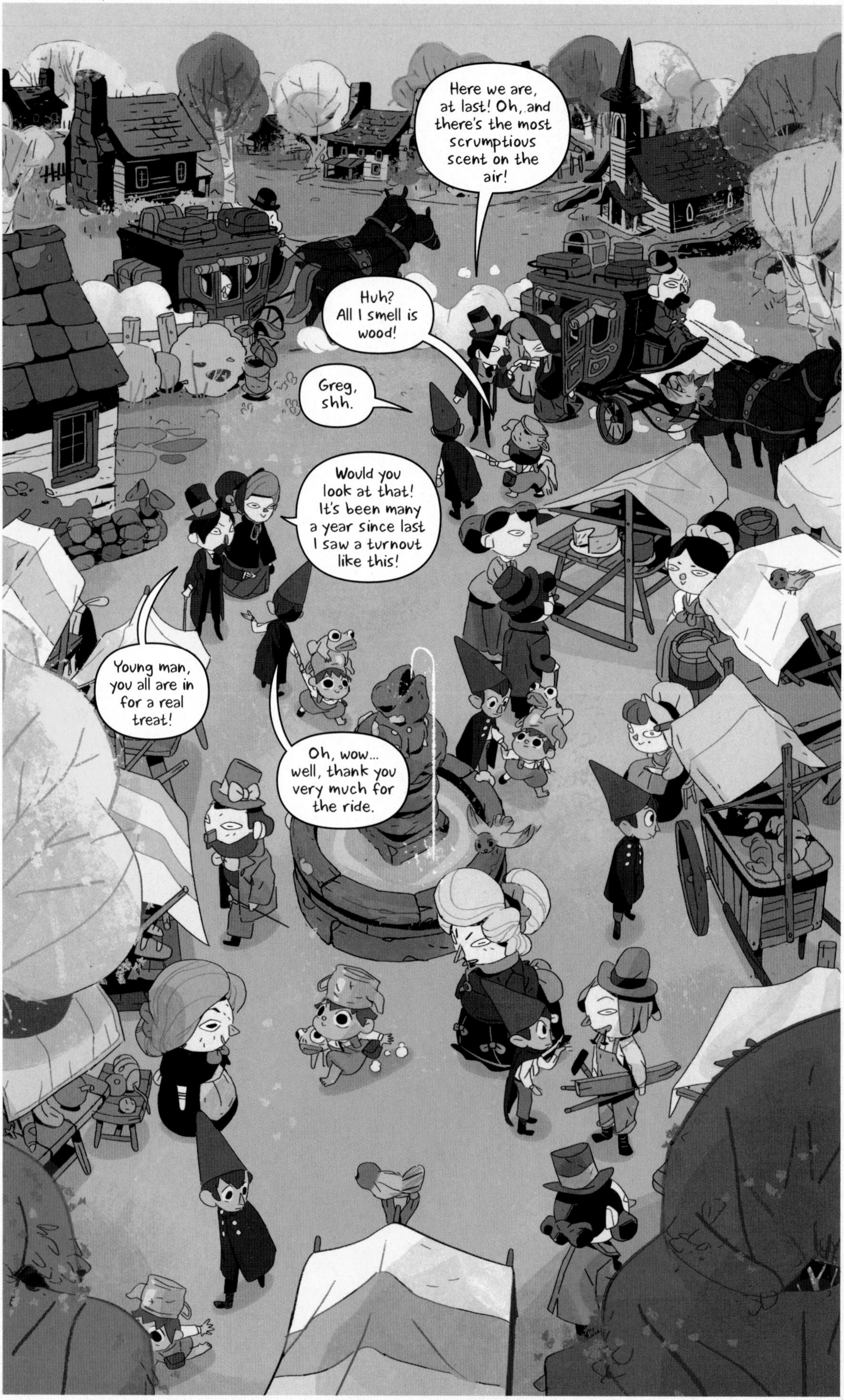
Here we are, at last! Oh, and there's the most scrumptious scent on the air!
Huh? All I smell is wood!
Greg, shh.
Would you look at that! It's been many a year since last I saw a turnout like this!
Young man, you all are in for a real treat!
Oh, wow... well, thank you very much for the ride.

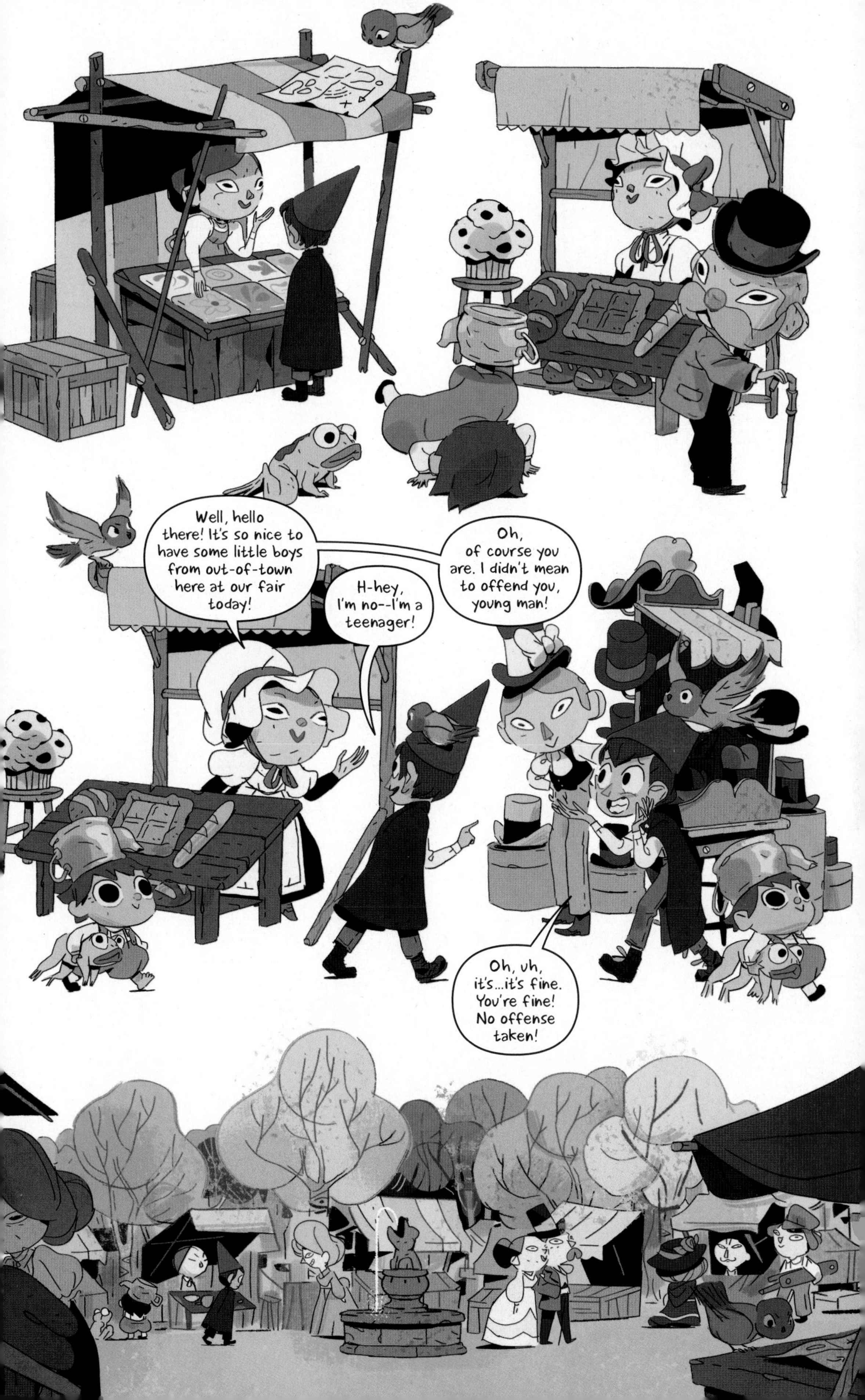
Well, hello there! It's so nice to have some little boys from out-of-town here at our fair today!
H-hey, I'm no--I'm a teenager!
Oh, of course you are. I didn't mean to offend you, young man!
Oh, uh, it's...it's fine. You're fine! No offense taken!

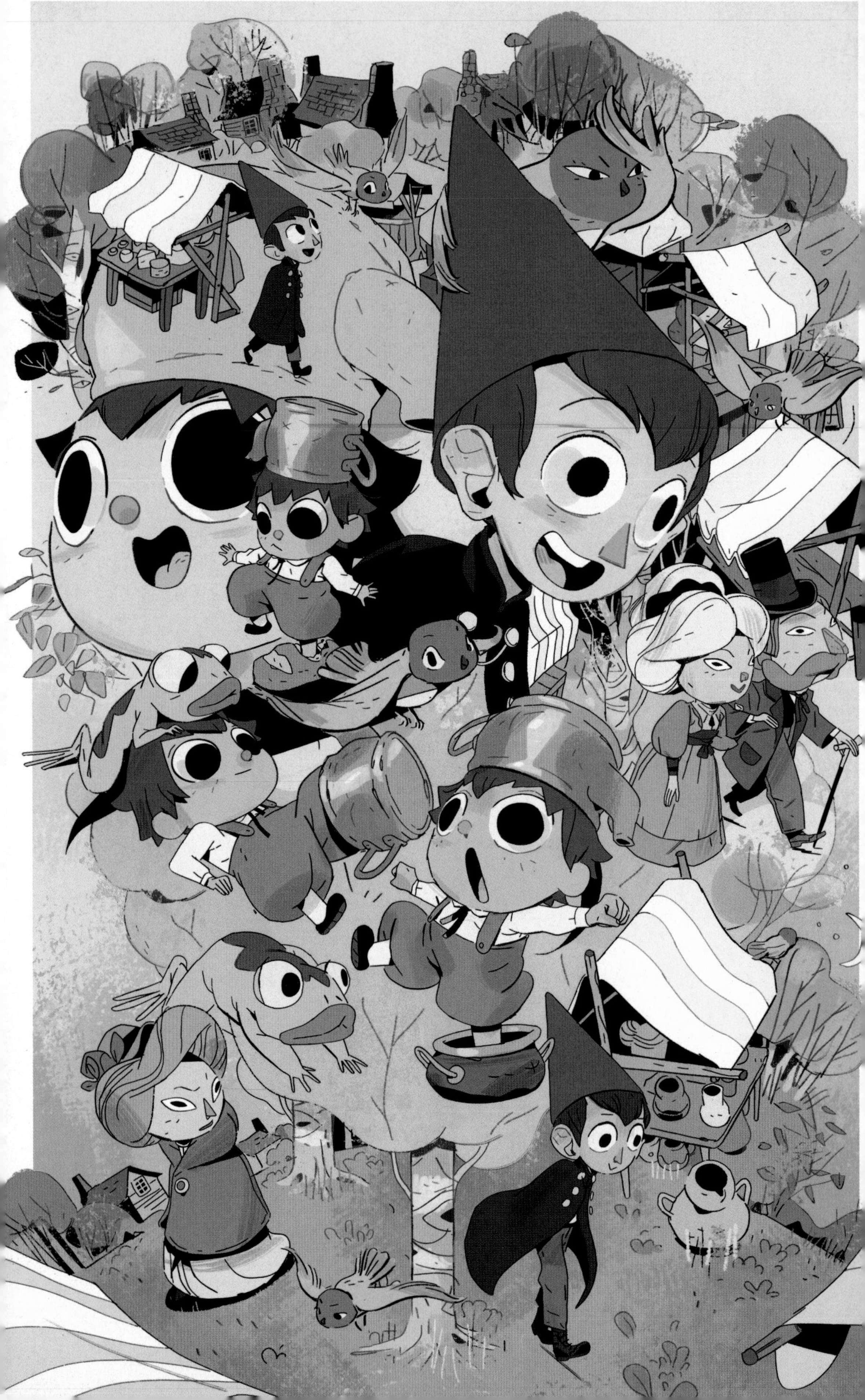

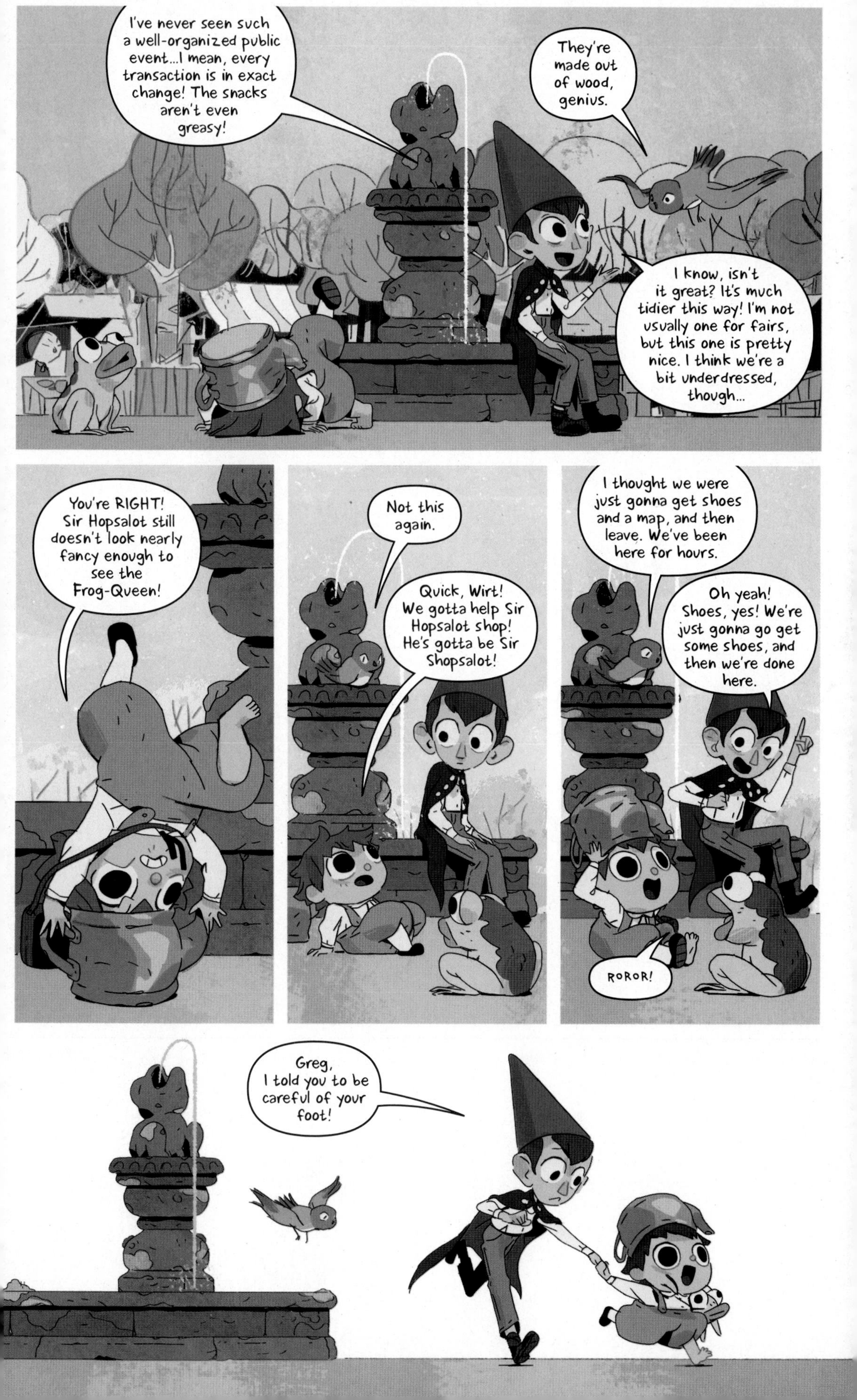

I've never seen such a well-organized public event...I mean, every transaction is in exact change! The snacks aren't even greasy!
They're made out of wood, genius.
I know, isn't it great? It's much tidier this way! I'm not usually one for fairs, but this one is pretty nice. I think we're a bit underdressed, though...
You're RIGHT! Sir Hopsalot still doesn't look nearly fancy enough to see the Frog-Queen!
Not this again.
Quick, Wirt! We gotta help Sir Hopsalot shop! He's gotta be Sir Shopsalot!
I thought we were just gonna get shoes and a map, and then leave. We've been here for hours.
Oh yeah! Shoes, yes! We're just gonna go get some shoes, and then we're done here.
ROROR!
Greg, I told you to be careful of your foot!

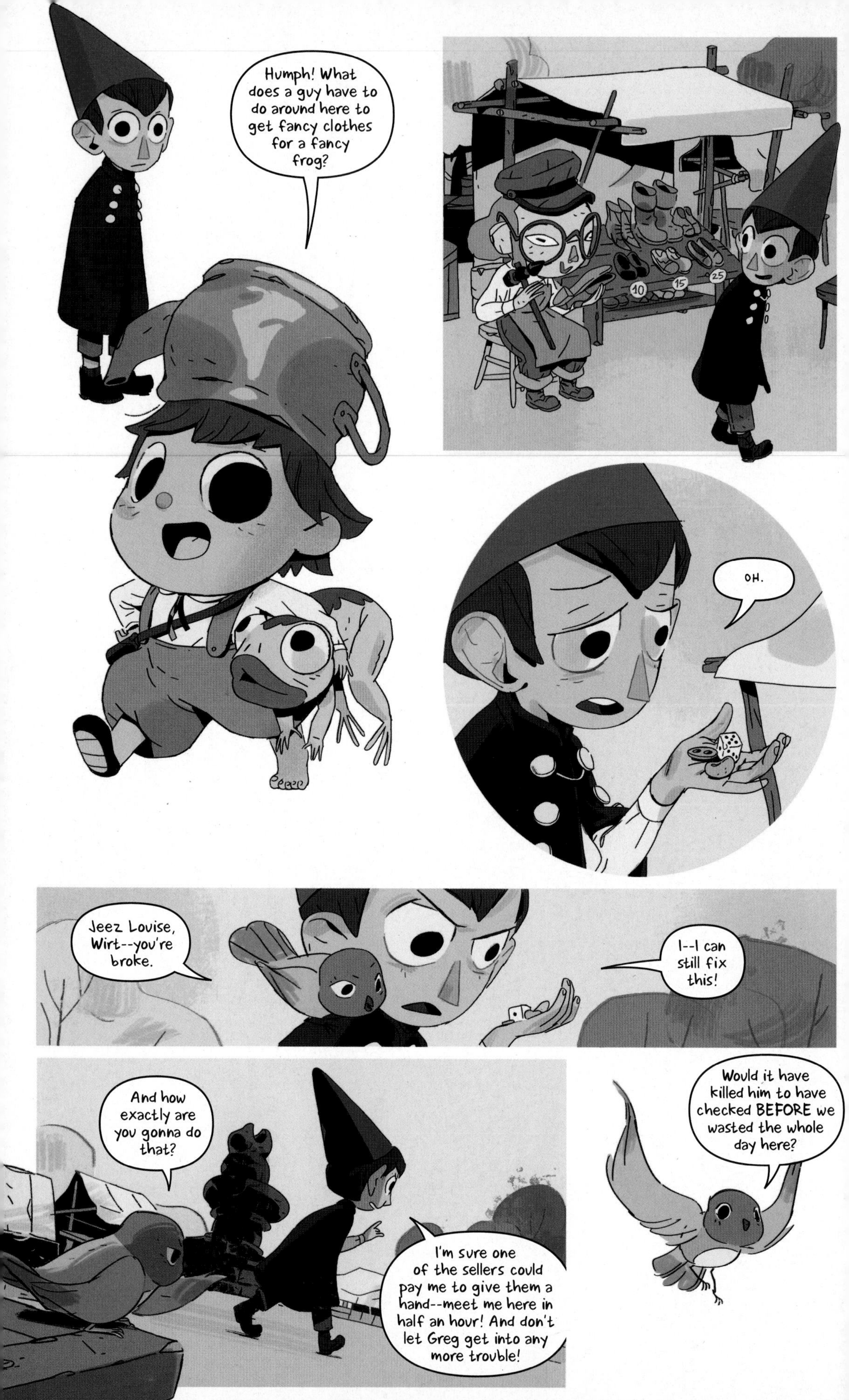
Humph! What does a guy have to do around here to get fancy clothes for a fancy frog?
10
15
25
OH.
Jeez Louise, Wirt--you're broke.
I--I can still fix this!
And how exactly are you gonna do that?
I'm sure one of the sellers could pay me to give them a hand--meet me here in half an hour! And don't let Greg get into any more trouble!
Would it have killed him to have checked BEFORE we wasted the whole day here?

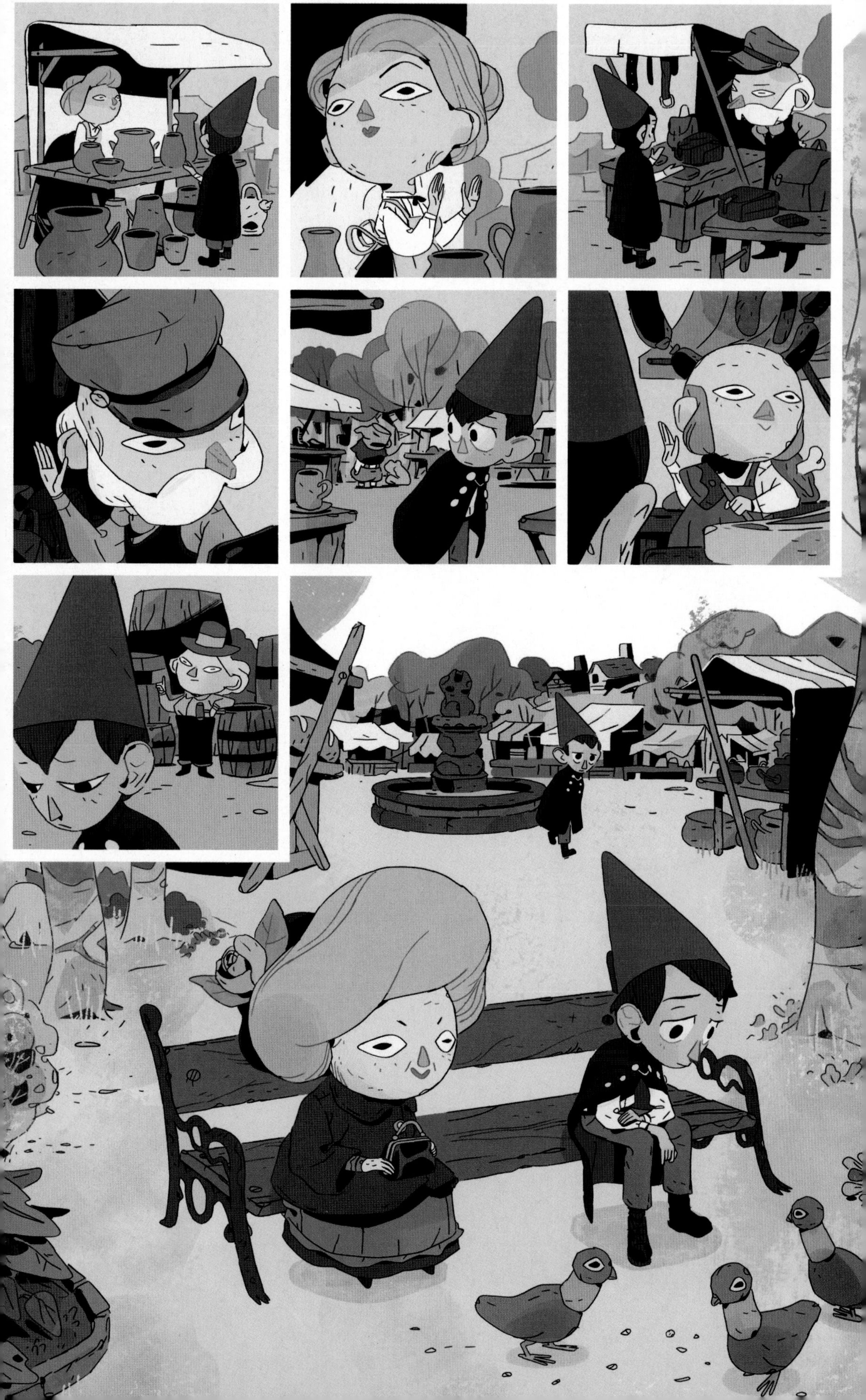

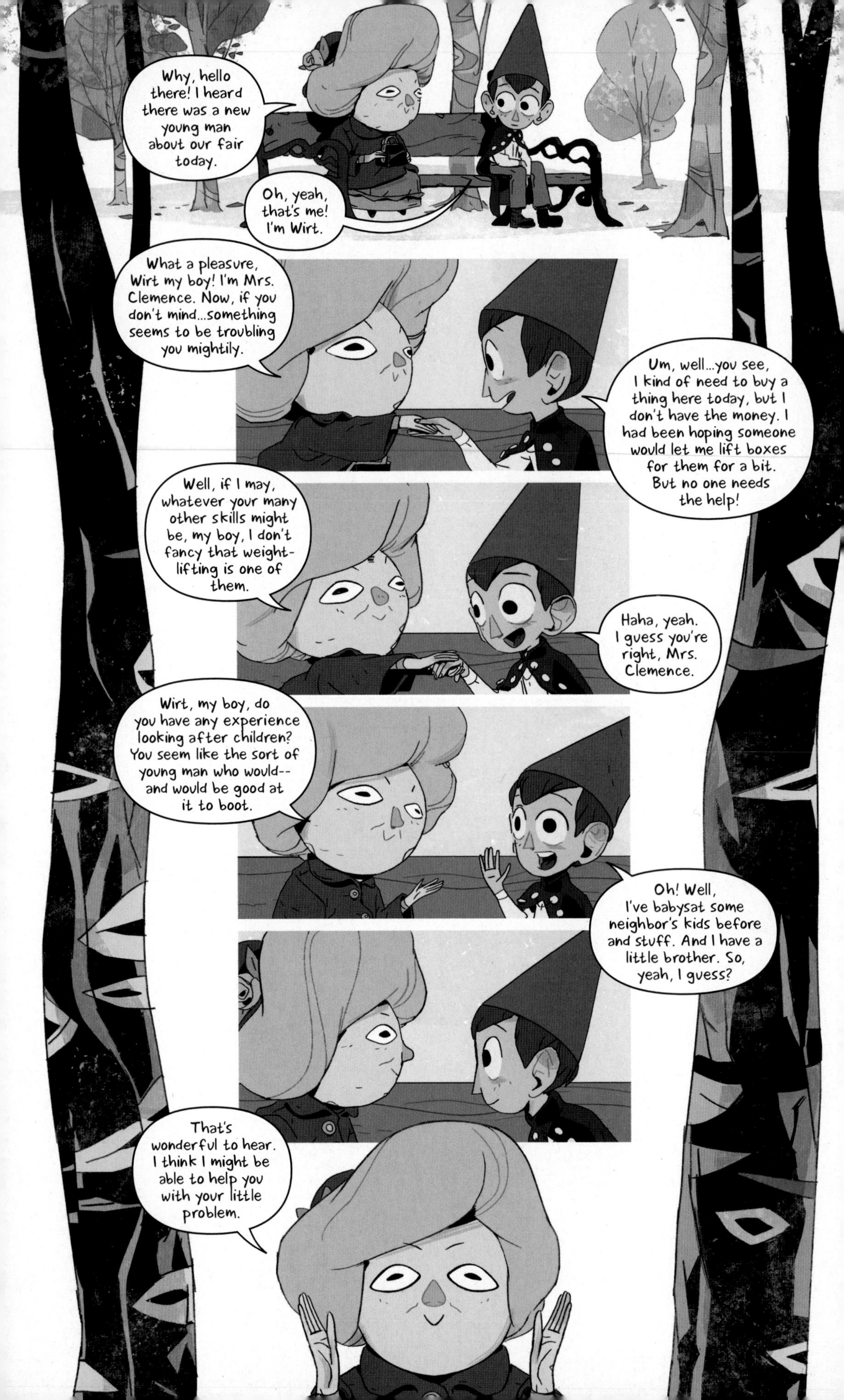
Why, hello there! I heard there was a new young man about our fair today.
Oh, yeah, that's me! I'm Wirt.
What a pleasure, Wirt my boy! I'm Mrs. Clemence. Now, if you don't mind...something seems to be troubling you mightily.
Um, well...you see, I kind of need to buy a thing here today, but I don't have the money. I had been hoping someone would let me lift boxes for them for a bit. But no one needs the help!
Well, if I may, whatever your many other skills might be, my boy, I don't fancy that weight-lifting is one of them.
Haha, yeah. I guess you're right, Mrs. Clemence.
Wirt, my boy, do you have any experience looking after children? You seem like the sort of young man who would-- and would be good at it to boot.
Oh! Well, I've babysat some neighbor's kids before and stuff. And I have a little brother. So, yeah, I guess?
That's wonderful to hear. I think I might be able to help you with your little problem.

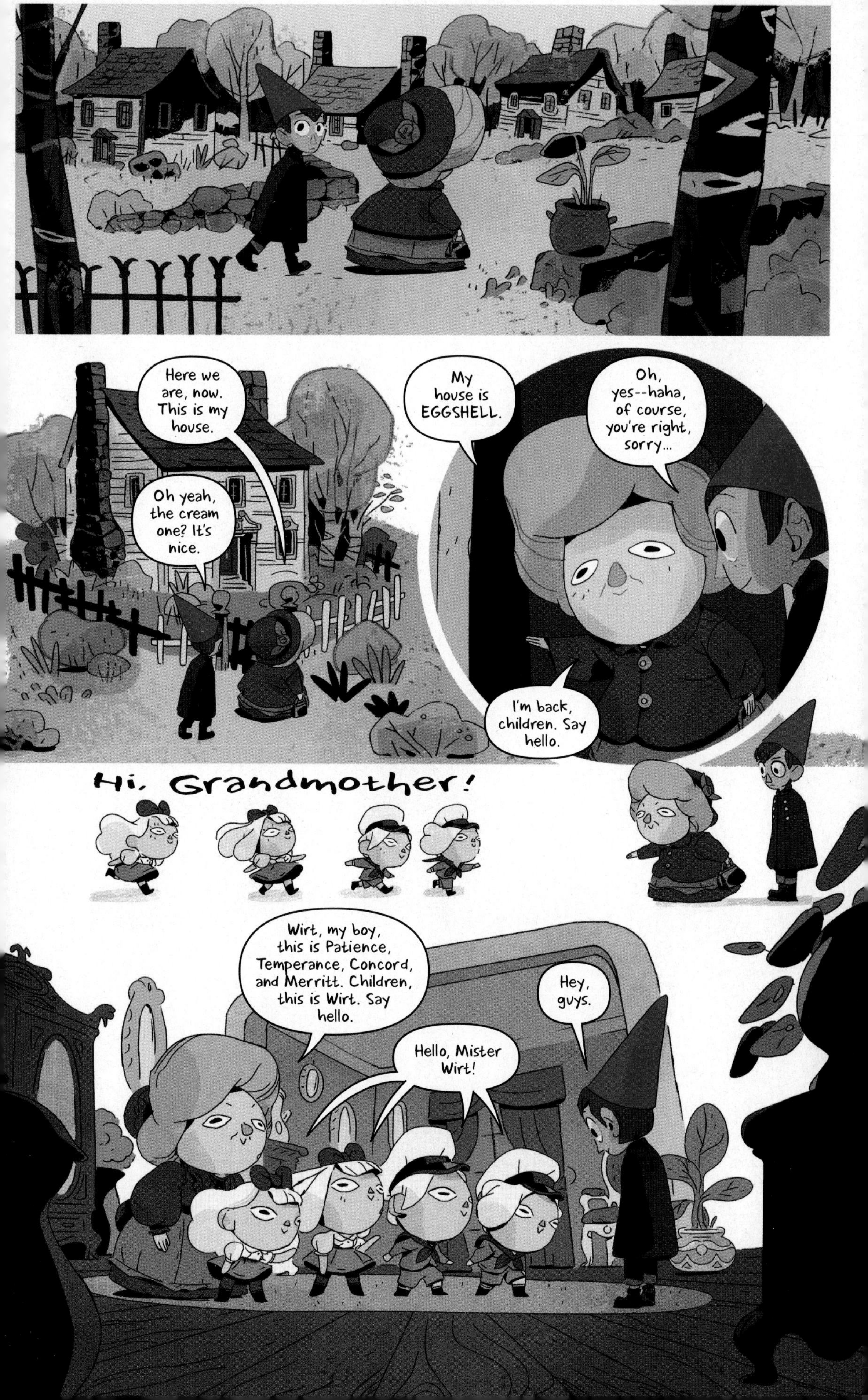
Here we are, now. This is my house.
Oh yeah, the cream one? It's nice.
My house is EGGSHELL.
Oh, yes--haha, of course, you're right, sorry...
I'm back, children. Say hello.
Hi, Grandmother!
Wirt, my boy, this is Patience, Temperance, Concord, and Merritt. Children, this is Wirt. Say hello.
Hello, Mister Wirt!
Hey, guys.

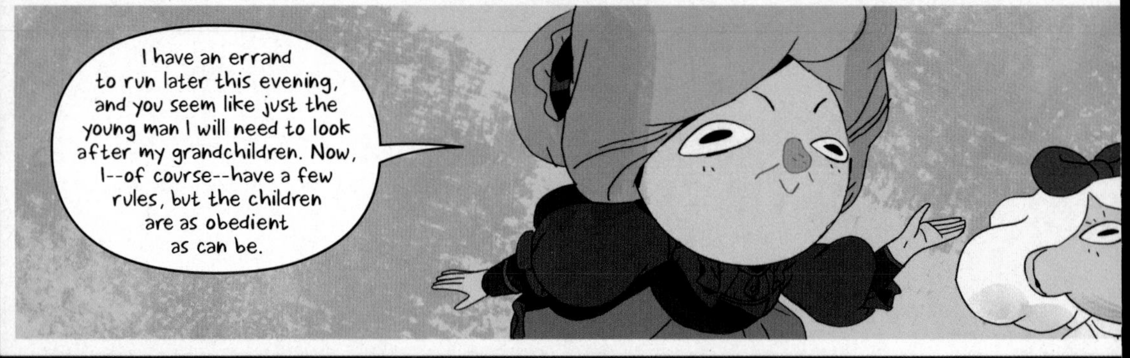
I have an errand to run later this evening, and you seem like just the young man I will need to look after my grandchildren. Now, I--of course--have a few rules, but the children are as obedient as can be.

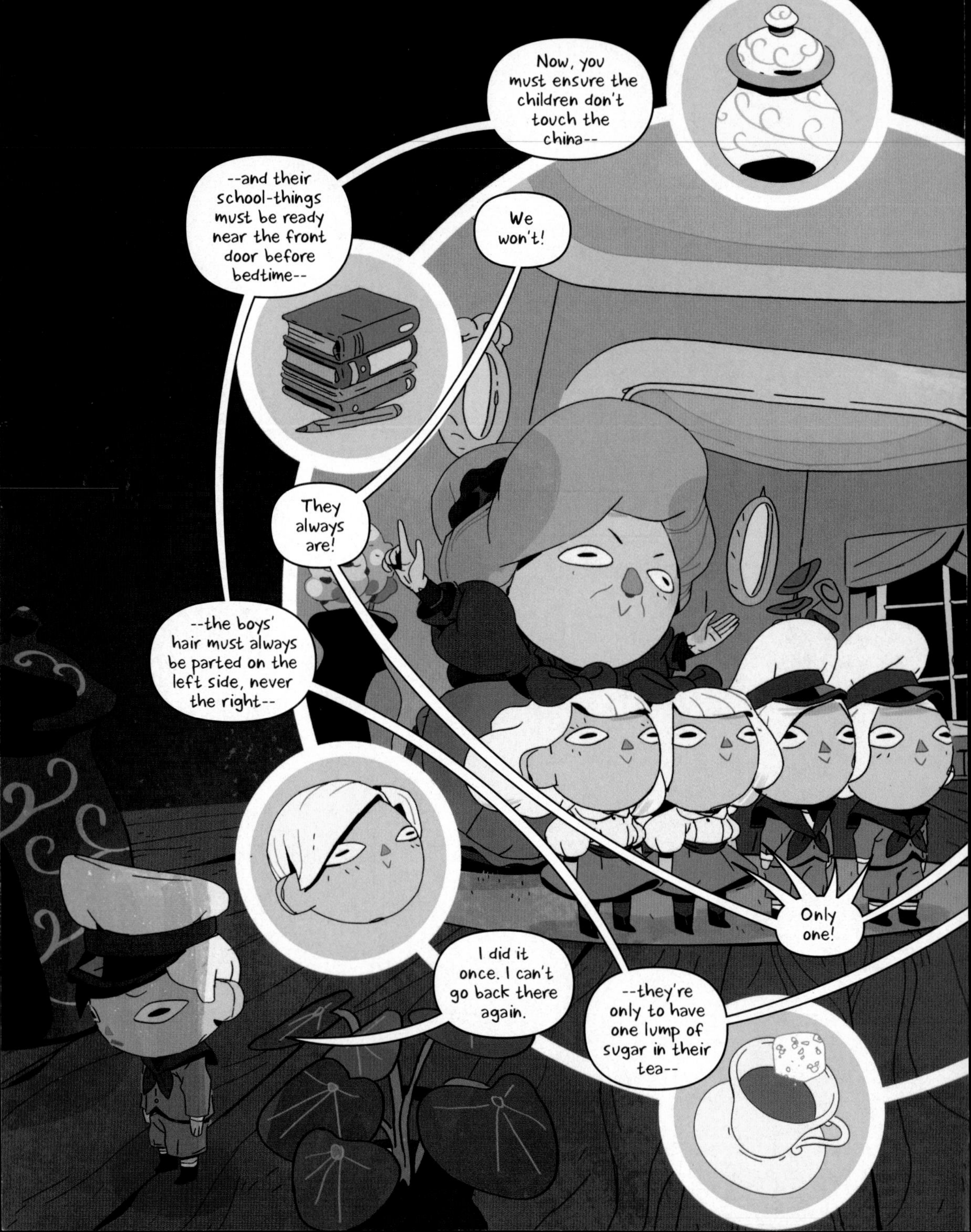
Now, you must ensure the children don't touch the china--
We won't!
--and their school-things must be ready near the front door before bedtime--
They always are!
--the boys' hair must always be parted on the left side, never the right--
I did it once. I can't go back there again.
--they're only to have one lump of sugar in their tea--
Only one!

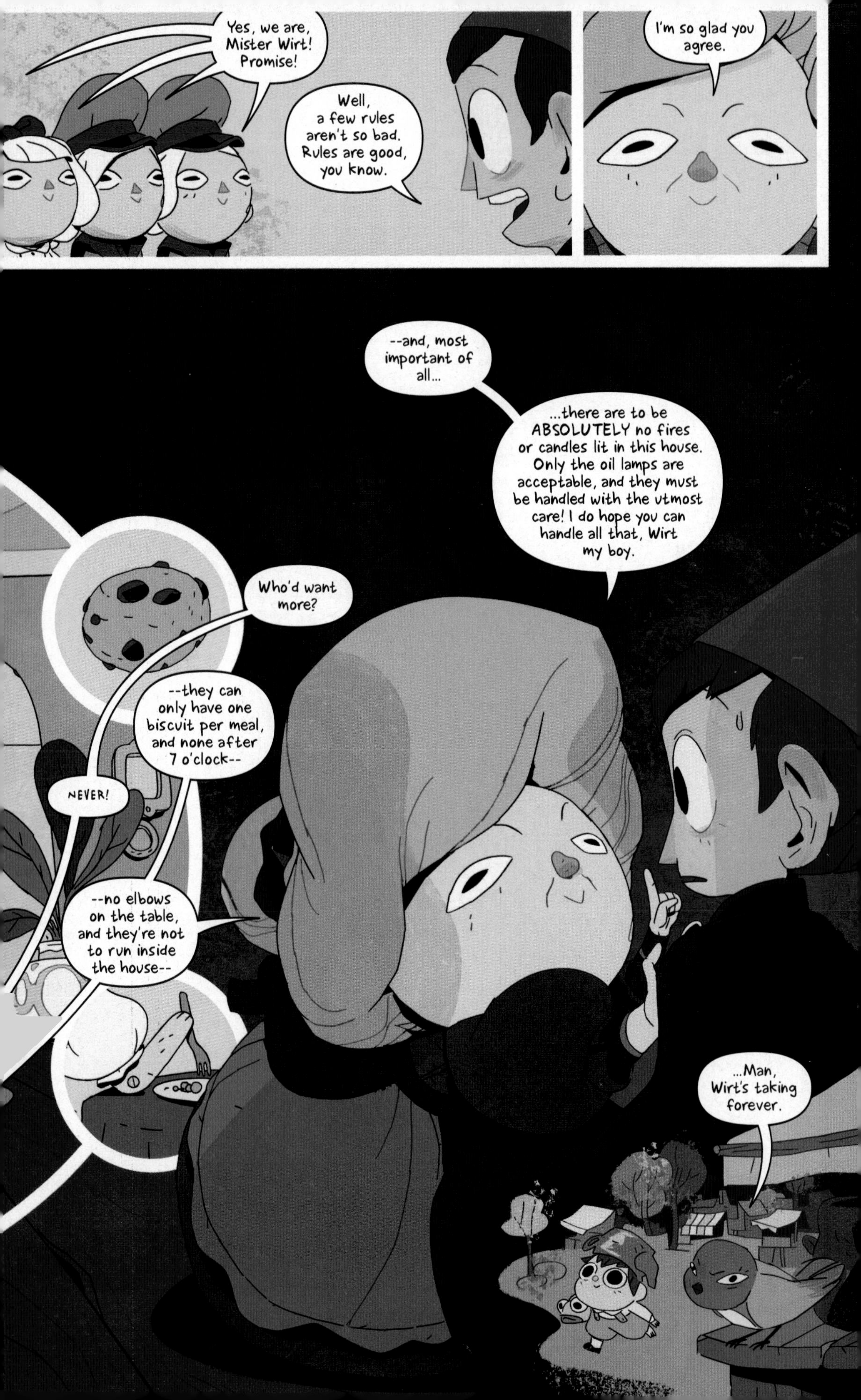
Yes, we are, Mister Wirt! Promise!
Well, a few rules aren't so bad. Rules are good, you know.
I'm so glad you agree.
--no elbows on the table, and they're not to run inside the house--
--they can only have one biscuit per meal, and none after 7 o'clock--
NEVER!
Who'd want more?
--and, most important of all...
...there are to be ABSOLUTELY no fires or candles lit in this house. Only the oil lamps are acceptable, and they must be handled with the utmost care! I do hope you can handle all that, Wirt my boy.
...Man, Wirt's taking forever.

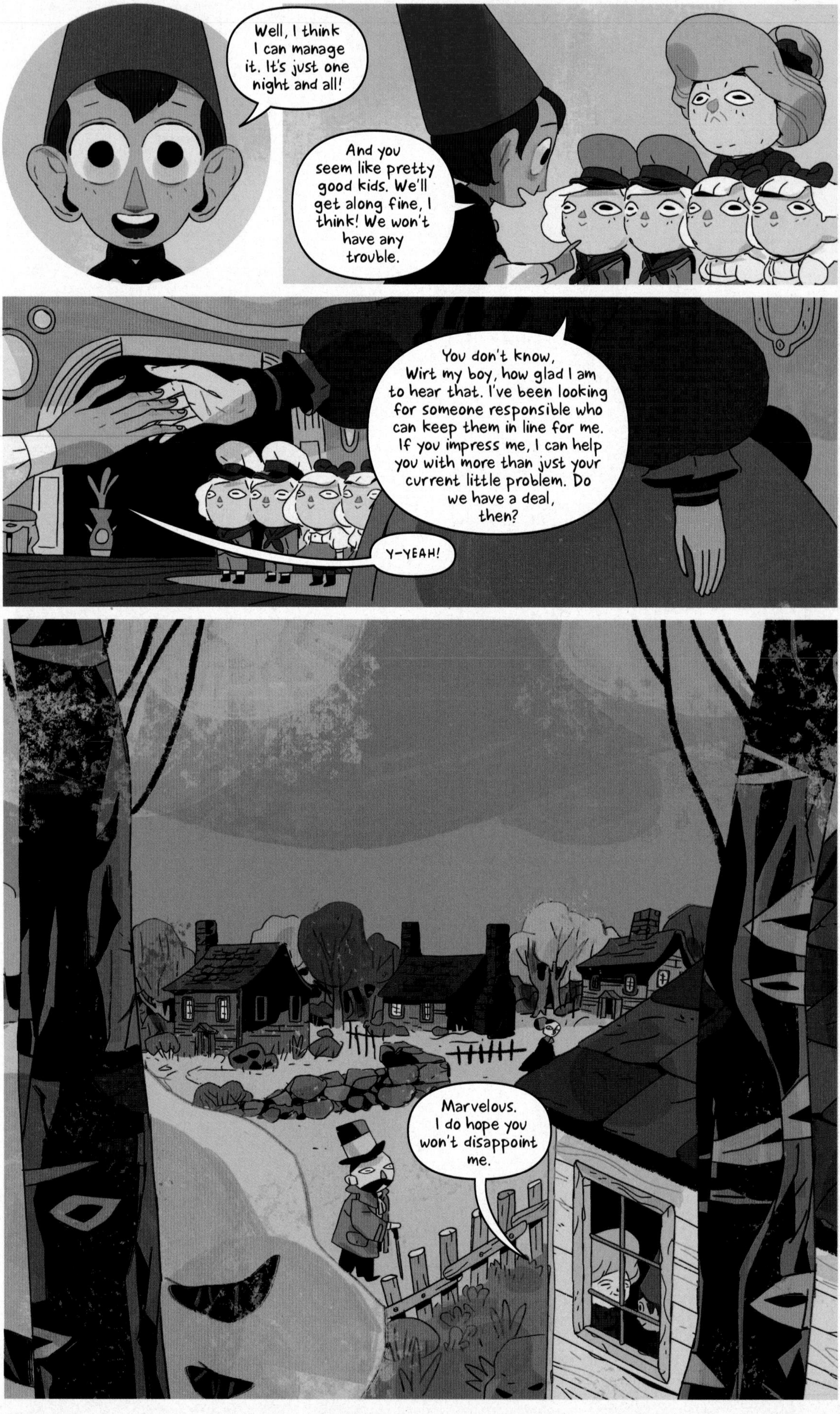
Well, I think I can manage it. It's just one night and all!
And you seem like pretty good kids. We'll get along fine, I think! We won't have any trouble.
You don't know, Wirt my boy, how glad I am to hear that. I've been looking for someone responsible who can keep them in line for me. If you impress me, I can help you with more than just your current little problem. Do we have a deal, then?
Y-YEAH!
Marvelous. I do hope you won't disappoint me.

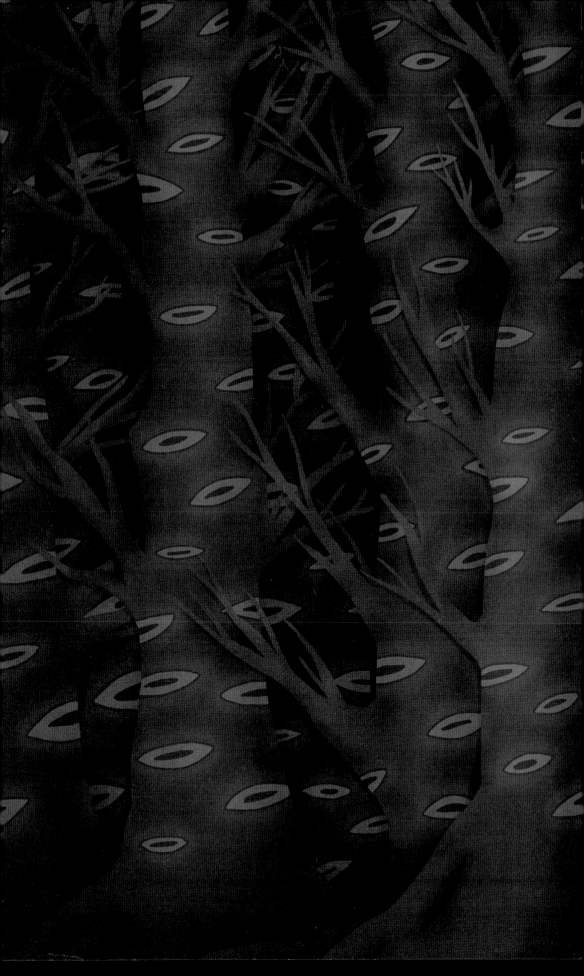

CHAPTER
2

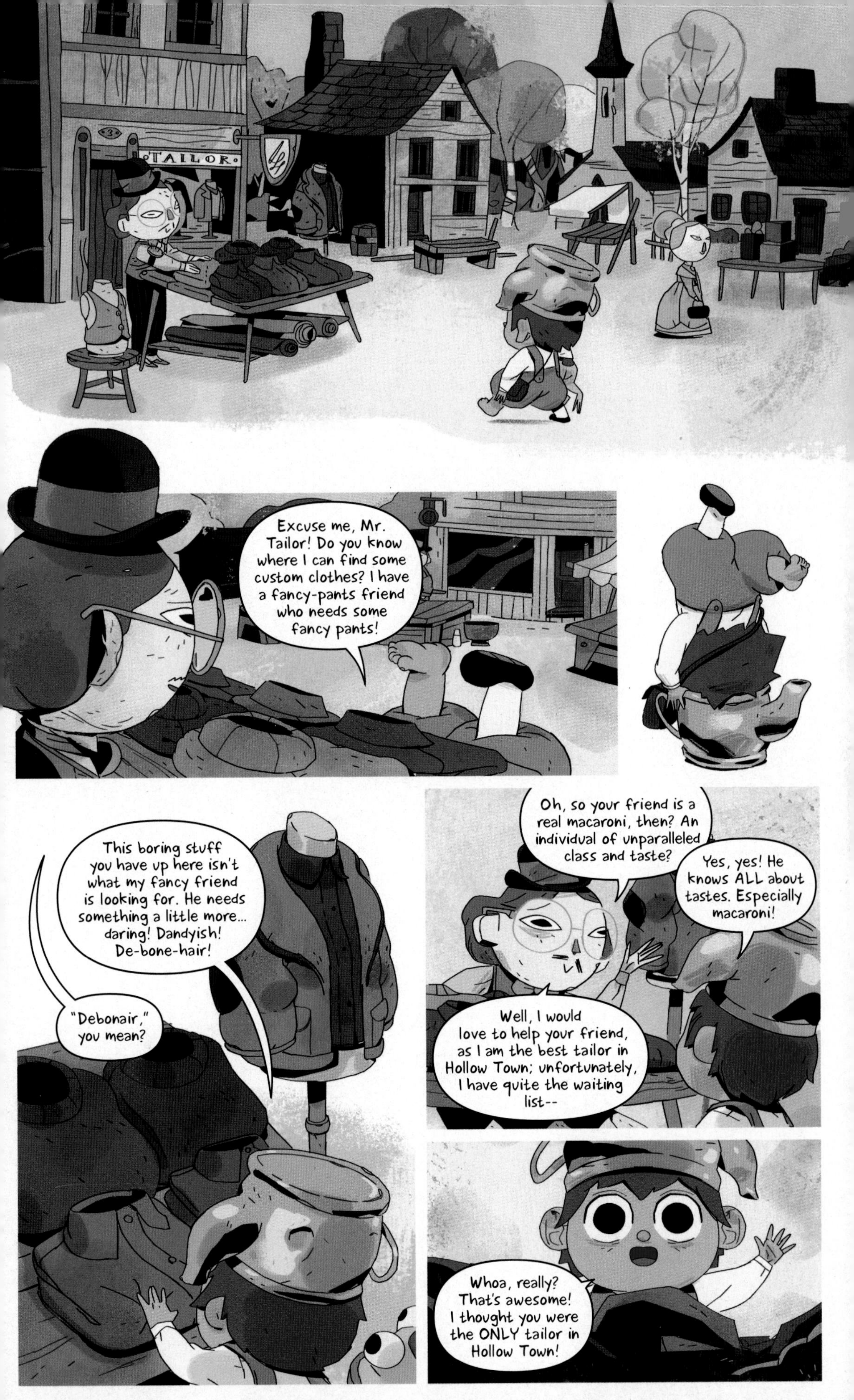

TAILOR
Excuse me, Mr. Tailor! Do you know where I can find some custom clothes? I have a fancy-pants friend who needs some fancy pants!
This boring stuff you have up here isn't what my fancy friend is looking for. He needs something a little more... daring! Dandyish! De-bone-hair!
"Debonair," you mean?
Oh, so your friend is a real macaroni, then? An individual of unparalleled class and taste?
Yes, yes! He knows ALL about tastes. Especially macaroni!
Well, I would love to help your friend, as I am the best tailor in Hollow Town; unfortunately, I have quite the waiting list--
Whoa, really? That's awesome! I thought you were the ONLY tailor in Hollow Town!

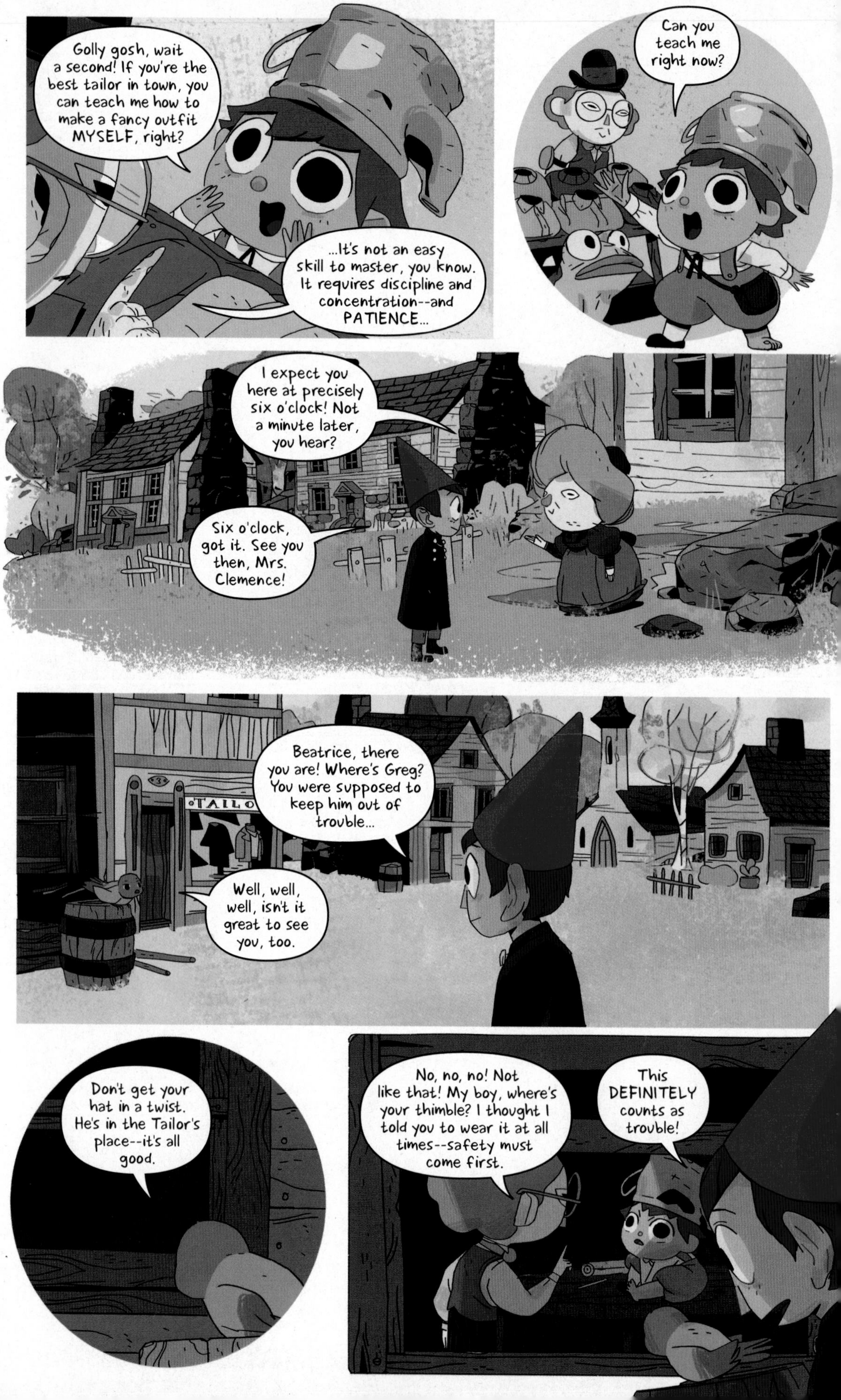
Golly gosh, wait a second! If you're the best tailor in town, you can teach me how to make a fancy outfit MYSELF, right?
...It's not an easy skill to master, you know. It requires discipline and concentration--and PATIENCE...
Can you teach me right now?
I expect you here at precisely six o'clock! Not a minute later, you hear?
Six o'clock, got it. See you then, Mrs. Clemence!
TAILO
Beatrice, there you are! Where's Greg? You were supposed to keep him out of trouble...
Well, well, well, isn't it great to see you, too.
Don't get your hat in a twist. He's in the Tailor's place--it's all good.
No, no, no! Not like that! My boy, where's your thimble? I thought I told you to wear it at all times--safety must come first.
This DEFINITELY counts as trouble!

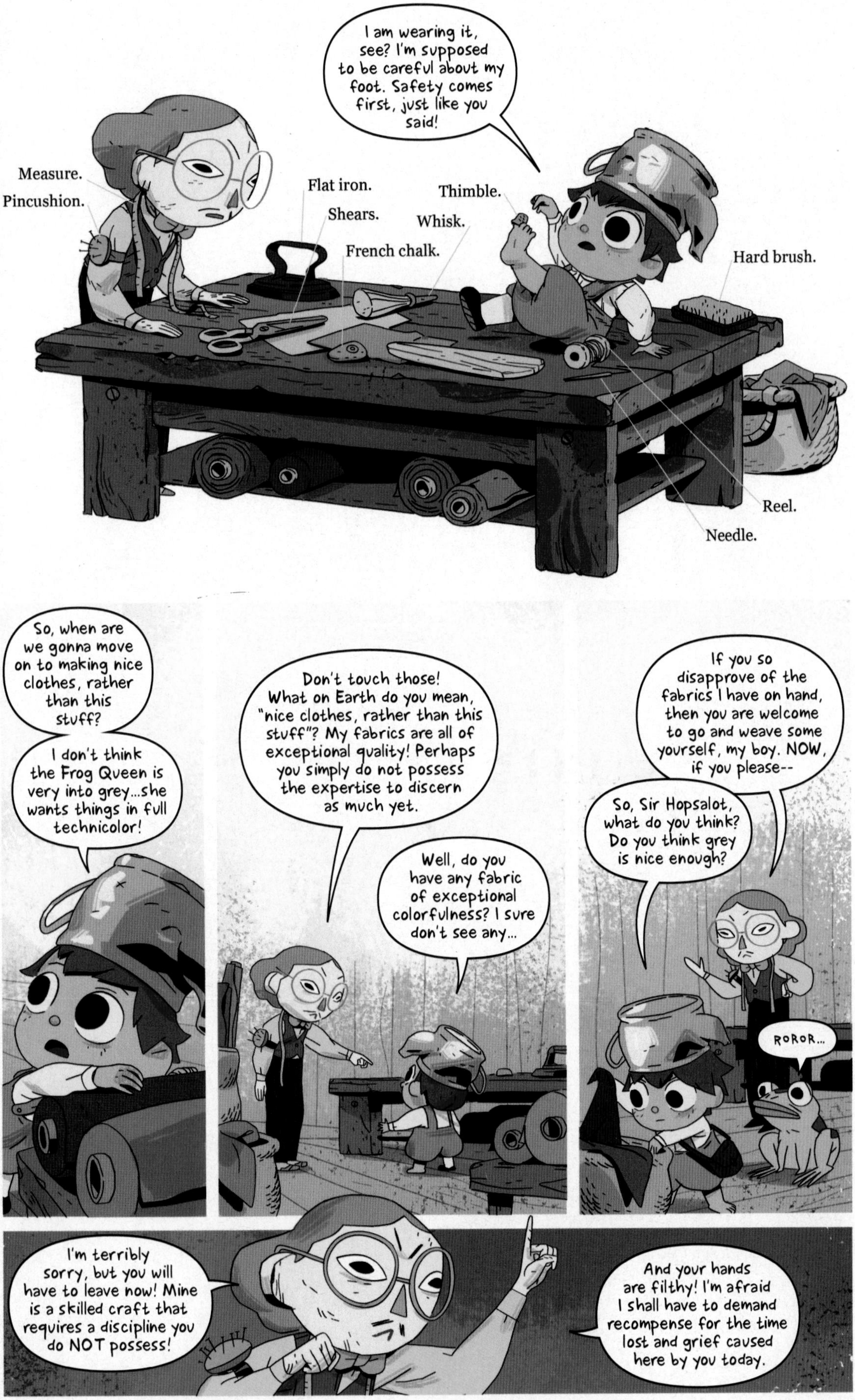

I am wearing it, see? I'm supposed to be careful about my foot. Safety comes first, just like you said!
Measure.
Pincushion.
Flat iron.
Shears.
French chalk.
Whisk.
Thimble.
Hard brush.
Reel.
Needle.
So, when are we gonna move on to making nice clothes, rather than this stuff?
I don't think the Frog Queen is very into grey...she wants things in full technicolor!
Don't touch those! What on Earth do you mean, "nice clothes, rather than this stuff"? My fabrics are all of exceptional quality! Perhaps you simply do not possess the expertise to discern as much yet.
Well, do you have any fabric of exceptional colorfulness? I sure don't see any...
If you so disapprove of the fabrics I have on hand, then you are welcome to go and weave some yourself, my boy. NOW, if you please--
So, Sir Hopsalot, what do you think? Do you think grey is nice enough?
ROROR...
I'm terribly sorry, but you will have to leave now! Mine is a skilled craft that requires a discipline you do NOT possess!
And your hands are filthy! I'm afraid I shall have to demand recompense for the time lost and grief caused here by you today.

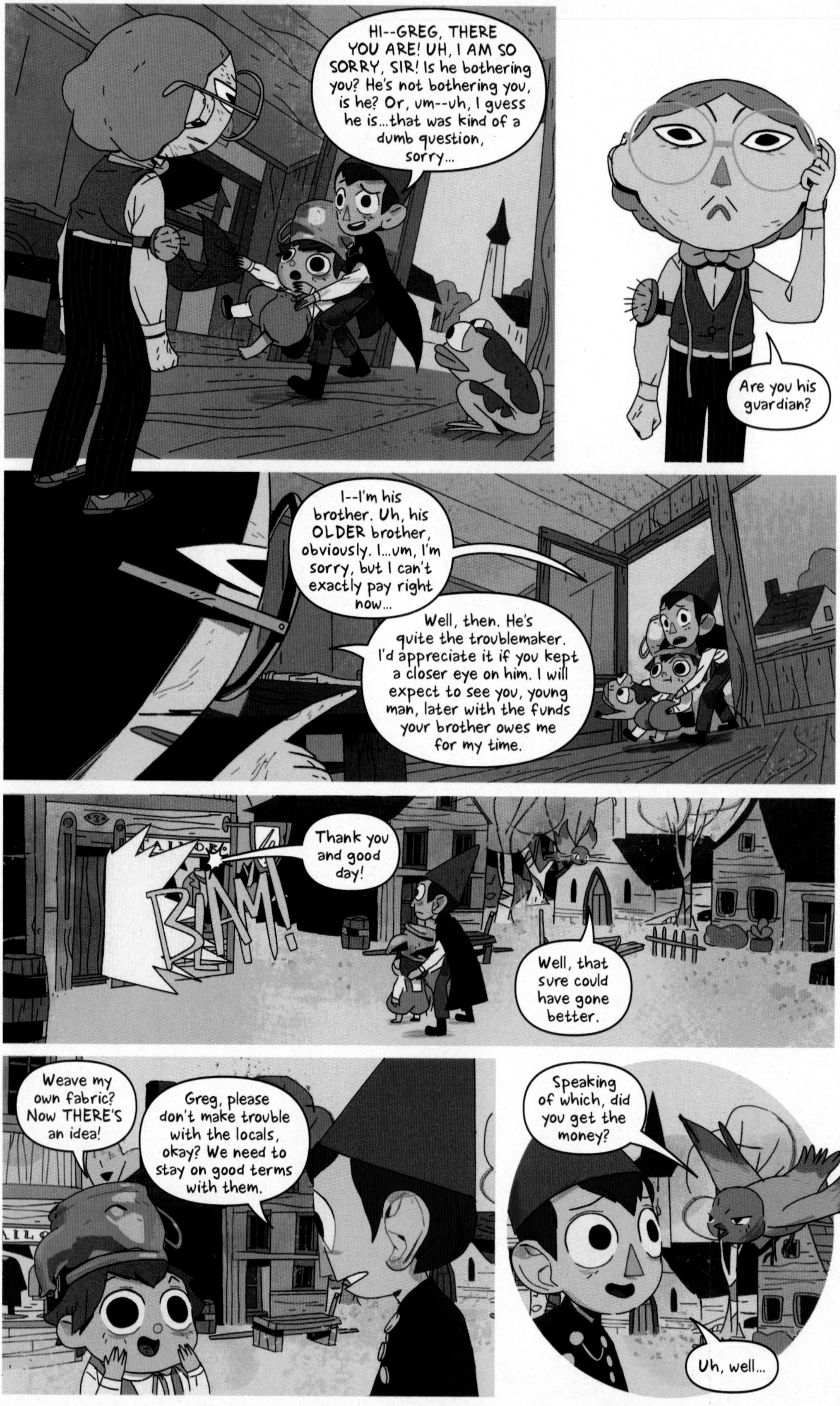
HI--GREG, THERE YOU ARE! UH, I AM SO SORRY, SIR! Is he bothering you? He's not bothering you, is he? Or, um--uh, I guess he is...that was kind of a dumb question, sorry...
Are you his guardian?
I--I'm his brother. Uh, his OLDER brother, obviously. I...um, I'm sorry, but I can't exactly pay right now...
Well, then. He's quite the troublemaker. I'd appreciate it if you kept a closer eye on him. I will expect to see you, young man, later with the funds your brother owes me for my time.
Thank you and good day!
BLAM!
Well, that sure could have gone better.
Weave my own fabric? Now THERE'S an idea!
Greg, please don't make trouble with the locals, okay? We need to stay on good terms with them.
Speaking of which, did you get the money?
Uh, well...

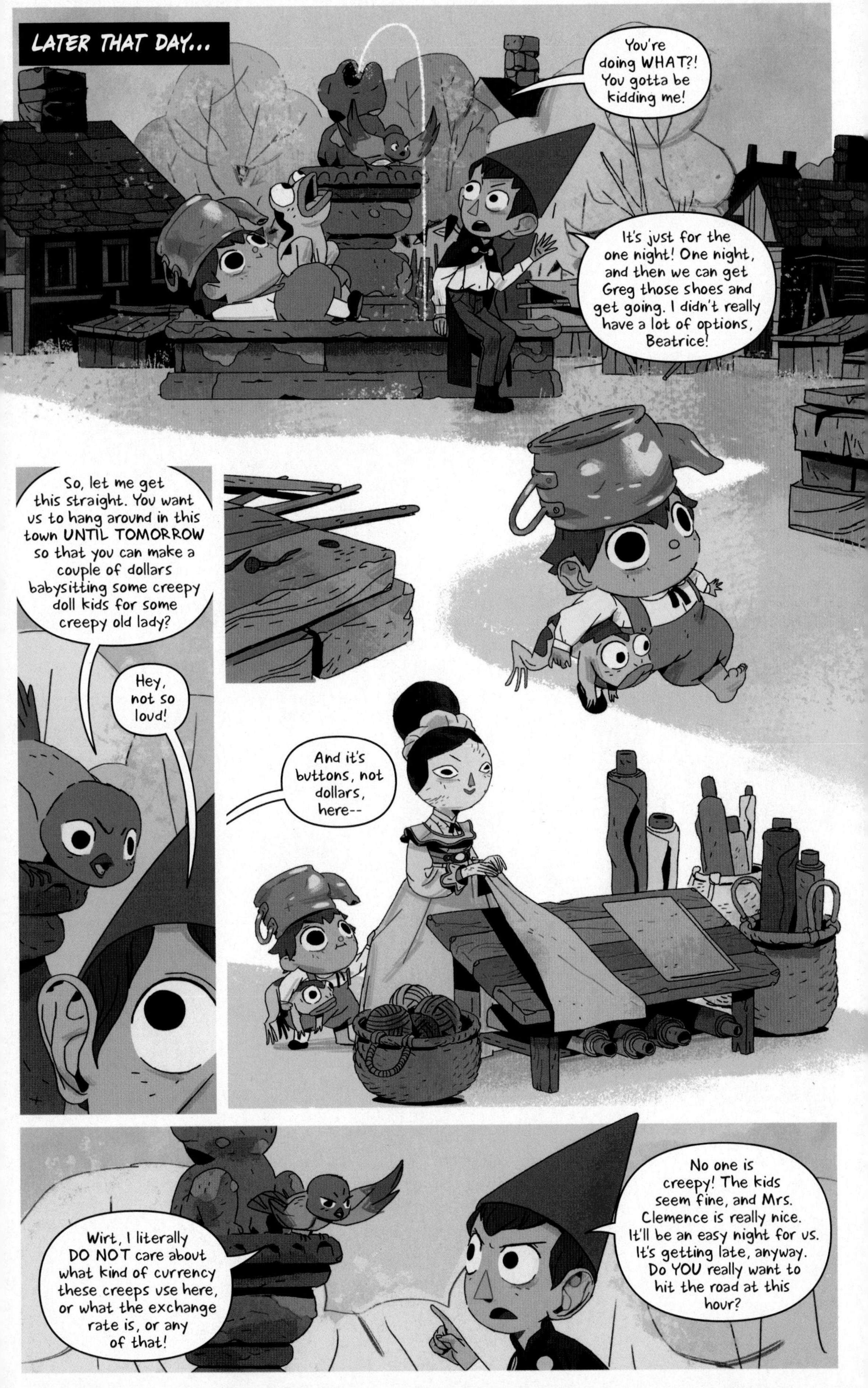
LATER THAT DAY...
You're doing WHAT?! You gotta be kidding me!
It's just for the one night! One night, and then we can get Greg those shoes and get going. I didn't really have a lot of options, Beatrice!
So, let me get this straight. You want us to hang around in this town UNTIL TOMORROW so that you can make a couple of dollars babysitting some creepy doll kids for some creepy old lady?
Hey, not so loud!
And it's buttons, not dollars, here--
Wirt, I literally DO NOT care about what kind of currency these creeps use here, or what the exchange rate is, or any of that!
No one is creepy! The kids seem fine, and Mrs. Clemence is really nice. It'll be an easy night for us. It's getting late, anyway. Do YOU really want to hit the road at this hour?

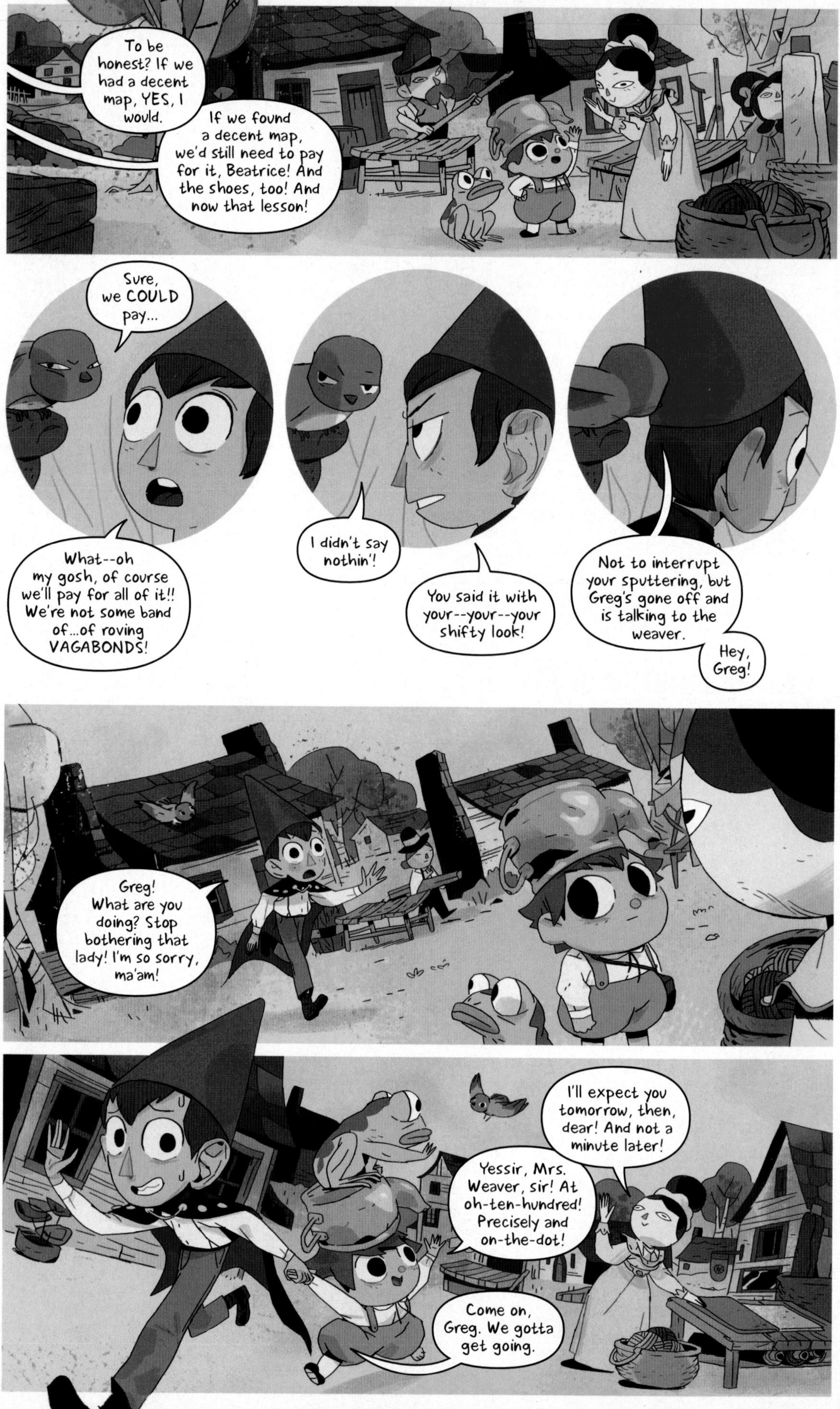
To be honest? If we had a decent map, YES, I would.
If we found a decent map, we'd still need to pay for it, Beatrice! And the shoes, too! And now that lesson!
Sure, we COULD pay...
What--oh my gosh, of course we'll pay for all of it!! We're not some band of...of roving VAGABONDS!
I didn't say nothin'!
You said it with your--your--your shifty look!
Not to interrupt your sputtering, but Greg's gone off and is talking to the weaver.
Hey, Greg!
Greg! What are you doing? Stop bothering that lady! I'm so sorry, ma'am!
I'll expect you tomorrow, then, dear! And not a minute later!
Yessir, Mrs. Weaver, sir! At oh-ten-hundred! Precisely and on-the-dot!
Come on, Greg. We gotta get going.

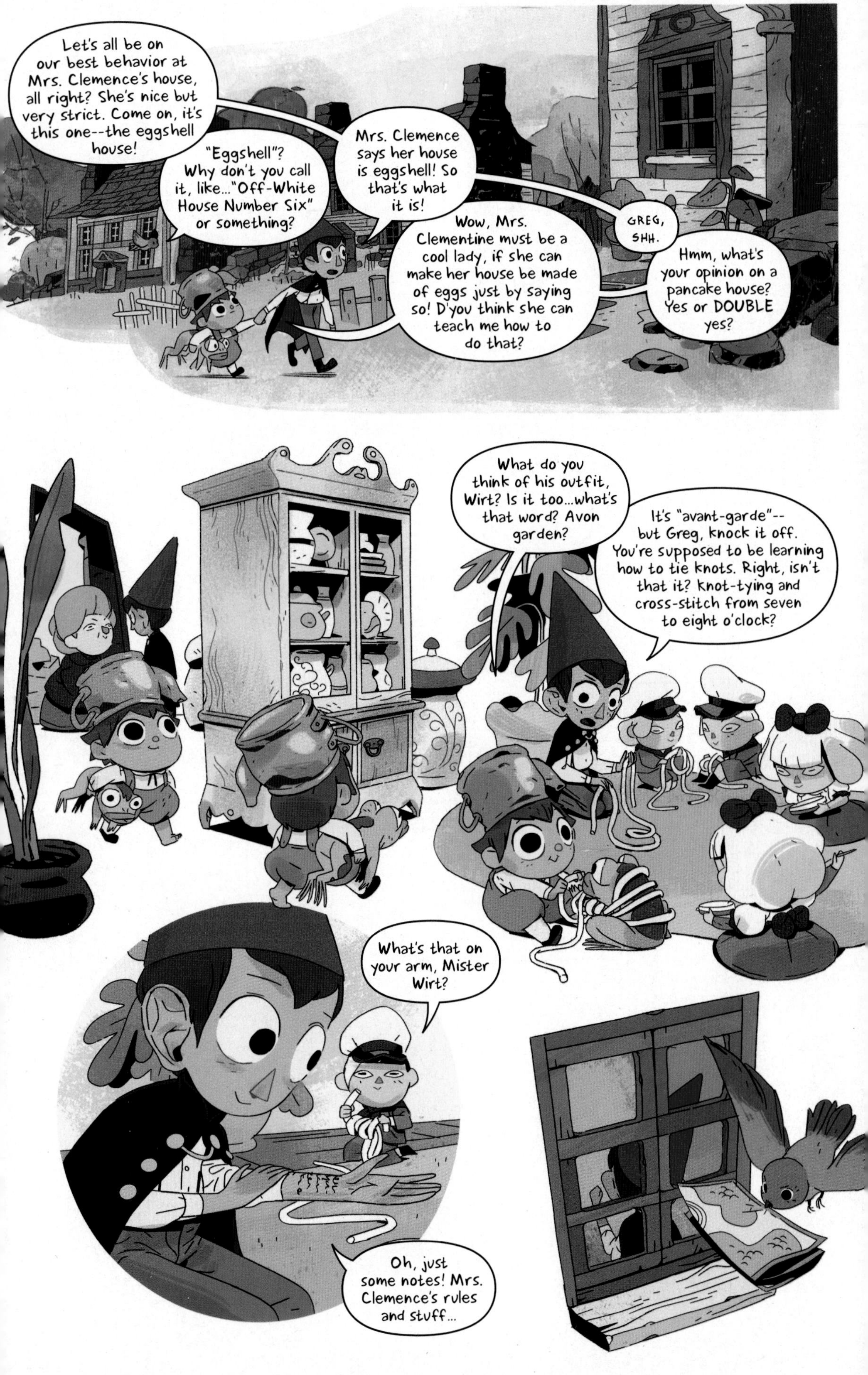
Let's all be on our best behavior at Mrs. Clemence's house, all right? She's nice but very strict. Come on, it's this one--the eggshell house!
"Eggshell"? Why don't you call it, like..."Off-White House Number Six" or something?
Mrs. Clemence says her house is eggshell! So that's what it is!
Wow, Mrs. Clementine must be a cool lady, if she can make her house be made of eggs just by saying so! D'you think she can teach me how to do that?
GREG, SHH.
Hmm, what's your opinion on a pancake house? Yes or DOUBLE yes?
What do you think of his outfit, Wirt? Is it too...what's that word? Avon garden?
It's "avant-garde"-- but Greg, knock it off. You're supposed to be learning how to tie knots. Right, isn't that it? Knot-tying and cross-stitch from seven to eight o'clock?
What's that on your arm, Mister Wirt?
Oh, just some notes! Mrs. Clemence's rules and stuff...

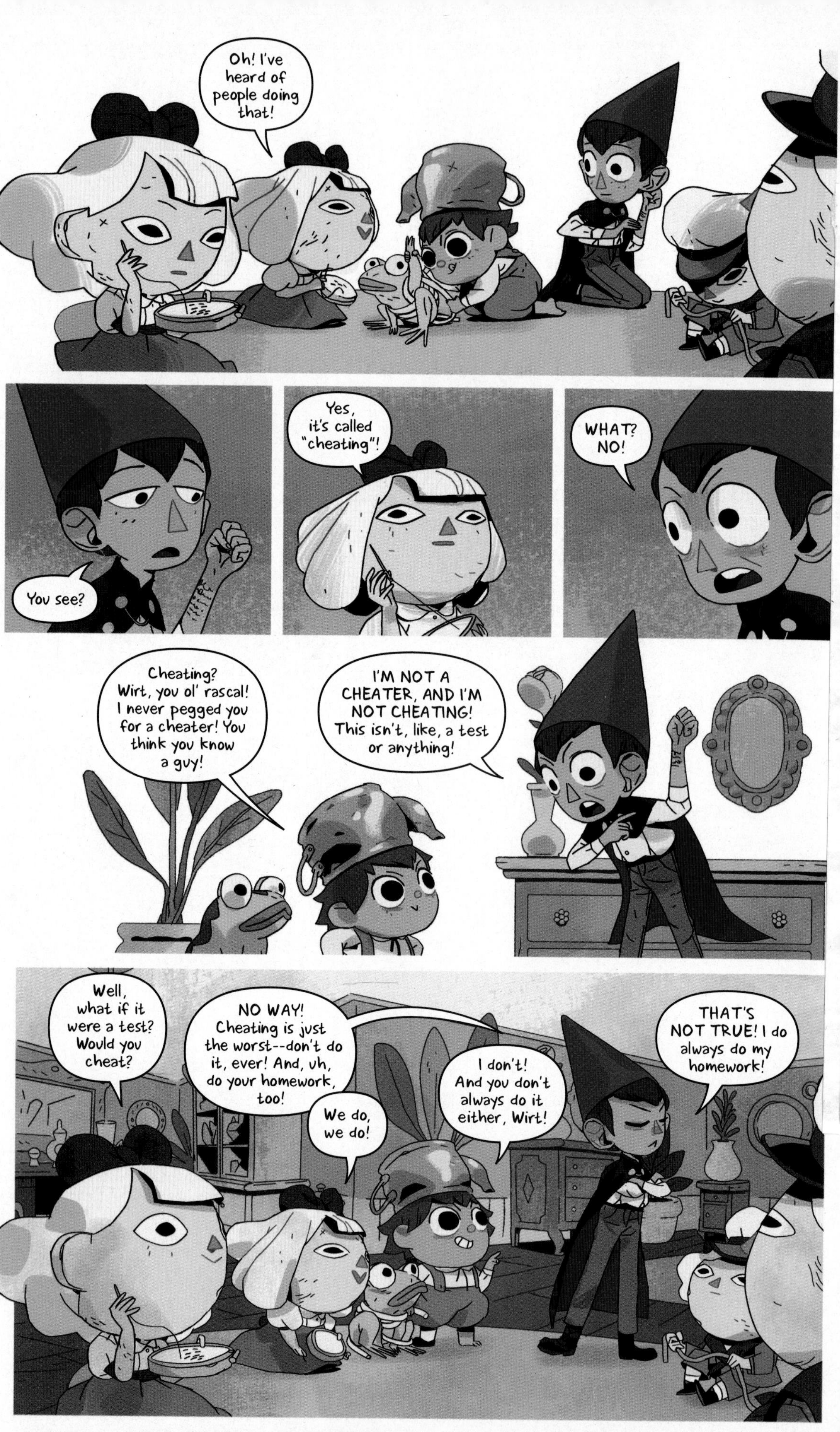
Oh! I've heard of people doing that!
You see?
Yes, it's called "cheating"!
WHAT? NO!
Cheating? Wirt, you ol' rascal! I never pegged you for a cheater! You think you know a guy!
I'M NOT A CHEATER, AND I'M NOT CHEATING! This isn't, like, a test or anything!
Well, what if it were a test? Would you cheat?
NO WAY! Cheating is just the worst--don't do it, ever! And, uh, do your homework, too!
We do, we do!
I don't! And you don't always do it either, Wirt!
THAT'S NOT TRUE! I do always do my homework!

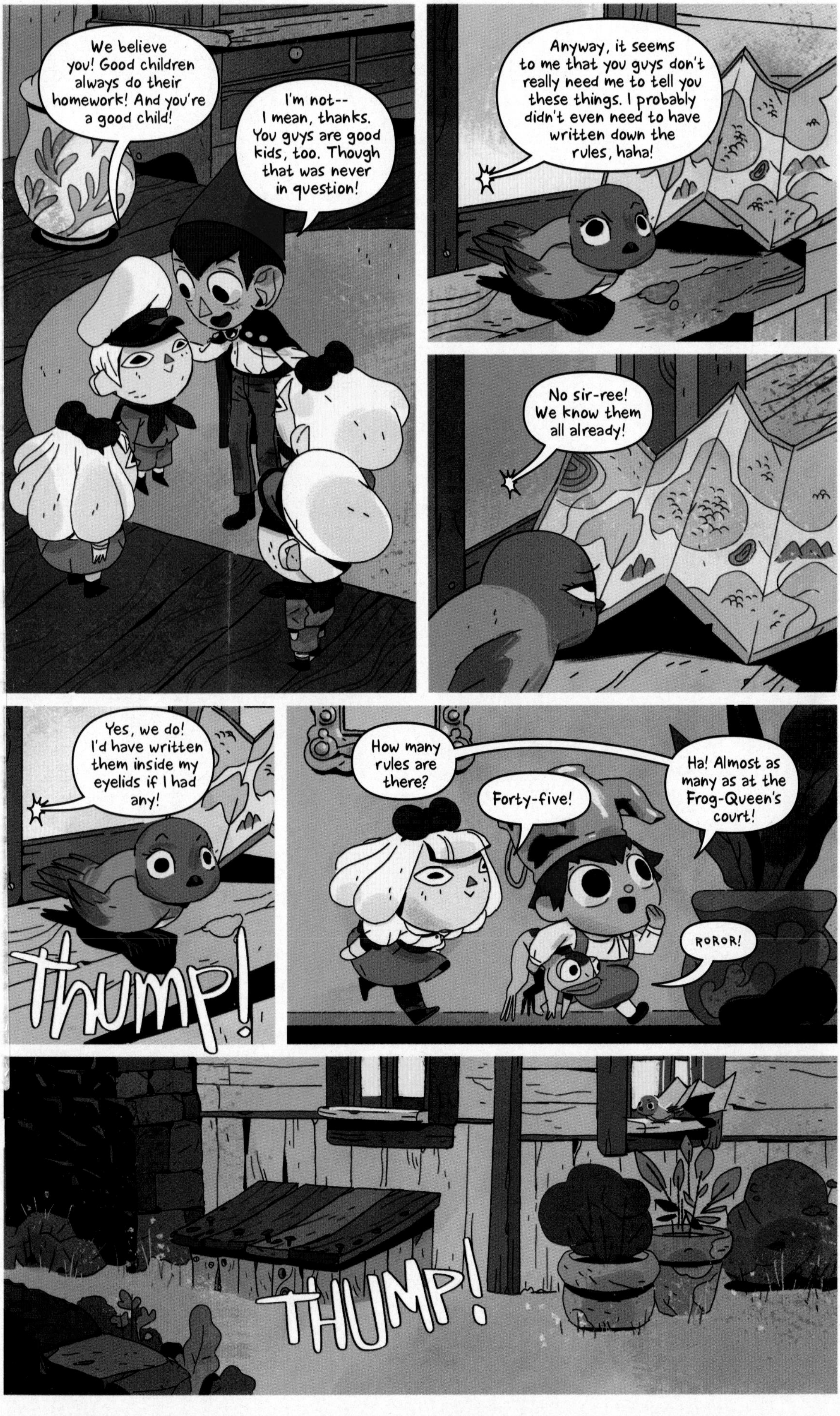
We believe you! Good children always do their homework! And you're a good child!
I'm not-- I mean, thanks. You guys are good kids, too. Though that was never in question!
Anyway, it seems to me that you guys don't really need me to tell you these things. I probably didn't even need to have written down the rules, haha!
No sir-ree! We know them all already!
Yes, we do! I'd have written them inside my eyelids if I had any!
THUMP!
How many rules are there?
Forty-five!
Ha! Almost as many as at the Frog-Queen's court!
ROROR!
THUMP!

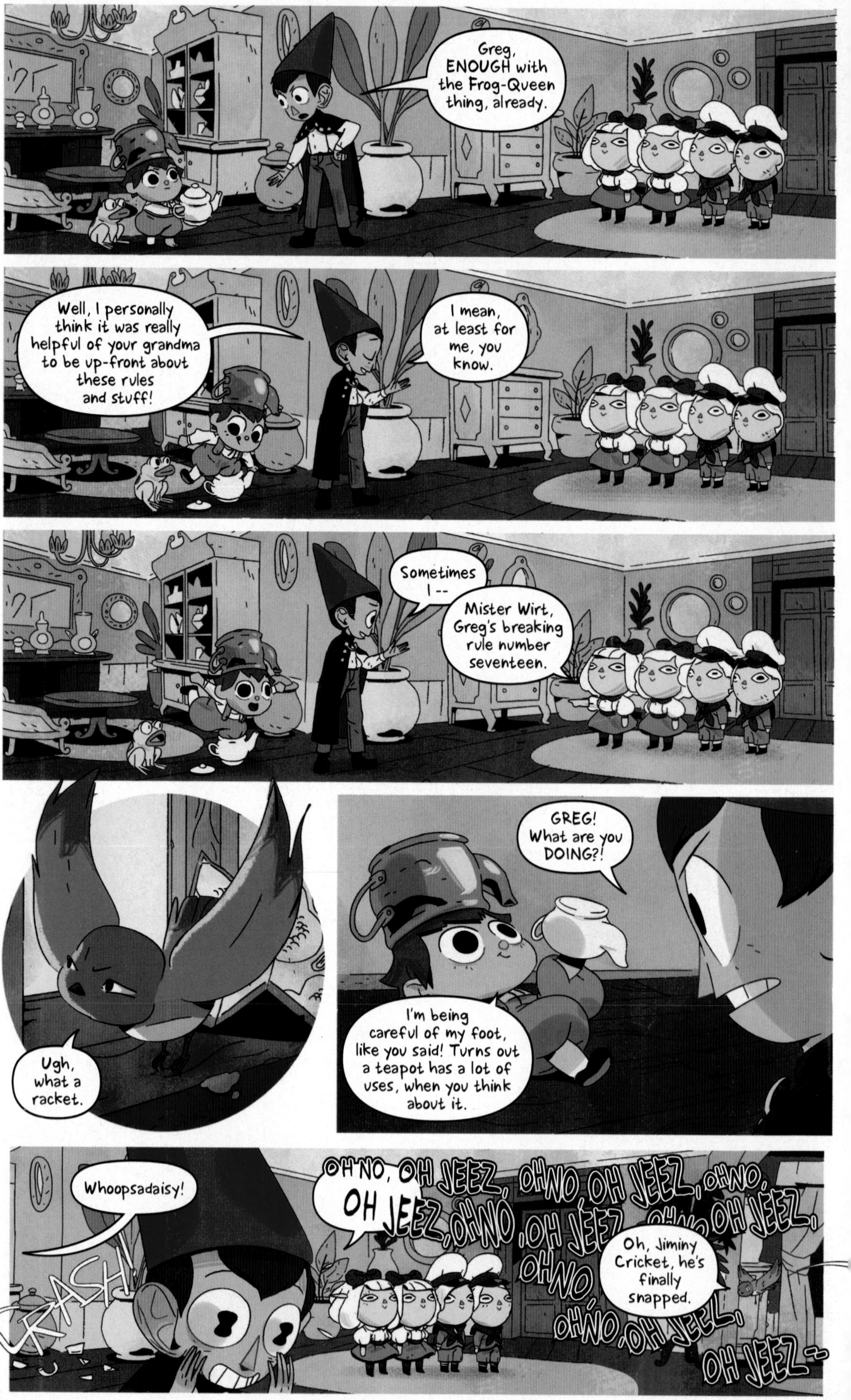
Greg, ENOUGH with the Frog-Queen thing, already.
Well, I personally think it was really helpful of your grandma to be up-front about these rules and stuff!
I mean, at least for me, you know.
Sometimes I --
Mister Wirt, Greg's breaking rule number seventeen.
Ugh, what a racket.
GREG! What are you DOING?!
I'm being careful of my foot, like you said! Turns out a teapot has a lot of uses, when you think about it.
Whoopsadaisy!
CRASH!
OH NO, OH JEEZ, OH NO, OH JEEZ, OH NO, OH JEEZ, OH NO, OH JEEZ, OH NO, OH JEEZ, OH NO, OH NO, OH JEEZ, OH JEEZ -
Oh, Jiminy Cricket, he's finally snapped.

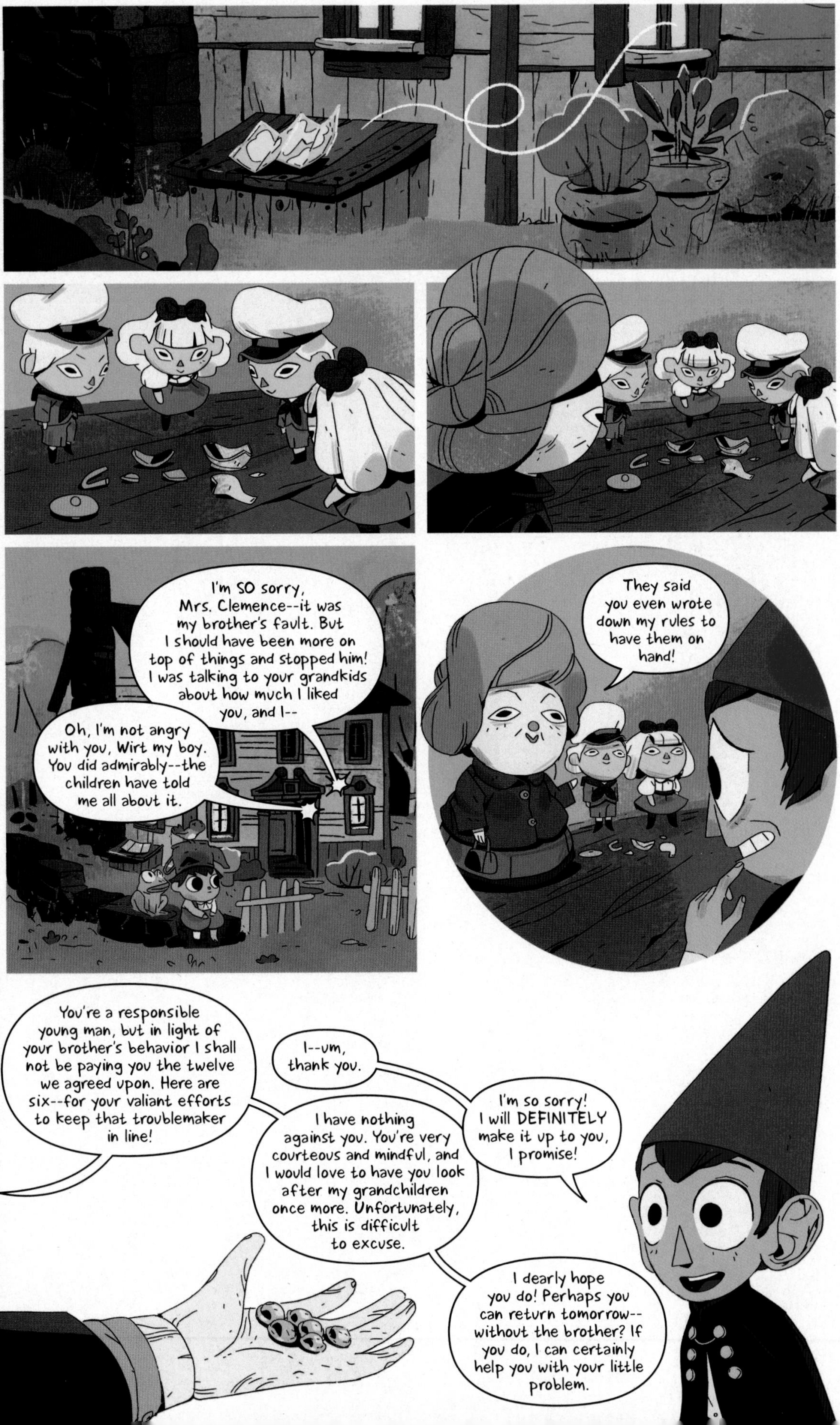
I'm SO sorry, Mrs. Clemence--it was my brother's fault. But I should have been more on top of things and stopped him! I was talking to your grandkids about how much I liked you, and I--
Oh, I'm not angry with you, Wirt my boy. You did admirably--the children have told me all about it.
They said you even wrote down my rules to have them on hand!
You're a responsible young man, but in light of your brother's behavior I shall not be paying you the twelve we agreed upon. Here are six--for your valiant efforts to keep that troublemaker in line!
I--um, thank you.
I have nothing against you. You're very courteous and mindful, and I would love to have you look after my grandchildren once more. Unfortunately, this is difficult to excuse.
I'm so sorry! I will DEFINITELY make it up to you, I promise!
I dearly hope you do! Perhaps you can return tomorrow--without the brother? If you do, I can certainly help you with your little problem.

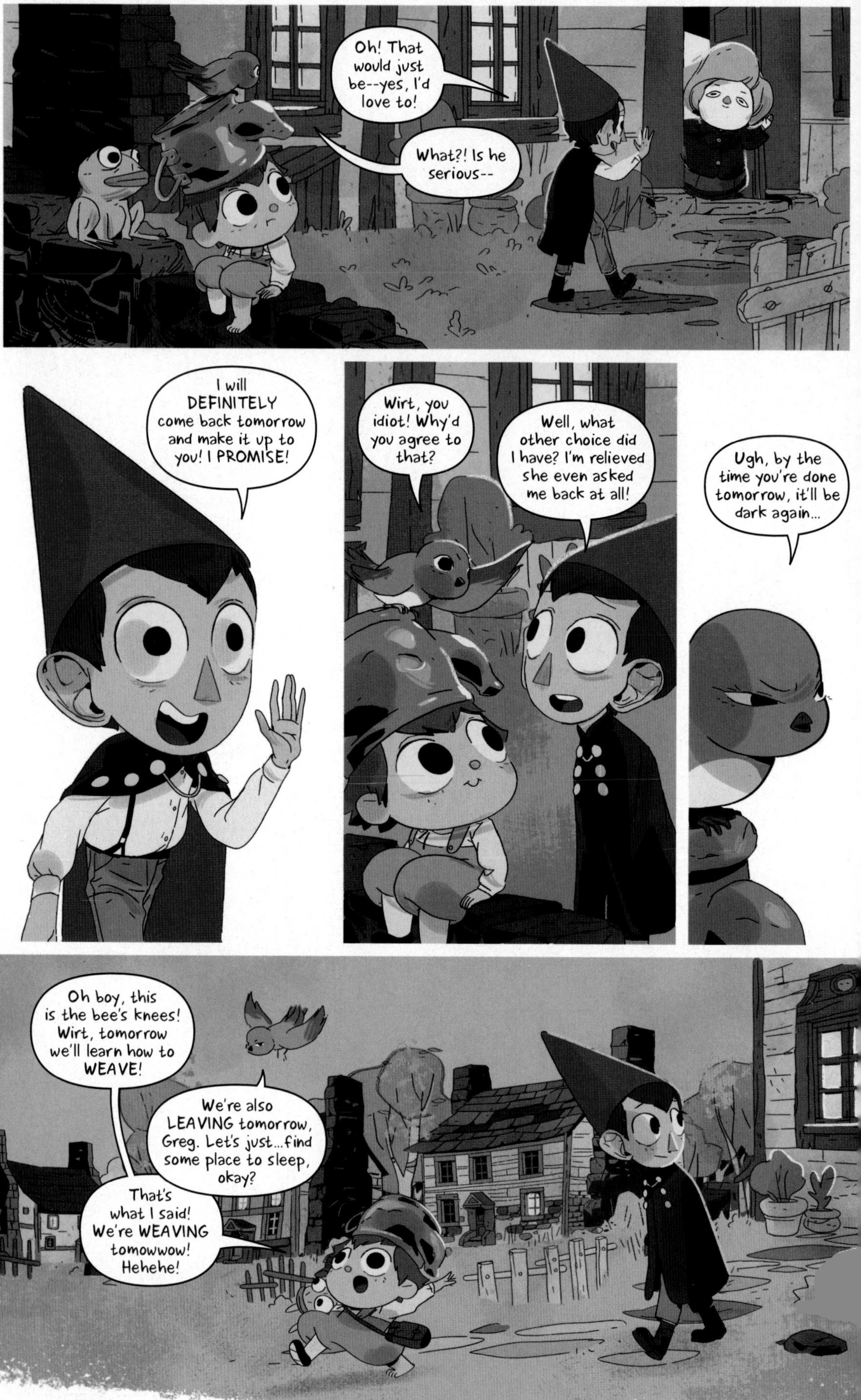
Oh! That would just be--yes, I'd love to!
What?! Is he serious--
I will DEFINITELY come back tomorrow and make it up to you! I PROMISE!
Wirt, you idiot! Why'd you agree to that?
Well, what other choice did I have? I'm relieved she even asked me back at all!
Ugh, by the time you're done tomorrow, it'll be dark again...
Oh boy, this is the bee's knees! Wirt, tomorrow we'll learn how to WEAVE!
We're also LEAVING tomorrow, Greg. Let's just...find some place to sleep, okay?
That's what I said! We're WEAVING tomowwow! Hehehe!

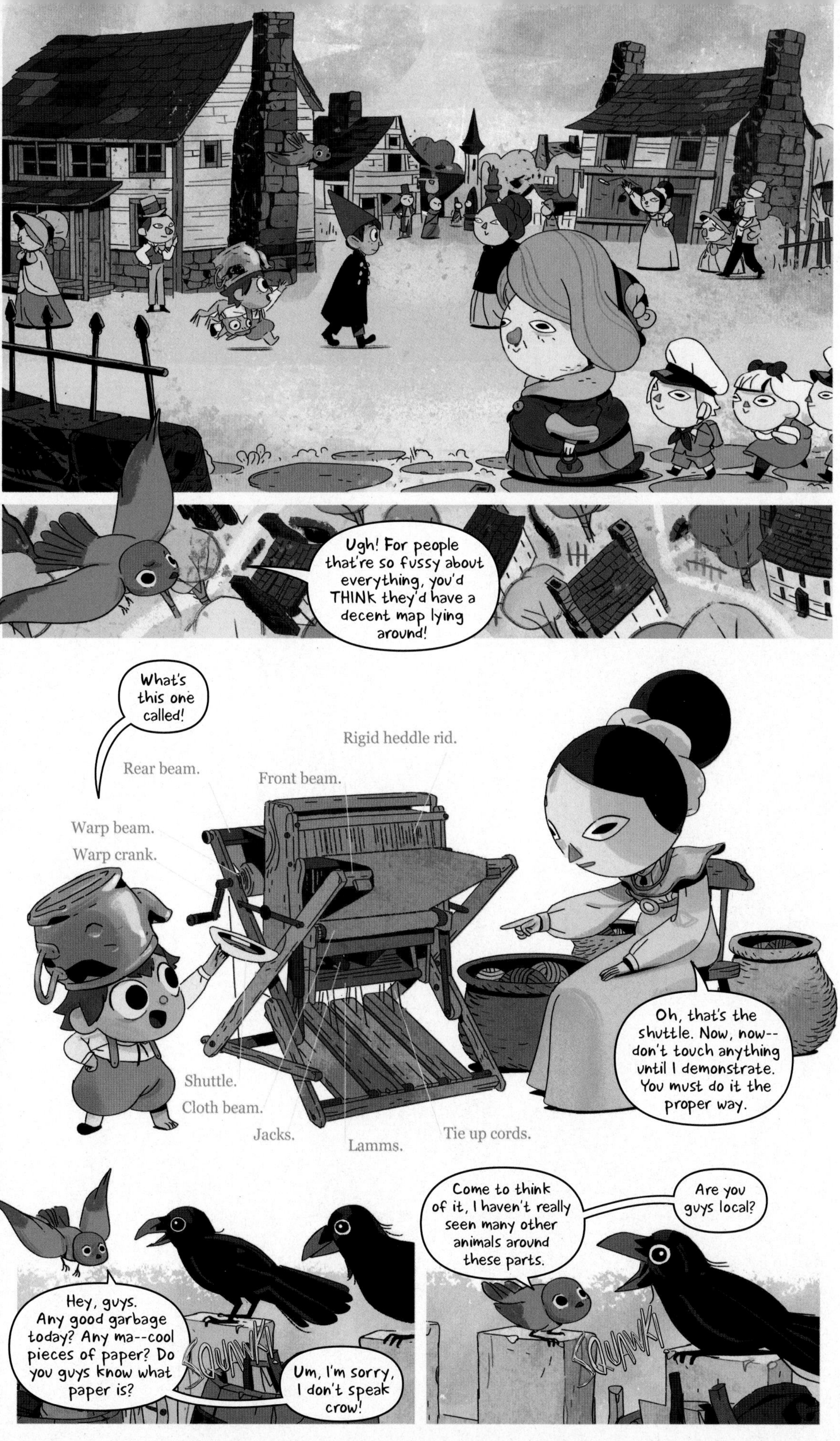
Ugh! For people that're so fussy about everything, you'd THINK they'd have a decent map lying around!
What's this one called!
Rigid heddle rid.
Rear beam.
Front beam.
Warp beam.
Warp crank.
Shuttle.
Cloth beam.
Jacks.
Lamms.
Tie up cords.
Oh, that's the shuttle. Now, now--don't touch anything until I demonstrate. You must do it the proper way.
Hey, guys. Any good garbage today? Any ma--cool pieces of paper? Do you guys know what paper is?
SQUAWK!
Um, I'm sorry, I don't speak crow!
Come to think of it, I haven't really seen many other animals around these parts.
Are you guys local?
SQUAWK!

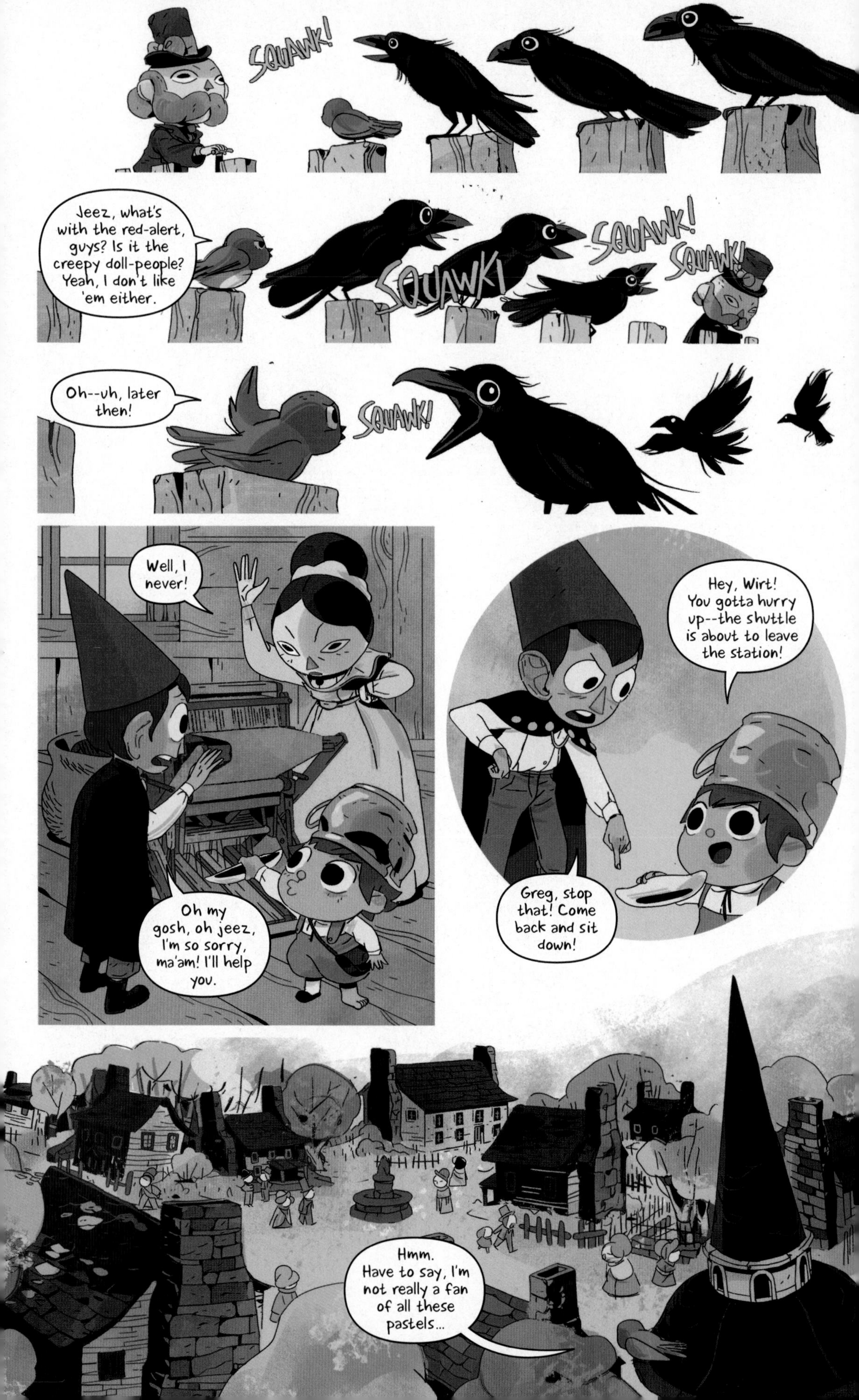
SQUAWK!
Jeez, what's with the red-alert, guys? Is it the creepy doll-people? Yeah, I don't like 'em either.
SQUAWK!
SQUAWK!
SQUAWK!
Oh--uh, later then!
SQUAWK!
Well, I never!
Oh my gosh, oh jeez, I'm so sorry, ma'am! I'll help you.
Hey, Wirt! You gotta hurry up--the shuttle is about to leave the station!
Greg, stop that! Come back and sit down!
Hmm. Have to say, I'm not really a fan of all these pastels...

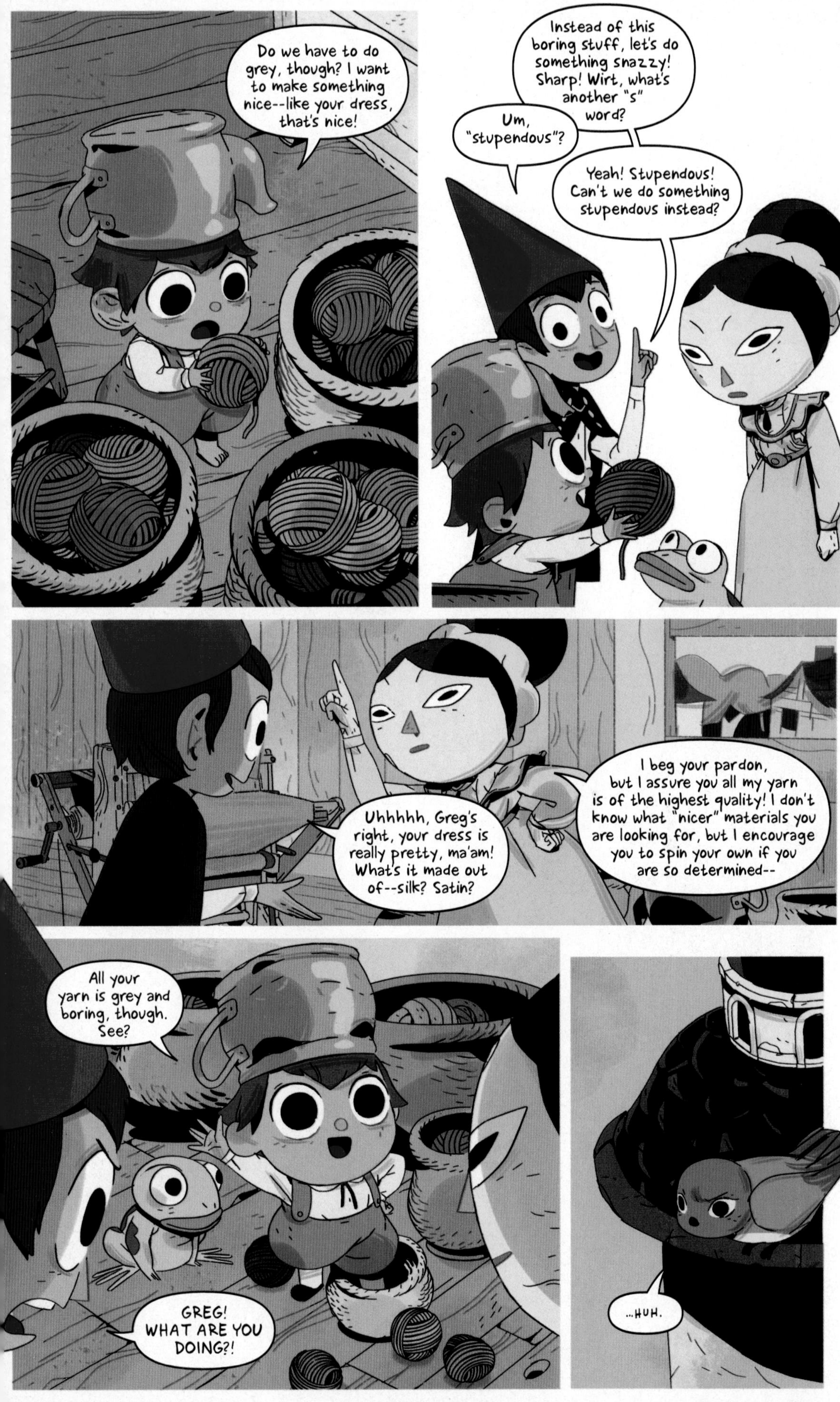
Do we have to do grey, though? I want to make something nice--like your dress, that's nice!
Instead of this boring stuff, let's do something snazzy! Sharp! Wirt, what's another "s" word?
Um, "stupendous"?
Yeah! Stupendous! Can't we do something stupendous instead?
Uhhhhh, Greg's right, your dress is really pretty, ma'am! What's it made out of--silk? Satin?
I beg your pardon, but I assure you all my yarn is of the highest quality! I don't know what "nicer" materials you are looking for, but I encourage you to spin your own if you are so determined--
All your yarn is grey and boring, though. See?
GREG! WHAT ARE YOU DOING?!
...HUH.

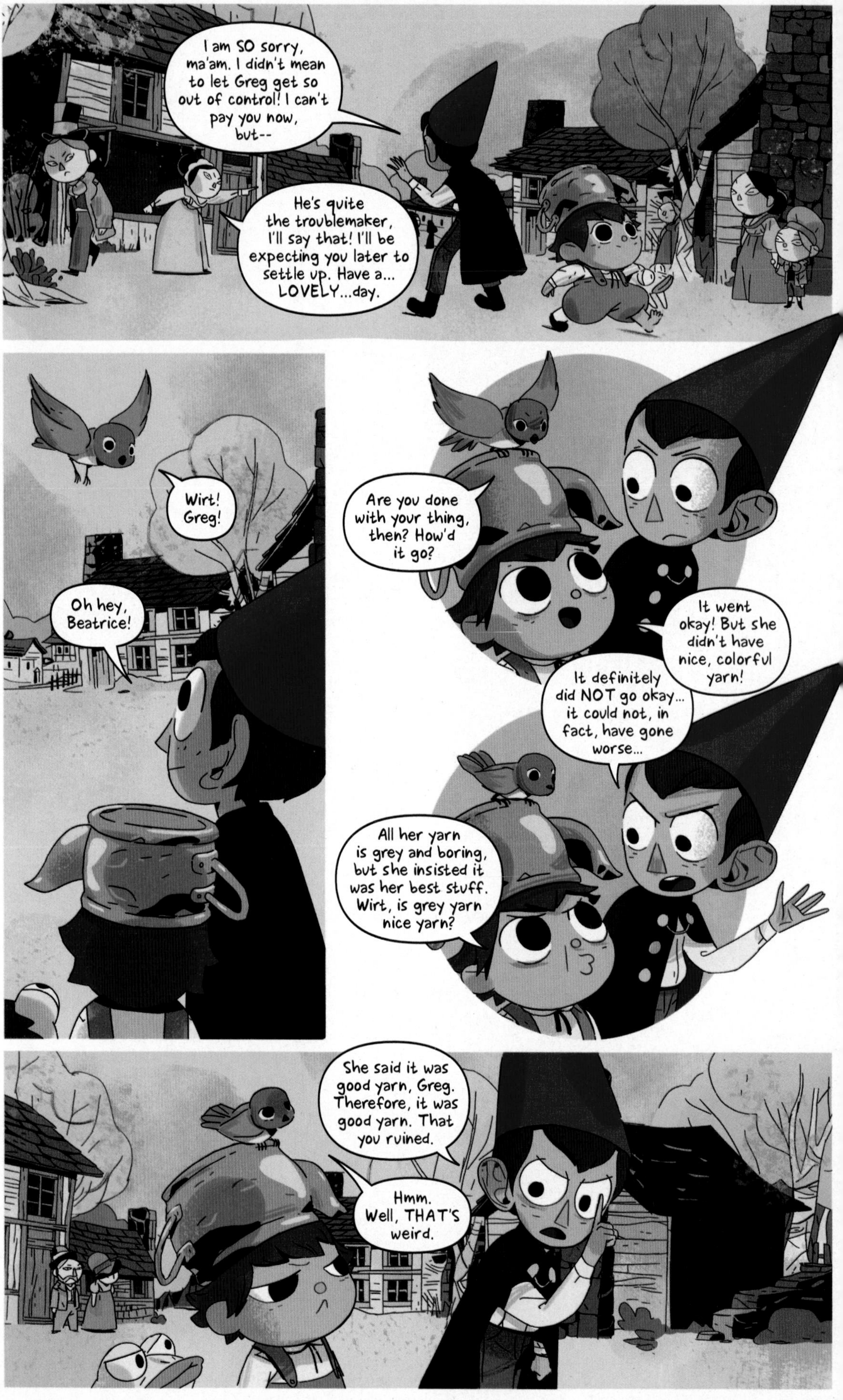
I am SO sorry, ma'am. I didn't mean to let Greg get so out of control! I can't pay you now, but--
He's quite the troublemaker, I'll say that! I'll be expecting you later to settle up. Have a... LOVELY...day.
Wirt! Greg!
Oh hey, Beatrice!
Are you done with your thing, then? How'd it go?
It went okay! But she didn't have nice, colorful yarn!
It definitely did NOT go okay... it could not, in fact, have gone worse...
All her yarn is grey and boring, but she insisted it was her best stuff. Wirt, is grey yarn nice yarn?
She said it was good yarn, Greg. Therefore, it was good yarn. That you ruined.
Hmm. Well, THAT'S weird.

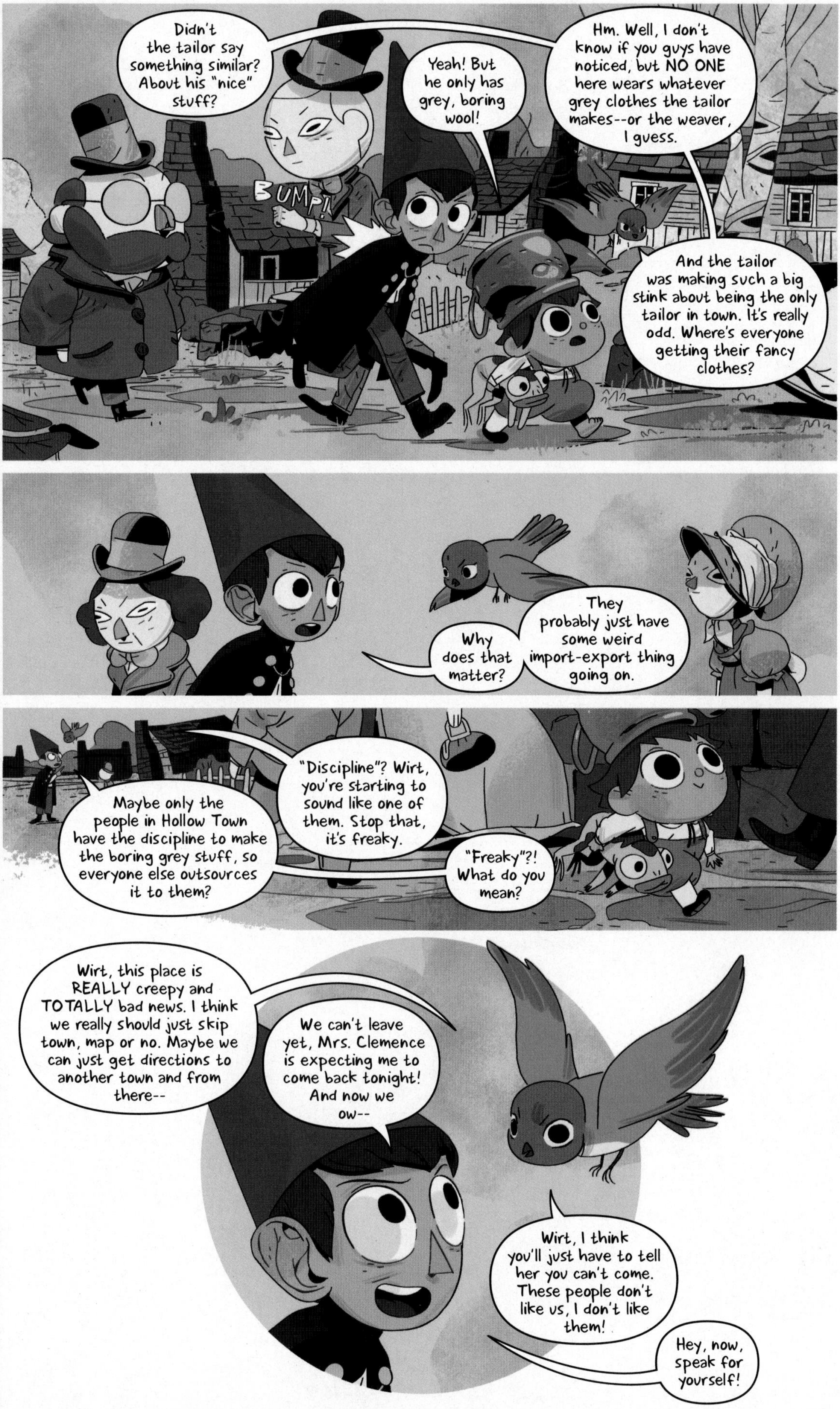
Didn't the tailor say something similar? About his "nice" stuff?
Yeah! But he only has grey, boring wool!
Hm. Well, I don't know if you guys have noticed, but NO ONE here wears whatever grey clothes the tailor makes--or the weaver, I guess.
BUMP!
And the tailor was making such a big stink about being the only tailor in town. It's really odd. Where's everyone getting their fancy clothes?
Why does that matter?
They probably just have some weird import-export thing going on.
Maybe only the people in Hollow Town have the discipline to make the boring grey stuff, so everyone else outsources it to them?
"Discipline"? Wirt, you're starting to sound like one of them. Stop that, it's freaky.
"Freaky"?! What do you mean?
Wirt, this place is REALLY creepy and TOTALLY bad news. I think we really should just skip town, map or no. Maybe we can just get directions to another town and from there--
We can't leave yet, Mrs. Clemence is expecting me to come back tonight! And now we ow--
Wirt, I think you'll just have to tell her you can't come. These people don't like us, I don't like them!
Hey, now, speak for yourself!

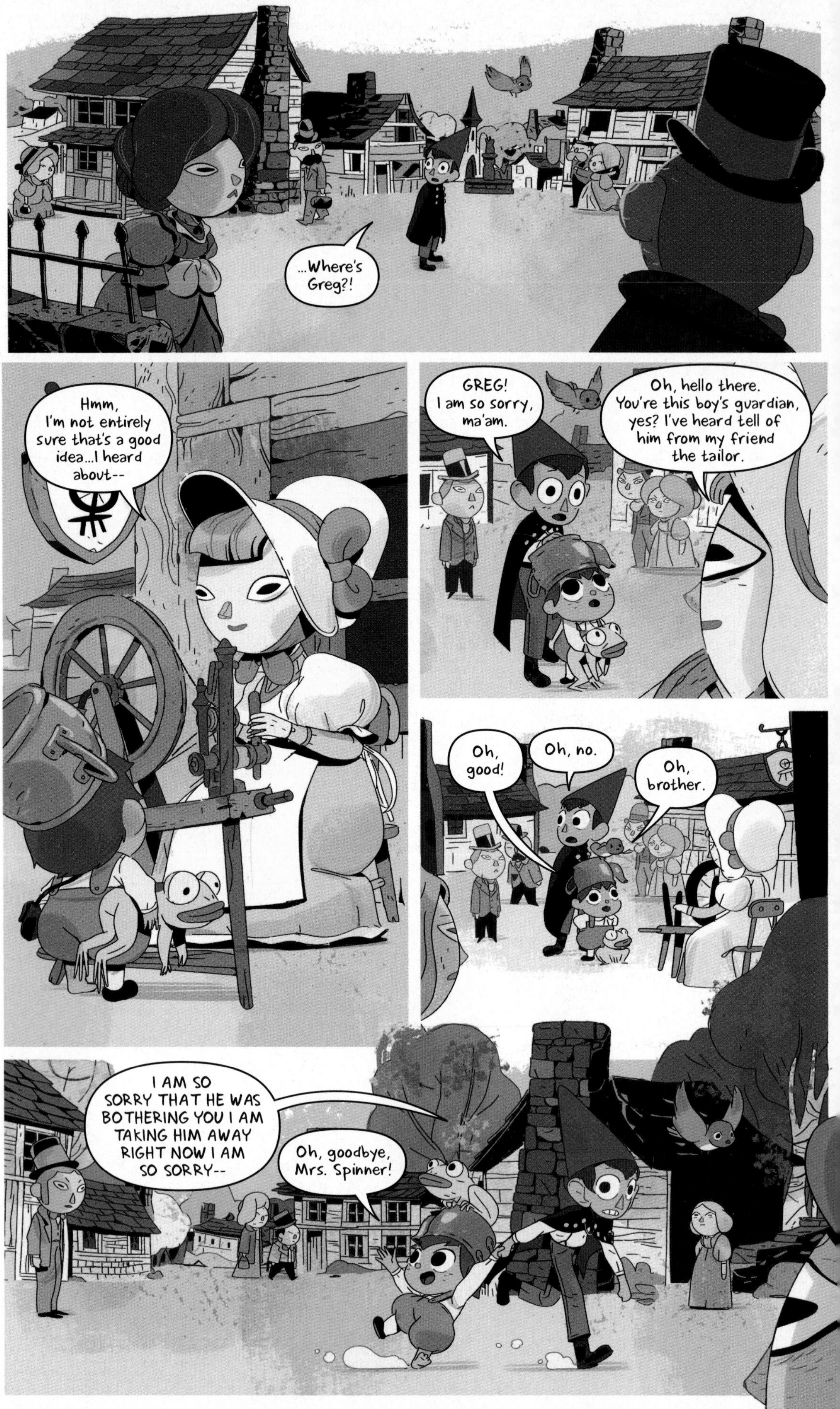
...Where's Greg?!
Hmm, I'm not entirely sure that's a good idea...I heard about--
GREG! I am so sorry, ma'am.
Oh, hello there. You're this boy's guardian, yes? I've heard tell of him from my friend the tailor.
Oh, good!
Oh, no.
Oh, brother.
I AM SO SORRY THAT HE WAS BOTHERING YOU I AM TAKING HIM AWAY RIGHT NOW I AM SO SORRY--
Oh, goodbye, Mrs. Spinner!

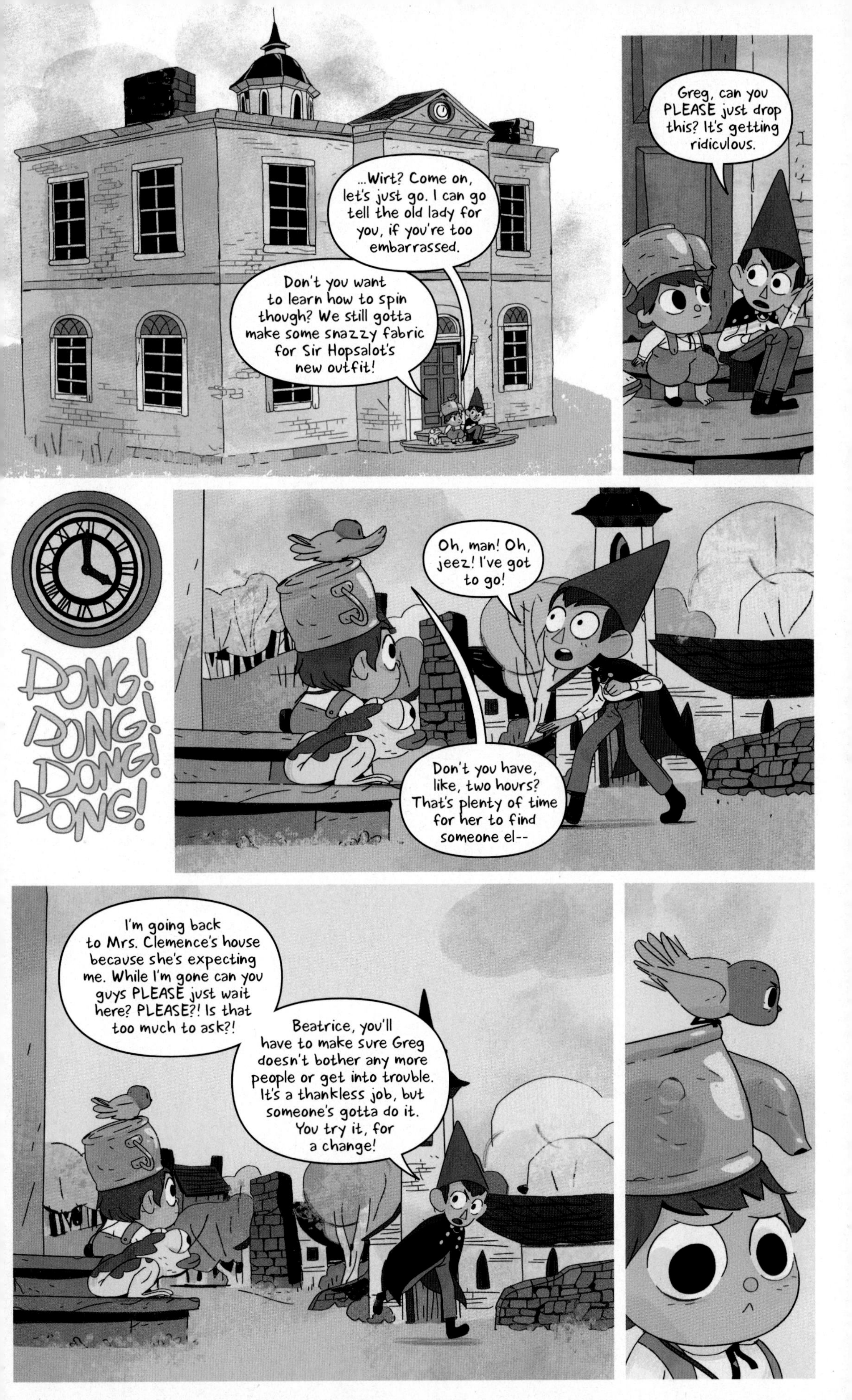
...Wirt? Come on, let's just go. I can go tell the old lady for you, if you're too embarrassed.
Don't you want to learn how to spin though? We still gotta make some snazzy fabric for Sir Hopsalot's new outfit!
Greg, can you PLEASE just drop this? It's getting ridiculous.
DONG! DONG! DONG! DONG!
Oh, man! Oh, jeez! I've got to go!
Don't you have, like, two hours? That's plenty of time for her to find someone el--
I'm going back to Mrs. Clemence's house because she's expecting me. While I'm gone can you guys PLEASE just wait here? PLEASE?! Is that too much to ask?!
Beatrice, you'll have to make sure Greg doesn't bother any more people or get into trouble. It's a thankless job, but someone's gotta do it. You try it, for a change!

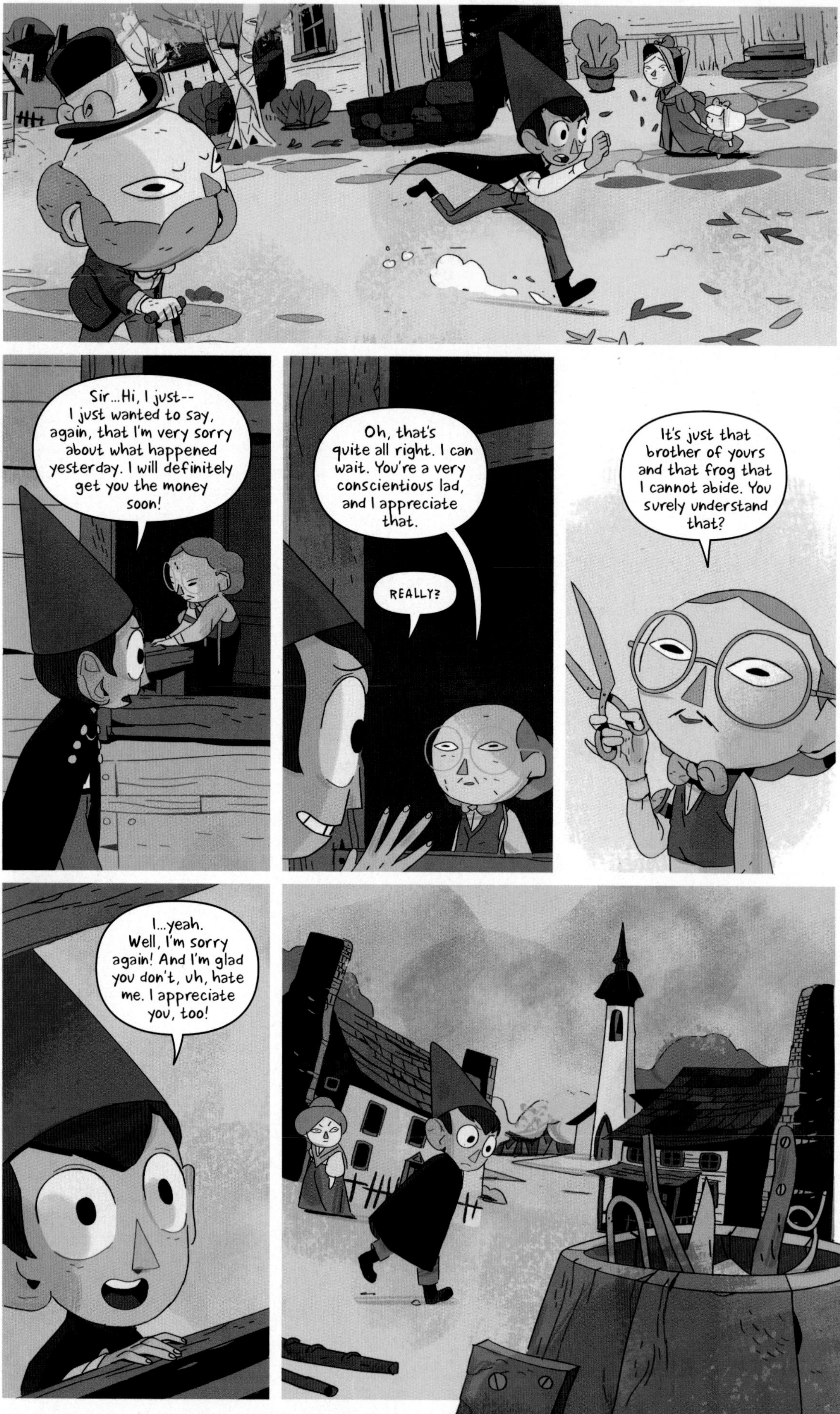
Sir...Hi, I just--
I just wanted to say, again, that I'm very sorry about what happened yesterday. I will definitely get you the money soon!
Oh, that's quite all right. I can wait. You're a very conscientious lad, and I appreciate that.
REALLY?
It's just that brother of yours and that frog that I cannot abide. You surely understand that?
I...yeah. Well, I'm sorry again! And I'm glad you don't, uh, hate me. I appreciate you, too!

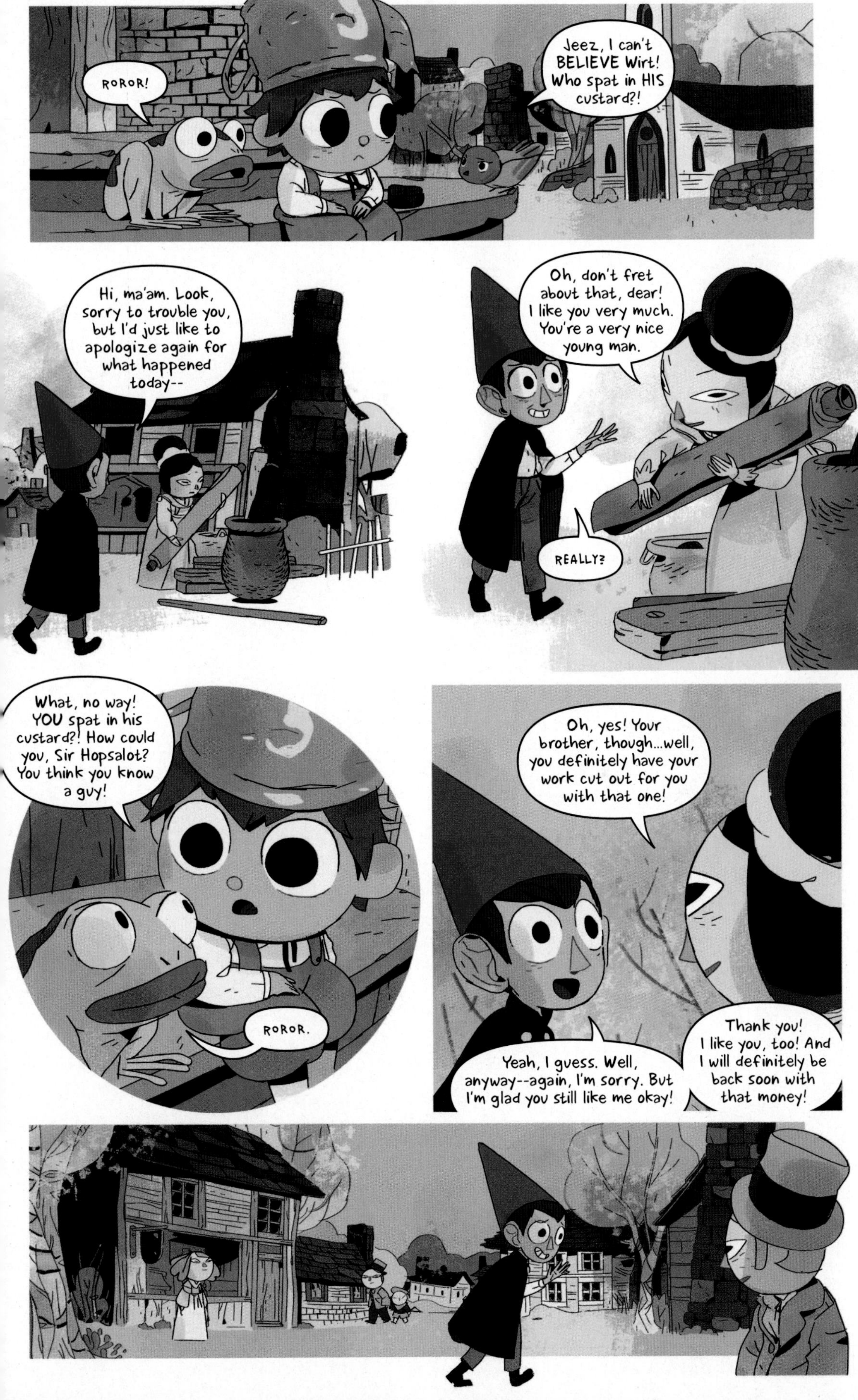
RoRoR!
Jeez, I can't BELIEVE Wirt! Who spat in HIS custard?!
Hi, ma'am. Look, sorry to trouble you, but I'd just like to apologize again for what happened today--
Oh, don't fret about that, dear! I like you very much. You're a very nice young man.
REALLY?
What, no way! YOU spat in his custard?! How could you, Sir Hopsalot? You think you know a guy!
RoRoR.
Oh, yes! Your brother, though...well, you definitely have your work cut out for you with that one!
Yeah, I guess. Well, anyway--again, I'm sorry. But I'm glad you still like me okay!
Thank you! I like you, too! And I will definitely be back soon with that money!

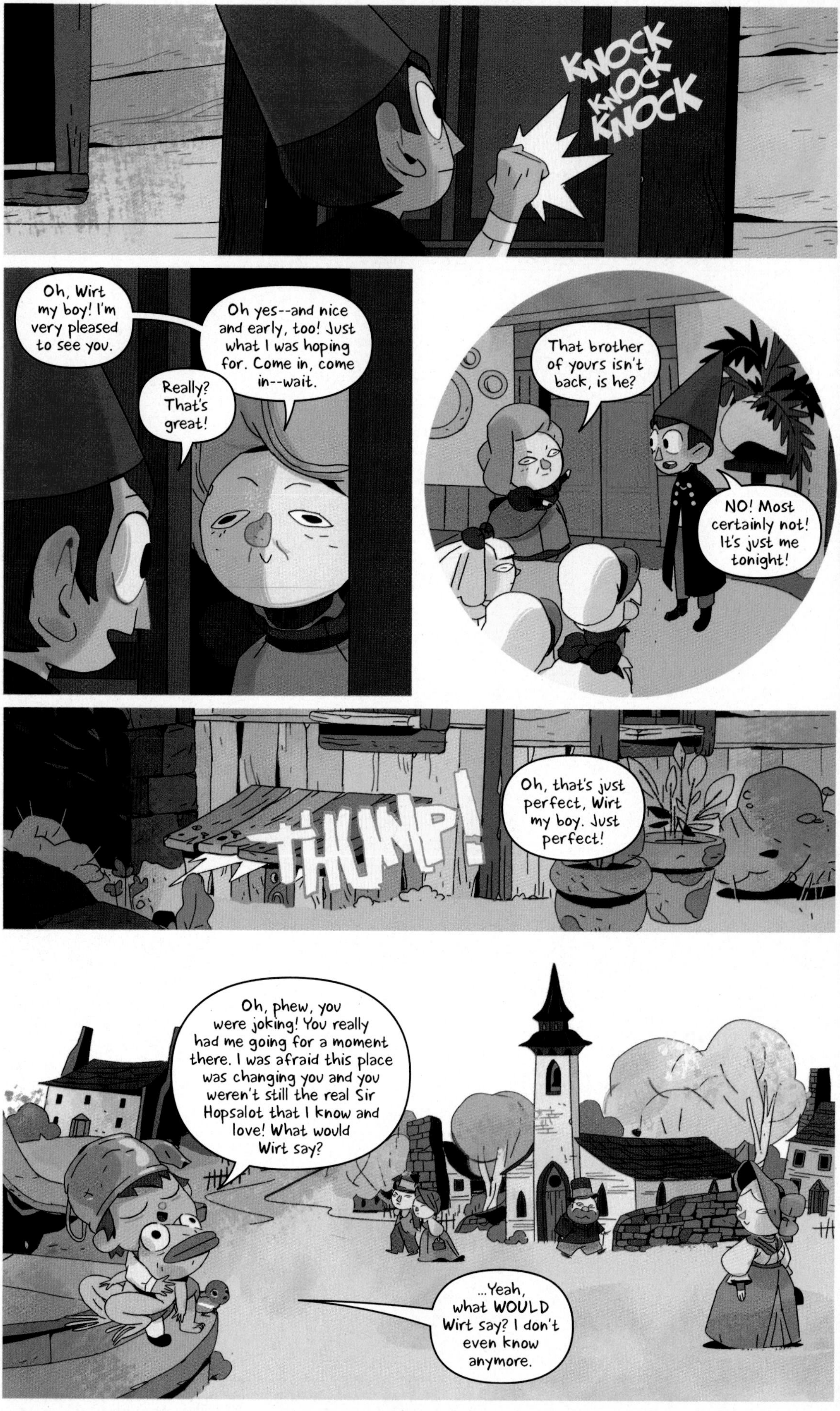
KNOCK KNOCK KNOCK
Oh, Wirt my boy! I'm very pleased to see you.
Really? That's great!
Oh yes--and nice and early, too! Just what I was hoping for. Come in, come in--wait.
That brother of yours isn't back, is he?
NO! Most certainly not! It's just me tonight!
THUMP!
Oh, that's just perfect, Wirt my boy. Just perfect!
Oh, phew, you were joking! You really had me going for a moment there. I was afraid this place was changing you and you weren't still the real Sir Hopsalot that I know and love! What would Wirt say?
...Yeah, what WOULD Wirt say? I don't even know anymore.

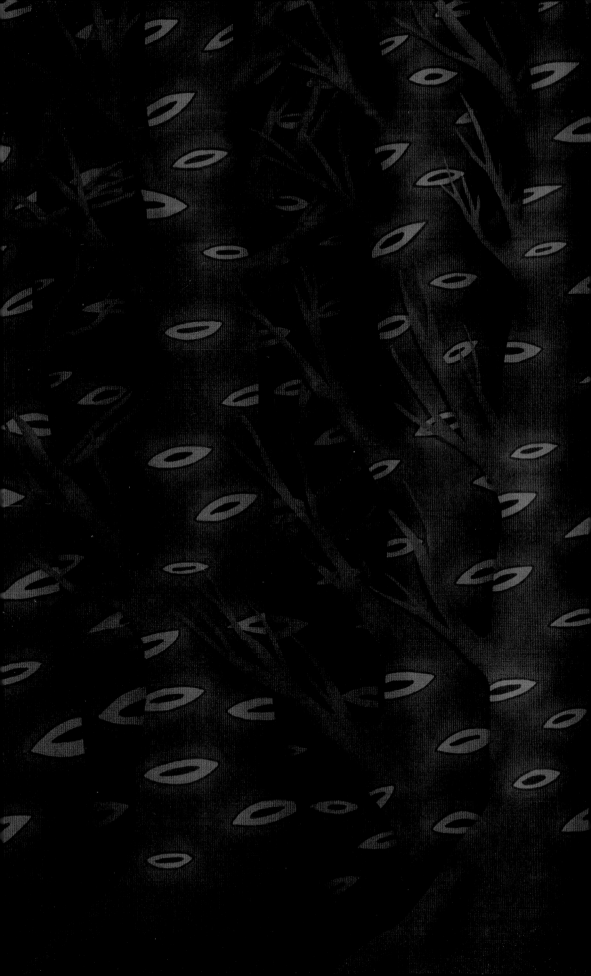

CHAPTER

3

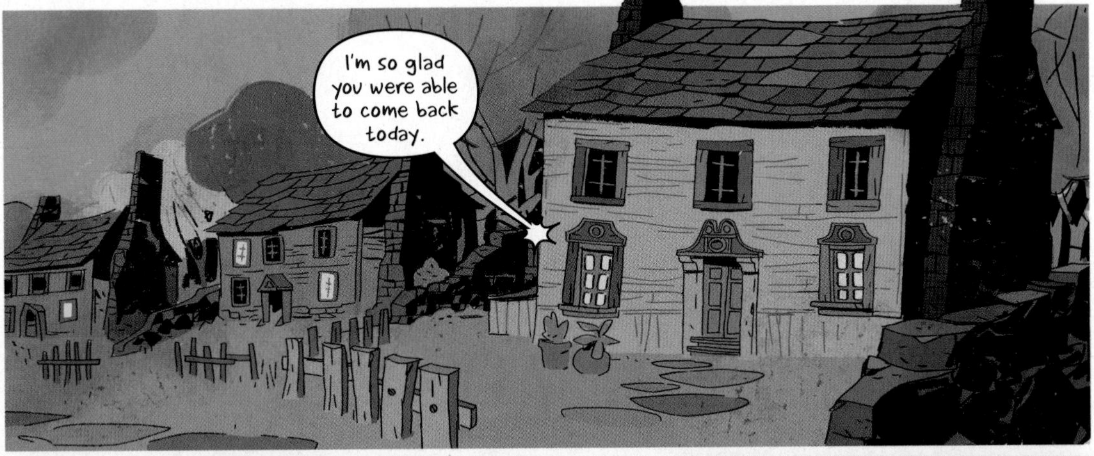
I'm so glad you were able to come back today.

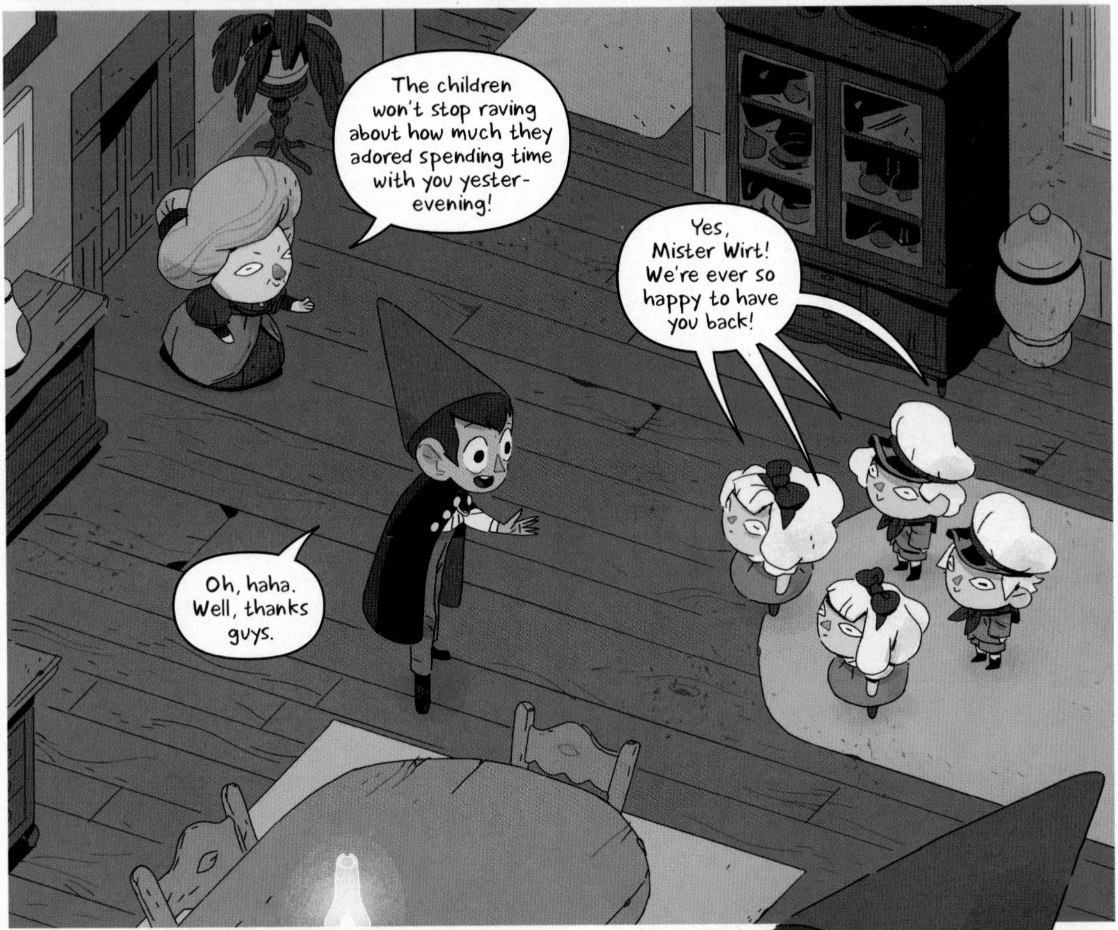
The children won't stop raving about how much they adored spending time with you yester-evening!
Yes, Mister Wirt! We're ever so happy to have you back!
Oh, haha. Well, thanks guys.

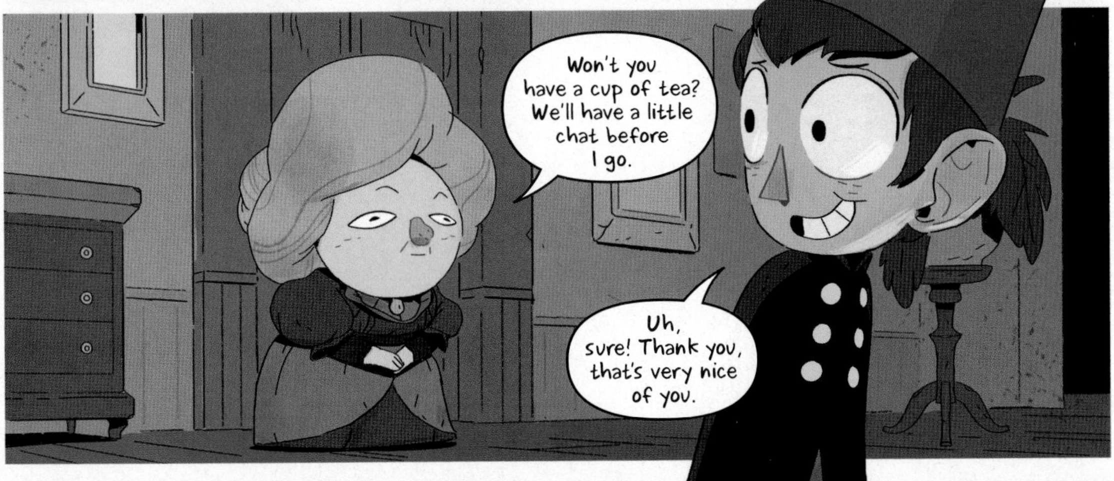
Won't you have a cup of tea? We'll have a little chat before I go.
Uh, sure! Thank you, that's very nice of you.

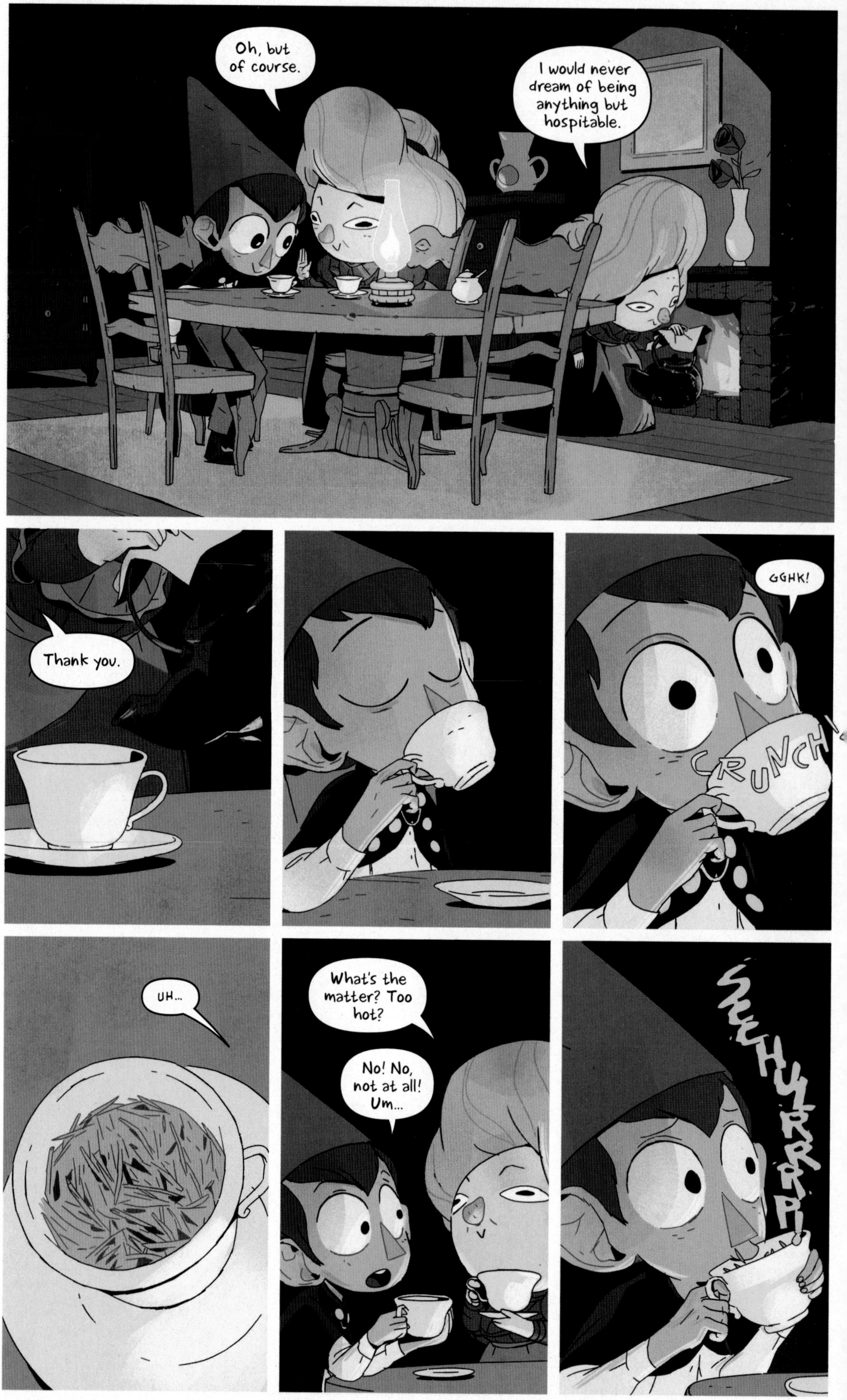
Oh, but of course.
I would never dream of being anything but hospitable.
Thank you.
GGHK!
CRUNCH!
UH...
What's the matter? Too hot?
No! No, not at all! Um...
SCHURRRP!

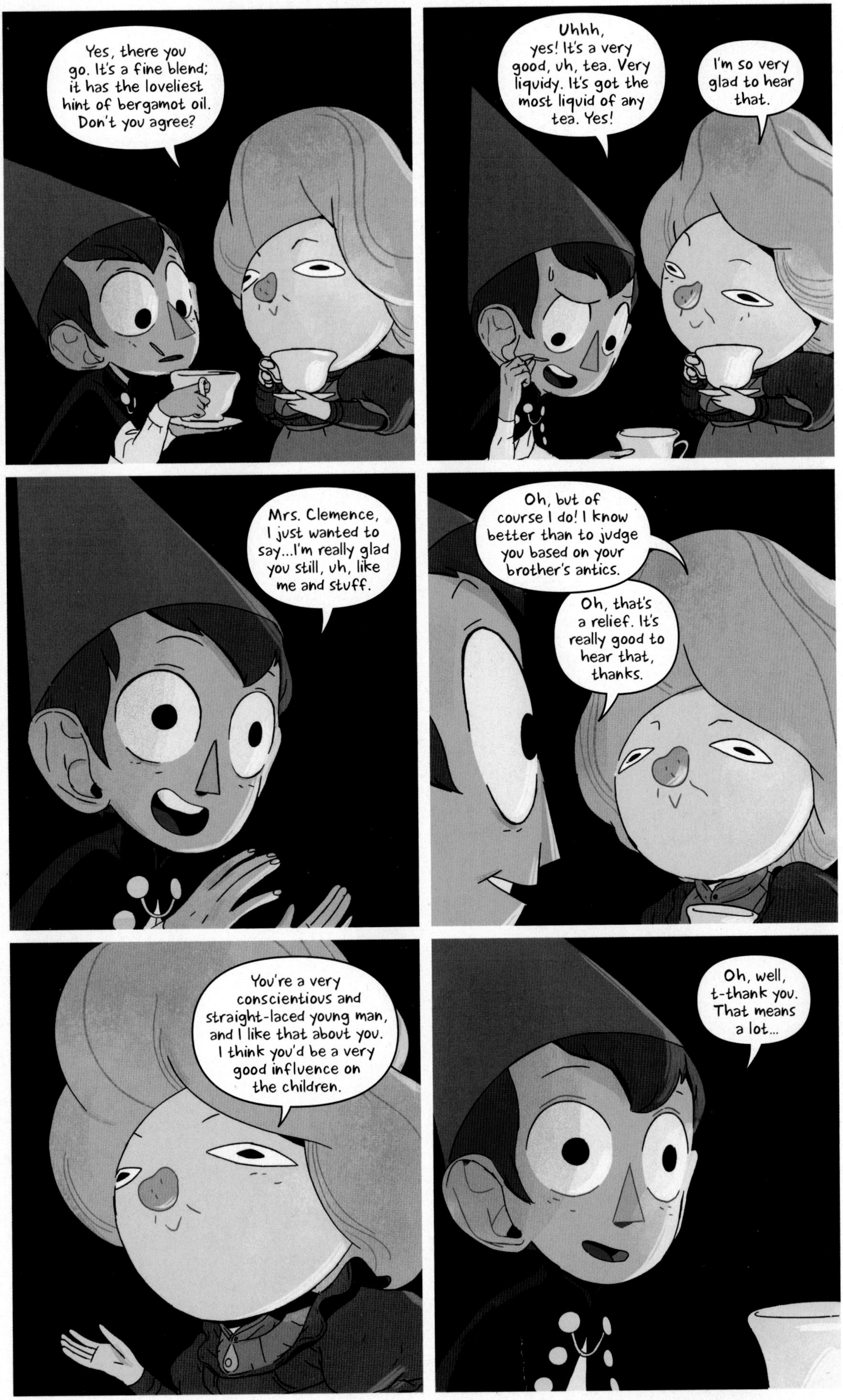
Yes, there you go. It's a fine blend; it has the loveliest hint of bergamot oil. Don't you agree?
Uhhh, yes! It's a very good, uh, tea. Very liquidy. It's got the most liquid of any tea. Yes!
I'm so very glad to hear that.
Mrs. Clemence, I just wanted to say...I'm really glad you still, uh, like me and stuff.
Oh, but of course I do! I know better than to judge you based on your brother's antics.
Oh, that's a relief. It's really good to hear that, thanks.
You're a very conscientious and straight-laced young man, and I like that about you. I think you'd be a very good influence on the children.
Oh, well, t-thank you. That means a lot...

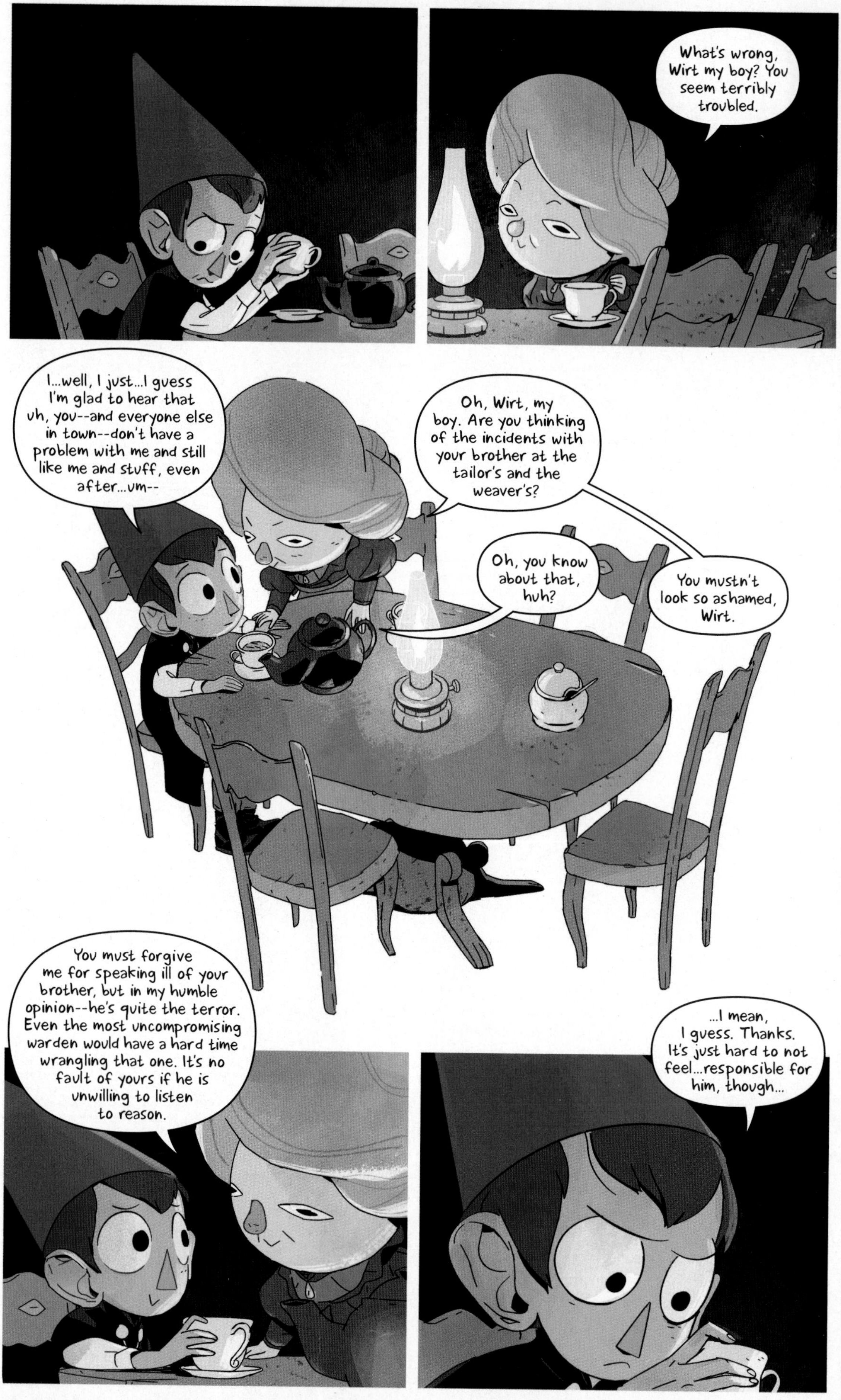
What's wrong, Wirt my boy? You seem terribly troubled.
I...well, I just...I guess I'm glad to hear that uh, you--and everyone else in town--don't have a problem with me and still like me and stuff, even after...um--
Oh, Wirt, my boy. Are you thinking of the incidents with your brother at the tailor's and the weaver's?
Oh, you know about that, huh?
You mustn't look so ashamed, Wirt.
You must forgive me for speaking ill of your brother, but in my humble opinion--he's quite the terror. Even the most uncompromising warden would have a hard time wrangling that one. It's no fault of yours if he is unwilling to listen to reason.
...I mean, I guess. Thanks. It's just hard to not feel...responsible for him, though...

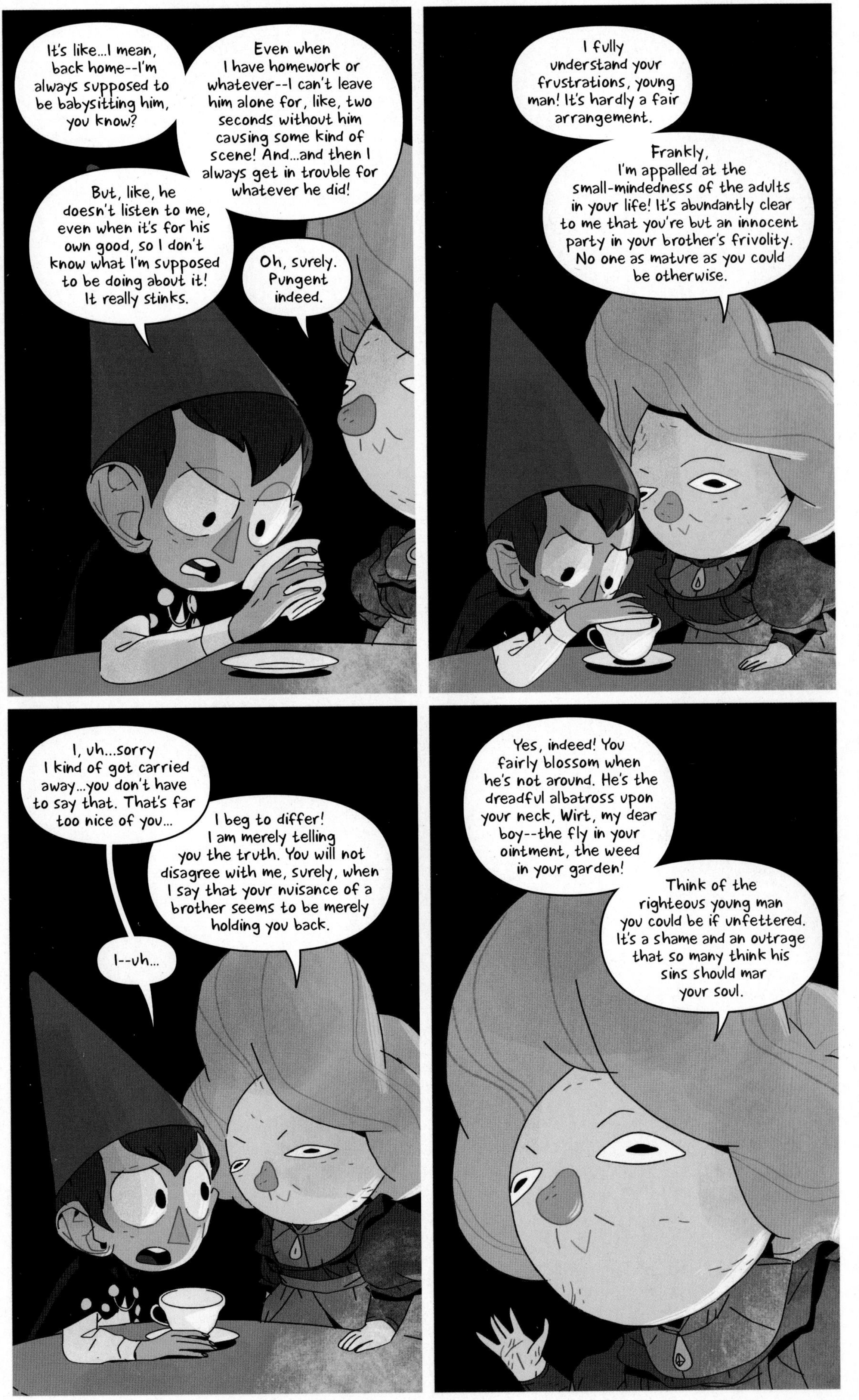
It's like...I mean, back home--I'm always supposed to be babysitting him, you know?
Even when I have homework or whatever--I can't leave him alone for, like, two seconds without him causing some kind of scene! And...and then I always get in trouble for whatever he did!
But, like, he doesn't listen to me, even when it's for his own good, so I don't know what I'm supposed to be doing about it! It really stinks.
Oh, surely. Pungent indeed.
I fully understand your frustrations, young man! It's hardly a fair arrangement.
Frankly, I'm appalled at the small-mindedness of the adults in your life! It's abundantly clear to me that you're but an innocent party in your brother's frivolity. No one as mature as you could be otherwise.
I, uh...sorry I kind of got carried away...you don't have to say that. That's far too nice of you...
I beg to differ! I am merely telling you the truth. You will not disagree with me, surely, when I say that your nuisance of a brother seems to be merely holding you back.
I--uh...
Yes, indeed! You fairly blossom when he's not around. He's the dreadful albatross upon your neck, Wirt, my dear boy--the fly in your ointment, the weed in your garden!
Think of the righteous young man you could be if unfettered. It's a shame and an outrage that so many think his sins should mar your soul.

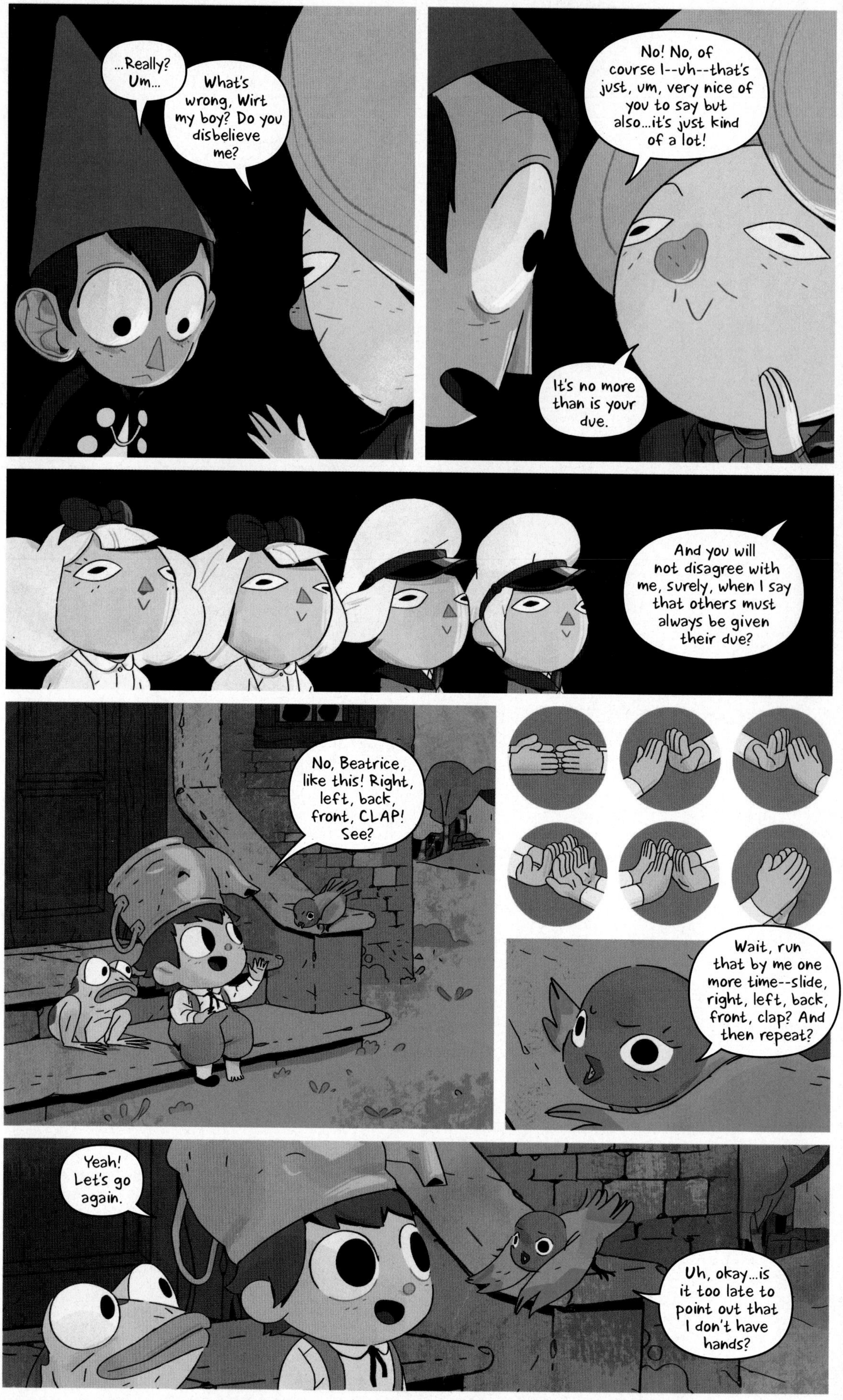
...Really? Um...
What's wrong, Wirt my boy? Do you disbelieve me?
No! No, of course I--uh--that's just, um, very nice of you to say but also...it's just kind of a lot!
It's no more than is your due.
And you will not disagree with me, surely, when I say that others must always be given their due?
No, Beatrice, like this! Right, left, back, front, CLAP! See?
Wait, run that by me one more time--slide, right, left, back, front, clap? And then repeat?
Yeah! Let's go again.
Uh, okay...is it too late to point out that I don't have hands?

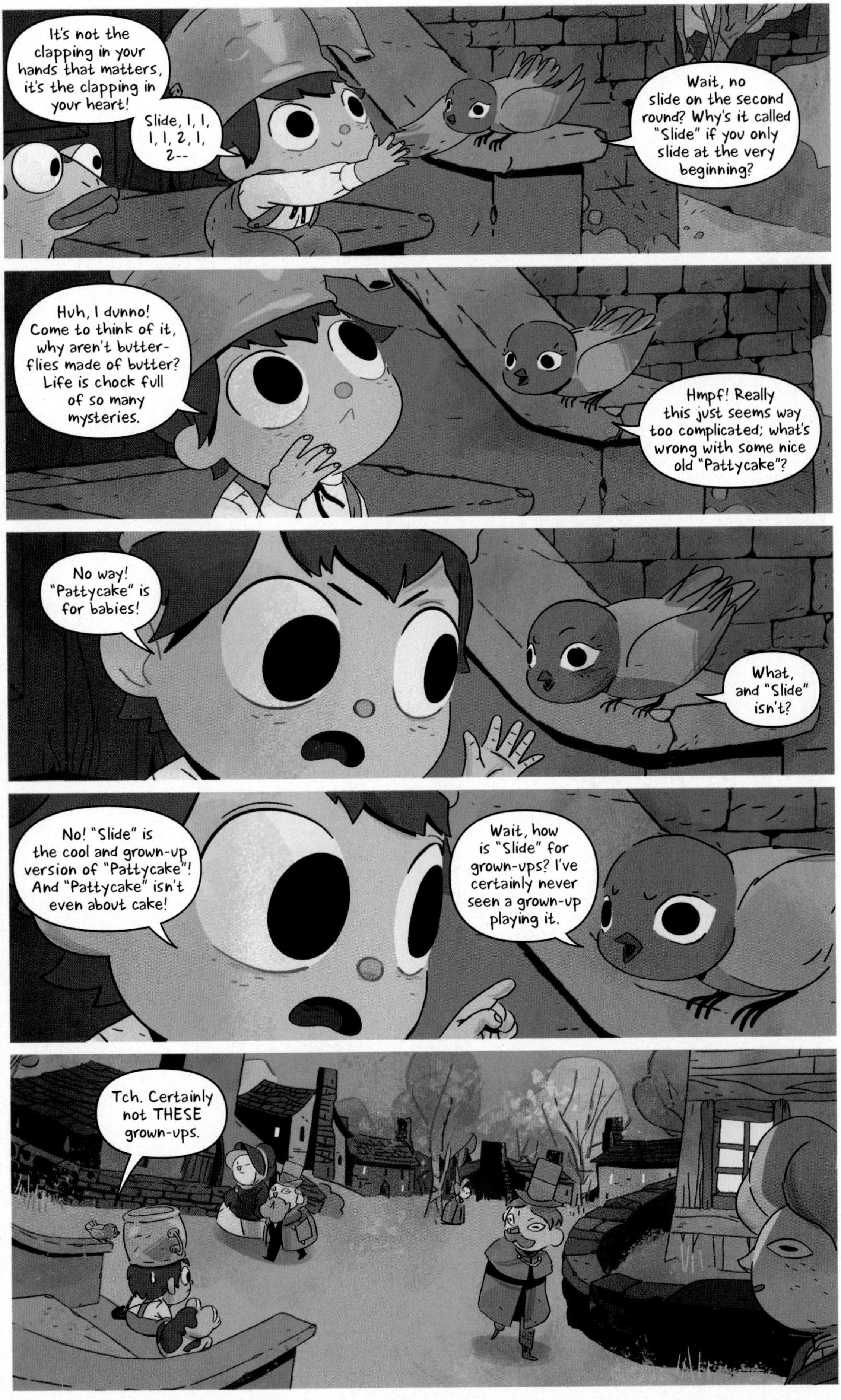
It's not the clapping in your hands that matters, it's the clapping in your heart!
Slide, 1, 1, 1, 1, 2, 1, 2--
Wait, no slide on the second round? Why's it called "Slide" if you only slide at the very beginning?
Huh, I dunno! Come to think of it, why aren't butter-flies made of butter? Life is chock full of so many mysteries.
Hmpf! Really this just seems way too complicated; what's wrong with some nice old "Pattycake"?
No way! "Pattycake" is for babies!
What, and "Slide" isn't?
No! "Slide" is the cool and grown-up version of "Pattycake"! And "Pattycake" isn't even about cake!
Wait, how is "Slide" for grown-ups? I've certainly never seen a grown-up playing it.
Tch. Certainly not THESE grown-ups.

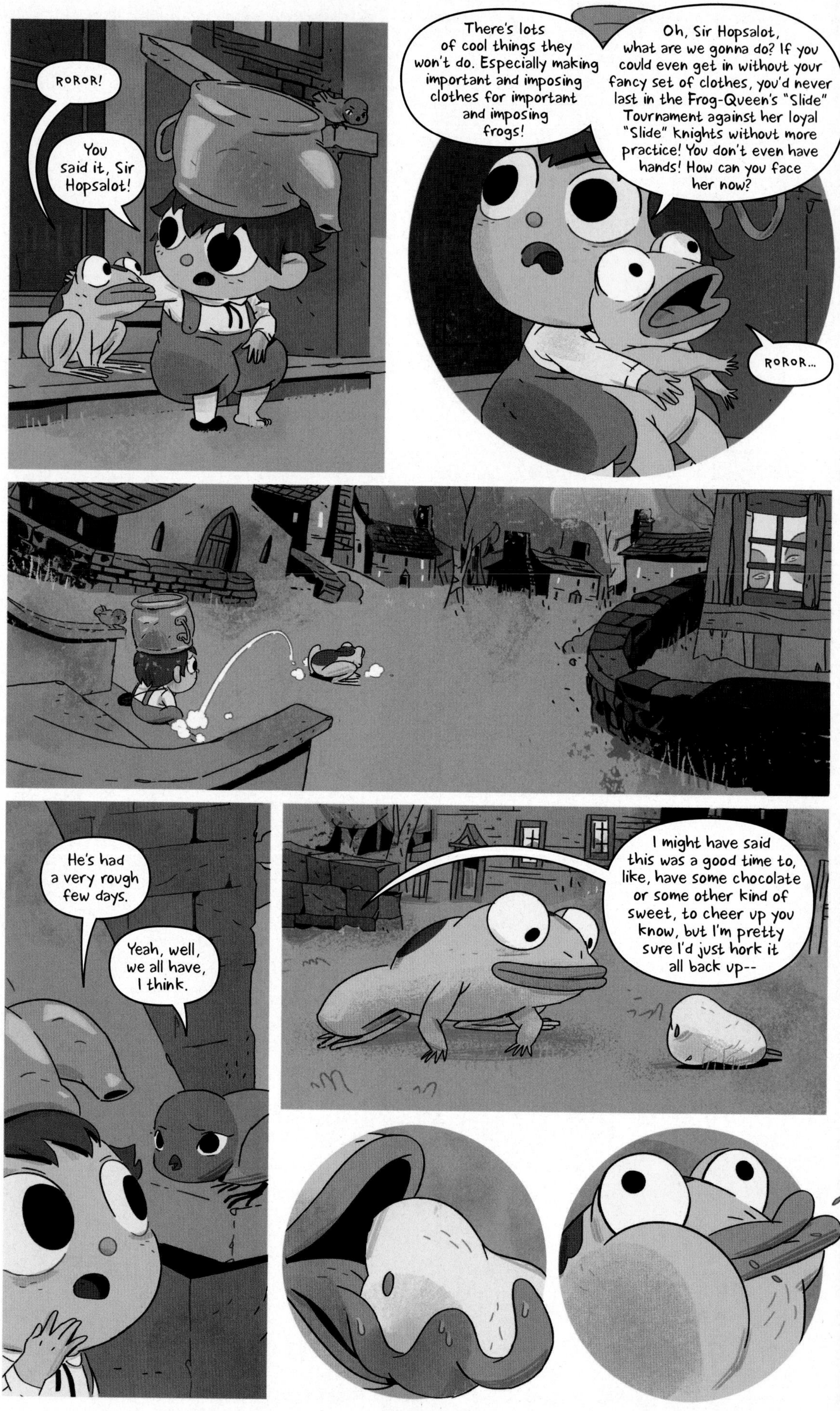
RoROR!
You said it, Sir Hopsalot!
There's lots of cool things they won't do. Especially making important and imposing clothes for important and imposing frogs!
Oh, Sir Hopsalot, what are we gonna do? If you could even get in without your fancy set of clothes, you'd never last in the Frog-Queen's "Slide" Tournament against her loyal "Slide" knights without more practice! You don't even have hands! How can you face her now?
RoROR...
He's had a very rough few days.
Yeah, well, we all have, I think.
I might have said this was a good time to, like, have some chocolate or some other kind of sweet, to cheer up you know, but I'm pretty sure I'd just hork it all back up--

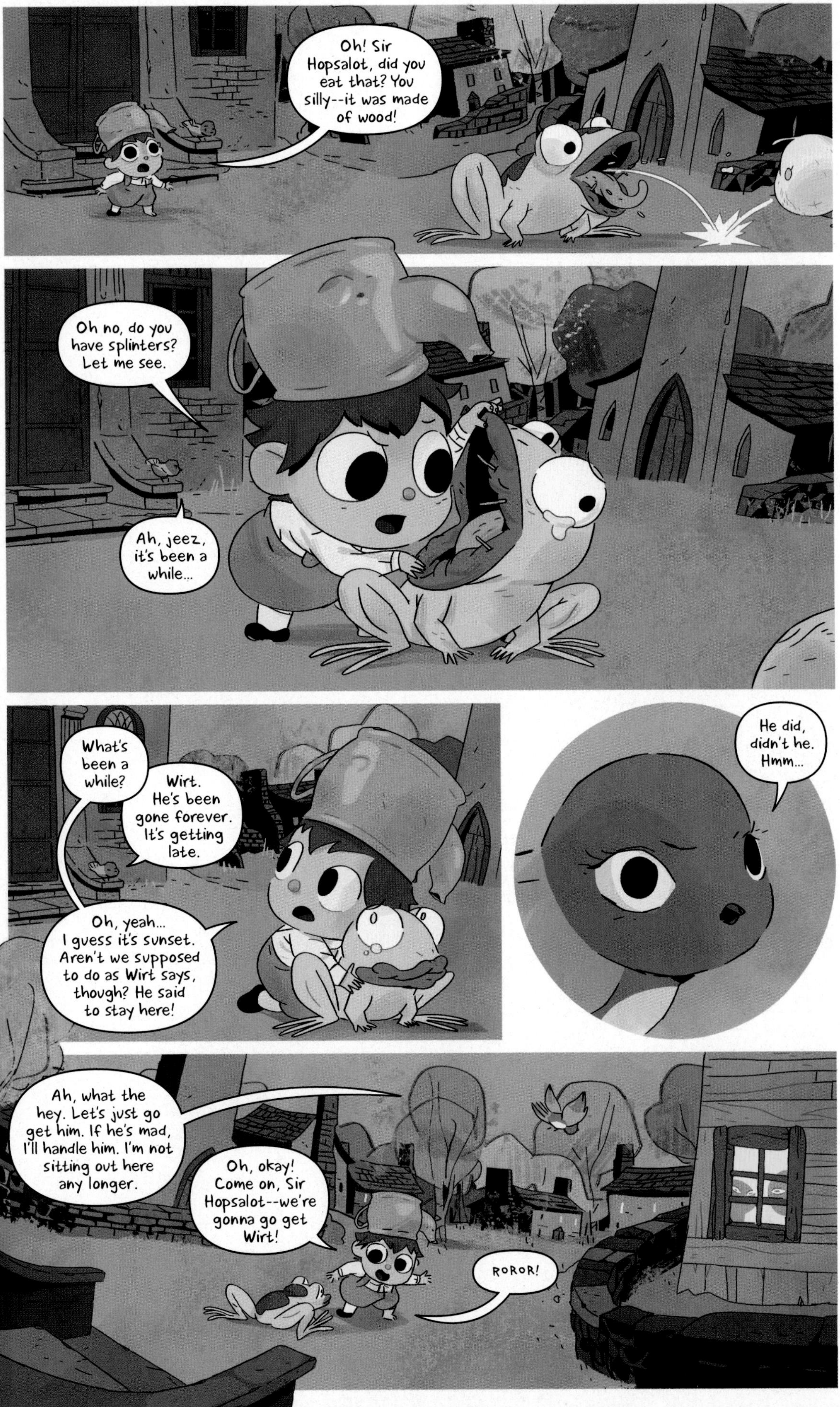
Oh! Sir Hopsalot, did you eat that? You silly--it was made of wood!
Oh no, do you have splinters? Let me see.
Ah, jeez, it's been a while...
What's been a while?
Wirt. He's been gone forever. It's getting late.
Oh, yeah... I guess it's sunset. Aren't we supposed to do as Wirt says, though? He said to stay here!
He did, didn't he. Hmm...
Ah, what the hey. Let's just go get him. If he's mad, I'll handle him. I'm not sitting out here any longer.
Oh, okay! Come on, Sir Hopsalot--we're gonna go get Wirt!
RORОR!

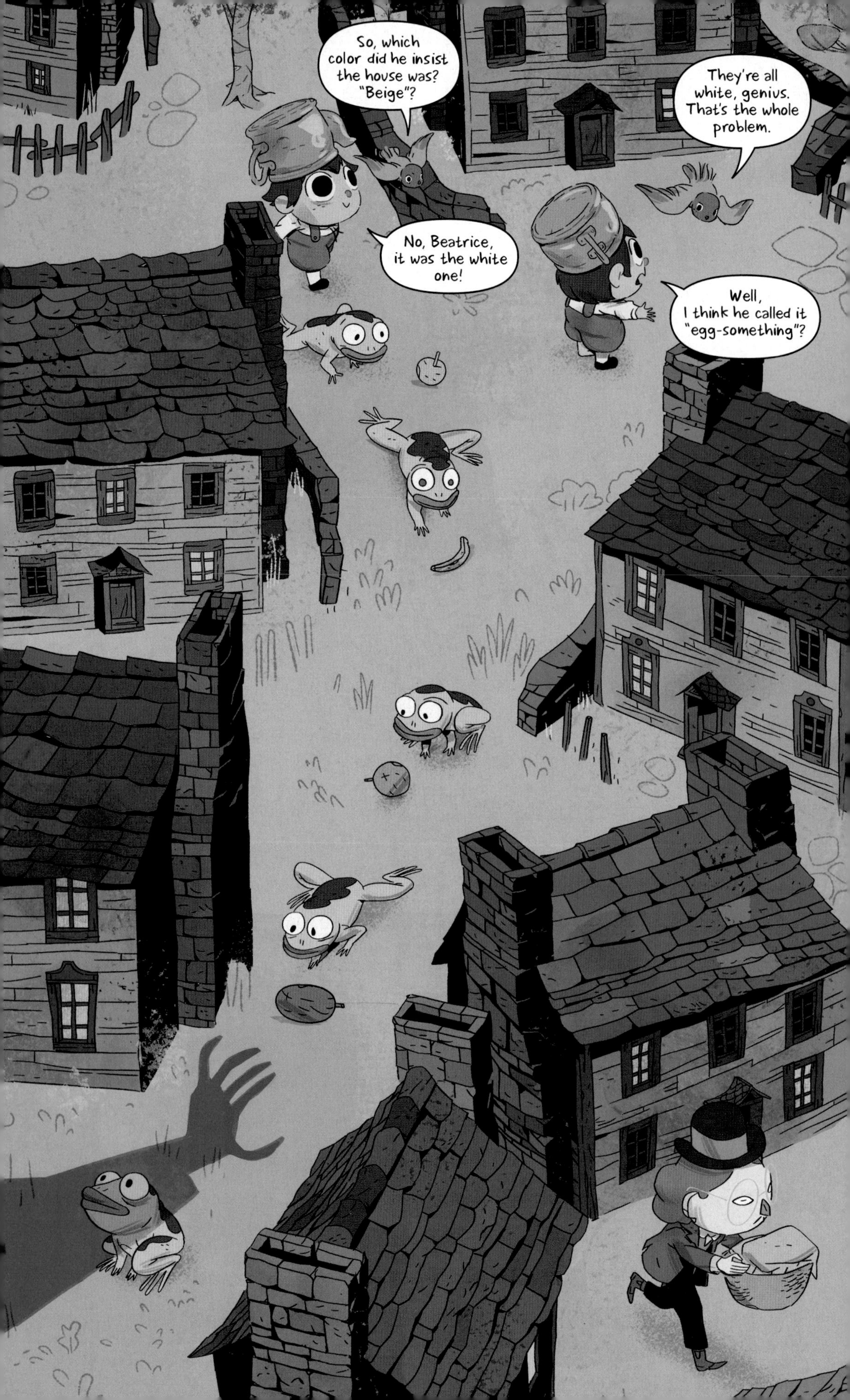
So, which color did he insist the house was? "Beige"?
They're all white, genius. That's the whole problem.
No, Beatrice, it was the white one!
Well, I think he called it "egg-something"?

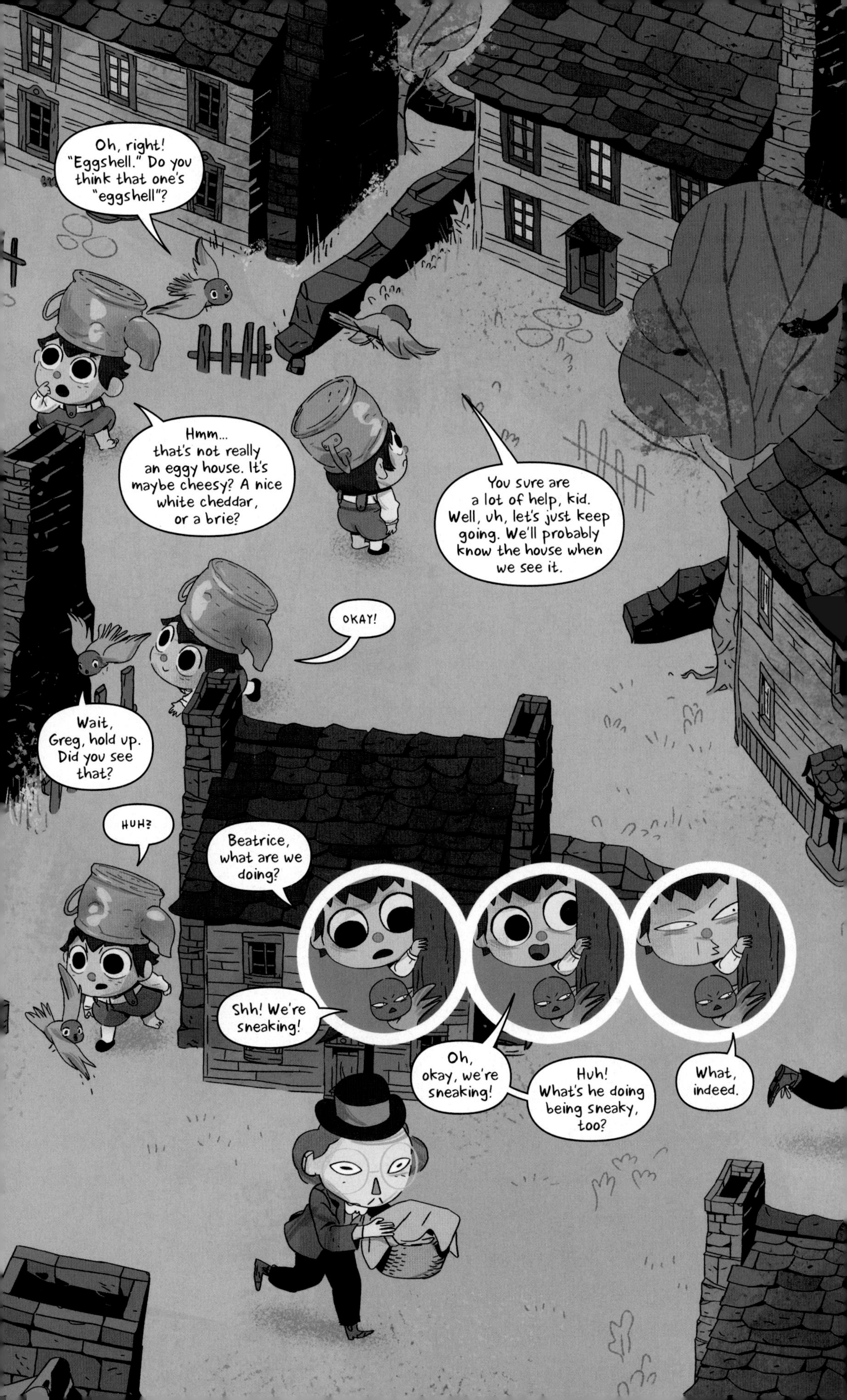

Oh, right! "Eggshell." Do you think that one's "eggshell"?
Hmm... that's not really an eggy house. It's maybe cheesy? A nice white cheddar, or a brie?
You sure are a lot of help, kid. Well, uh, let's just keep going. We'll probably know the house when we see it.
OKAY!
Wait, Greg, hold up. Did you see that?
HUH?
Beatrice, what are we doing?
Shh! We're sneaking!
Oh, okay, we're sneaking!
Huh! What's he doing being sneaky, too?
What, indeed.

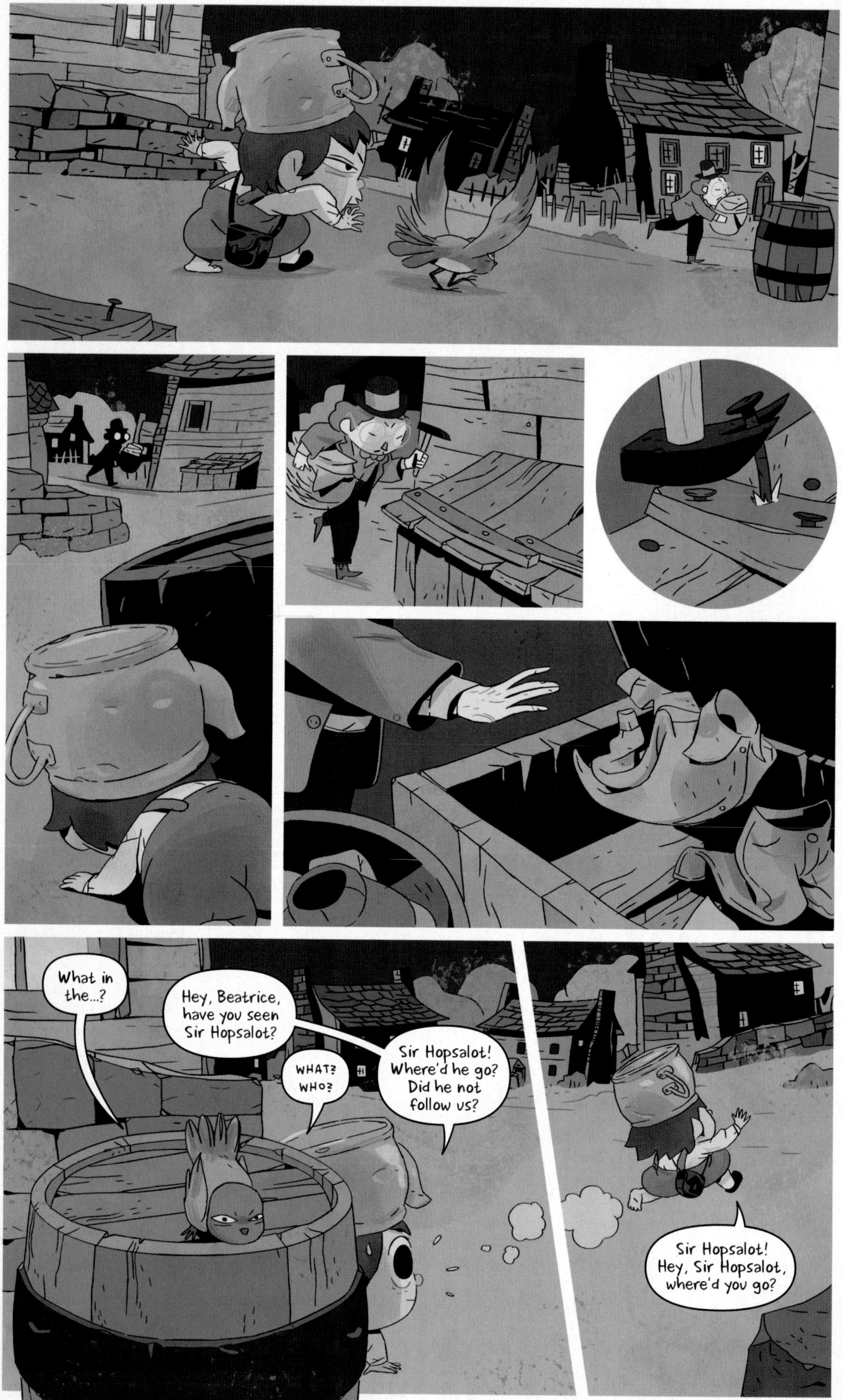
What in the...?
Hey, Beatrice, have you seen Sir Hopsalot?
WHAT? WHO?
Sir Hopsalot! Where'd he go? Did he not follow us?
Sir Hopsalot! Hey, Sir Hopsalot, where'd you go?

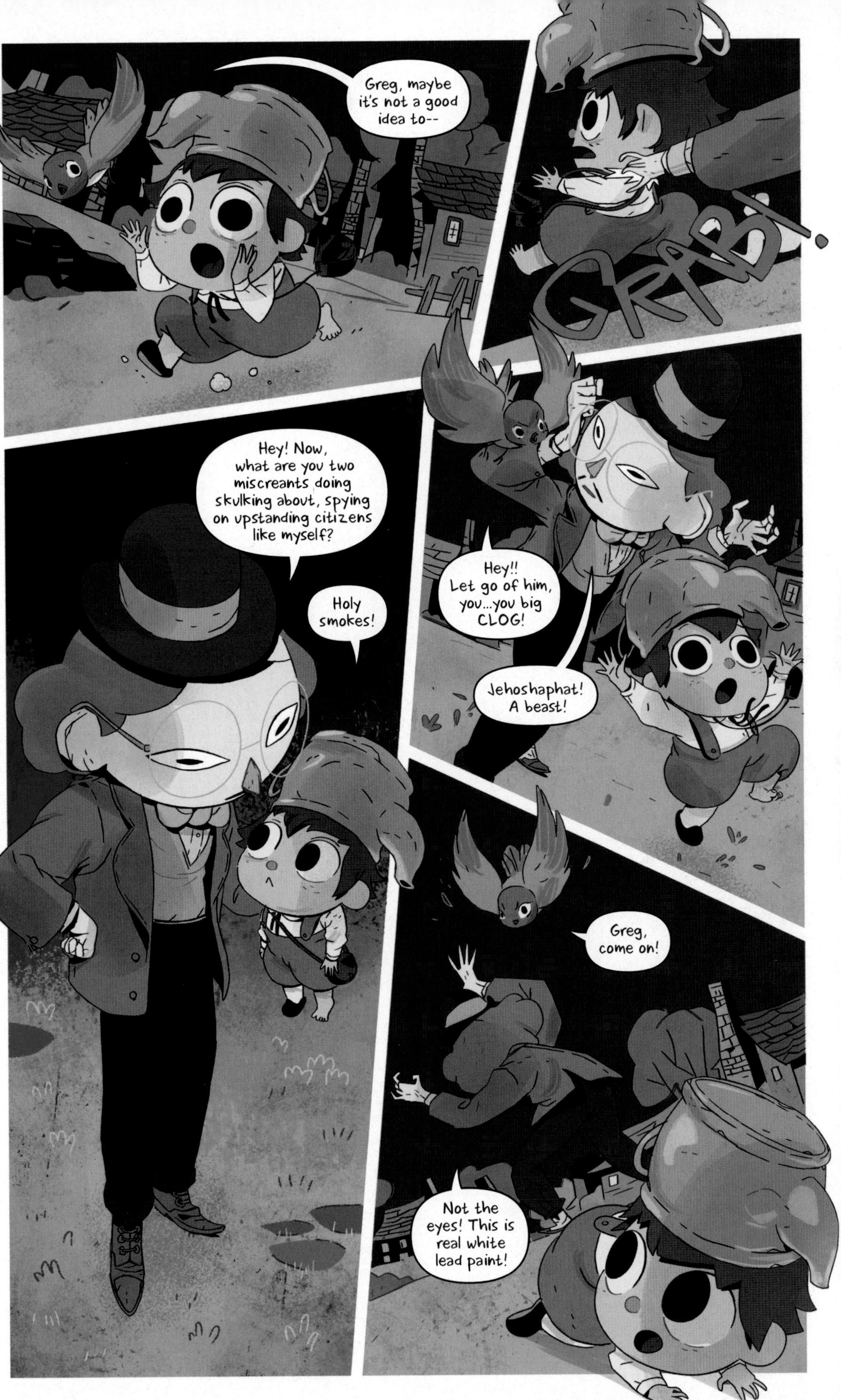
Greg, maybe it's not a good idea to--
GRAB!
Hey! Now, what are you two miscreants doing skulking about, spying on upstanding citizens like myself?
Holy smokes!
Hey!! Let go of him, you...you big CLOG!
Jehoshaphat! A beast!
Greg, come on!
Not the eyes! This is real white lead paint!

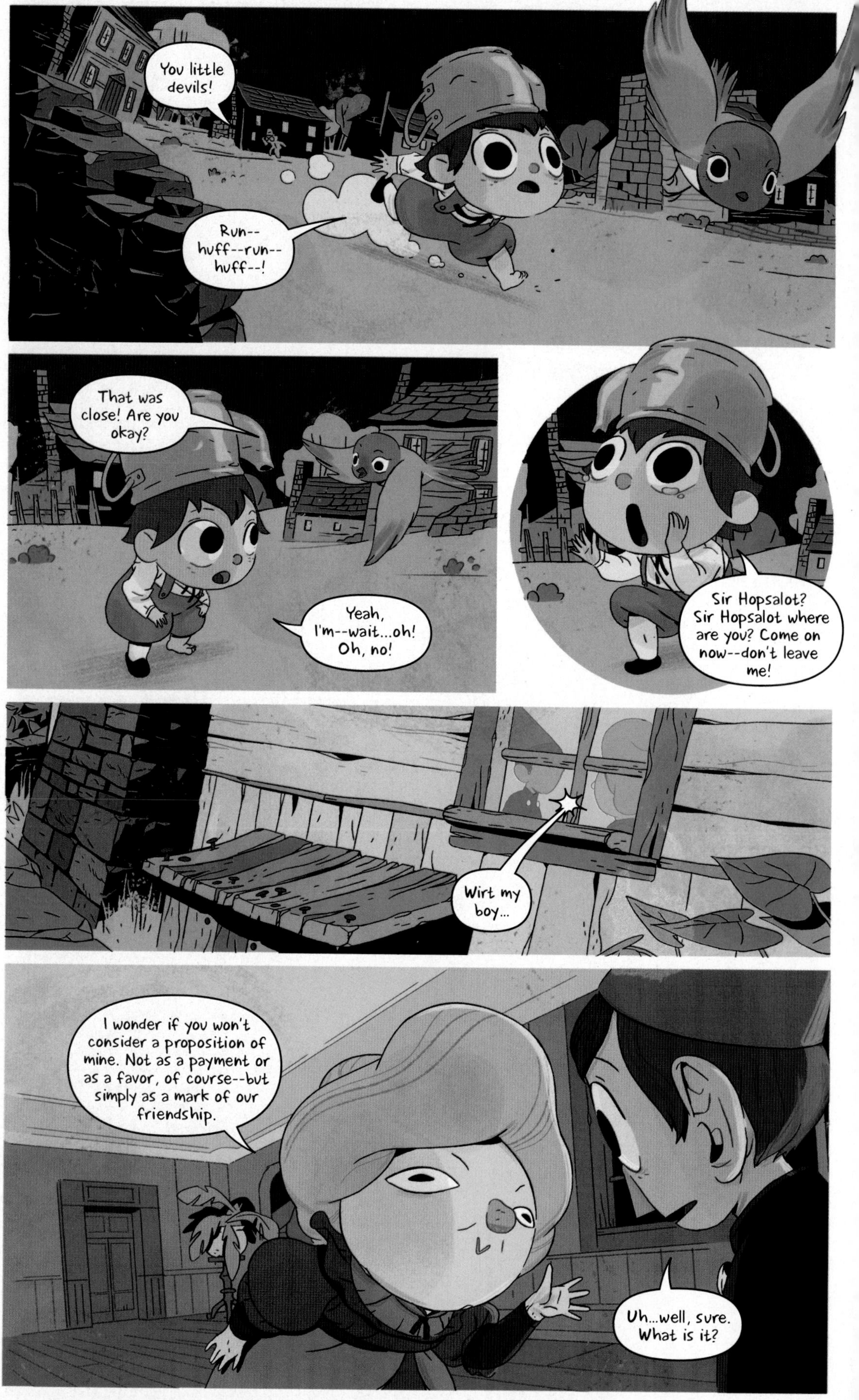
You little devils!
Run--huff--run--huff--!
That was close! Are you okay?
Yeah, I'm--wait...oh! Oh, no!
Sir Hopsalot? Sir Hopsalot where are you? Come on now--don't leave me!
Wirt my boy...
I wonder if you won't consider a proposition of mine. Not as a payment or as a favor, of course--but simply as a mark of our friendship.
Uh...well, sure. What is it?

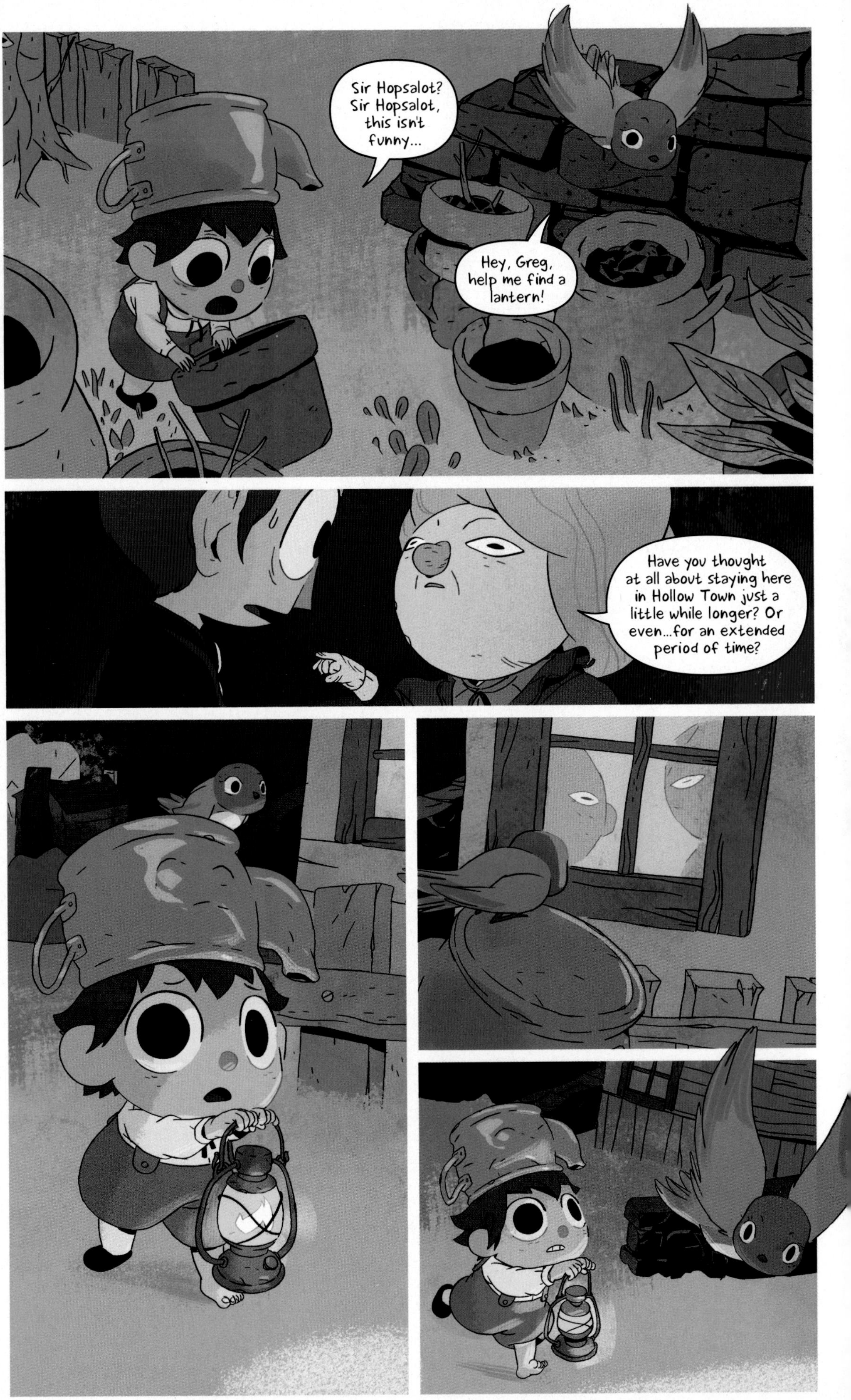
Sir Hopsalot? Sir Hopsalot, this isn't funny...
Hey, Greg, help me find a lantern!
Have you thought at all about staying here in Hollow Town just a little while longer? Or even...for an extended period of time?

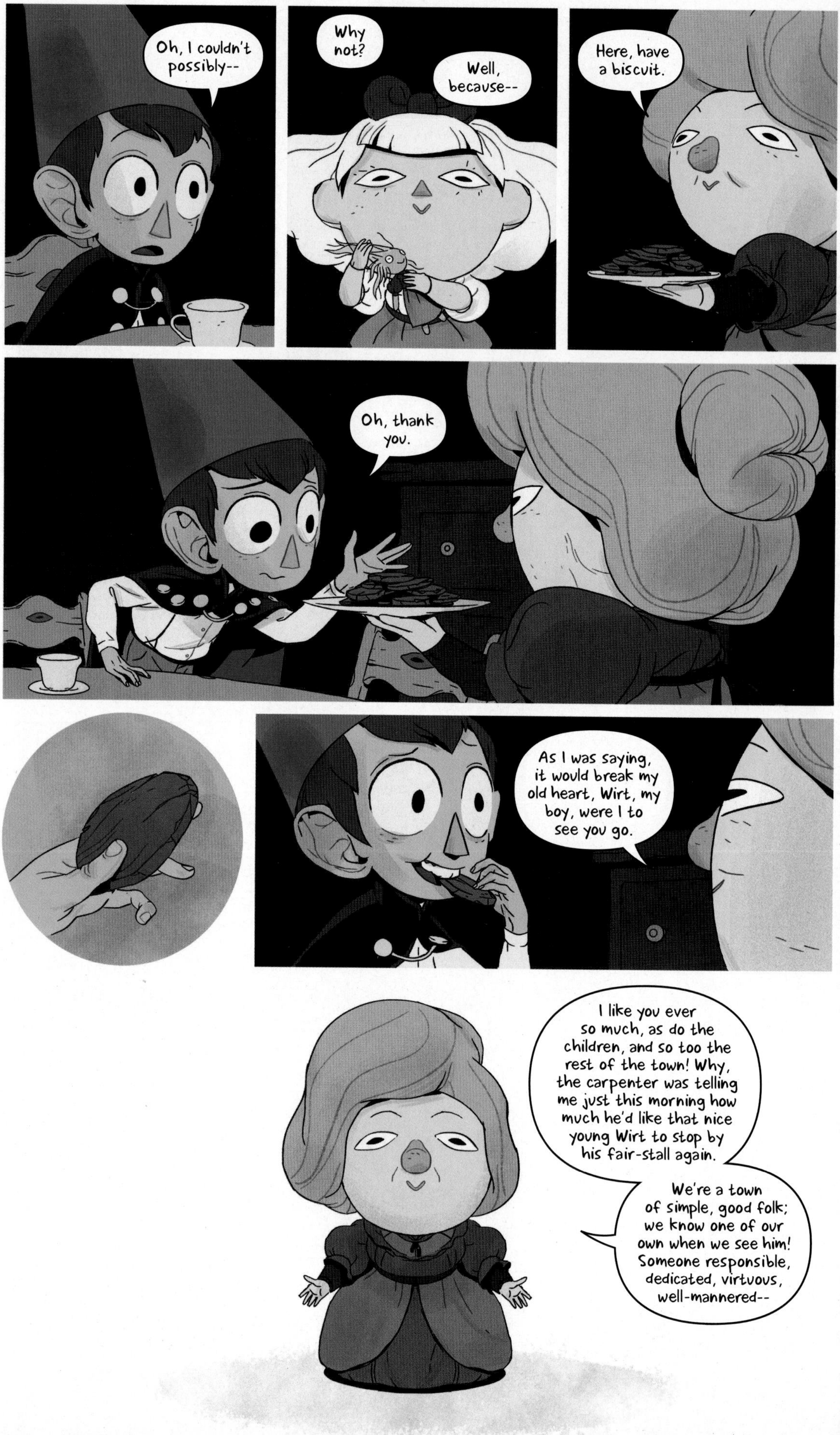
Oh, I couldn't possibly--
Why not?
Well, because--
Here, have a biscuit.
Oh, thank you.
As I was saying, it would break my old heart, Wirt, my boy, were I to see you go.
I like you ever so much, as do the children, and so too the rest of the town! Why, the carpenter was telling me just this morning how much he'd like that nice young Wirt to stop by his fair-stall again.
We're a town of simple, good folk; we know one of our own when we see him! Someone responsible, dedicated, virtuous, well-mannered--

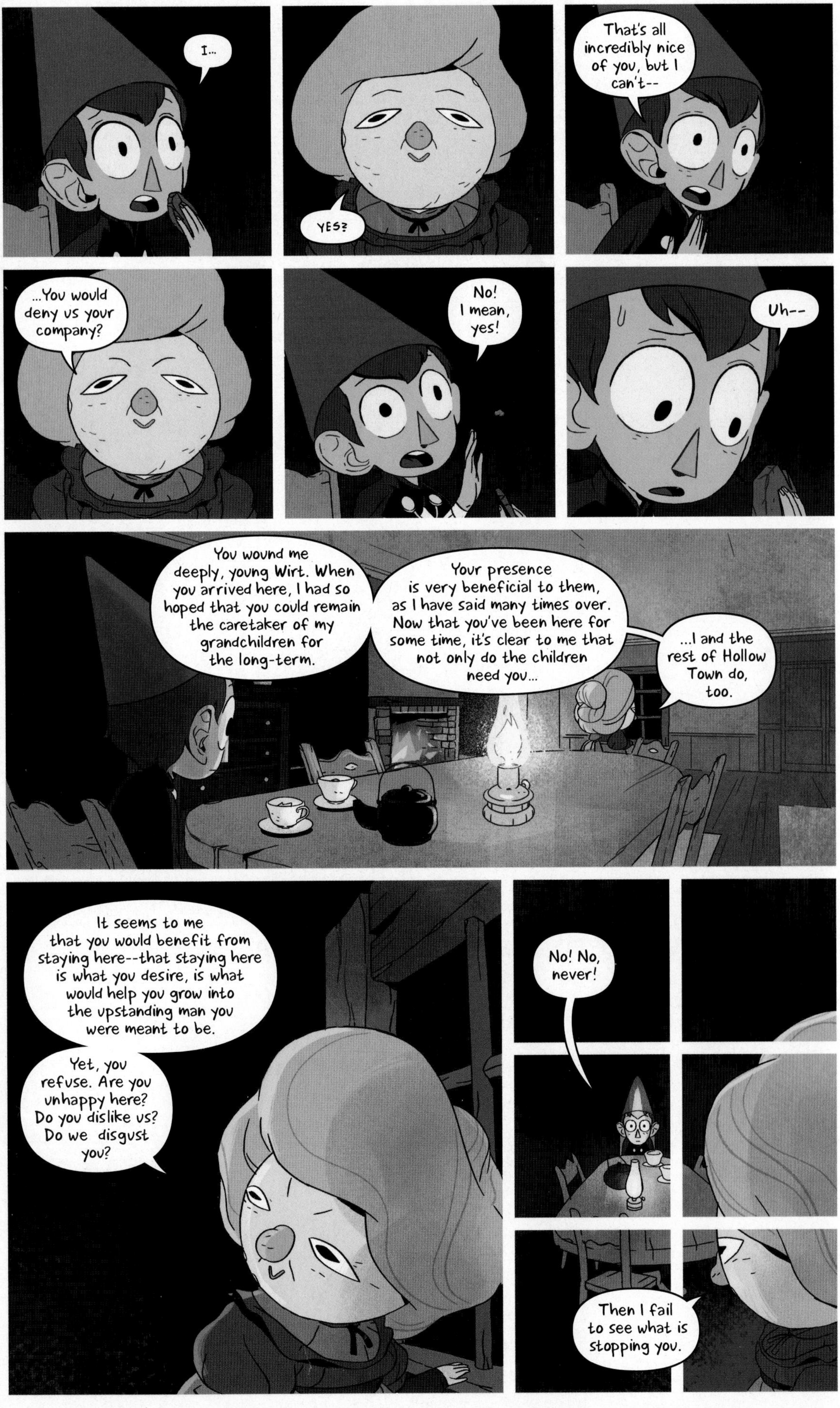
I...
YES?
That's all incredibly nice of you, but I can't--
...You would deny us your company?
No! I mean, yes!
Uh--
You wound me deeply, young Wirt. When you arrived here, I had so hoped that you could remain the caretaker of my grandchildren for the long-term.
Your presence is very beneficial to them, as I have said many times over. Now that you've been here for some time, it's clear to me that not only do the children need you...
...I and the rest of Hollow Town do, too.
It seems to me that you would benefit from staying here--that staying here is what you desire, is what would help you grow into the upstanding man you were meant to be.
Yet, you refuse. Are you unhappy here? Do you dislike us? Do we disgust you?
No! No, never!
Then I fail to see what is stopping you.

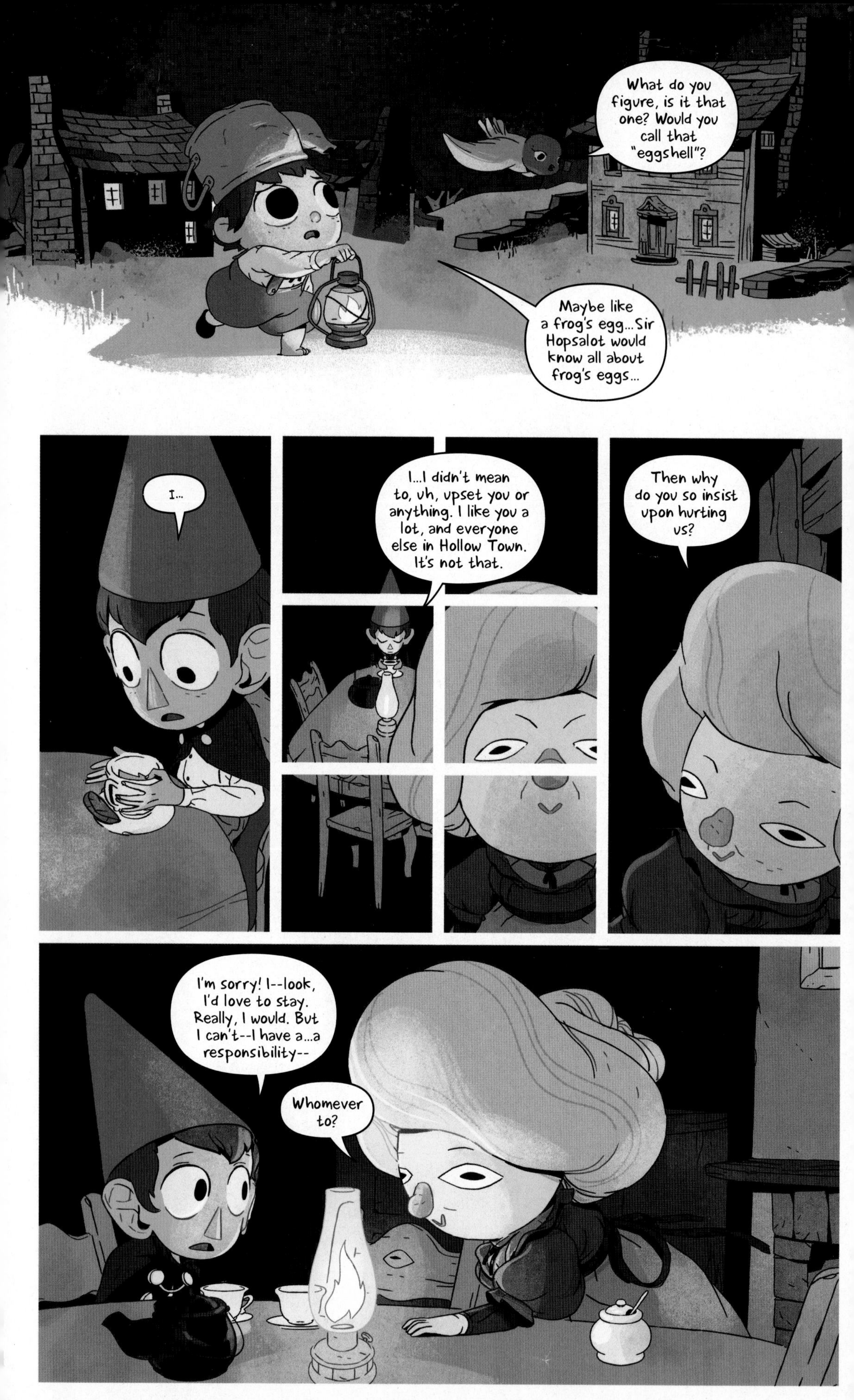
What do you figure, is it that one? Would you call that "eggshell"?
Maybe like a frog's egg...Sir Hopsalot would know all about frog's eggs...
I...
I...I didn't mean to, uh, upset you or anything. I like you a lot, and everyone else in Hollow Town. It's not that.
Then why do you so insist upon hurting us?
I'm sorry! I--look, I'd love to stay. Really, I would. But I can't--I have a...a responsibility--
Whomever to?

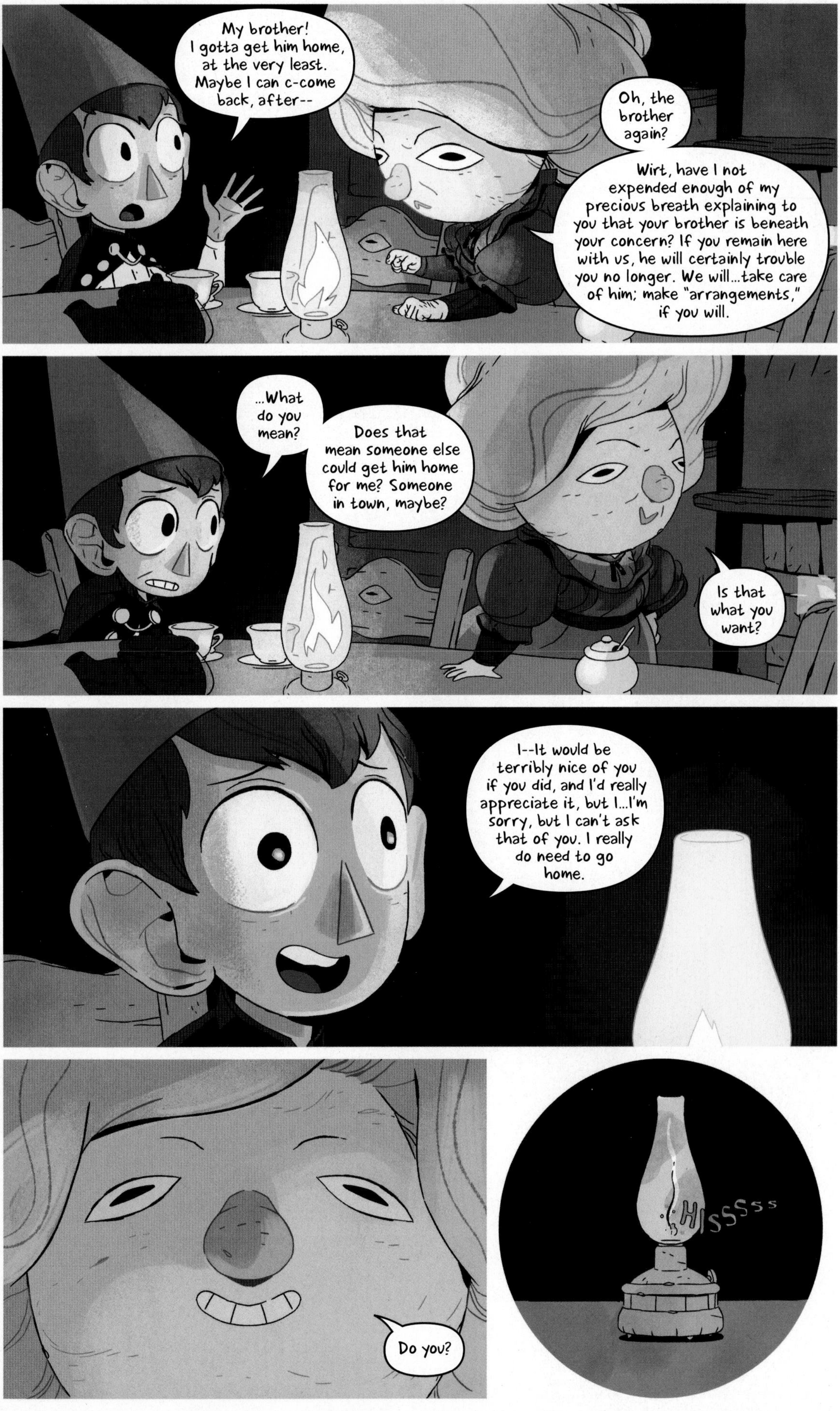
My brother! I gotta get him home, at the very least. Maybe I can c-come back, after--
Oh, the brother again?
Wirt, have I not expended enough of my precious breath explaining to you that your brother is beneath your concern? If you remain here with us, he will certainly trouble you no longer. We will...take care of him; make "arrangements," if you will.
...What do you mean?
Does that mean someone else could get him home for me? Someone in town, maybe?
Is that what you want?
I--It would be terribly nice of you if you did, and I'd really appreciate it, but I...I'm sorry, but I can't ask that of you. I really do need to go home.
Do you?
HISSSsss

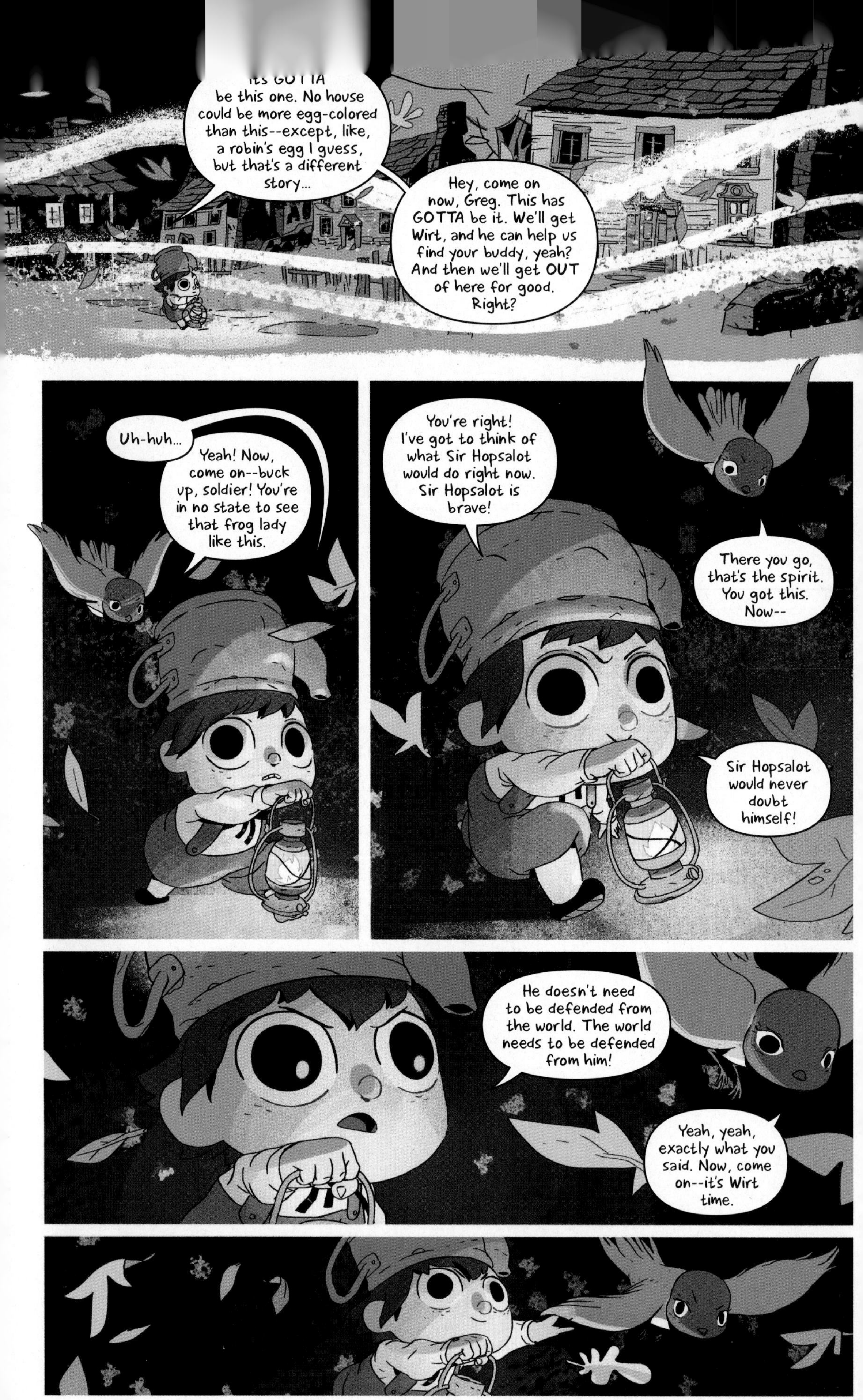
it's GOTTA be this one. No house could be more egg-colored than this--except, like, a robin's egg I guess, but that's a different story...
Hey, come on now, Greg. This has GOTTA be it. We'll get Wirt, and he can help us find your buddy, yeah? And then we'll get OUT of here for good. Right?
Uh-huh...
Yeah! Now, come on--buck up, soldier! You're in no state to see that frog lady like this.
You're right! I've got to think of what Sir Hopsalot would do right now. Sir Hopsalot is brave!
There you go, that's the spirit. You got this. Now--
Sir Hopsalot would never doubt himself!
He doesn't need to be defended from the world. The world needs to be defended from him!
Yeah, yeah, exactly what you said. Now, come on--it's Wirt time.

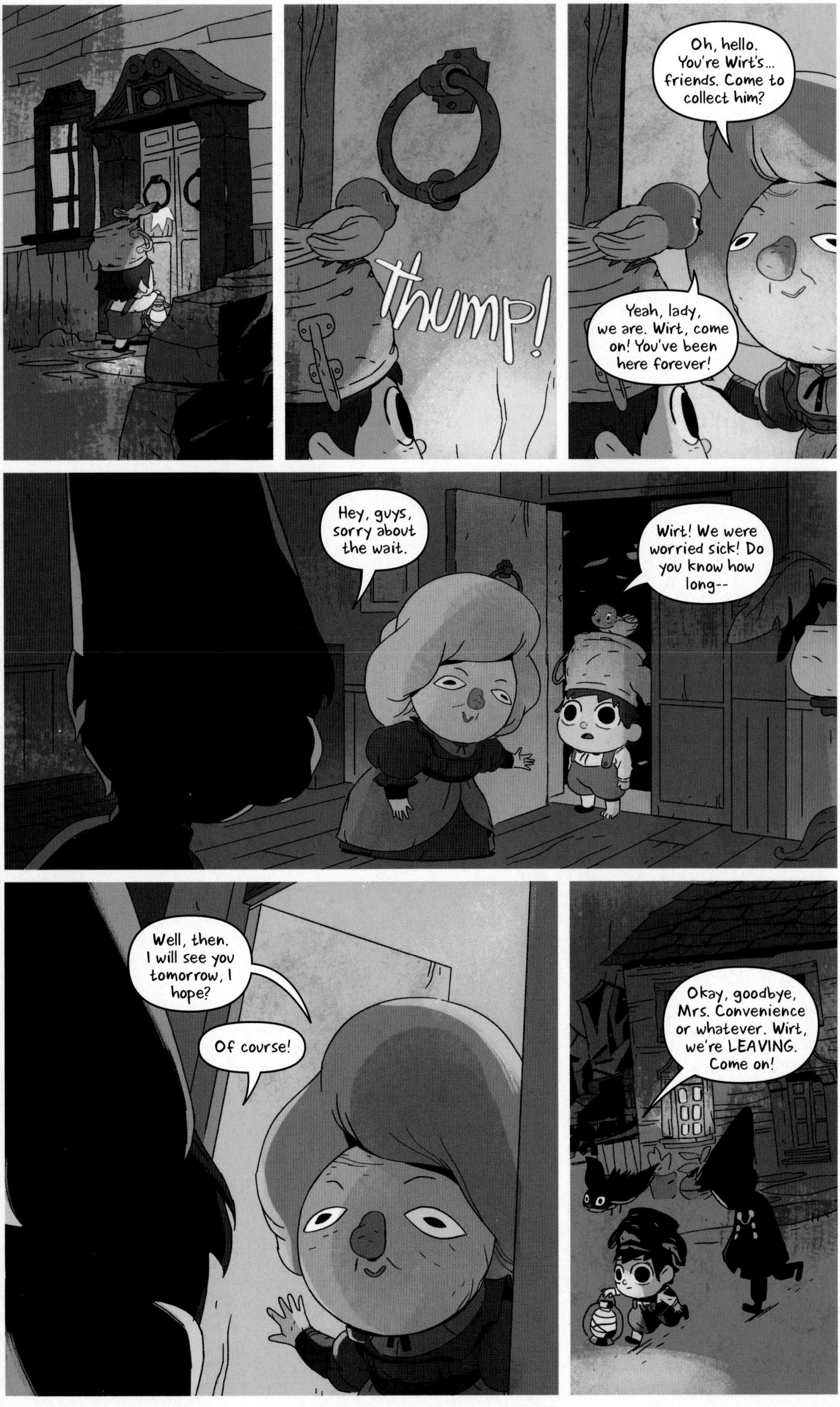
thump!
Oh, hello. You're Wirt's... friends. Come to collect him?
Yeah, lady, we are. Wirt, come on! You've been here forever!
Hey, guys, sorry about the wait.
Wirt! We were worried sick! Do you know how long--
Well, then. I will see you tomorrow, I hope?
Of course!
Okay, goodbye, Mrs. Convenience or whatever. Wirt, we're LEAVING. Come on!

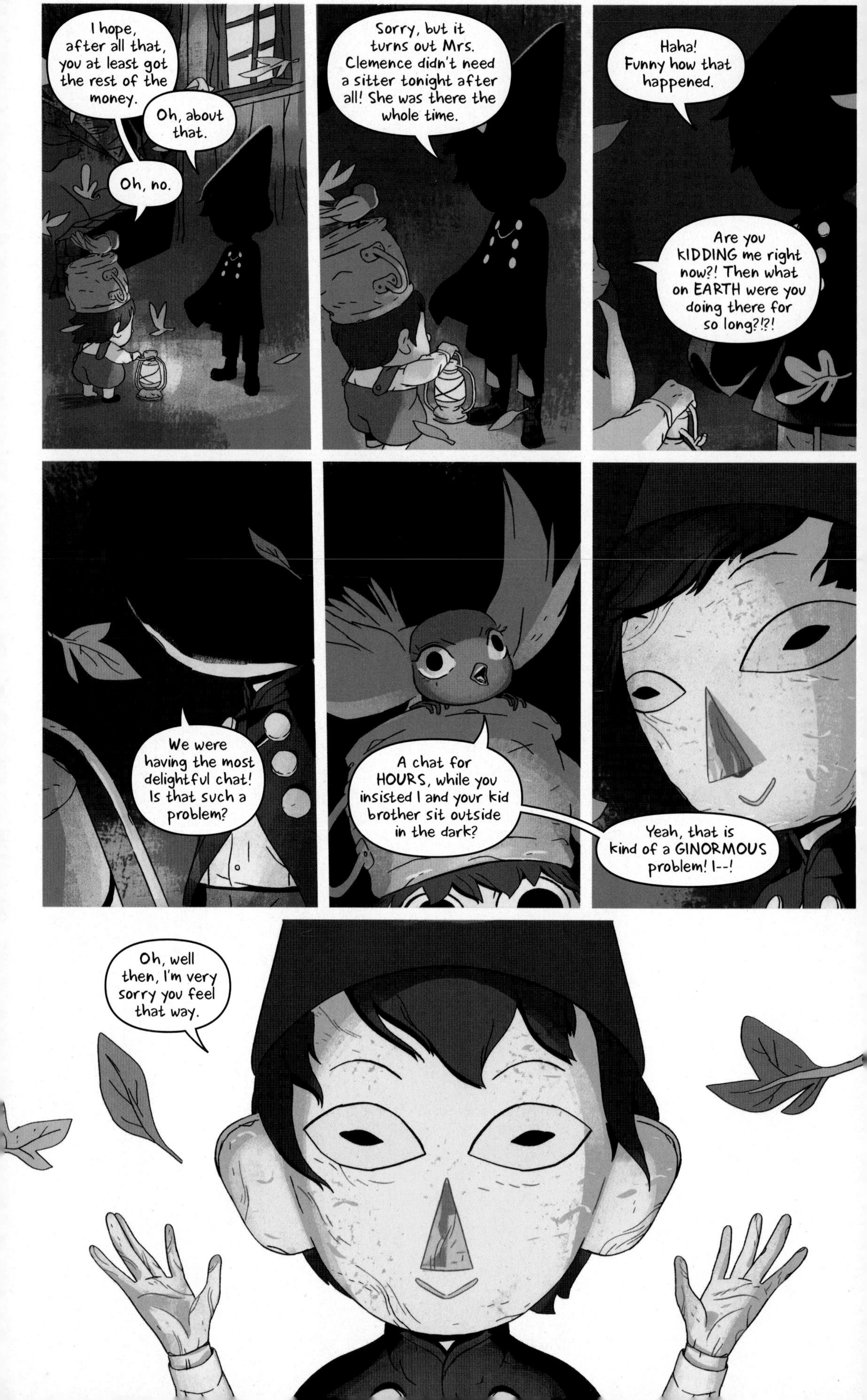

I hope, after all that, you at least got the rest of the money.
Oh, about that.
Oh, no.
Sorry, but it turns out Mrs. Clemence didn't need a sitter tonight after all! She was there the whole time.
Haha! Funny how that happened.
Are you KIDDING me right now?! Then what on EARTH were you doing there for so long?!?!
We were having the most delightful chat! Is that such a problem?
A chat for HOURS, while you insisted I and your kid brother sit outside in the dark?
Yeah, that is kind of a GINORMOUS problem! I--!
Oh, well then, I'm very sorry you feel that way.

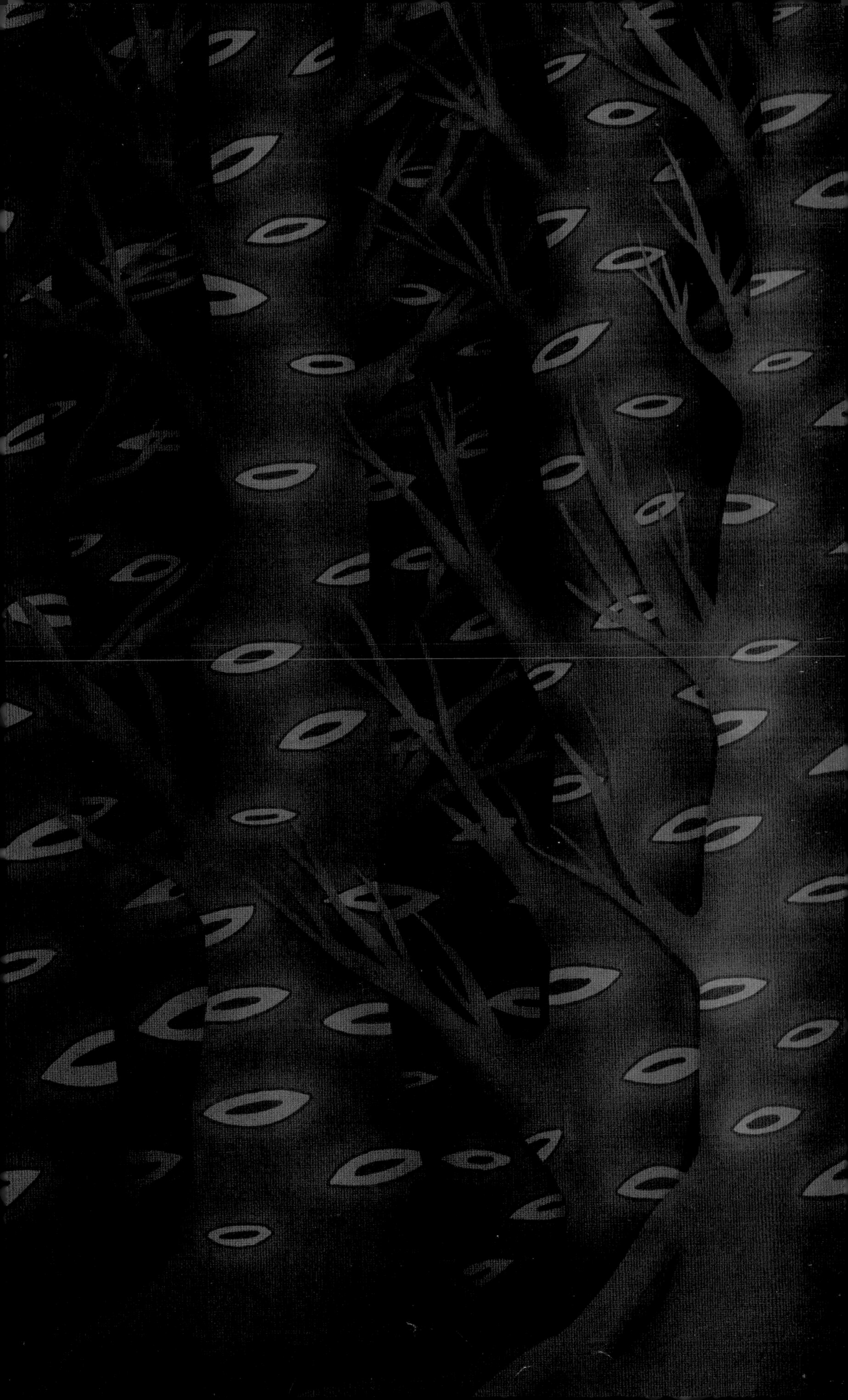

CHAPTER

4

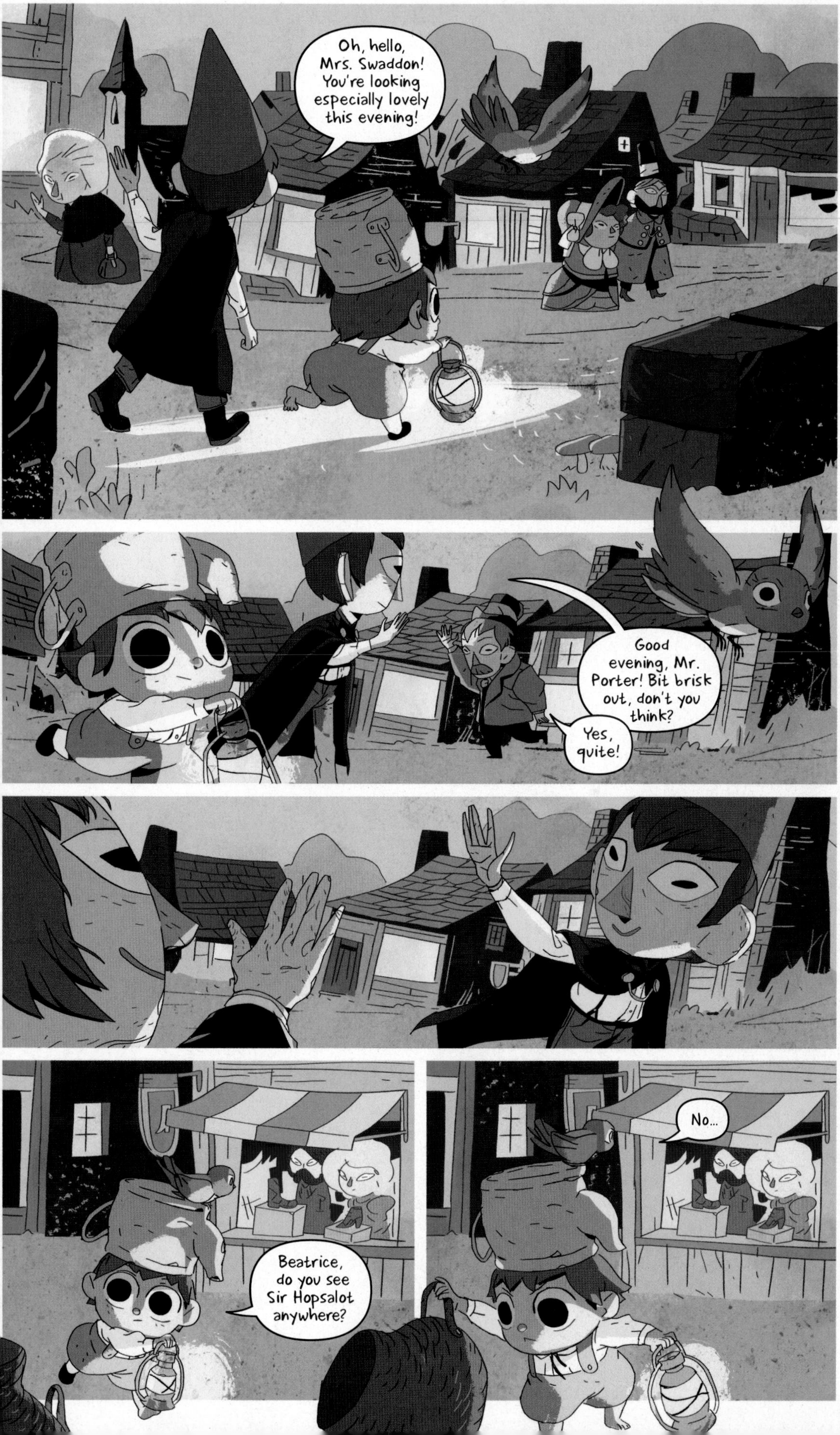
Oh, hello, Mrs. Swaddon! You're looking especially lovely this evening!
Good evening, Mr. Porter! Bit brisk out, don't you think?
Yes, quite!
Beatrice, do you see Sir Hopsalot anywhere?
No...

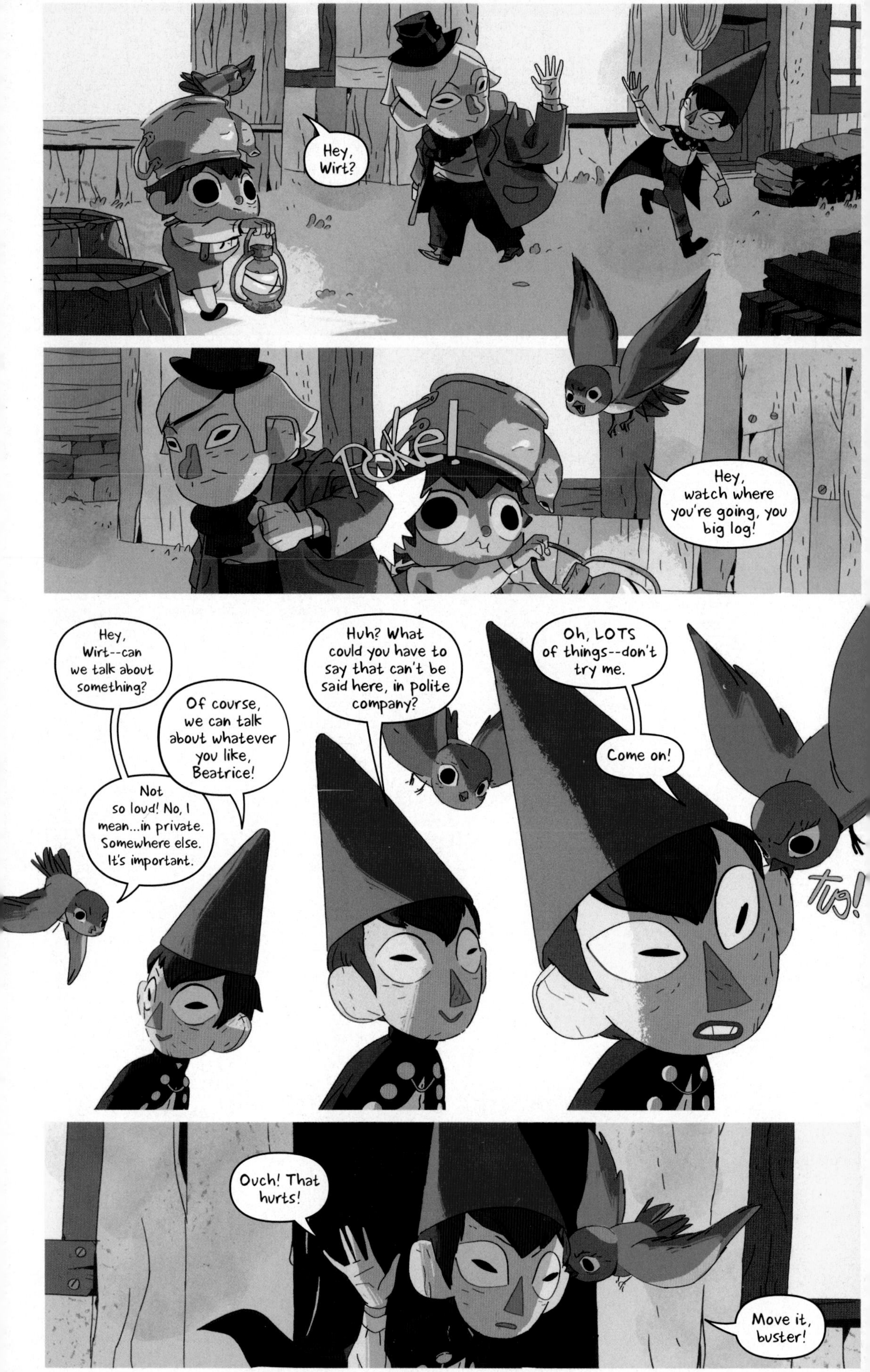
Hey, Wirt?
POKE!
Hey, watch where you're going, you big log!
Hey, Wirt--can we talk about something?
Of course, we can talk about whatever you like, Beatrice!
Not so loud! No, I mean...in private. Somewhere else. It's important.
Huh? What could you have to say that can't be said here, in polite company?
Oh, LOTS of things--don't try me.
Come on!
TUG!
Ouch! That hurts!
Move it, buster!

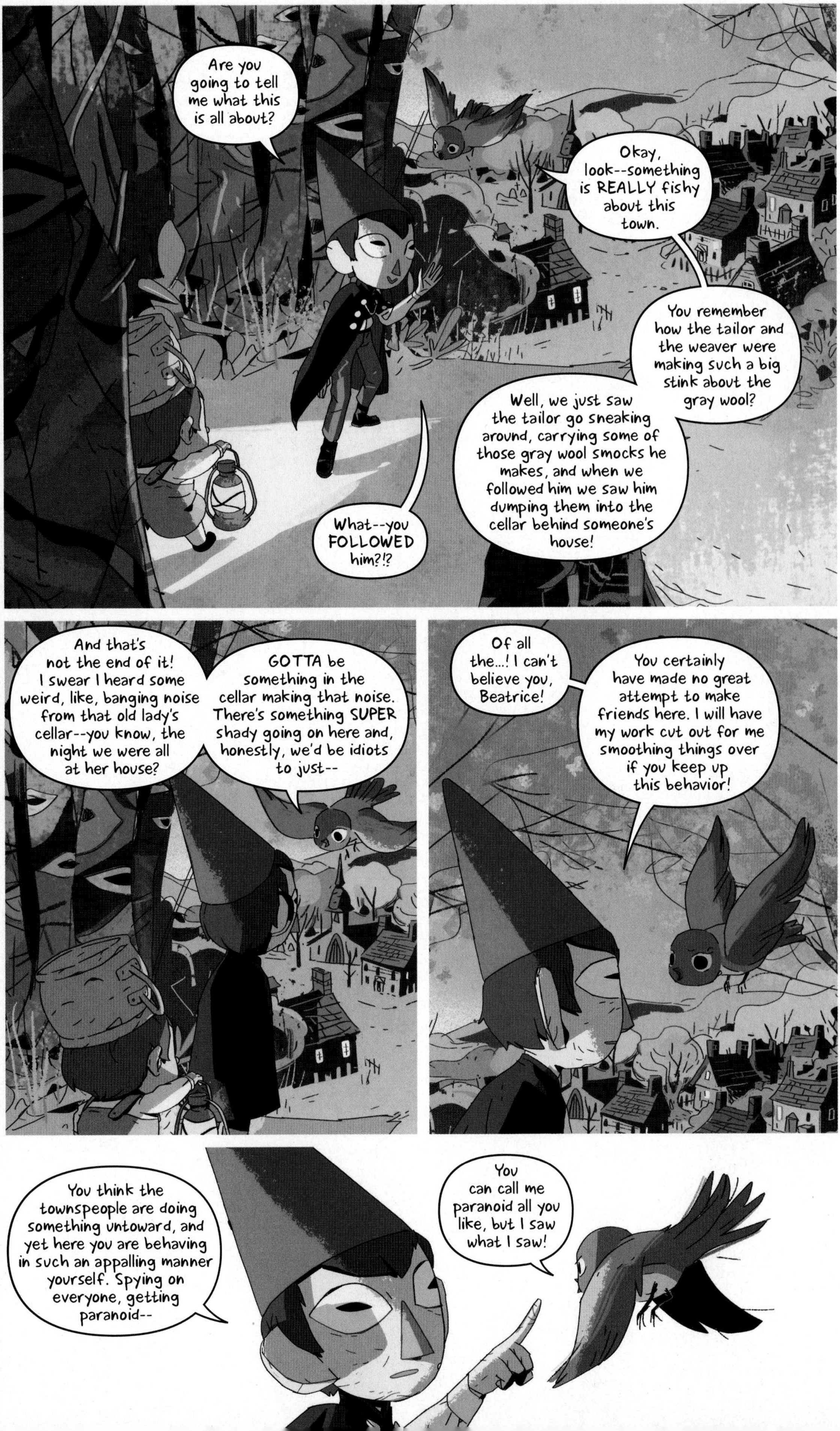
Are you going to tell me what this is all about?
Okay, look--something is REALLY fishy about this town.
You remember how the tailor and the weaver were making such a big stink about the gray wool?
Well, we just saw the tailor go sneaking around, carrying some of those gray wool smocks he makes, and when we followed him we saw him dumping them into the cellar behind someone's house!
What--you FOLLOWED him?!?
And that's not the end of it! I swear I heard some weird, like, banging noise from that old lady's cellar--you know, the night we were all at her house?
GOTTA be something in the cellar making that noise. There's something SUPER shady going on here and, honestly, we'd be idiots to just--
Of all the...! I can't believe you, Beatrice!
You certainly have made no great attempt to make friends here. I will have my work cut out for me smoothing things over if you keep up this behavior!
You think the townspeople are doing something untoward, and yet here you are behaving in such an appalling manner yourself. Spying on everyone, getting paranoid--
You can call me paranoid all you like, but I saw what I saw!

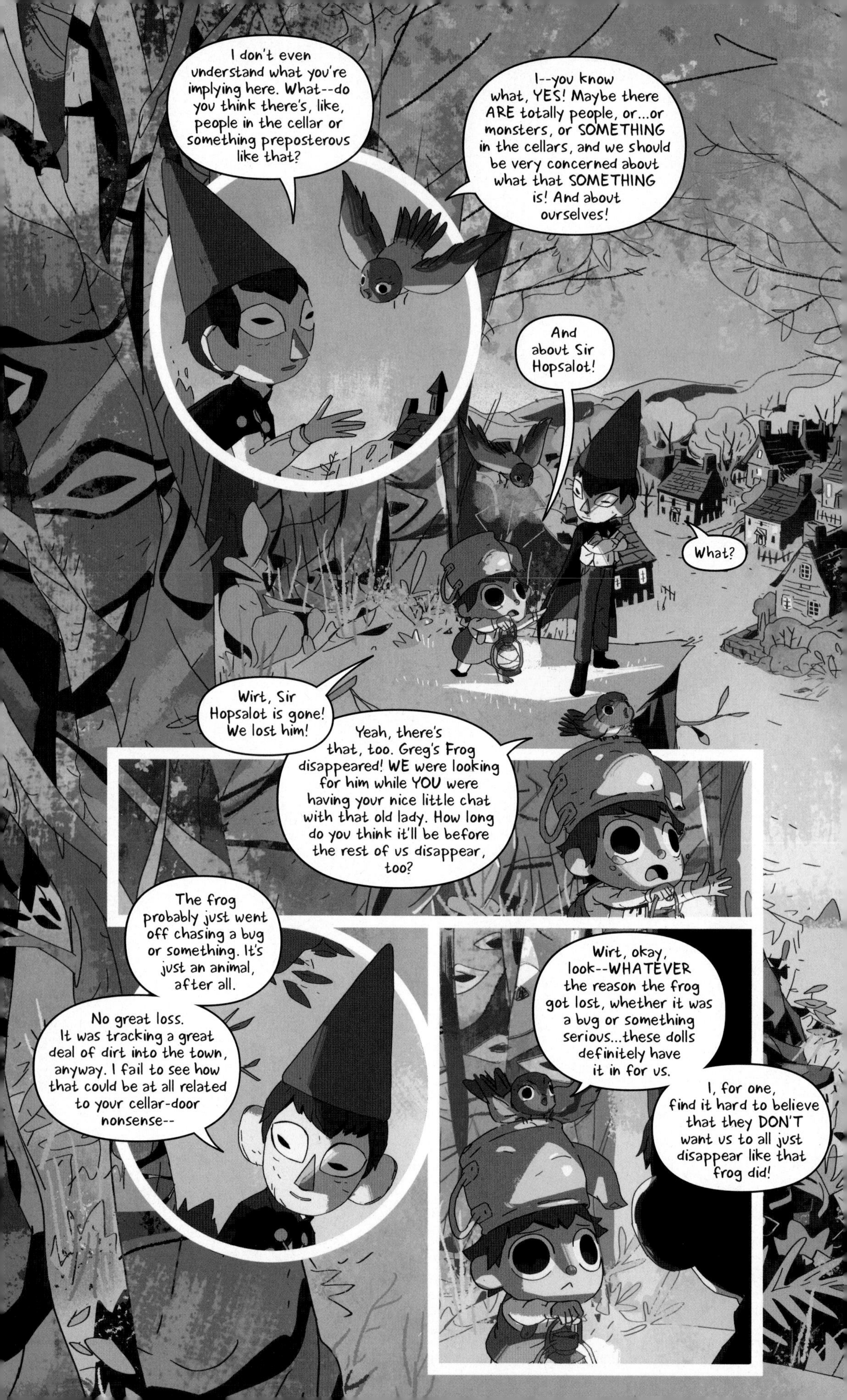

I don't even understand what you're implying here. What--do you think there's, like, people in the cellar or something preposterous like that?
I--you know what, YES! Maybe there ARE totally people, or...or monsters, or SOMETHING in the cellars, and we should be very concerned about what that SOMETHING is! And about ourselves!
And about Sir Hopsalot!
What?
Wirt, Sir Hopsalot is gone! We lost him!
Yeah, there's that, too. Greg's Frog disappeared! WE were looking for him while YOU were having your nice little chat with that old lady. How long do you think it'll be before the rest of us disappear, too?
The frog probably just went off chasing a bug or something. It's just an animal, after all.
No great loss. It was tracking a great deal of dirt into the town, anyway. I fail to see how that could be at all related to your cellar-door nonsense--
Wirt, okay, look--WHATEVER the reason the frog got lost, whether it was a bug or something serious...these dolls definitely have it in for us.
I, for one, find it hard to believe that they DON'T want us to all just disappear like that frog did!

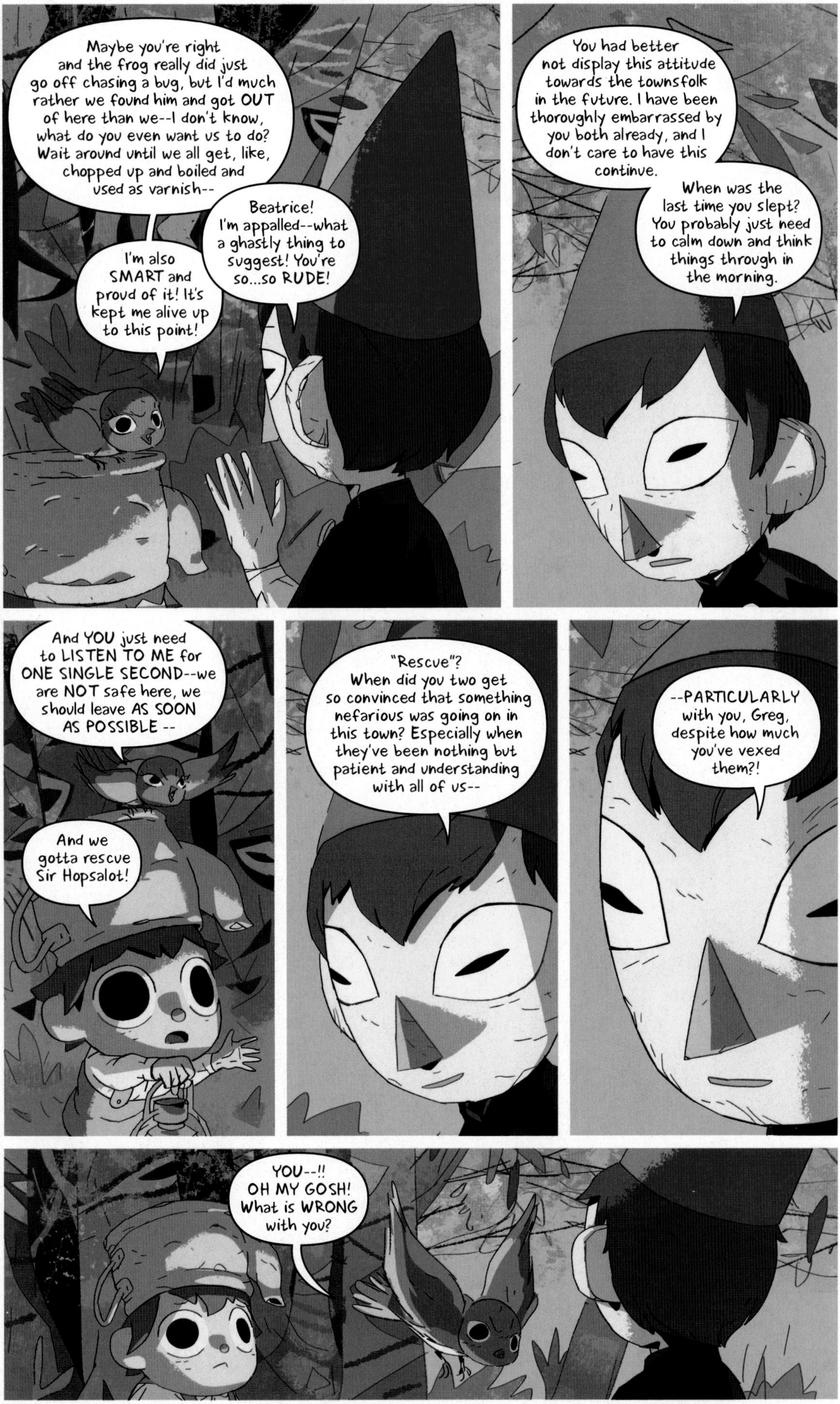
Maybe you're right and the frog really did just go off chasing a bug, but I'd much rather we found him and got OUT of here than we--I don't know, what do you even want us to do? Wait around until we all get, like, chopped up and boiled and used as varnish--
I'm also SMART and proud of it! It's kept me alive up to this point!
Beatrice! I'm appalled--what a ghastly thing to suggest! You're so...so RUDE!
You had better not display this attitude towards the townsfolk in the future. I have been thoroughly embarrassed by you both already, and I don't care to have this continue.
When was the last time you slept? You probably just need to calm down and think things through in the morning.
And YOU just need to LISTEN TO ME for ONE SINGLE SECOND--we are NOT safe here, we should leave AS SOON AS POSSIBLE --
And we gotta rescue Sir Hopsalot!
"Rescue"? When did you two get so convinced that something nefarious was going on in this town? Especially when they've been nothing but patient and understanding with all of us--
--PARTICULARLY with you, Greg, despite how much you've vexed them?!
YOU--!! OH MY GOSH! What is WRONG with you?

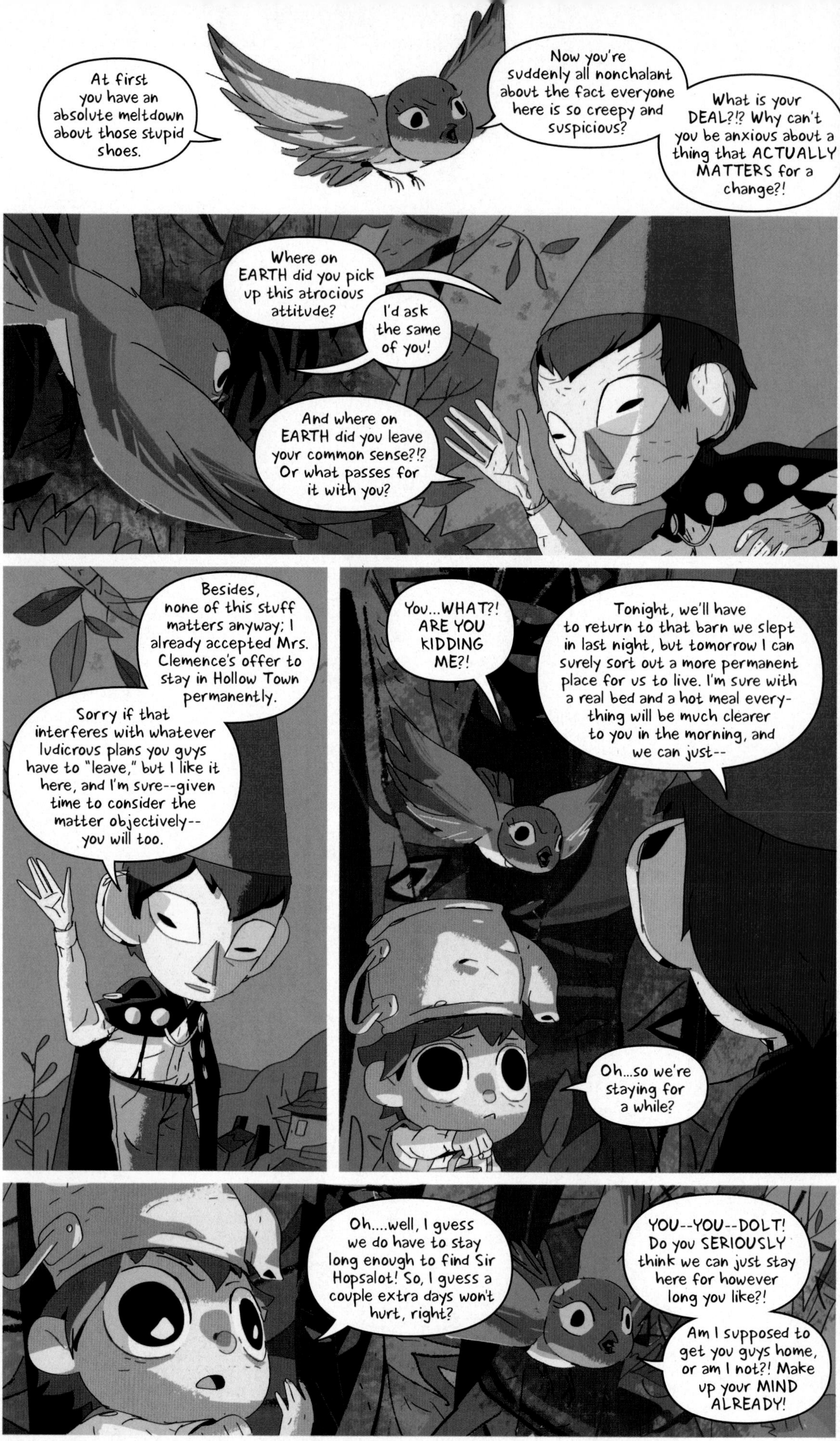
At first you have an absolute meltdown about those stupid shoes.
Now you're suddenly all nonchalant about the fact everyone here is so creepy and suspicious?
What is your DEAL?!? Why can't you be anxious about a thing that ACTUALLY MATTERS for a change?!
Where on EARTH did you pick up this atrocious attitude?
I'd ask the same of you!
And where on EARTH did you leave your common sense?!? Or what passes for it with you?
Besides, none of this stuff matters anyway; I already accepted Mrs. Clemence's offer to stay in Hollow Town permanently.
Sorry if that interferes with whatever ludicrous plans you guys have to "leave," but I like it here, and I'm sure--given time to consider the matter objectively--you will too.
You...WHAT?! ARE YOU KIDDING ME?!
Tonight, we'll have to return to that barn we slept in last night, but tomorrow I can surely sort out a more permanent place for us to live. I'm sure with a real bed and a hot meal everything will be much clearer to you in the morning, and we can just--
Oh...so we're staying for a while?
Oh....well, I guess we do have to stay long enough to find Sir Hopsalot! So, I guess a couple extra days won't hurt, right?
YOU--YOU--DOLT! Do you SERIOUSLY think we can just stay here for however long you like?!
Am I supposed to get you guys home, or am I not?! Make up your MIND ALREADY!

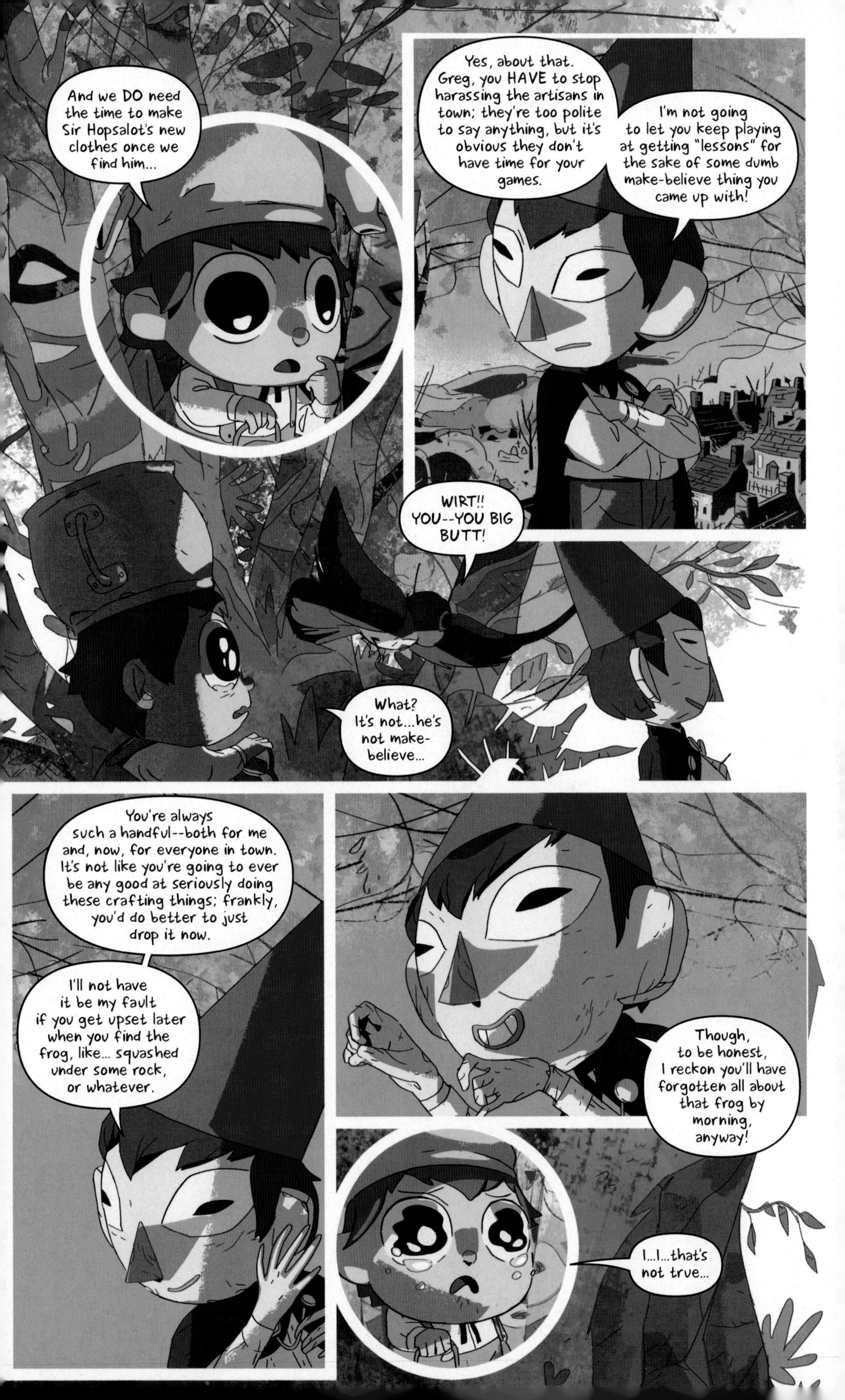
And we DO need the time to make Sir Hopsalot's new clothes once we find him...
Yes, about that. Greg, you HAVE to stop harassing the artisans in town; they're too polite to say anything, but it's obvious they don't have time for your games.
I'm not going to let you keep playing at getting "lessons" for the sake of some dumb make-believe thing you came up with!
WIRT!! YOU--YOU BIG BUTT!
What? It's not...he's not make-believe...
You're always such a handful--both for me and, now, for everyone in town. It's not like you're going to ever be any good at seriously doing these crafting things; frankly, you'd do better to just drop it now.
I'll not have it be my fault if you get upset later when you find the frog, like... squashed under some rock, or whatever.
Though, to be honest, I reckon you'll have forgotten all about that frog by morning, anyway!
I...I...that's not true...

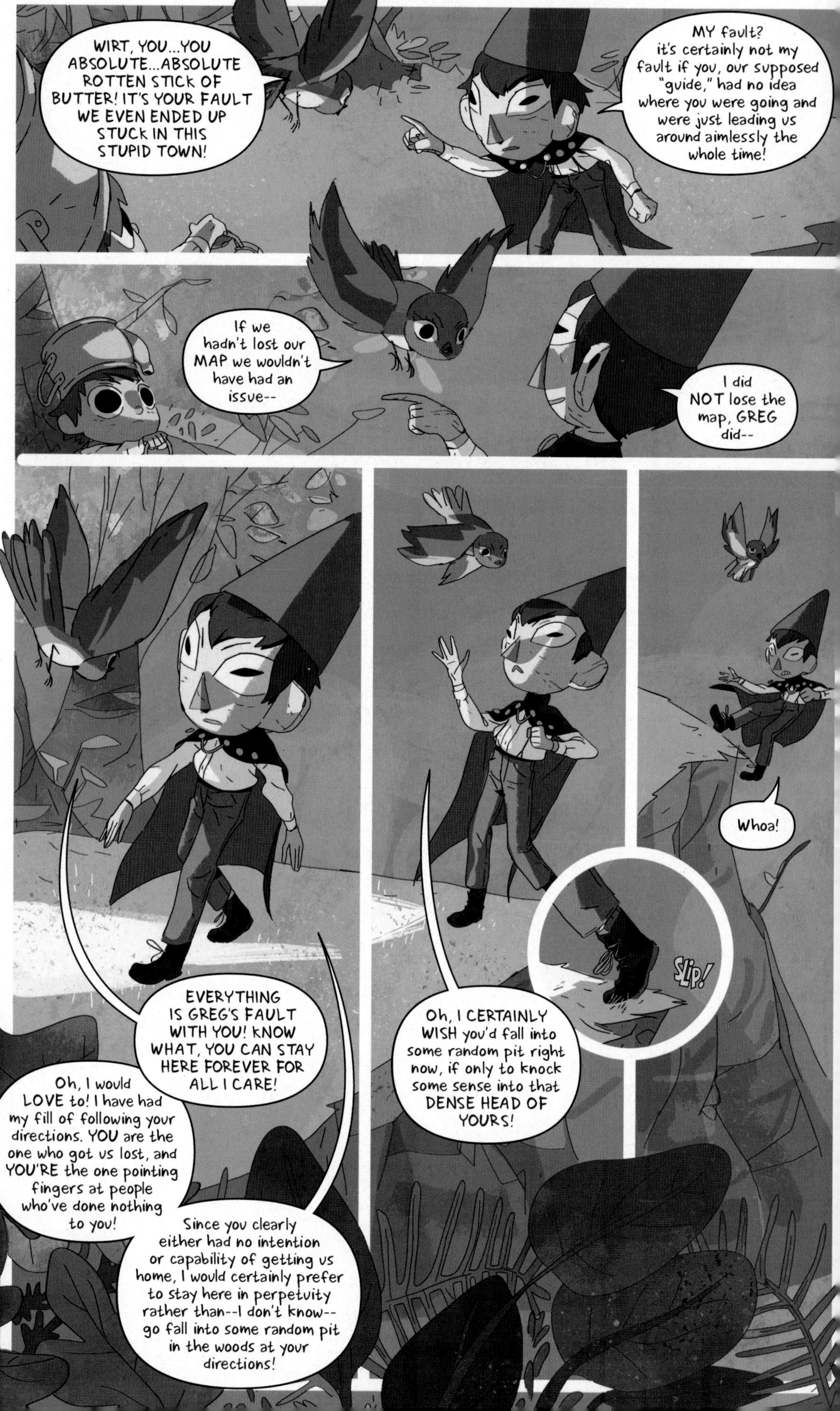

WIRT, YOU...YOU ABSOLUTE...ABSOLUTE ROTTEN STICK OF BUTTER! IT'S YOUR FAULT WE EVEN ENDED UP STUCK IN THIS STUPID TOWN!
MY fault? it's certainly not my fault if you, our supposed "guide," had no idea where you were going and were just leading us around aimlessly the whole time!
If we hadn't lost our MAP we wouldn't have had an issue--
I did NOT lose the map, GREG did--
EVERYTHING IS GREG'S FAULT WITH YOU! KNOW WHAT, YOU CAN STAY HERE FOREVER FOR ALL I CARE!
Oh, I would LOVE to! I have had my fill of following your directions. YOU are the one who got us lost, and YOU'RE the one pointing fingers at people who've done nothing to you!
Since you clearly either had no intention or capability of getting us home, I would certainly prefer to stay here in perpetuity rather than--I don't know--go fall into some random pit in the woods at your directions!
Oh, I CERTAINLY WISH you'd fall into some random pit right now, if only to knock some sense into that DENSE HEAD OF YOURS!
SLIP!
Whoa!

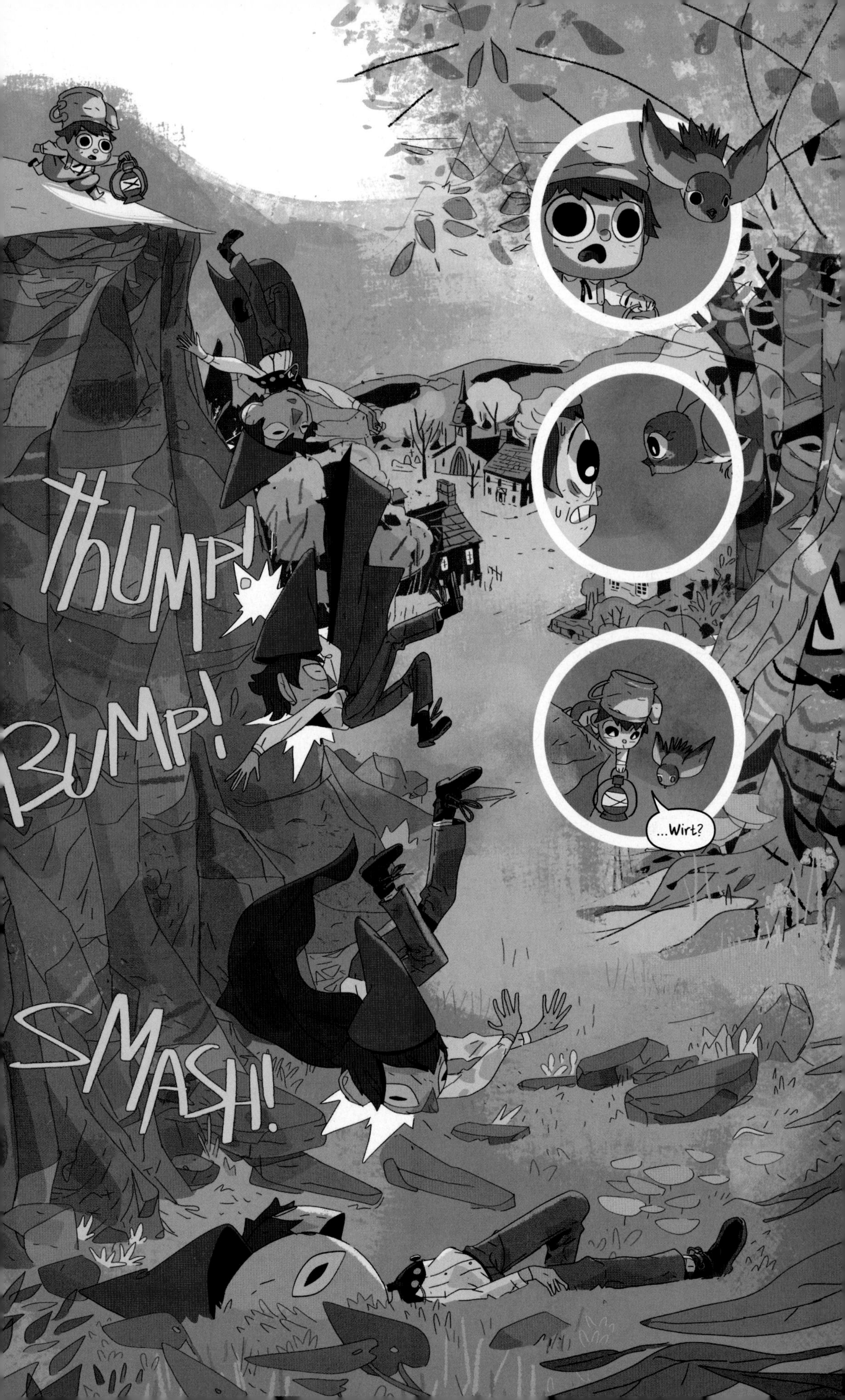
THUMP!
BUMP!
...Wirt?
SMASH!

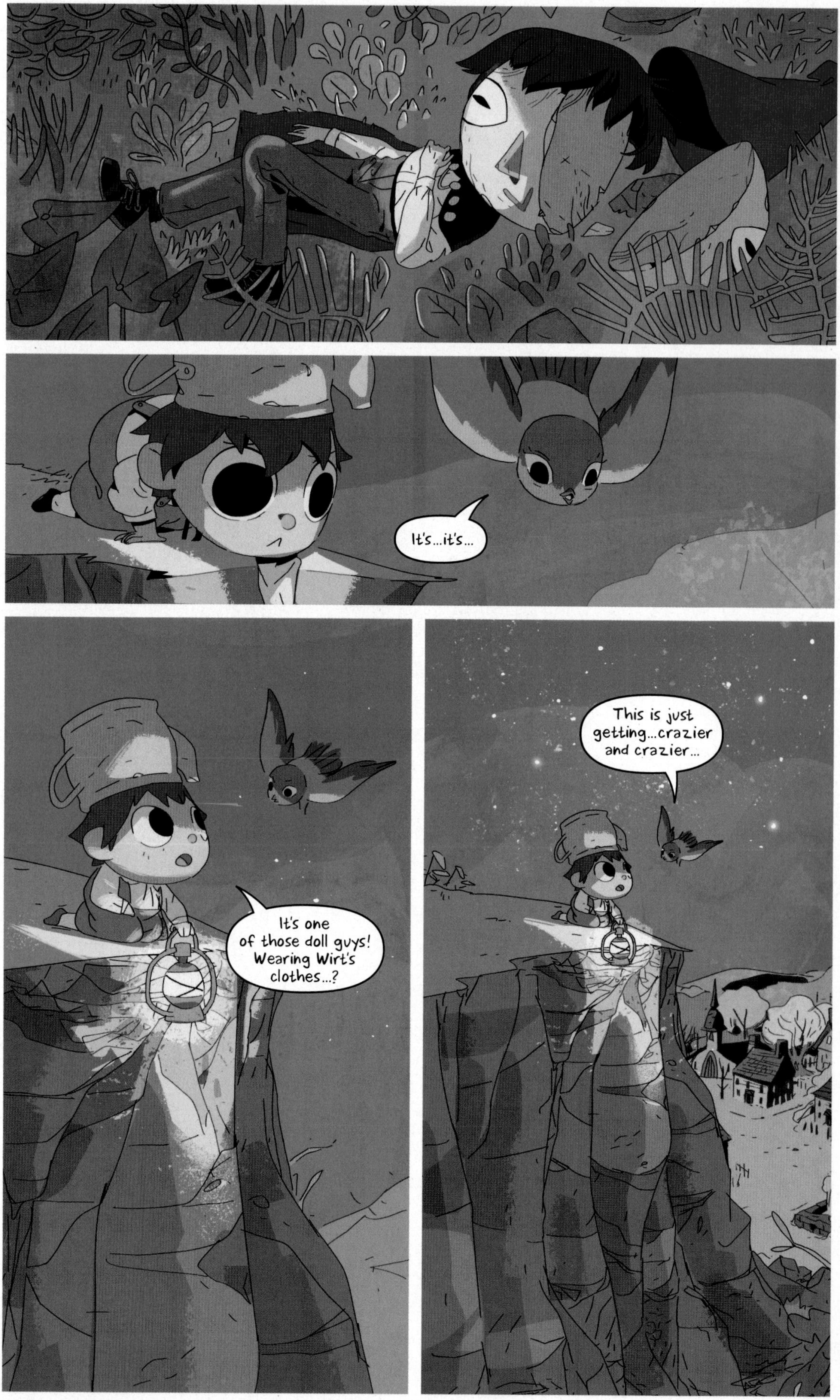

It's...it's...
It's one of those doll guys! Wearing Wirt's clothes...?
This is just getting...crazier and crazier...

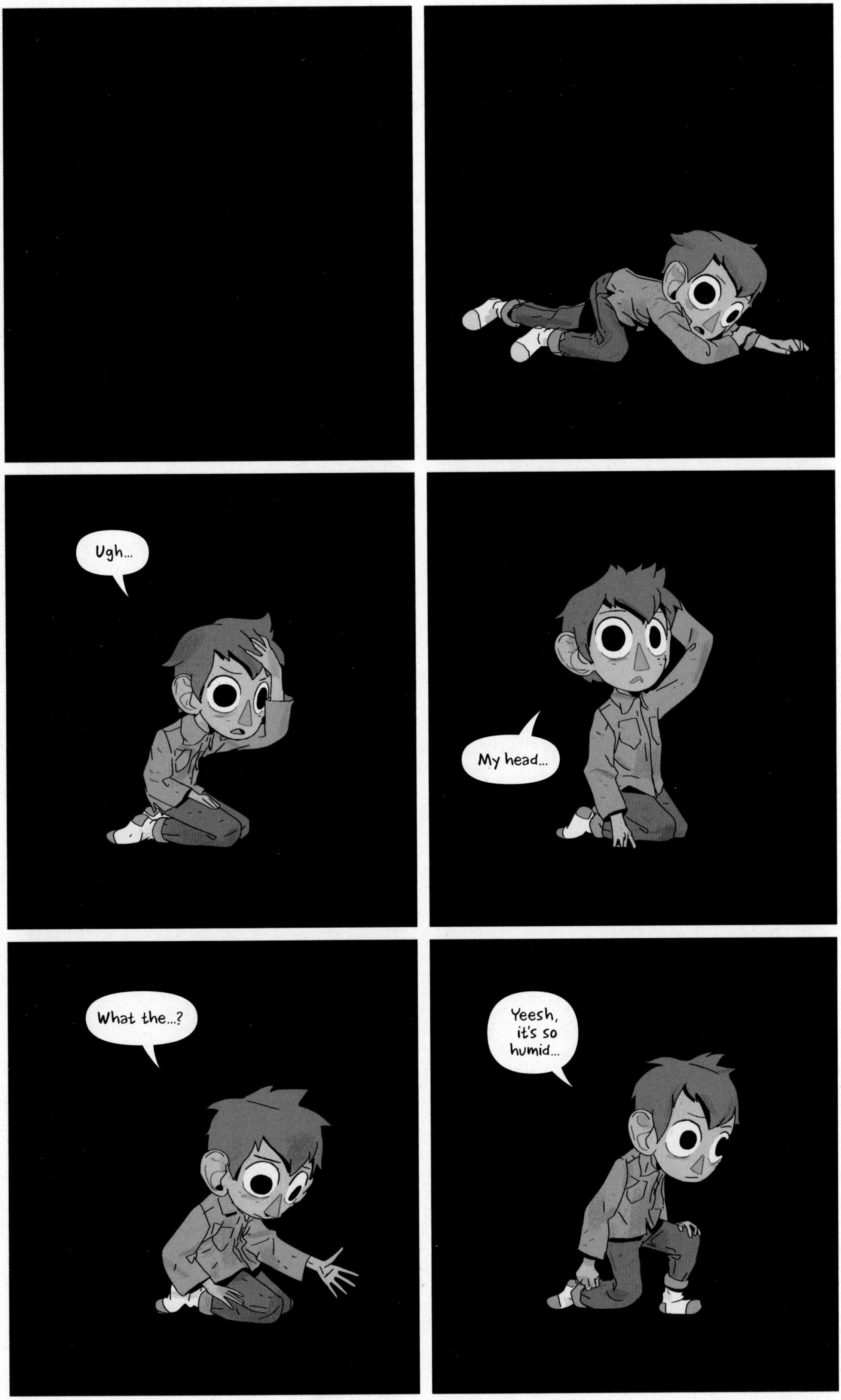
Ugh...
My head...
What the...?
Yeesh, it's so humid...

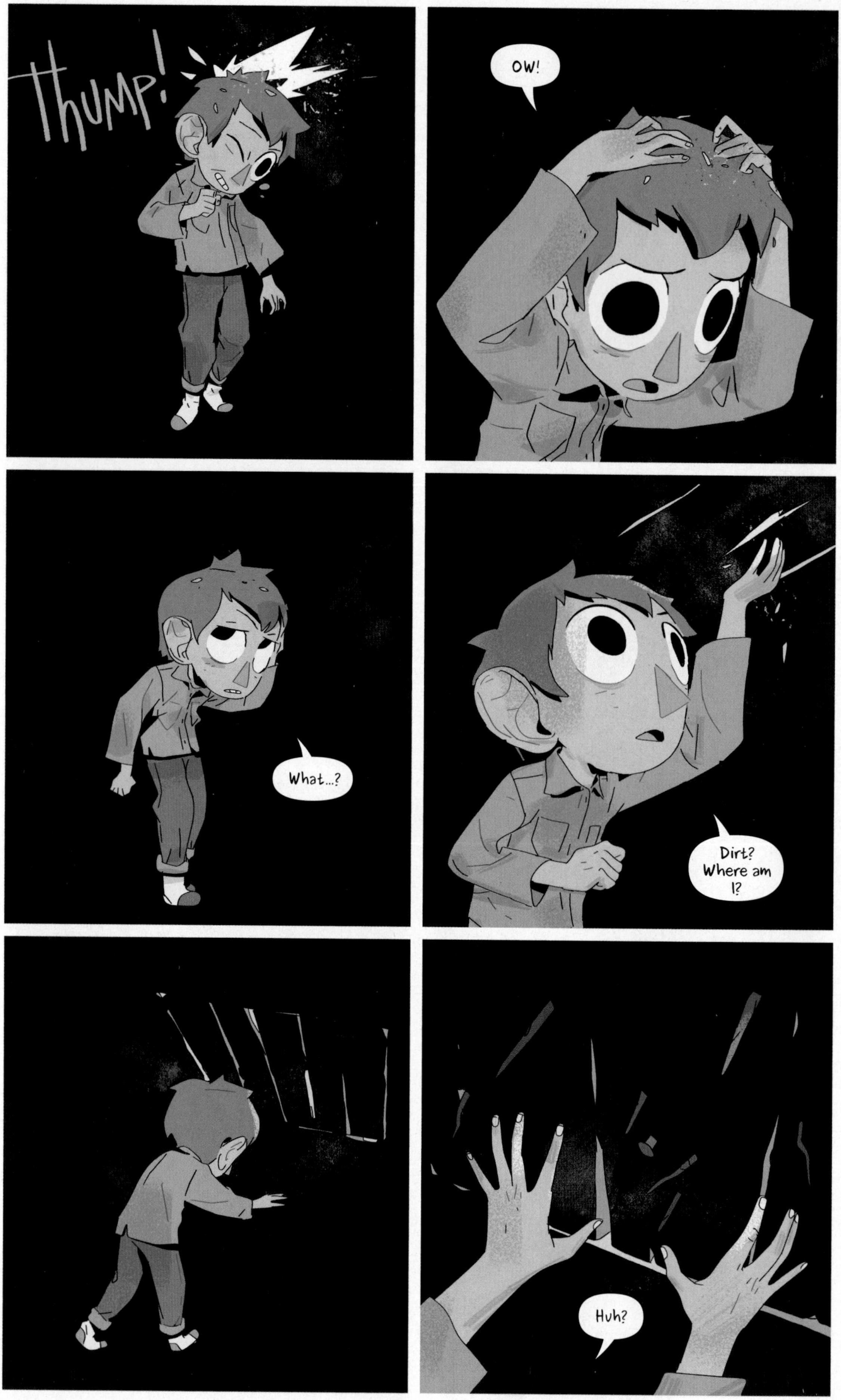
THUMP!
OW!
What...?
Dirt?
Where am
I?
Huh?

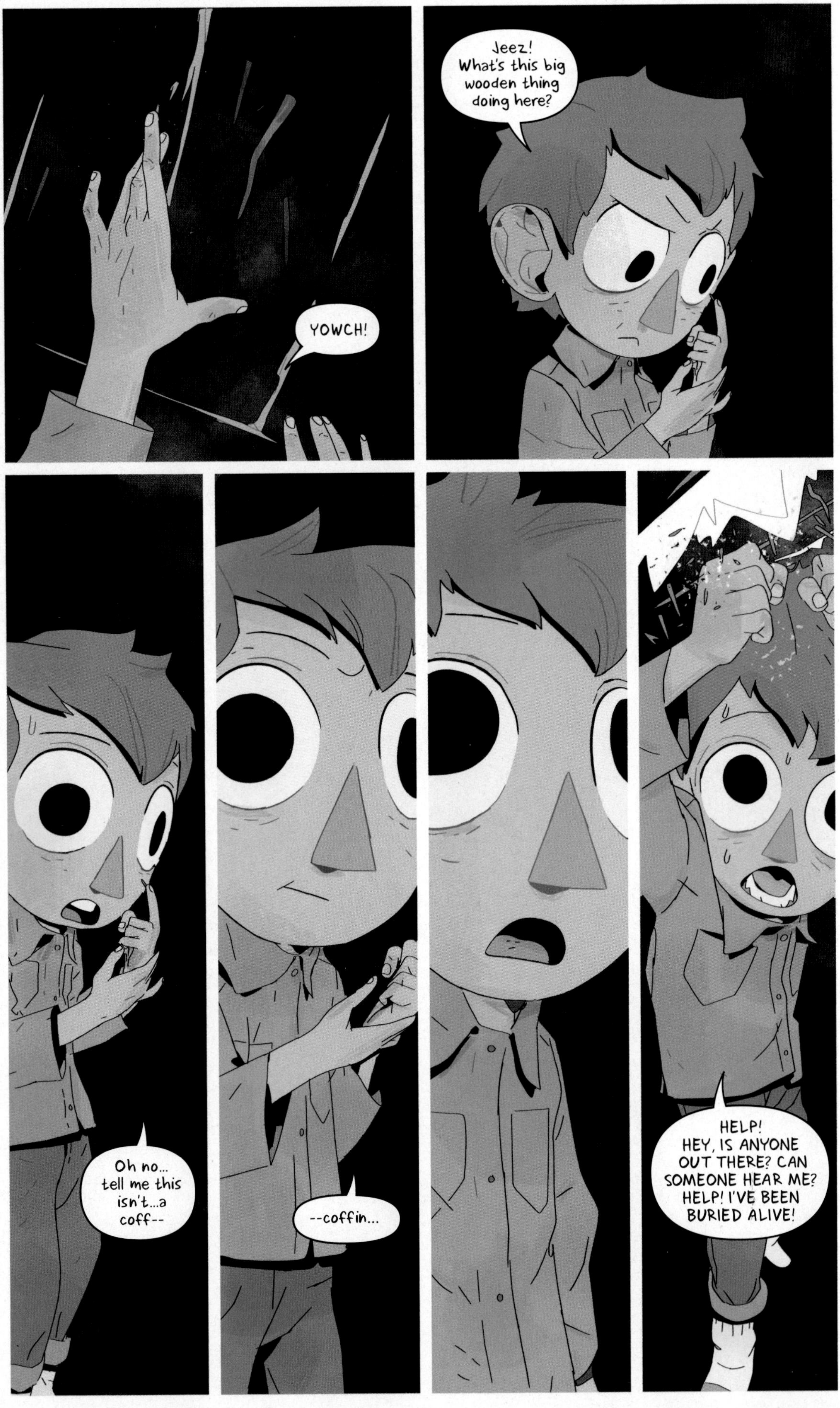
YOWCH!
Jeez! What's this big wooden thing doing here?
Oh no... tell me this isn't...a coff--
--coffin...
HELP! HEY, IS ANYONE OUT THERE? CAN SOMEONE HEAR ME? HELP! I'VE BEEN BURIED ALIVE!

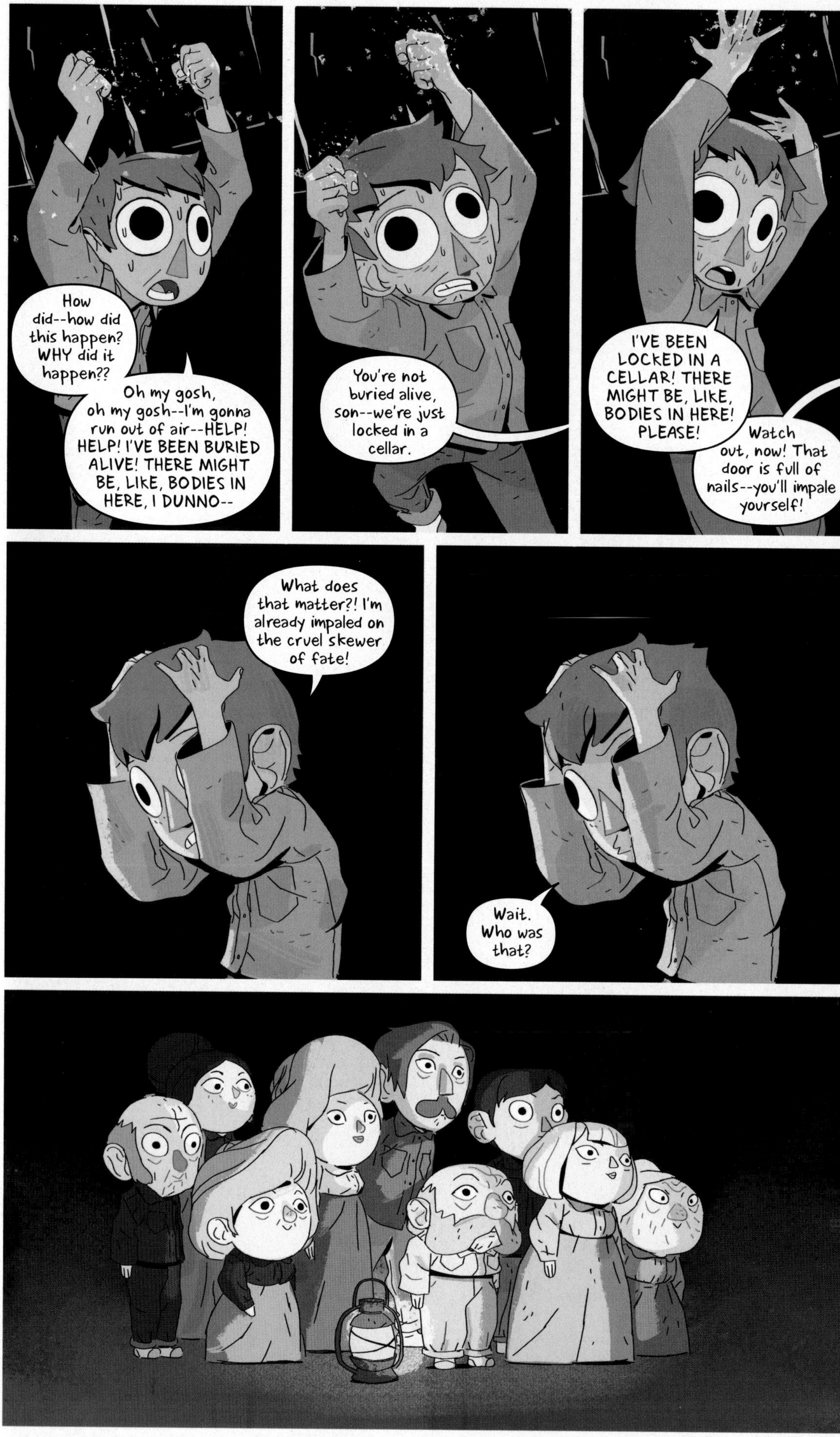
How did--how did this happen? WHY did it happen??
Oh my gosh, oh my gosh--I'm gonna run out of air--HELP! HELP! I'VE BEEN BURIED ALIVE! THERE MIGHT BE, LIKE, BODIES IN HERE, I DUNNO--
You're not buried alive, son--we're just locked in a cellar.
I'VE BEEN LOCKED IN A CELLAR! THERE MIGHT BE, LIKE, BODIES IN HERE! PLEASE!
Watch out, now! That door is full of nails--you'll impale yourself!
What does that matter?! I'm already impaled on the cruel skewer of fate!
Wait. Who was that?

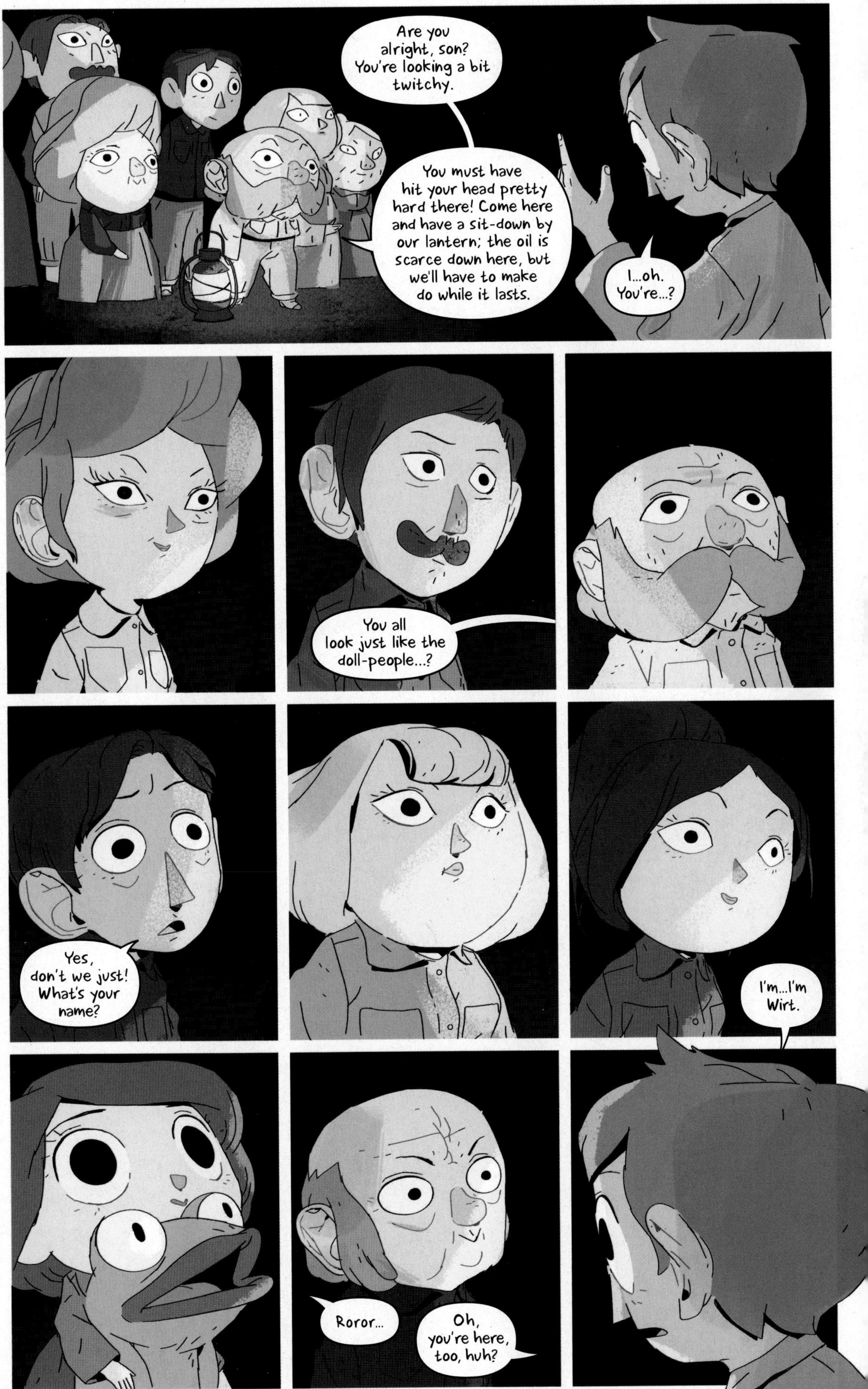
Are you alright, son? You're looking a bit twitchy.
You must have hit your head pretty hard there! Come here and have a sit-down by our lantern; the oil is scarce down here, but we'll have to make do while it lasts.
I...oh. You're...?
You all look just like the doll-people...?
Yes, don't we just! What's your name?
I'm...I'm Wirt.
Roror...
Oh, you're here, too, huh?

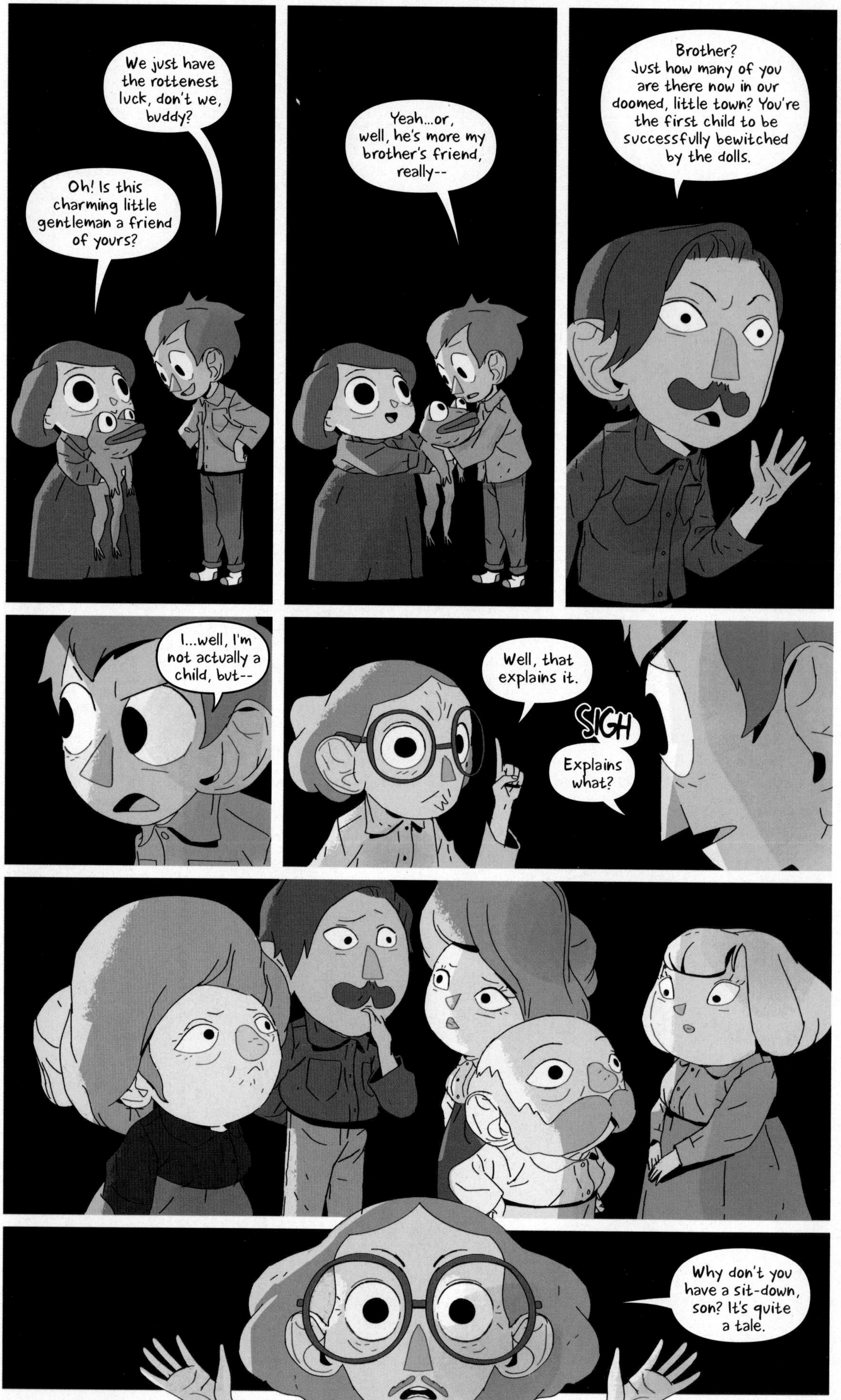
Oh! Is this charming little gentleman a friend of yours?
We just have the rottenest luck, don't we, buddy?
Yeah...or, well, he's more my brother's friend, really--
Brother? Just how many of you are there now in our doomed, little town? You're the first child to be successfully bewitched by the dolls.
I...well, I'm not actually a child, but--
Well, that explains it.
SIGH
Explains what?
Why don't you have a sit-down, son? It's quite a tale.

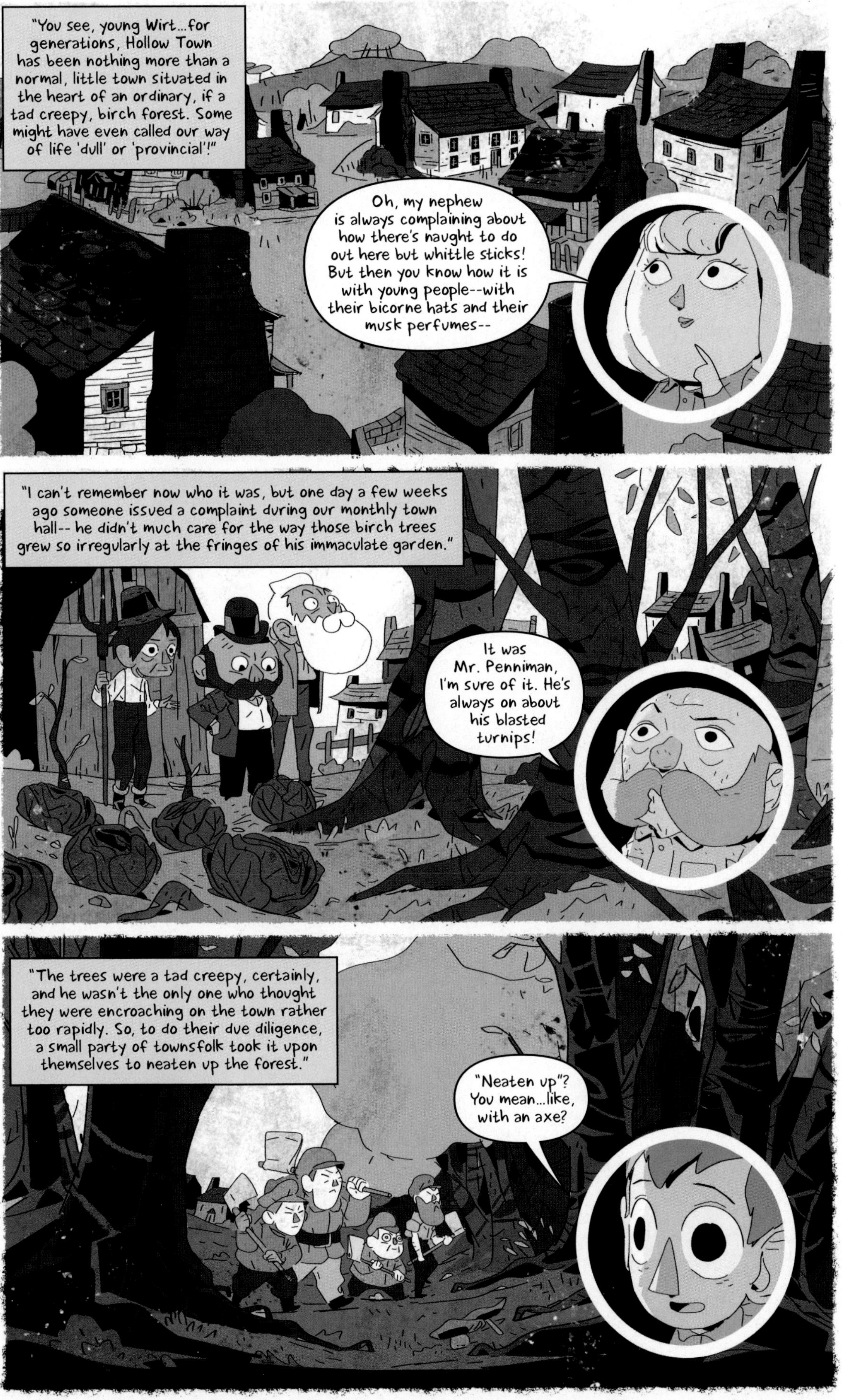
"You see, young Wirt...for generations, Hollow Town has been nothing more than a normal, little town situated in the heart of an ordinary, if a tad creepy, birch forest. Some might have even called our way of life 'dull' or 'provincial'!"
Oh, my nephew is always complaining about how there's naught to do out here but whittle sticks! But then you know how it is with young people--with their bicorne hats and their musk perfumes--
"I can't remember now who it was, but one day a few weeks ago someone issued a complaint during our monthly town hall-- he didn't much care for the way those birch trees grew so irregularly at the fringes of his immaculate garden."
It was Mr. Penniman, I'm sure of it. He's always on about his blasted turnips!
"The trees were a tad creepy, certainly, and he wasn't the only one who thought they were encroaching on the town rather too rapidly. So, to do their due diligence, a small party of townsfolk took it upon themselves to neaten up the forest."
"Neaten up"? You mean...like, with an axe?

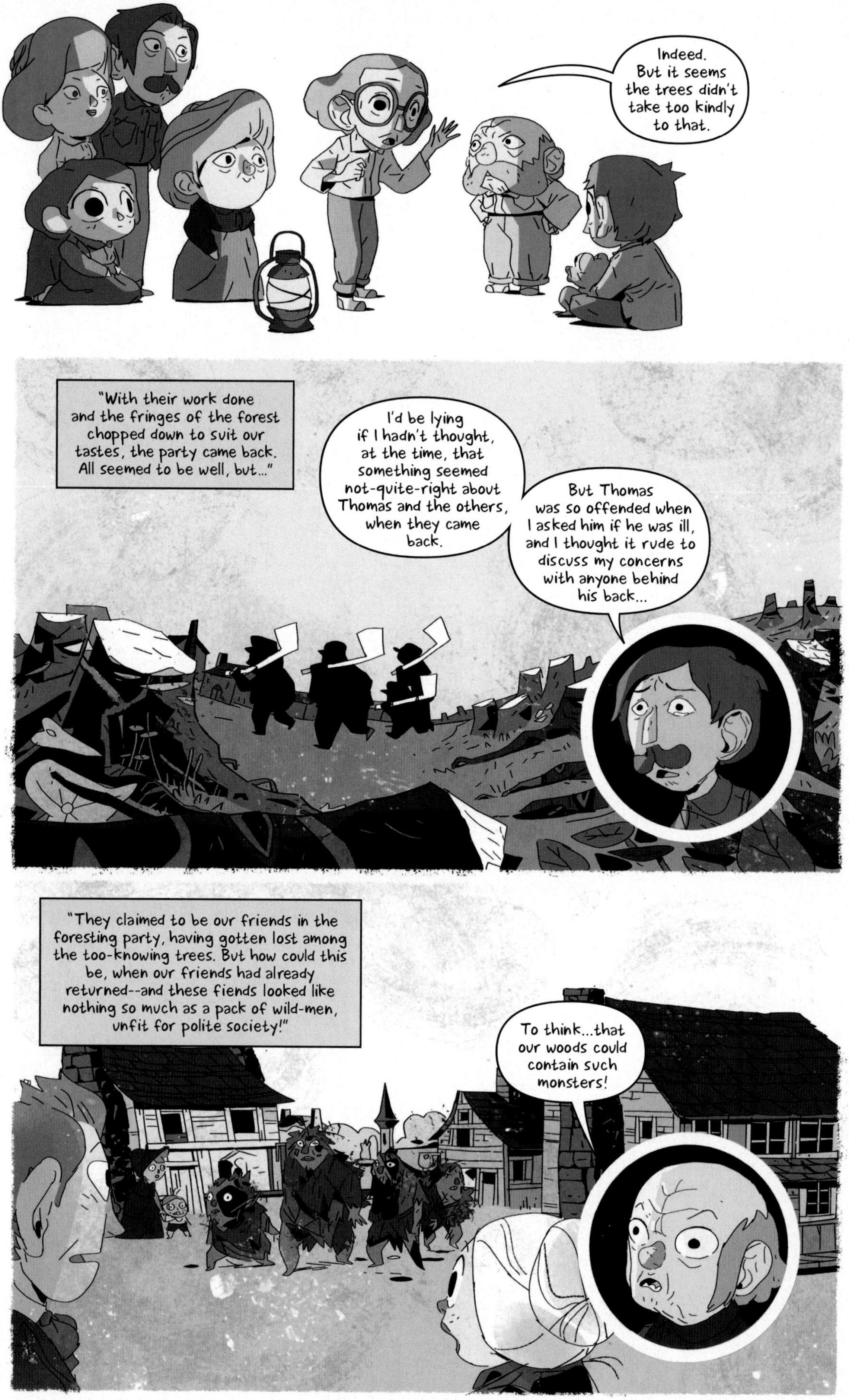
Indeed. But it seems the trees didn't take too kindly to that.
"With their work done and the fringes of the forest chopped down to suit our tastes, the party came back. All seemed to be well, but..."
I'd be lying if I hadn't thought, at the time, that something seemed not-quite-right about Thomas and the others, when they came back.
But Thomas was so offended when I asked him if he was ill, and I thought it rude to discuss my concerns with anyone behind his back...
"They claimed to be our friends in the foresting party, having gotten lost among the too-knowing trees. But how could this be, when our friends had already returned--and these fiends looked like nothing so much as a pack of wild-men, unfit for polite society!"
To think...that our woods could contain such monsters!

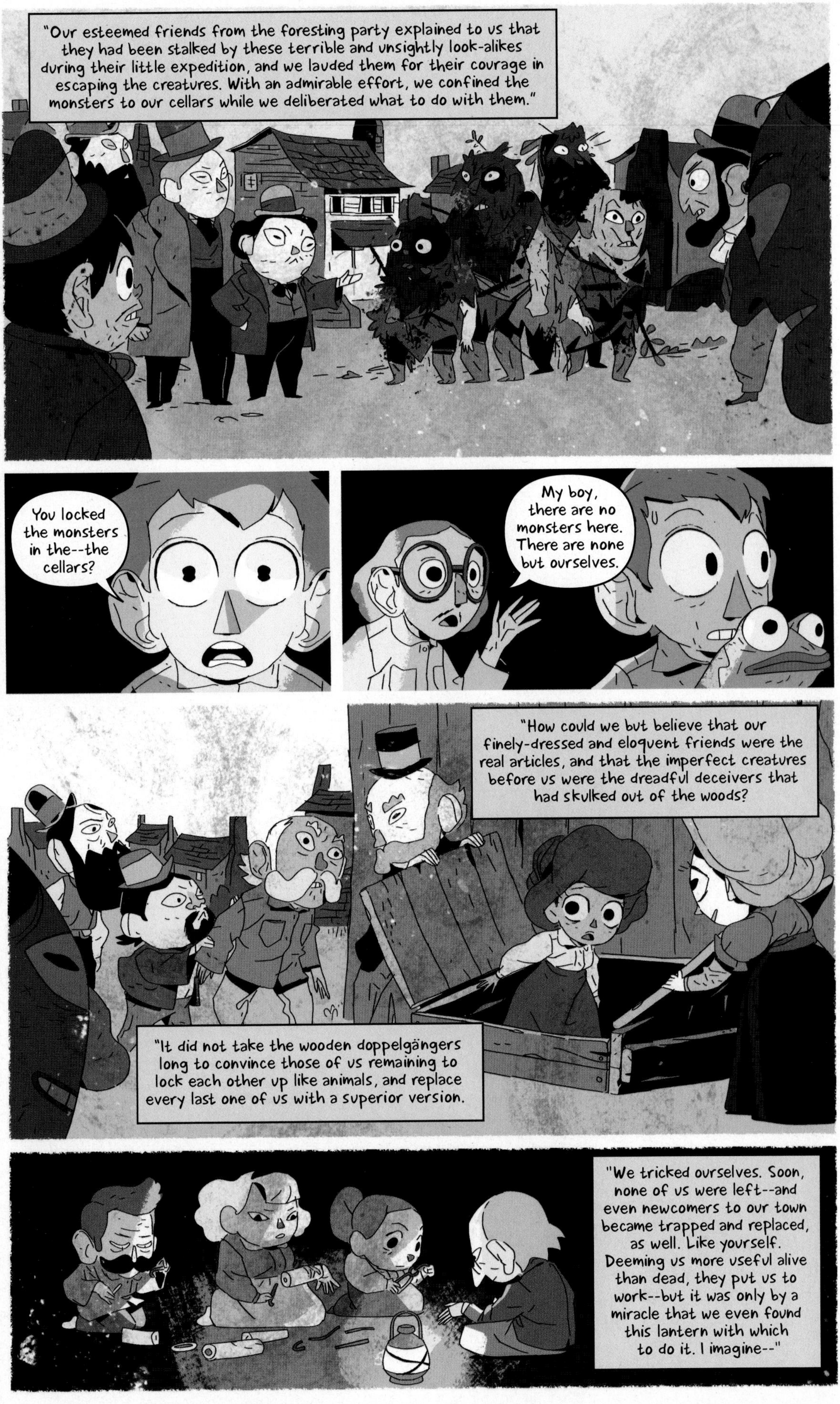
"Our esteemed friends from the foresting party explained to us that they had been stalked by these terrible and unsightly look-alikes during their little expedition, and we lauded them for their courage in escaping the creatures. With an admirable effort, we confined the monsters to our cellars while we deliberated what to do with them."
You locked the monsters in the--the cellars?
My boy, there are no monsters here. There are none but ourselves.
"How could we but believe that our finely-dressed and eloquent friends were the real articles, and that the imperfect creatures before us were the dreadful deceivers that had skulked out of the woods?
"It did not take the wooden doppelgängers long to convince those of us remaining to lock each other up like animals, and replace every last one of us with a superior version.
"We tricked ourselves. Soon, none of us were left--and even newcomers to our town became trapped and replaced, as well. Like yourself. Deeming us more useful alive than dead, they put us to work--but it was only by a miracle that we even found this lantern with which to do it. I imagine--"

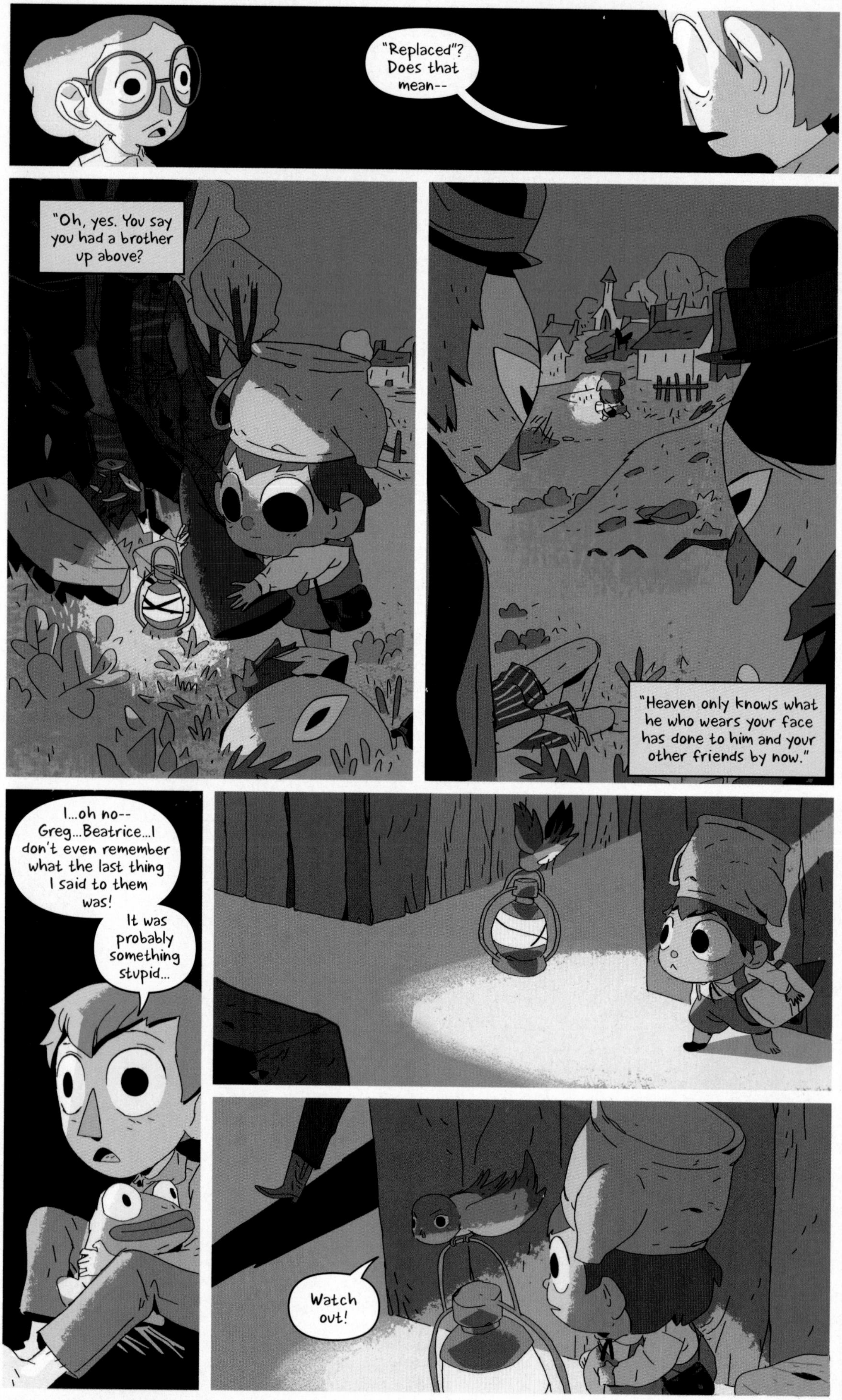
"Replaced"? Does that mean--
"Oh, yes. You say you had a brother up above?
"Heaven only knows what he who wears your face has done to him and your other friends by now."
I...oh no-- Greg...Beatrice...I don't even remember what the last thing I said to them was!
It was probably something stupid...
Watch out!

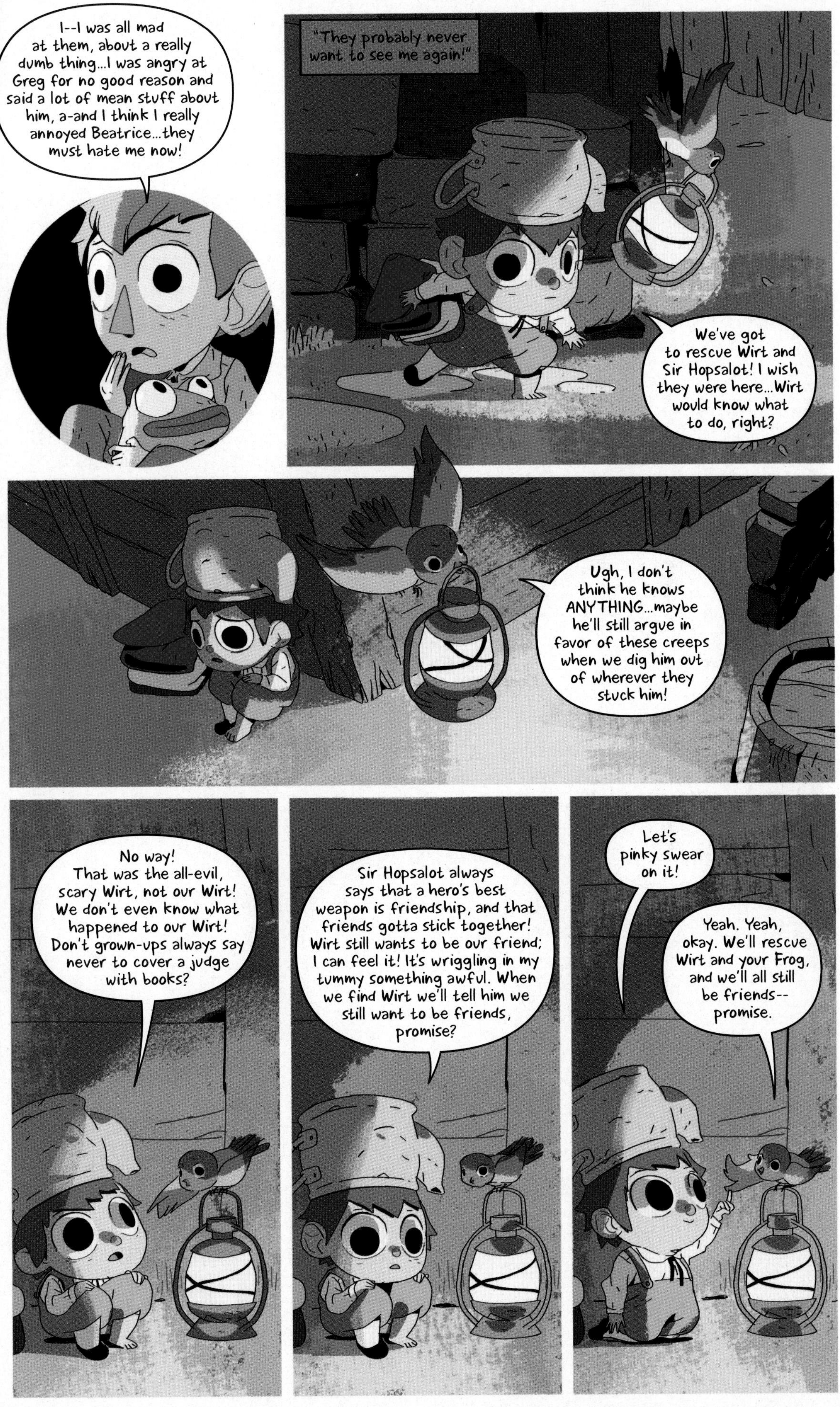
I--I was all mad at them, about a really dumb thing...I was angry at Greg for no good reason and said a lot of mean stuff about him, a-and I think I really annoyed Beatrice...they must hate me now!
"They probably never want to see me again!"
We've got to rescue Wirt and Sir Hopsalot! I wish they were here...Wirt would know what to do, right?
Ugh, I don't think he knows ANYTHING...maybe he'll still argue in favor of these creeps when we dig him out of wherever they stuck him!
No way! That was the all-evil, scary Wirt, not our Wirt! We don't even know what happened to our Wirt! Don't grown-ups always say never to cover a judge with books?
Sir Hopsalot always says that a hero's best weapon is friendship, and that friends gotta stick together! Wirt still wants to be our friend; I can feel it! It's wriggling in my tummy something awful. When we find Wirt we'll tell him we still want to be friends, promise?
Let's pinky swear on it!
Yeah. Yeah, okay. We'll rescue Wirt and your Frog, and we'll all still be friends--promise.

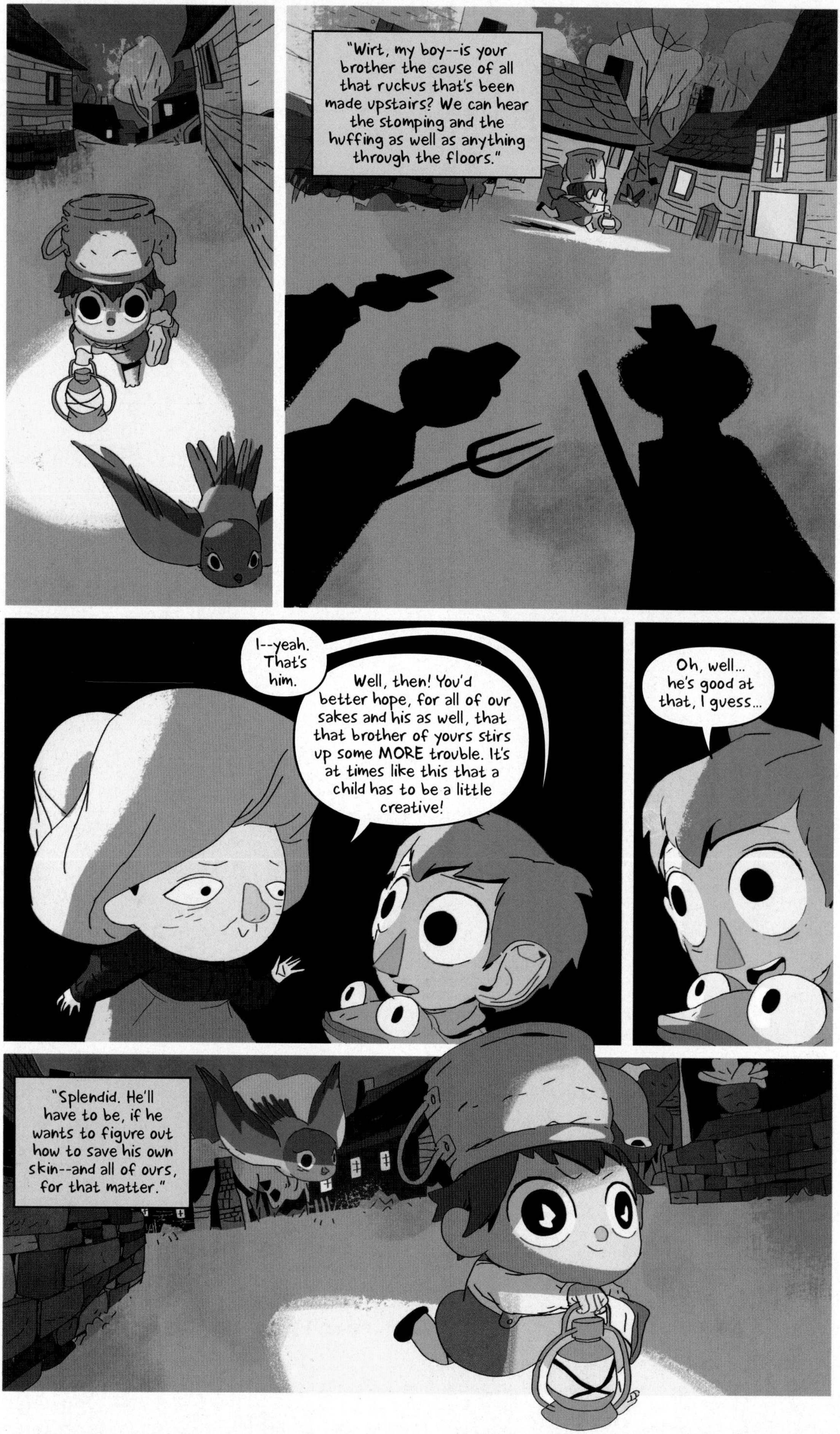
"Wirt, my boy--is your brother the cause of all that ruckus that's been made upstairs? We can hear the stomping and the huffing as well as anything through the floors."
I--yeah. That's him.
Well, then! You'd better hope, for all of our sakes and his as well, that that brother of yours stirs up some MORE trouble. It's at times like this that a child has to be a little creative!
Oh, well... he's good at that, I guess...
"Splendid. He'll have to be, if he wants to figure out how to save his own skin--and all of ours, for that matter."

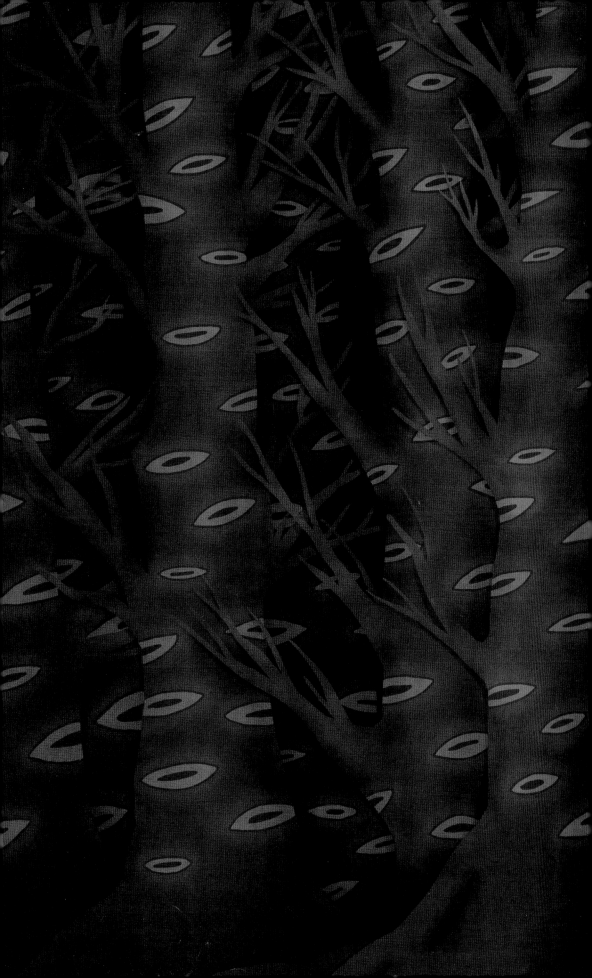

CHAPTER

5

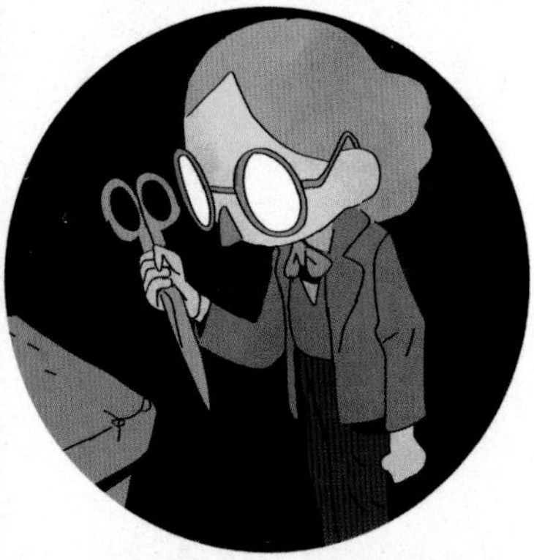
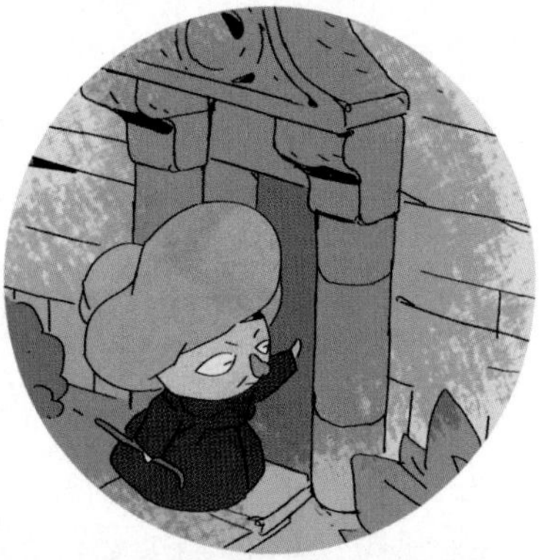
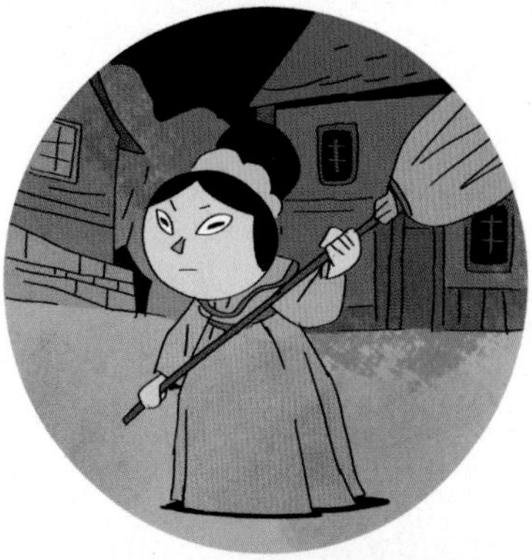
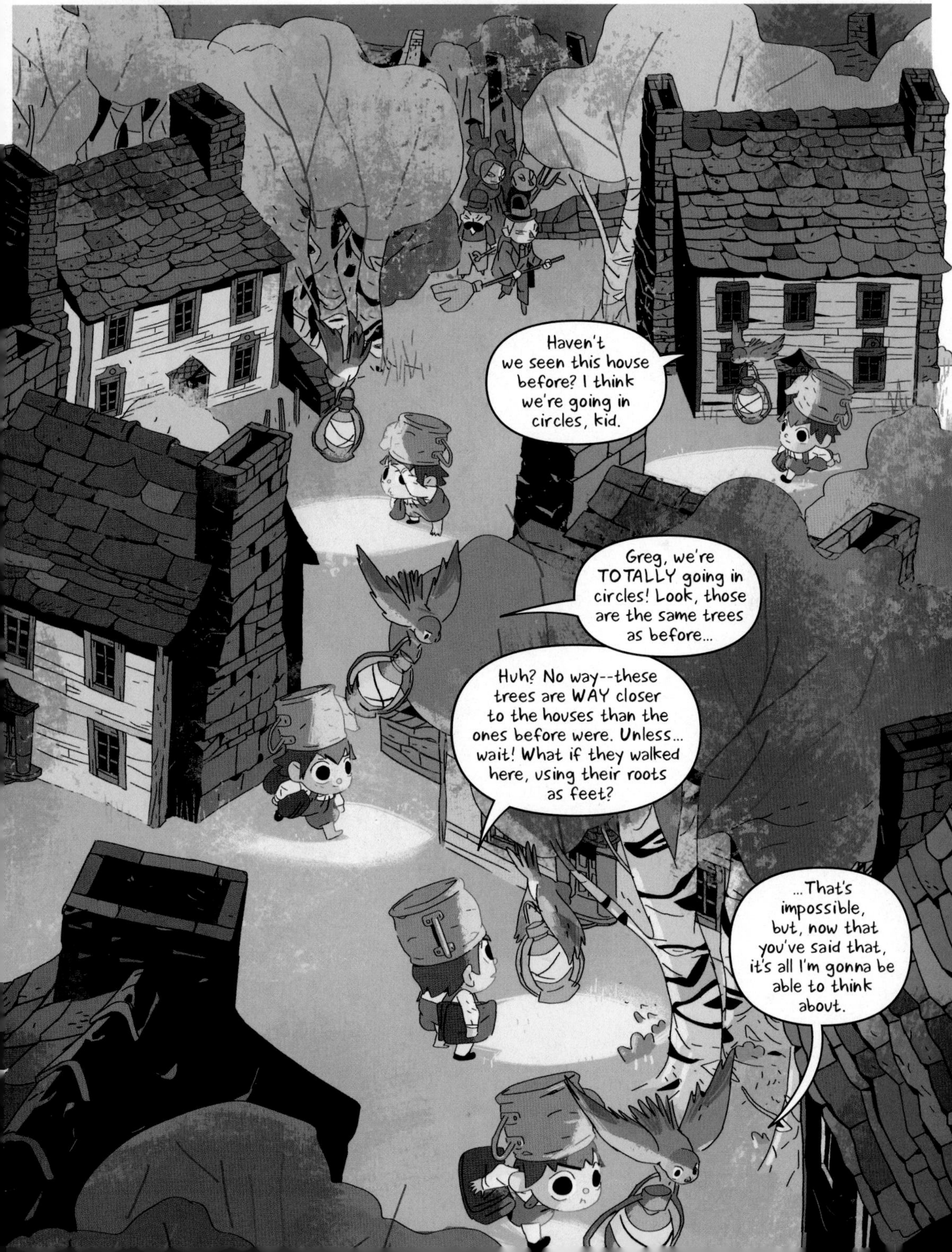
Haven't we seen this house before? I think we're going in circles, kid.
Greg, we're TOTALLY going in circles! Look, those are the same trees as before...
Huh? No way--these trees are WAY closer to the houses than the ones before were. Unless... wait! What if they walked here, using their roots as feet?
...That's impossible, but, now that you've said that, it's all I'm gonna be able to think about.

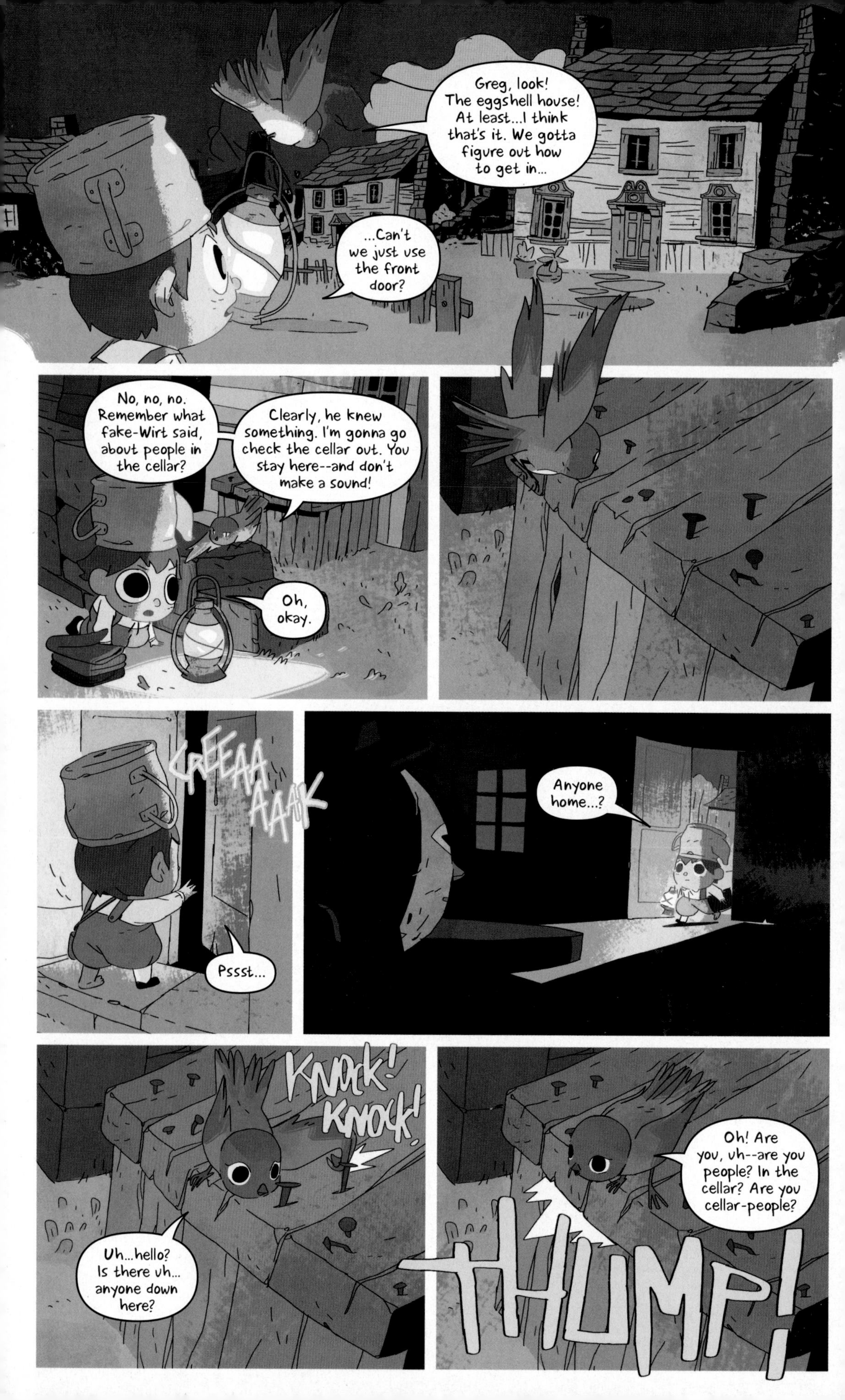

Greg, look! The eggshell house! At least...I think that's it. We gotta figure out how to get in...
...Can't we just use the front door?
No, no, no. Remember what fake-Wirt said, about people in the cellar?
Clearly, he knew something. I'm gonna go check the cellar out. You stay here--and don't make a sound!
Oh, okay.
CREEAAAAAK
Pssst...
Anyone home...?
KNOCK! KNOCK!
Uh...hello? Is there uh... anyone down here?
Oh! Are you, uh--are you people? In the cellar? Are you cellar-people?
THUMP!

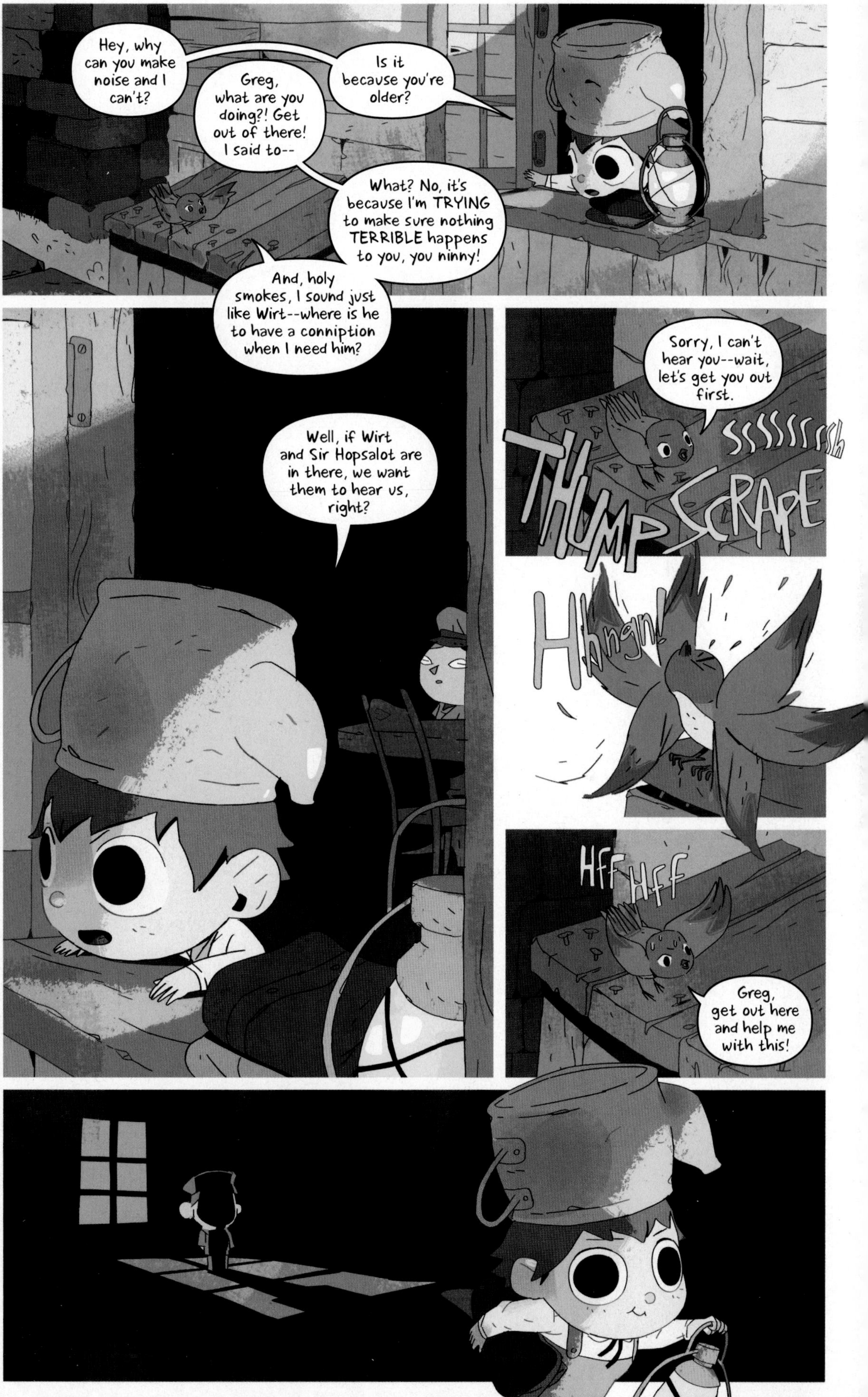
Hey, why can you make noise and I can't?
Greg, what are you doing?! Get out of there! I said to--
Is it because you're older?
What? No, it's because I'm TRYING to make sure nothing TERRIBLE happens to you, you ninny!
And, holy smokes, I sound just like Wirt--where is he to have a conniption when I need him?
Well, if Wirt and Sir Hopsalot are in there, we want them to hear us, right?
Sorry, I can't hear you--wait, let's get you out first.
Ssssssrrsh
THUMP
SCRAPE
Hhngn!
Hff Hff
Greg, get out here and help me with this!

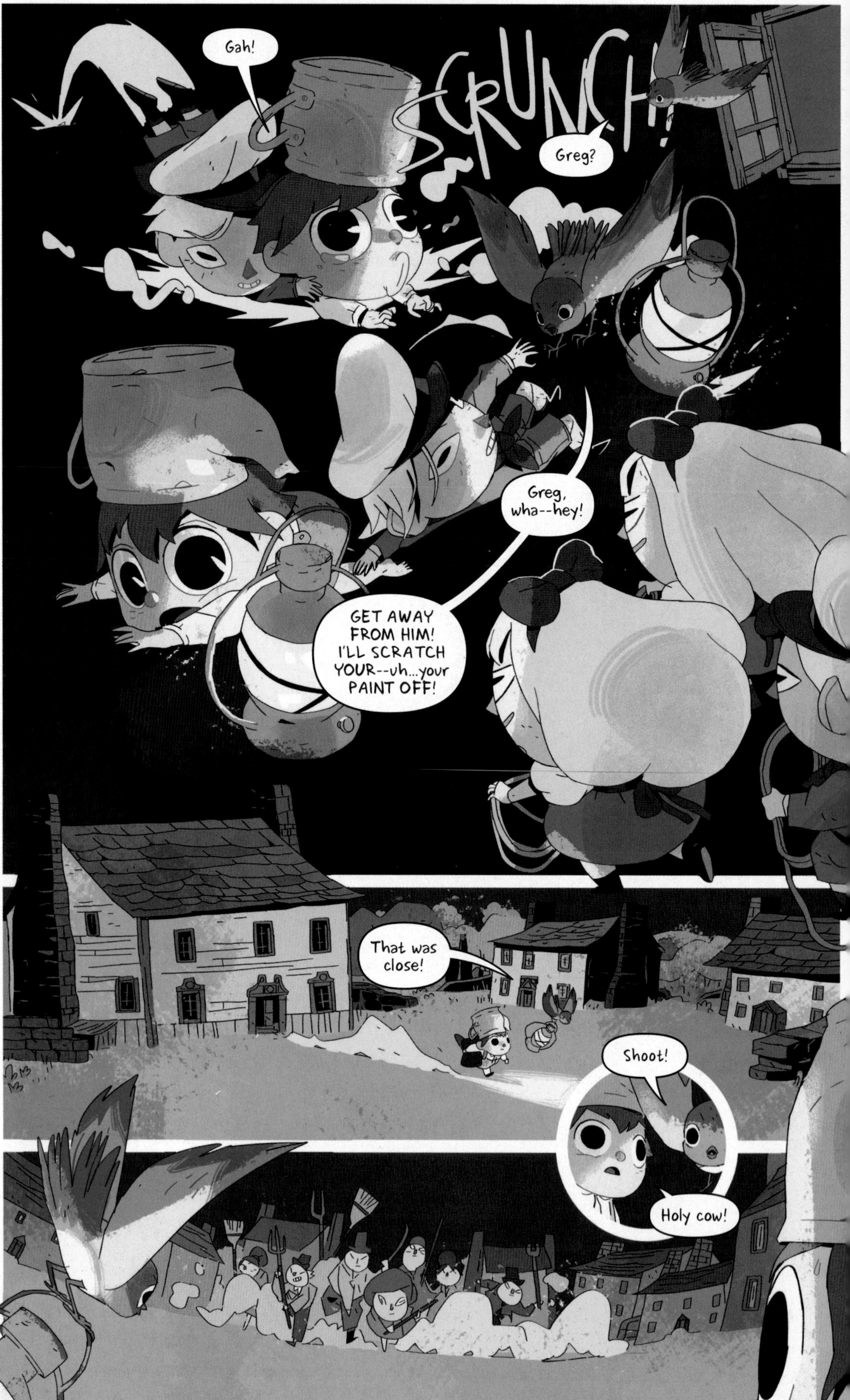
Gah!
SCRUNCH!
Greg?
Greg, wha--hey!
GET AWAY FROM HIM! I'LL SCRATCH YOUR--uh...your PAINT OFF!
That was close!
Shoot!
Holy cow!

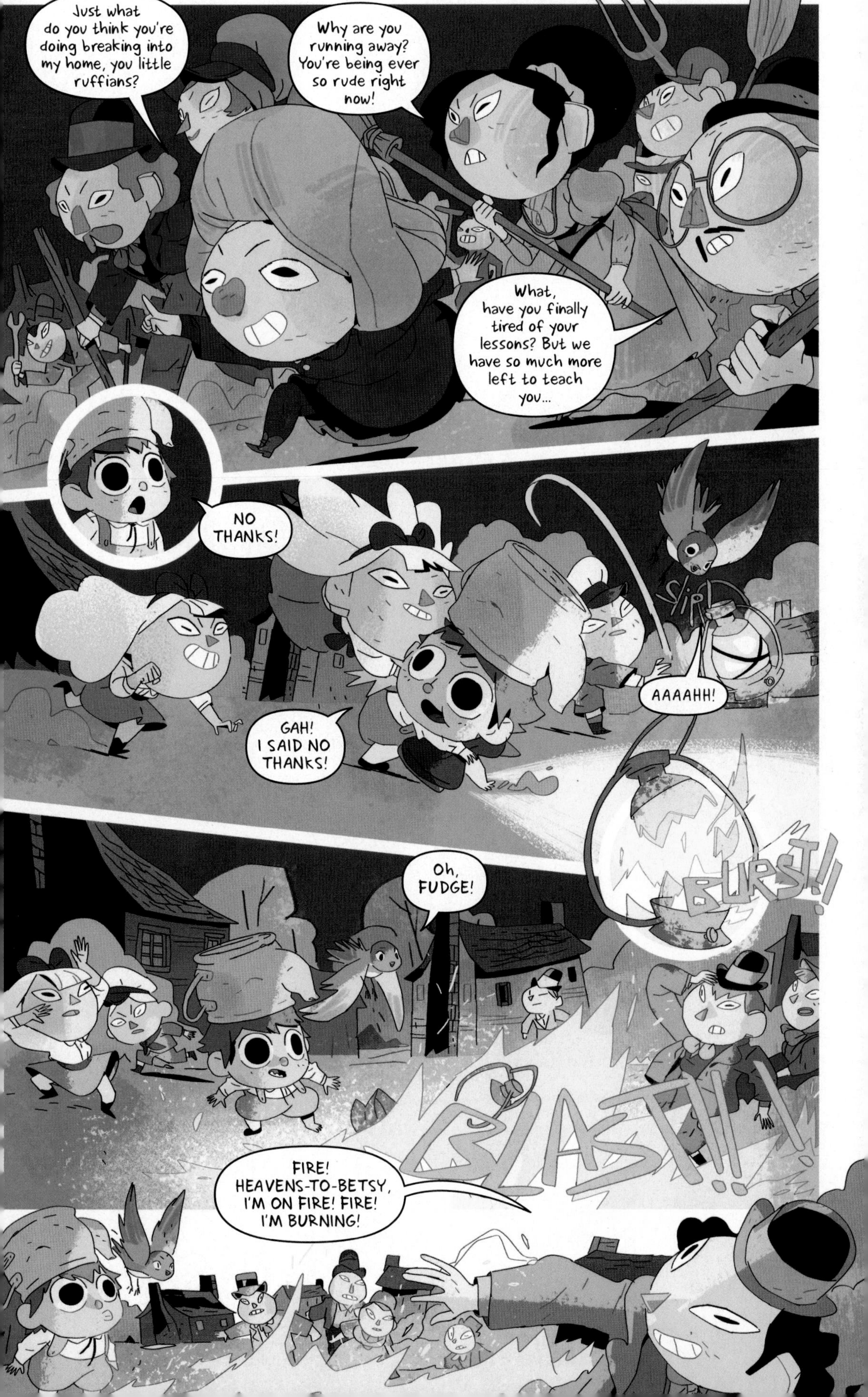
Just what do you think you're doing breaking into my home, you little ruffians?
Why are you running away? You're being ever so rude right now!
What, have you finally tired of your lessons? But we have so much more left to teach you...
NO THANKS!
GAH! I SAID NO THANKS!
SLIP!
AAAAHH!
BURST!!
Oh, FUDGE!
BLAST!!
FIRE! HEAVENS-TO-BETSY, I'M ON FIRE! FIRE! I'M BURNING!

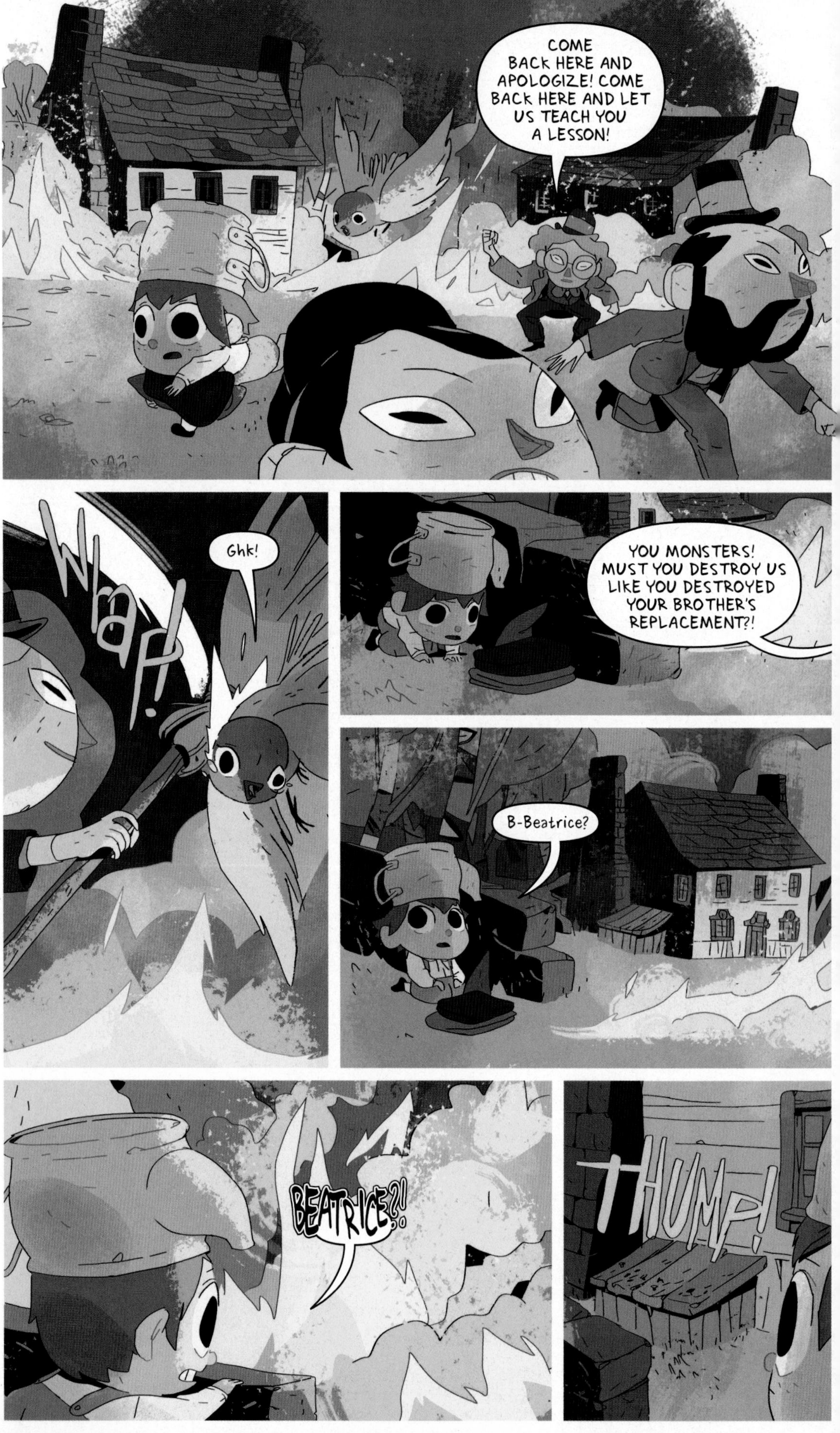
COME BACK HERE AND APOLOGIZE! COME BACK HERE AND LET US TEACH YOU A LESSON!
Whap!
Ghk!
YOU MONSTERS! MUST YOU DESTROY US LIKE YOU DESTROYED YOUR BROTHER'S REPLACEMENT?!
B-Beatrice?
BEATRICE?!
THUMP!

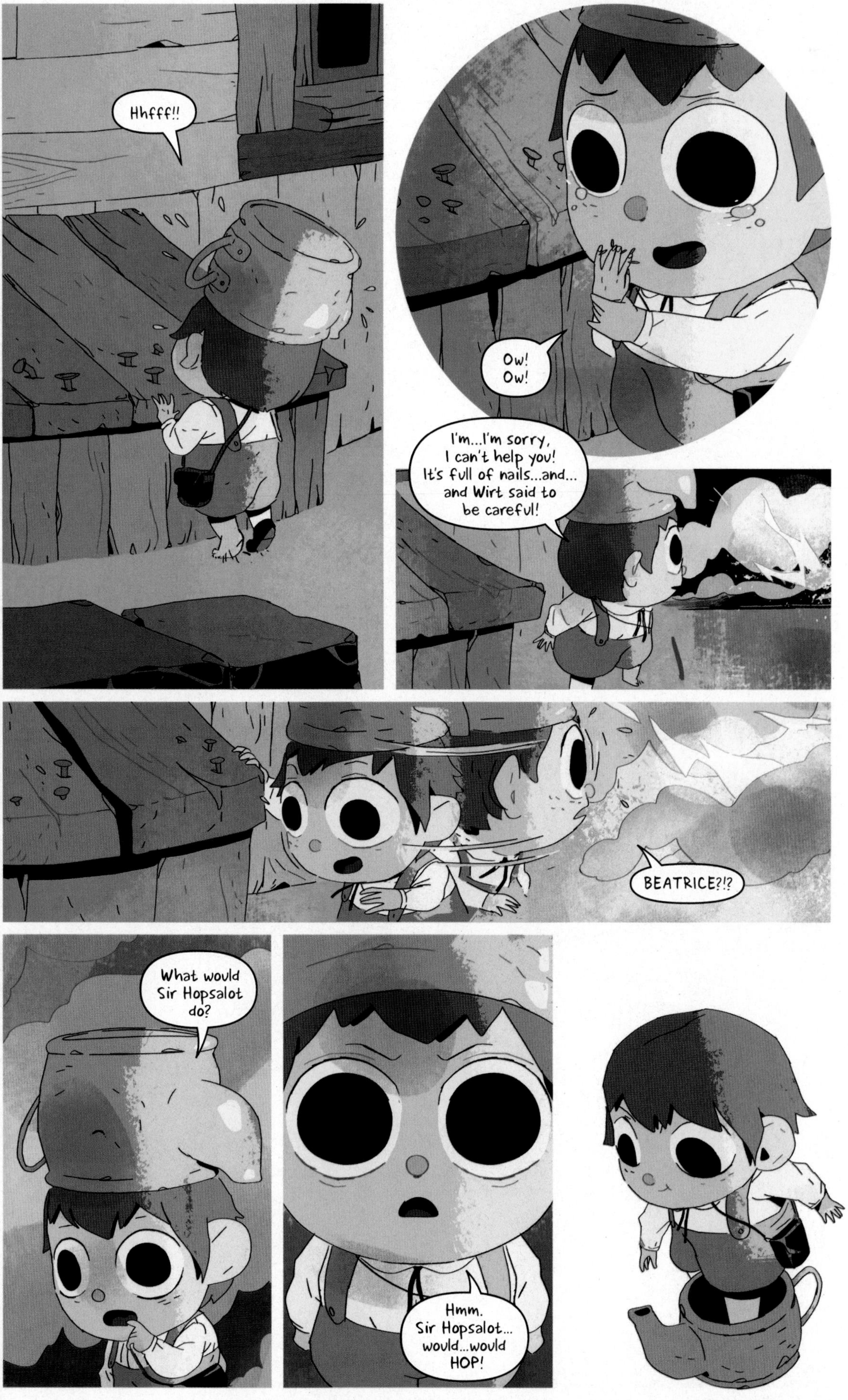
Hhfff!!
Ow! Ow!
I'm...I'm sorry, I can't help you! It's full of nails...and... and Wirt said to be careful!
BEATRICE?!?
What would Sir Hopsalot do?
Hmm. Sir Hopsalot... would...would HOP!

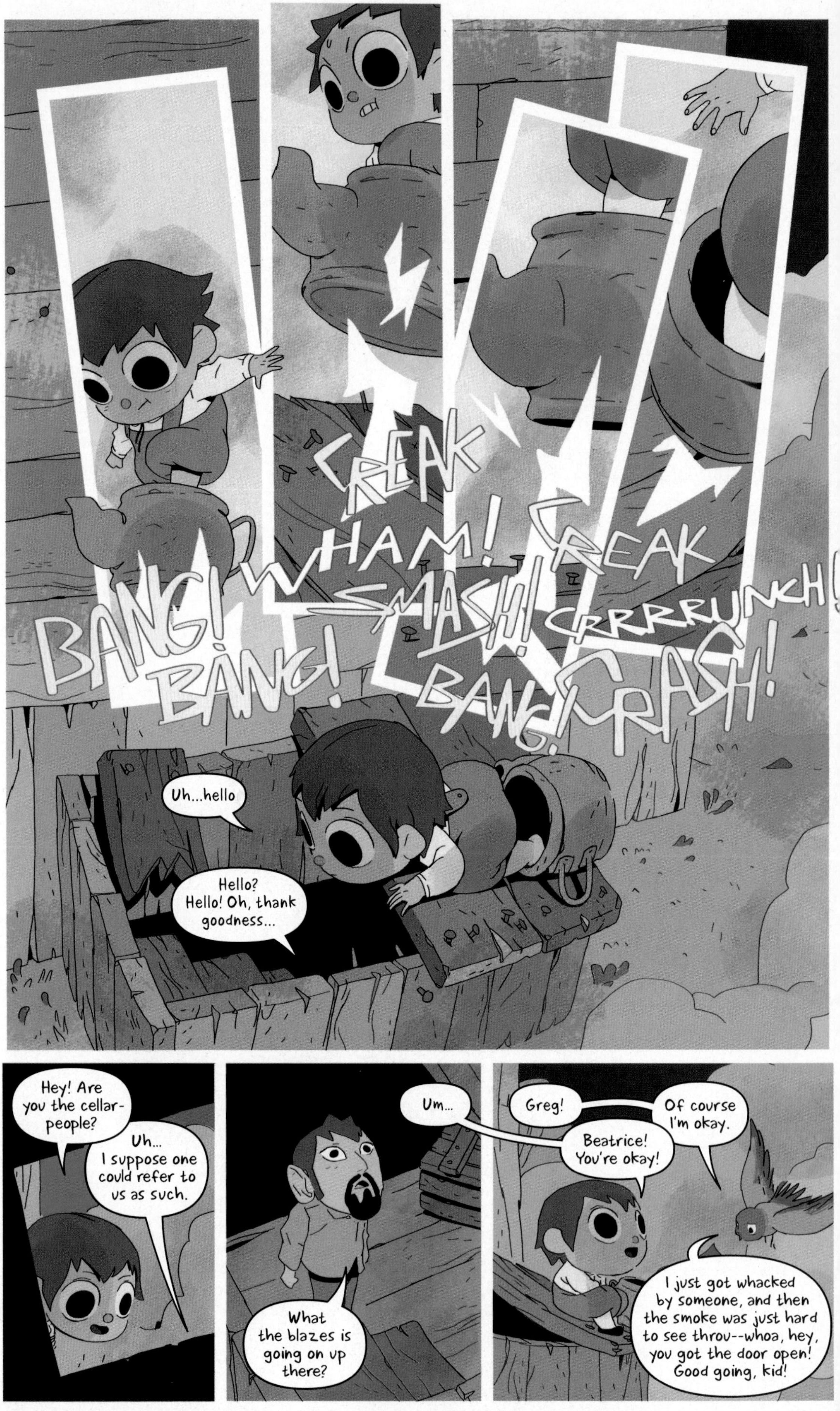
CREAK
WHAM!
CREAK
SMASH!
CRRRRUNCH!
BANG!
BANG!
BANG!
CRASH!
Uh...hello
Hello?
Hello! Oh, thank goodness...
Hey! Are you the cellar-people?
Uh... I suppose one could refer to us as such.
Um...
What the blazes is going on up there?
Greg!
Beatrice! You're okay!
Of course I'm okay.
I just got whacked by someone, and then the smoke was just hard to see throu--whoa, hey, you got the door open! Good going, kid!

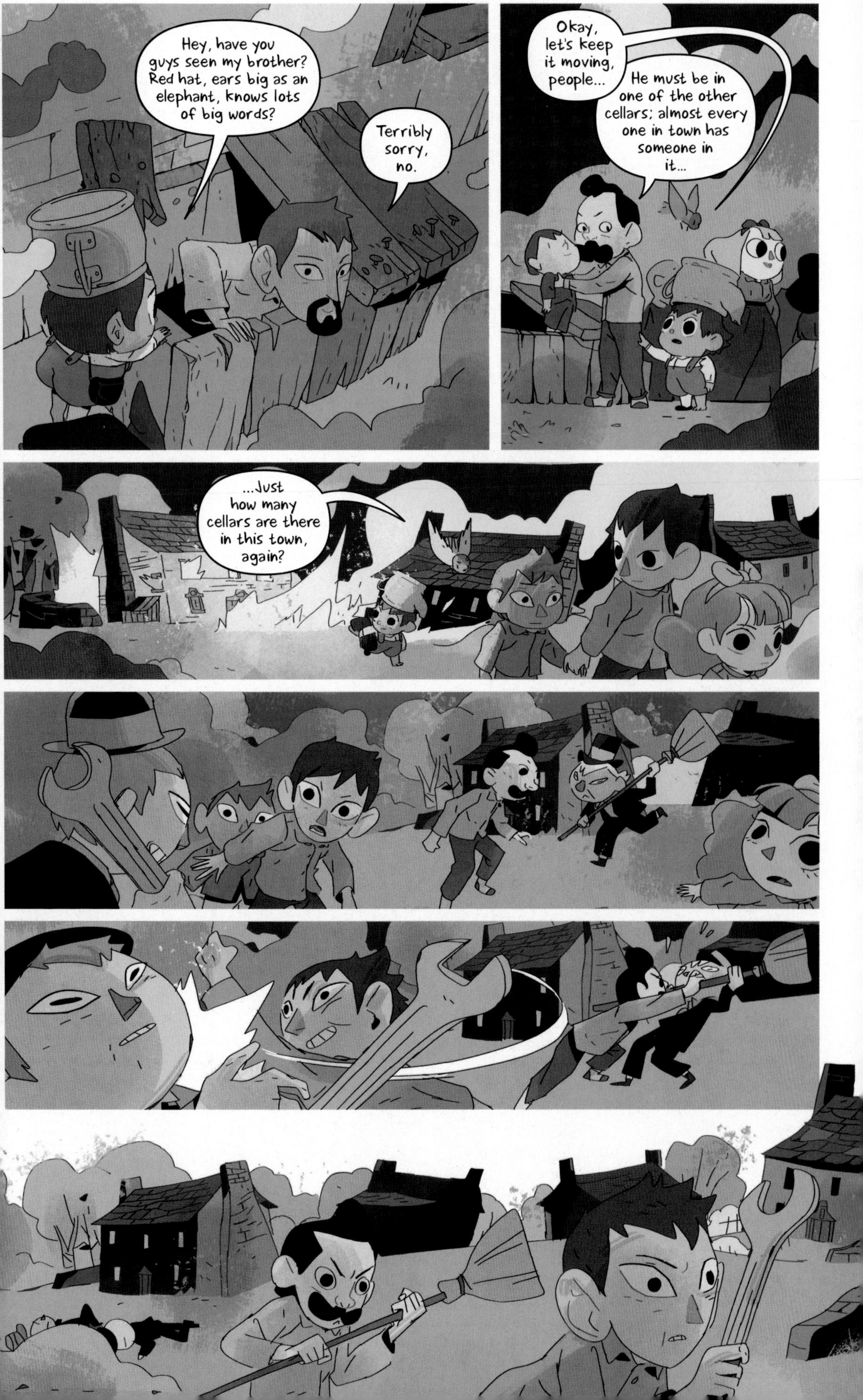
Hey, have you guys seen my brother? Red hat, ears big as an elephant, knows lots of big words?
Terribly sorry, no.
Okay, let's keep it moving, people...
He must be in one of the other cellars; almost every one in town has someone in it...
...Just how many cellars are there in this town, again?

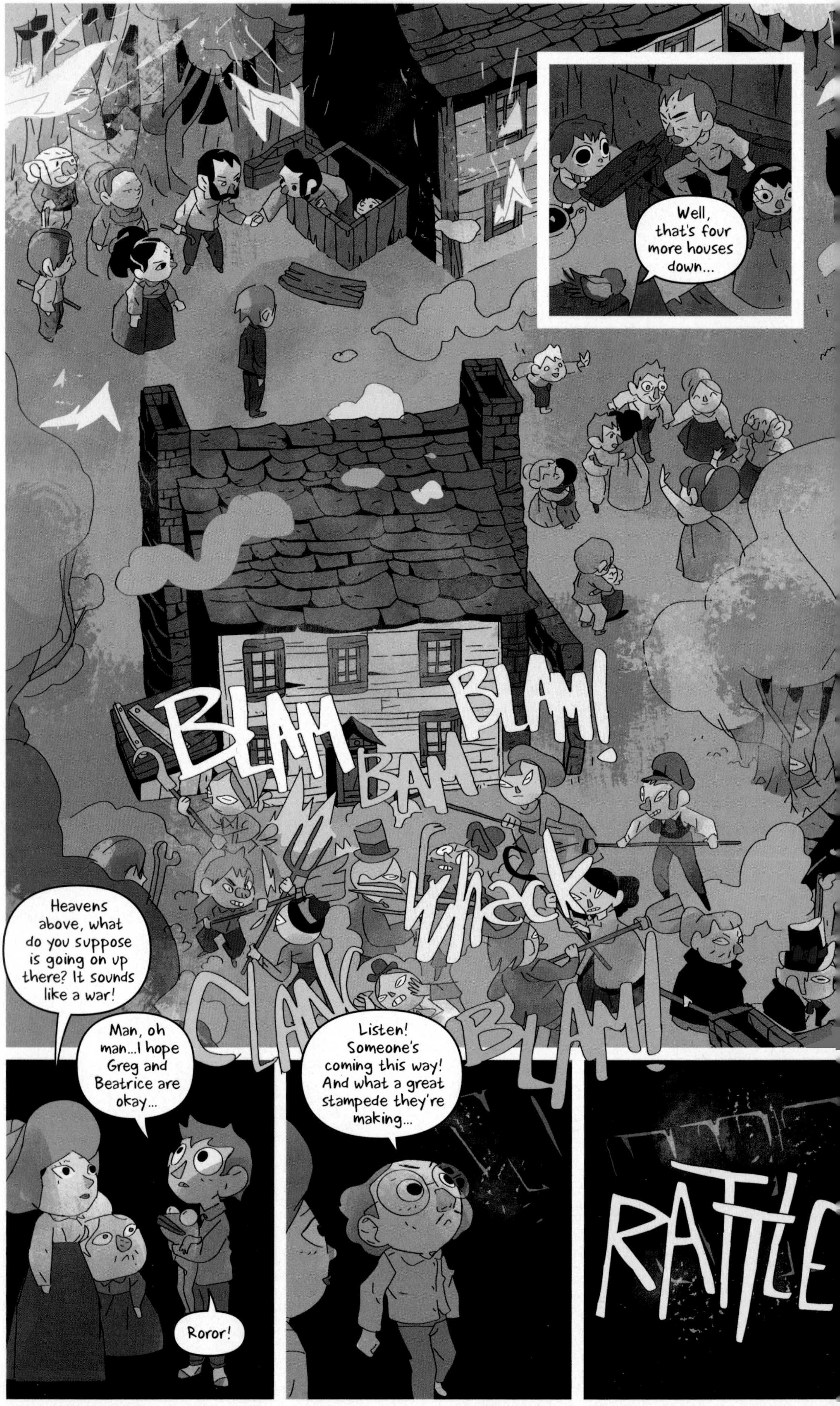
Well, that's four more houses down...
BLAM
BLAM!
BAM
WHACK
Heavens above, what do you suppose is going on up there? It sounds like a war!
CLANG
BLAM!
Man, oh man...I hope Greg and Beatrice are okay...
Roror!
Listen! Someone's coming this way! And what a great stampede they're making...
RATTLE

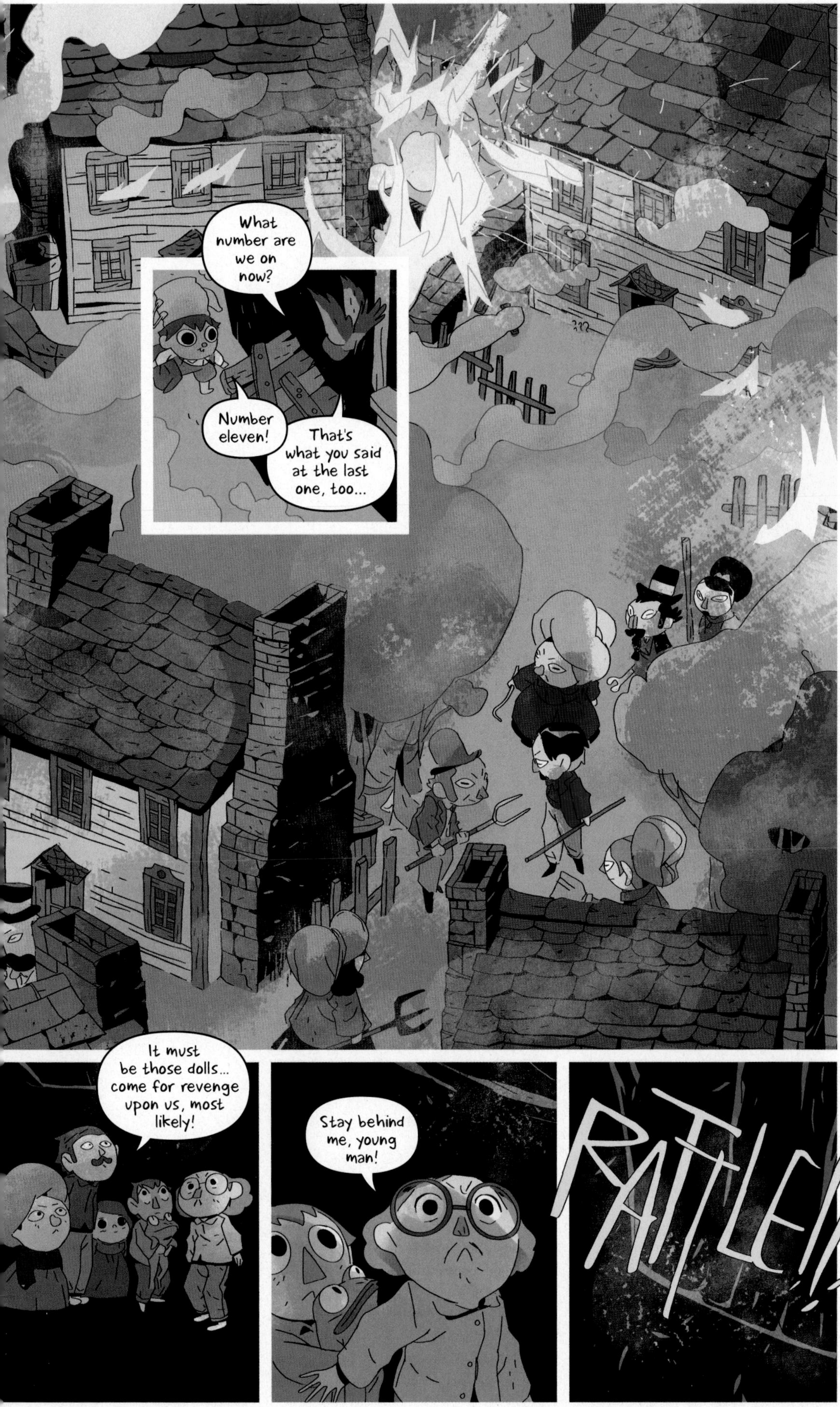

What number are we on now?
Number eleven!
That's what you said at the last one, too...
???
It must be those dolls... come for revenge upon us, most likely!
Stay behind me, young man!
RATTLE!!!

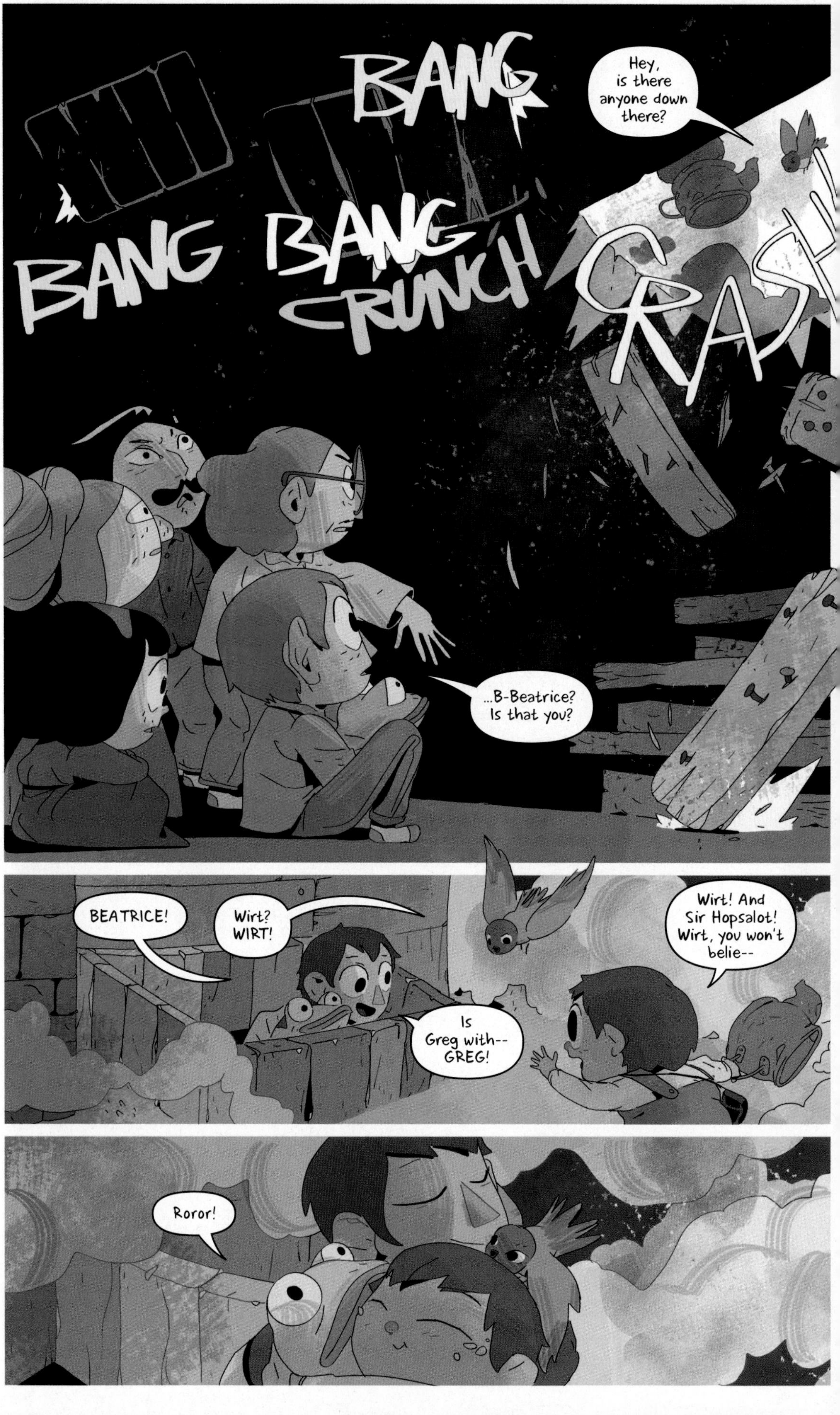
BANG
Hey, is there anyone down there?
BANG BANG
CRUNCH
CRASH
...B-Beatrice? Is that you?
BEATRICE!
Wirt? WIRT!
Is Greg with-- GREG!
Wirt! And Sir Hopsalot! Wirt, you won't belie--
Roror!

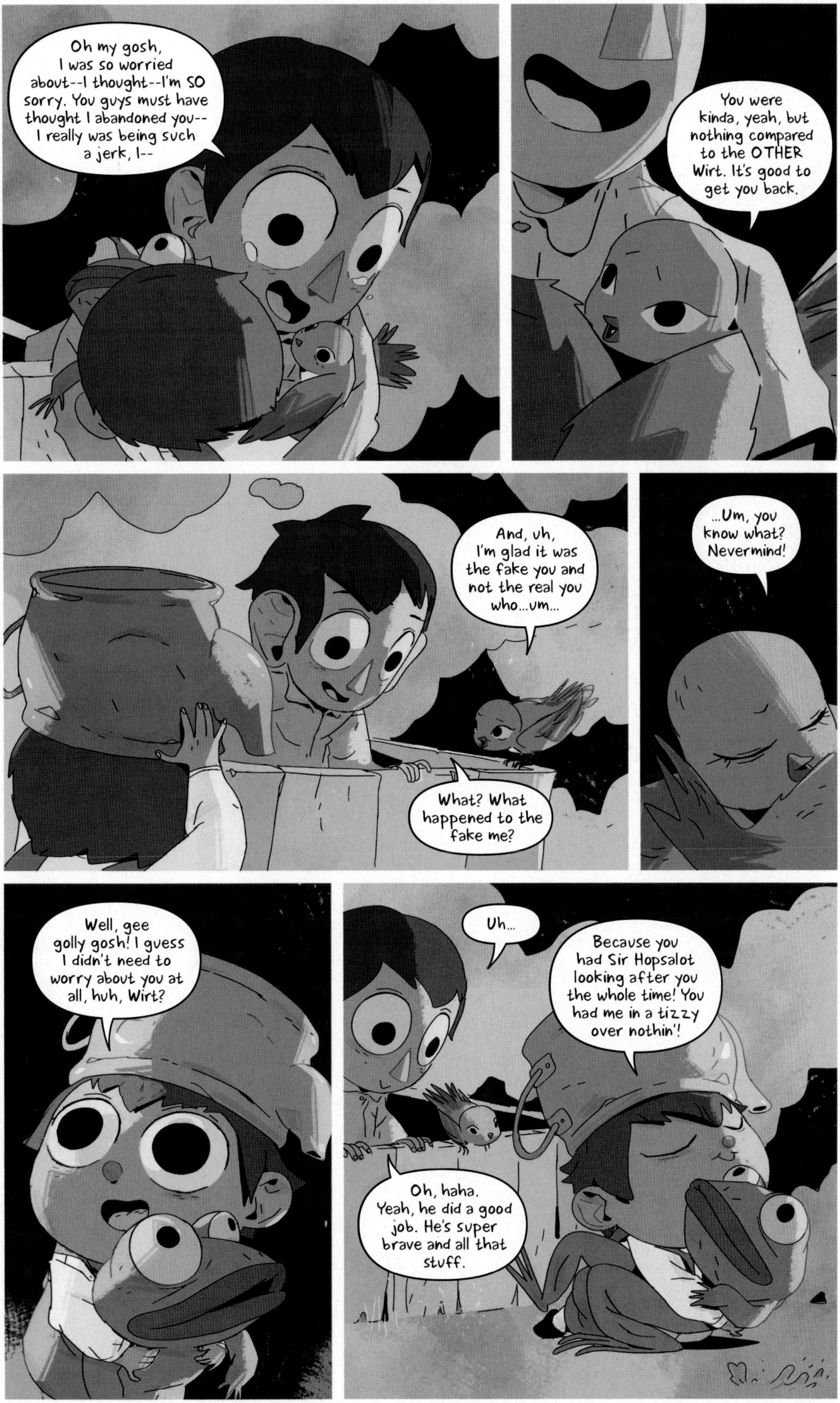
Oh my gosh, I was so worried about--I thought--I'm SO sorry. You guys must have thought I abandoned you--I really was being such a jerk, I--
You were kinda, yeah, but nothing compared to the OTHER Wirt. It's good to get you back.
And, uh, I'm glad it was the fake you and not the real you who...um...
What? What happened to the fake me?
...Um, you know what? Nevermind!
Well, gee golly gosh! I guess I didn't need to worry about you at all, huh, Wirt?
Uh...
Because you had Sir Hopsalot looking after you the whole time! You had me in a tizzy over nothin'!
Oh, haha. Yeah, he did a good job. He's super brave and all that stuff.

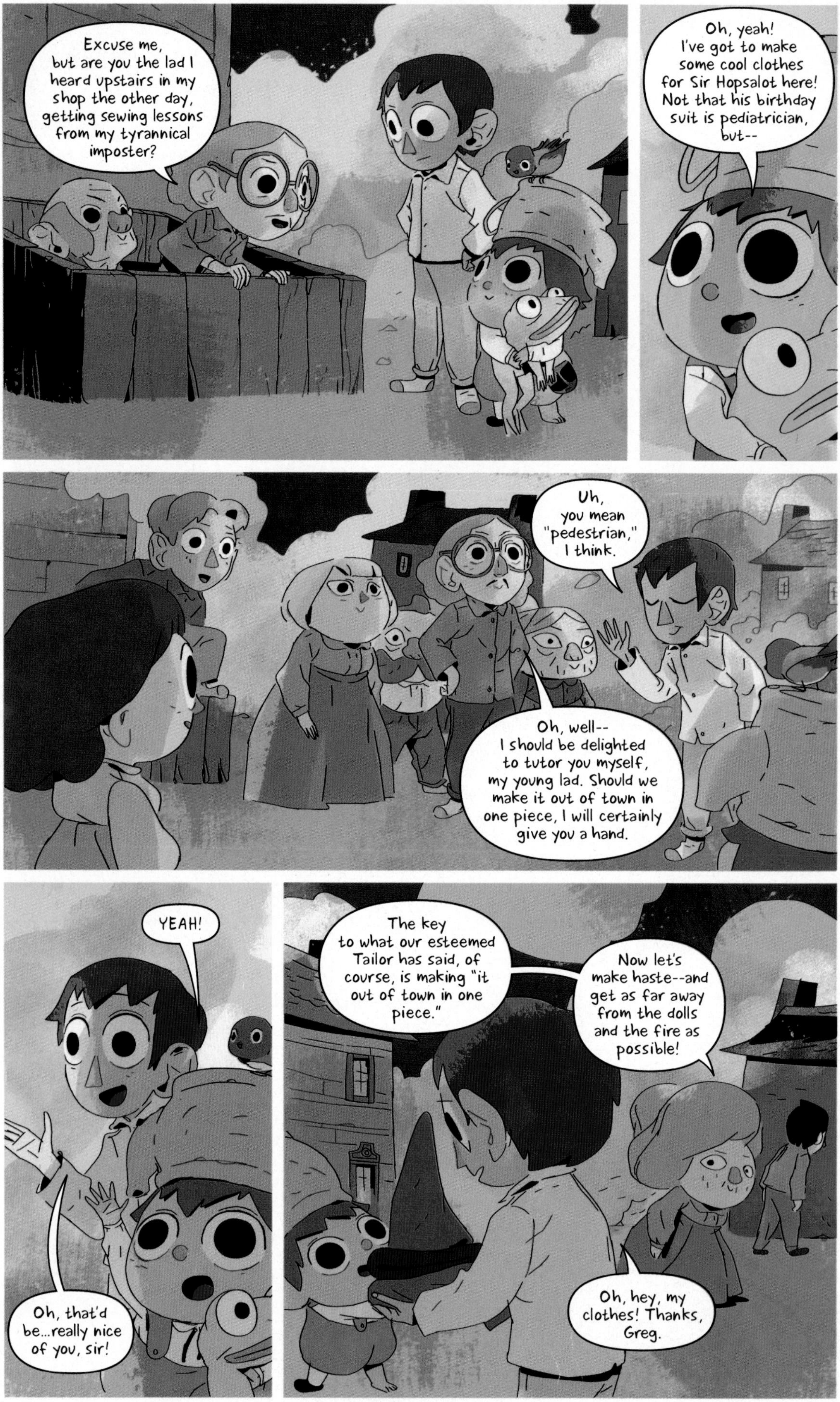

Excuse me, but are you the lad I heard upstairs in my shop the other day, getting sewing lessons from my tyrannical imposter?
Oh, yeah! I've got to make some cool clothes for Sir Hopsalot here! Not that his birthday suit is pediatrician, but--
Uh, you mean "pedestrian," I think.
Oh, well-- I should be delighted to tutor you myself, my young lad. Should we make it out of town in one piece, I will certainly give you a hand.
YEAH!
Oh, that'd be...really nice of you, sir!
The key to what our esteemed Tailor has said, of course, is making "it out of town in one piece."
Now let's make haste--and get as far away from the dolls and the fire as possible!
Oh, hey, my clothes! Thanks, Greg.

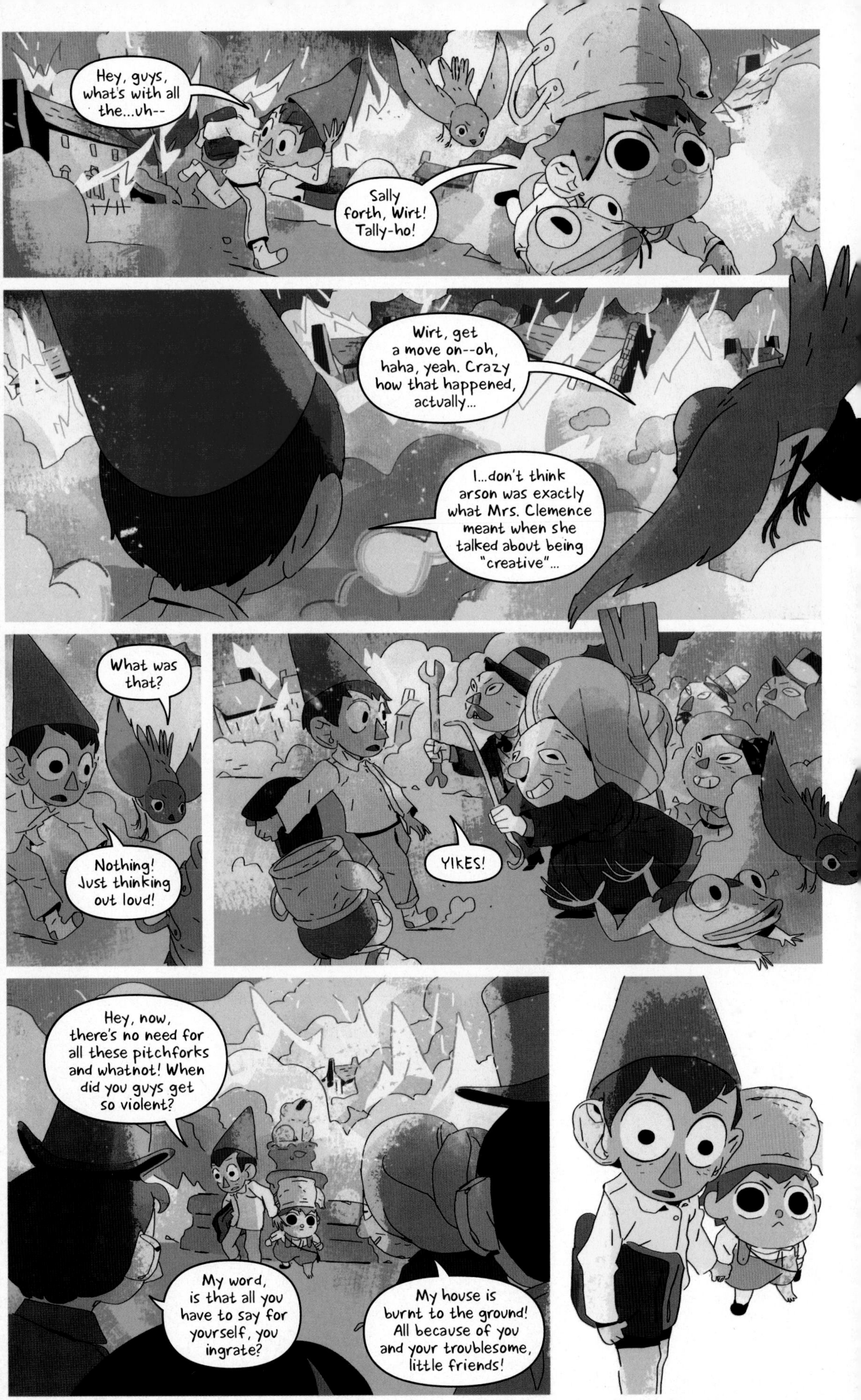
Hey, guys, what's with all the...uh--
Sally forth, Wirt! Tally-ho!
Wirt, get a move on--oh, haha, yeah. Crazy how that happened, actually...
I...don't think arson was exactly what Mrs. Clemence meant when she talked about being "creative"...
What was that?
Nothing! Just thinking out loud!
YIKES!
Hey, now, there's no need for all these pitchforks and whatnot! When did you guys get so violent?
My word, is that all you have to say for yourself, you ingrate?
My house is burnt to the ground! All because of you and your troublesome, little friends!

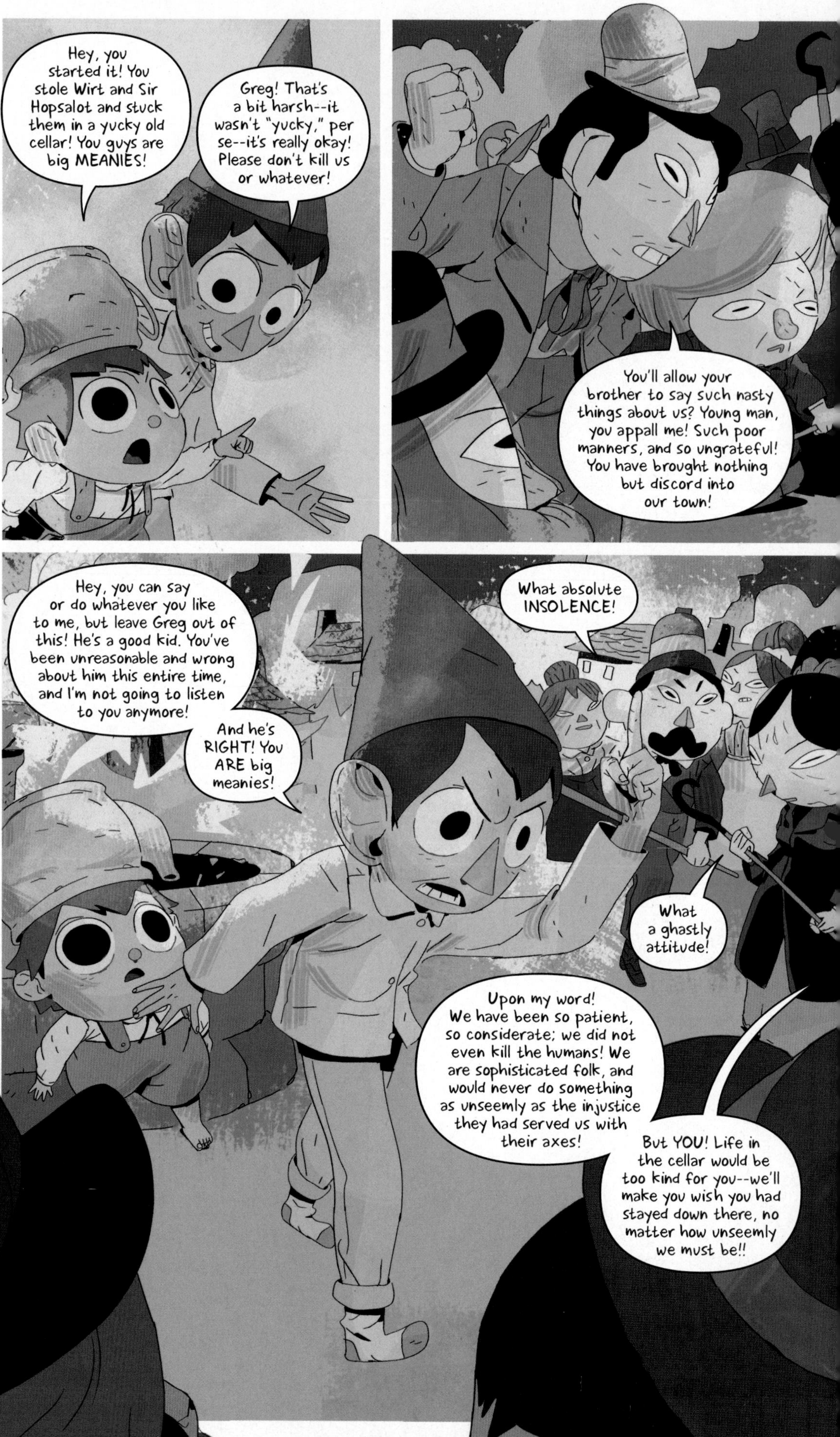
Hey, you started it! You stole Wirt and Sir Hopsalot and stuck them in a yucky old cellar! You guys are big MEANIES!
Greg! That's a bit harsh--it wasn't "yucky," per se--it's really okay! Please don't kill us or whatever!
You'll allow your brother to say such nasty things about us? Young man, you appall me! Such poor manners, and so ungrateful! You have brought nothing but discord into our town!
Hey, you can say or do whatever you like to me, but leave Greg out of this! He's a good kid. You've been unreasonable and wrong about him this entire time, and I'm not going to listen to you anymore!
And he's RIGHT! You ARE big meanies!
What absolute INSOLENCE!
What a ghastly attitude!
Upon my word! We have been so patient, so considerate; we did not even kill the humans! We are sophisticated folk, and would never do something as unseemly as the injustice they had served us with their axes!
But YOU! Life in the cellar would be too kind for you--we'll make you wish you had stayed down there, no matter how unseemly we must be!!

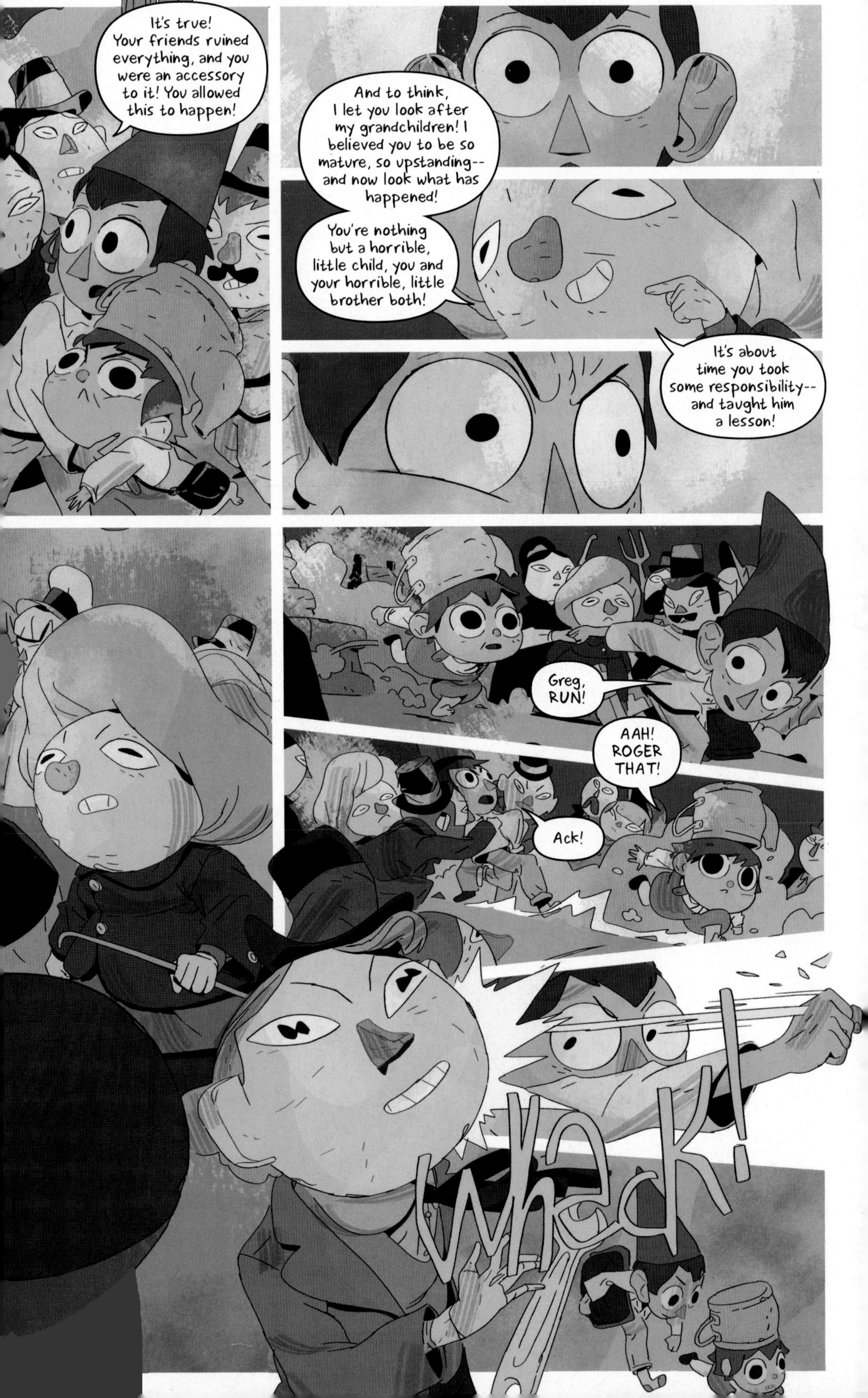
It's true! Your friends ruined everything, and you were an accessory to it! You allowed this to happen!
And to think, I let you look after my grandchildren! I believed you to be so mature, so upstanding-- and now look what has happened!
You're nothing but a horrible, little child, you and your horrible, little brother both!
It's about time you took some responsibility-- and taught him a lesson!
Greg, RUN!
AAH! ROGER THAT!
Ack!
Whack!

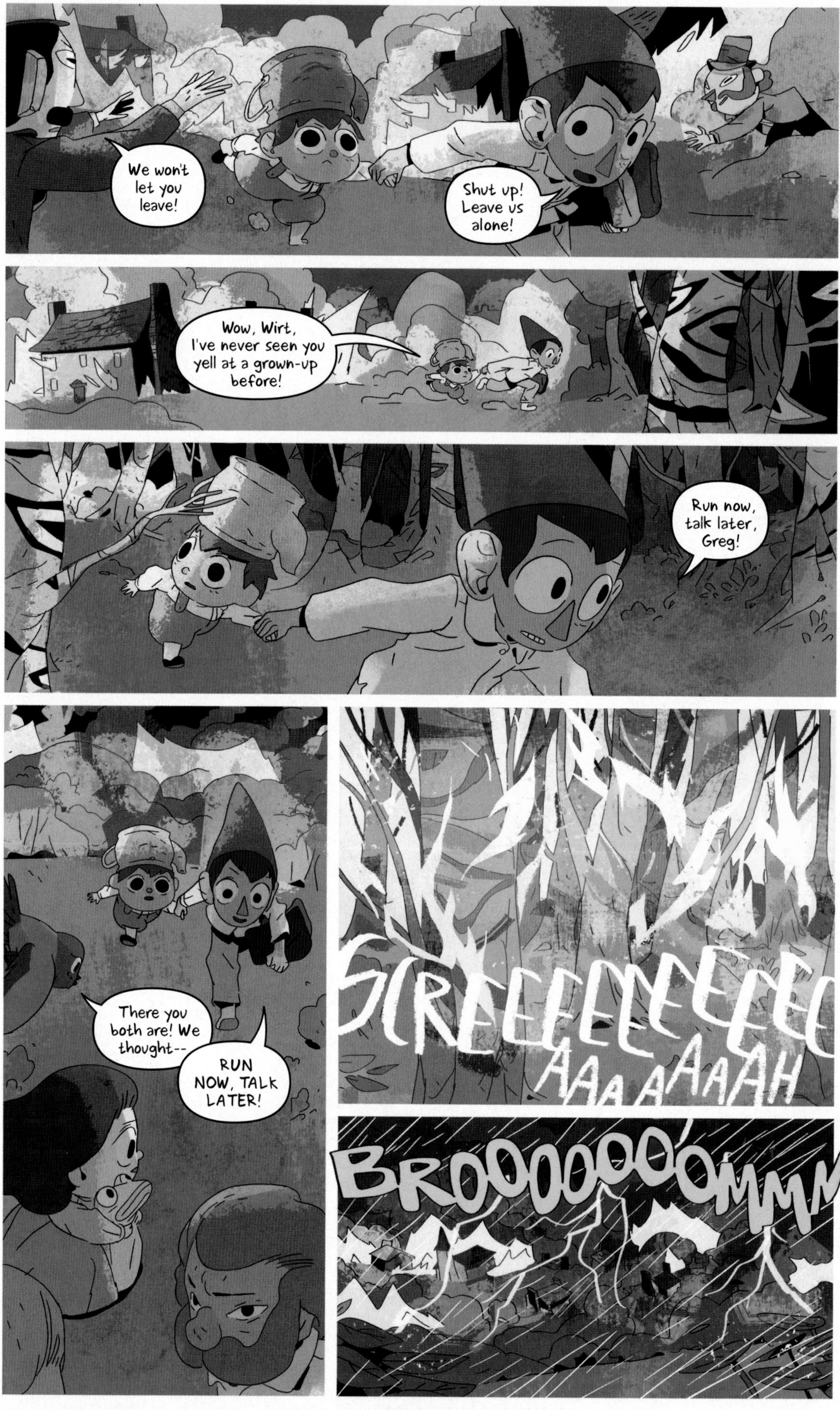
We won't let you leave!
Shut up! Leave us alone!
Wow, Wirt, I've never seen you yell at a grown-up before!
Run now, talk later, Greg!
There you both are! We thought--
RUN NOW, TALK LATER!
SCREEEEEEEEEEE AAAAAAAH
BROOOOOOOMMMM

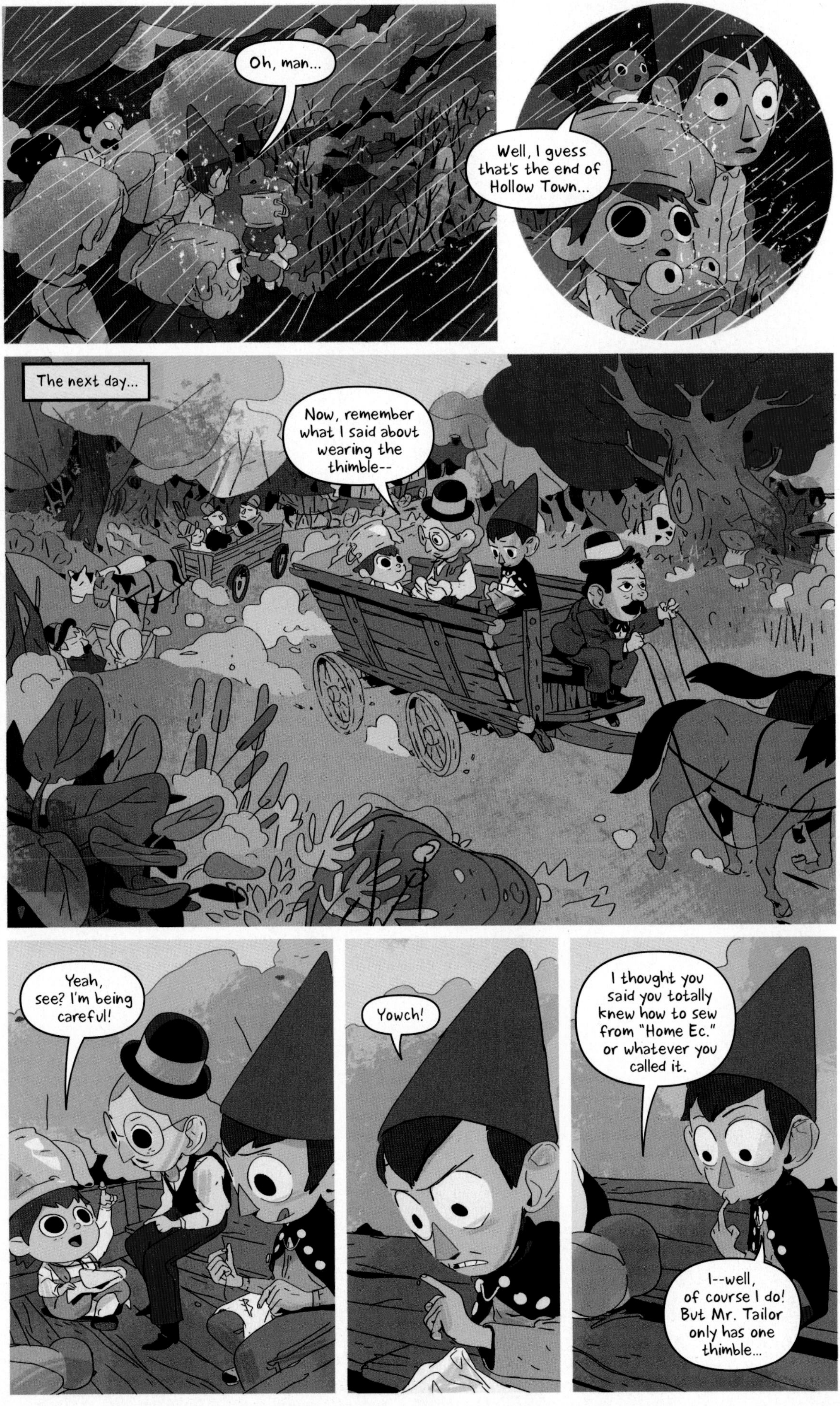
Oh, man...
Well, I guess that's the end of Hollow Town...
The next day...
Now, remember what I said about wearing the thimble--
Yeah, see? I'm being careful!
Yowch!
I thought you said you totally knew how to sew from "Home Ec." or whatever you called it.
I--well, of course I do! But Mr. Tailor only has one thimble...

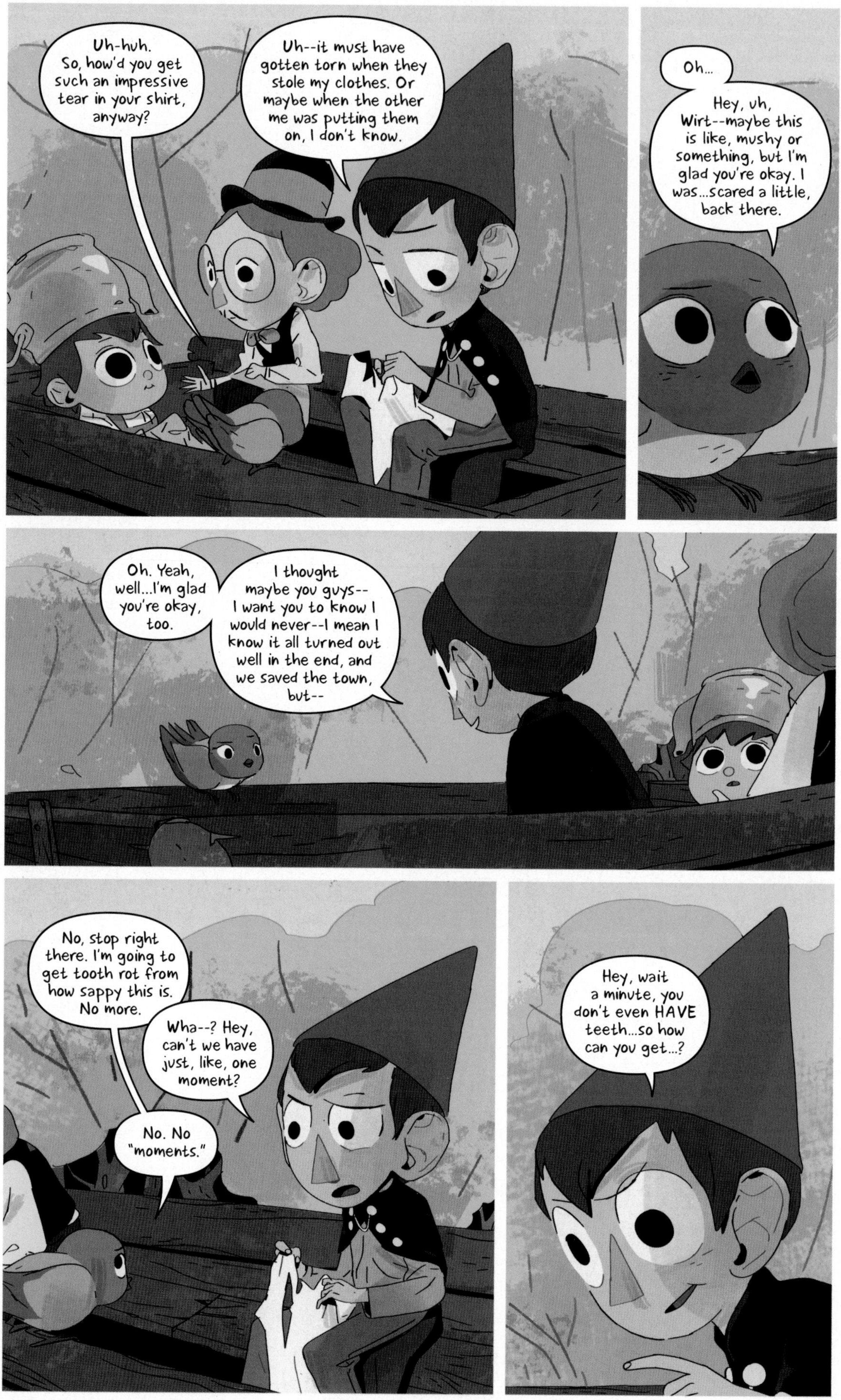
Uh-huh. So, how'd you get such an impressive tear in your shirt, anyway?
Uh--it must have gotten torn when they stole my clothes. Or maybe when the other me was putting them on, I don't know.
Oh...
Hey, uh, Wirt--maybe this is like, mushy or something, but I'm glad you're okay. I was...scared a little, back there.
Oh. Yeah, well...I'm glad you're okay, too.
I thought maybe you guys--I want you to know I would never--I mean I know it all turned out well in the end, and we saved the town, but--
No, stop right there. I'm going to get tooth rot from how sappy this is. No more.
Wha--? Hey, can't we have just, like, one moment?
No. No "moments."
Hey, wait a minute, you don't even HAVE teeth...so how can you get...?

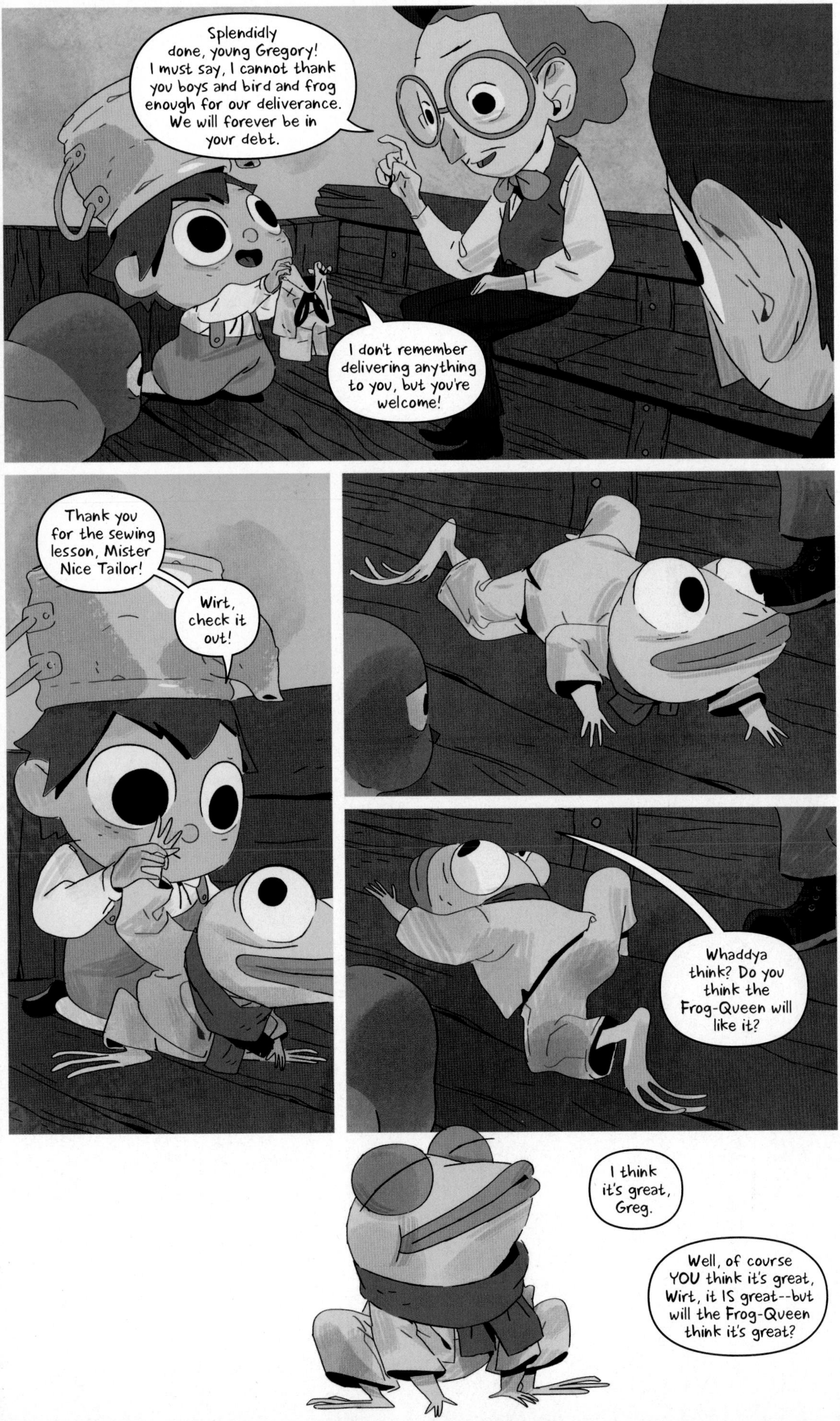

Splendidly done, young Gregory! I must say, I cannot thank you boys and bird and frog enough for our deliverance. We will forever be in your debt.
I don't remember delivering anything to you, but you're welcome!
Thank you for the sewing lesson, Mister Nice Tailor!
Wirt, check it out!
Whaddya think? Do you think the Frog-Queen will like it?
I think it's great, Greg.
Well, of course YOU think it's great, Wirt, it IS great--but will the Frog-Queen think it's great?

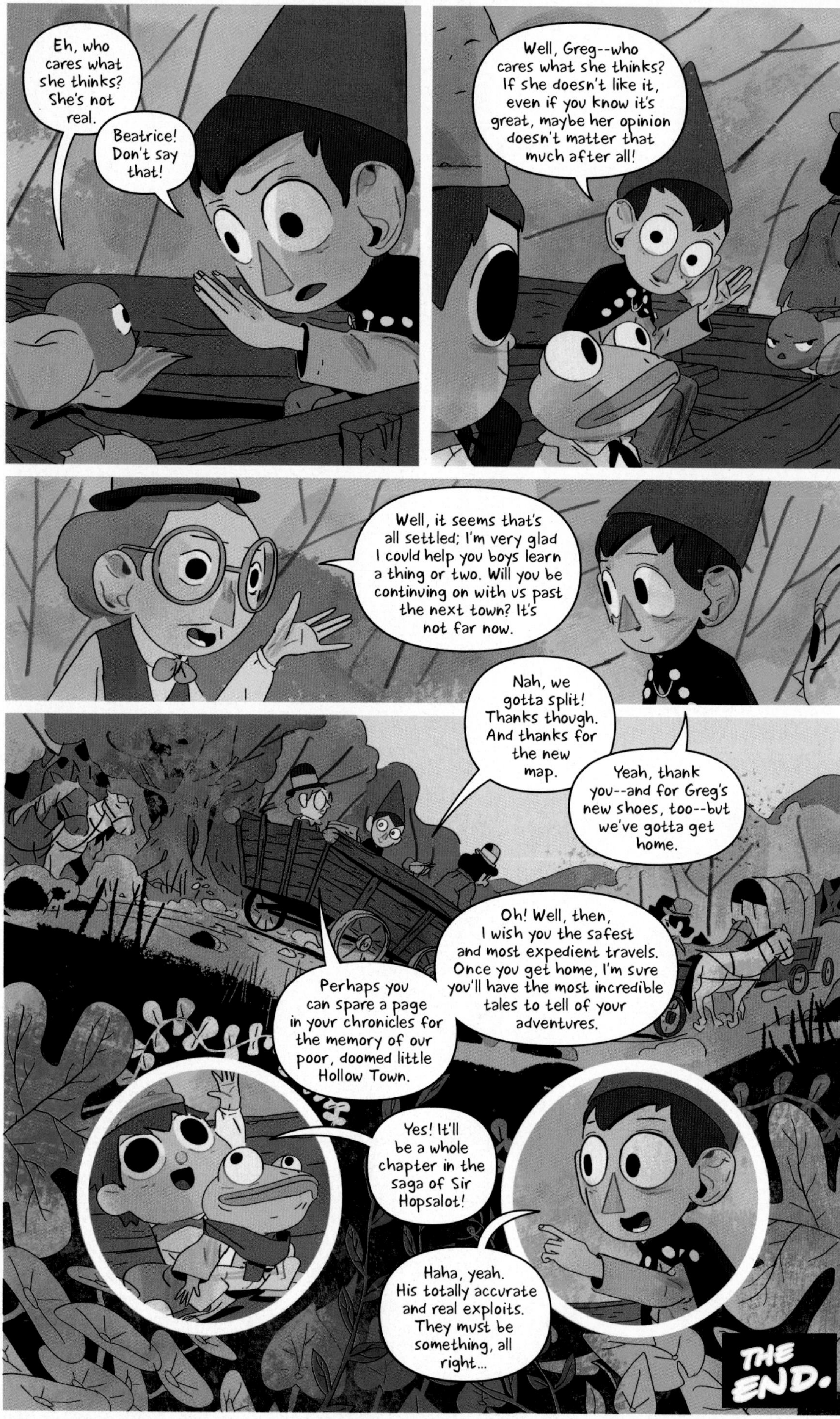
Eh, who cares what she thinks? She's not real.
Beatrice! Don't say that!
Well, Greg--who cares what she thinks? If she doesn't like it, even if you know it's great, maybe her opinion doesn't matter that much after all!
Well, it seems that's all settled; I'm very glad I could help you boys learn a thing or two. Will you be continuing on with us past the next town? It's not far now.
Nah, we gotta split! Thanks though. And thanks for the new map.
Yeah, thank you--and for Greg's new shoes, too--but we've gotta get home.
Oh! Well, then, I wish you the safest and most expedient travels. Once you get home, I'm sure you'll have the most incredible tales to tell of your adventures.
Perhaps you can spare a page in your chronicles for the memory of our poor, doomed little Hollow Town.
Yes! It'll be a whole chapter in the saga of Sir Hopsalot!
Haha, yeah. His totally accurate and real exploits. They must be something, all right...
THE END.

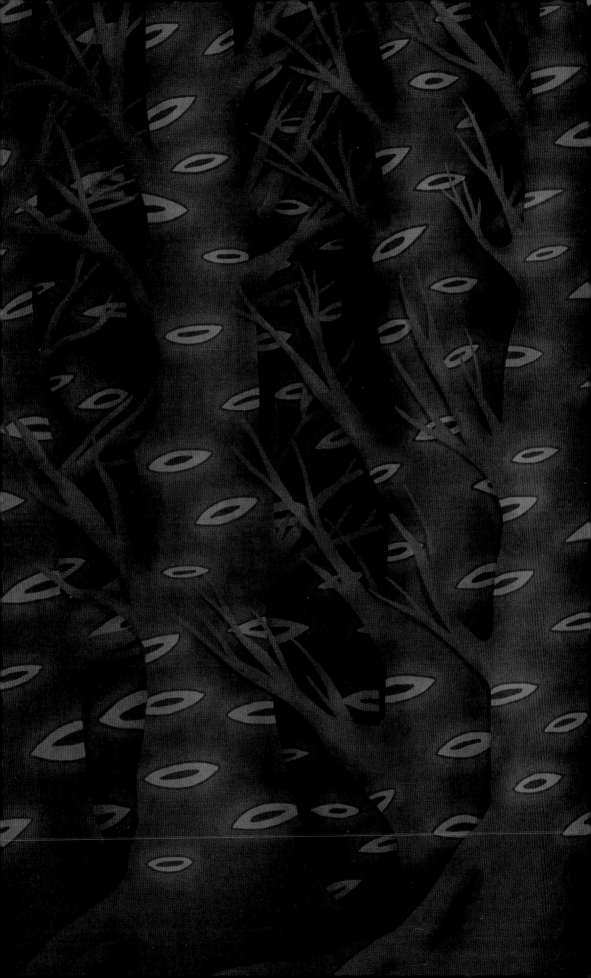

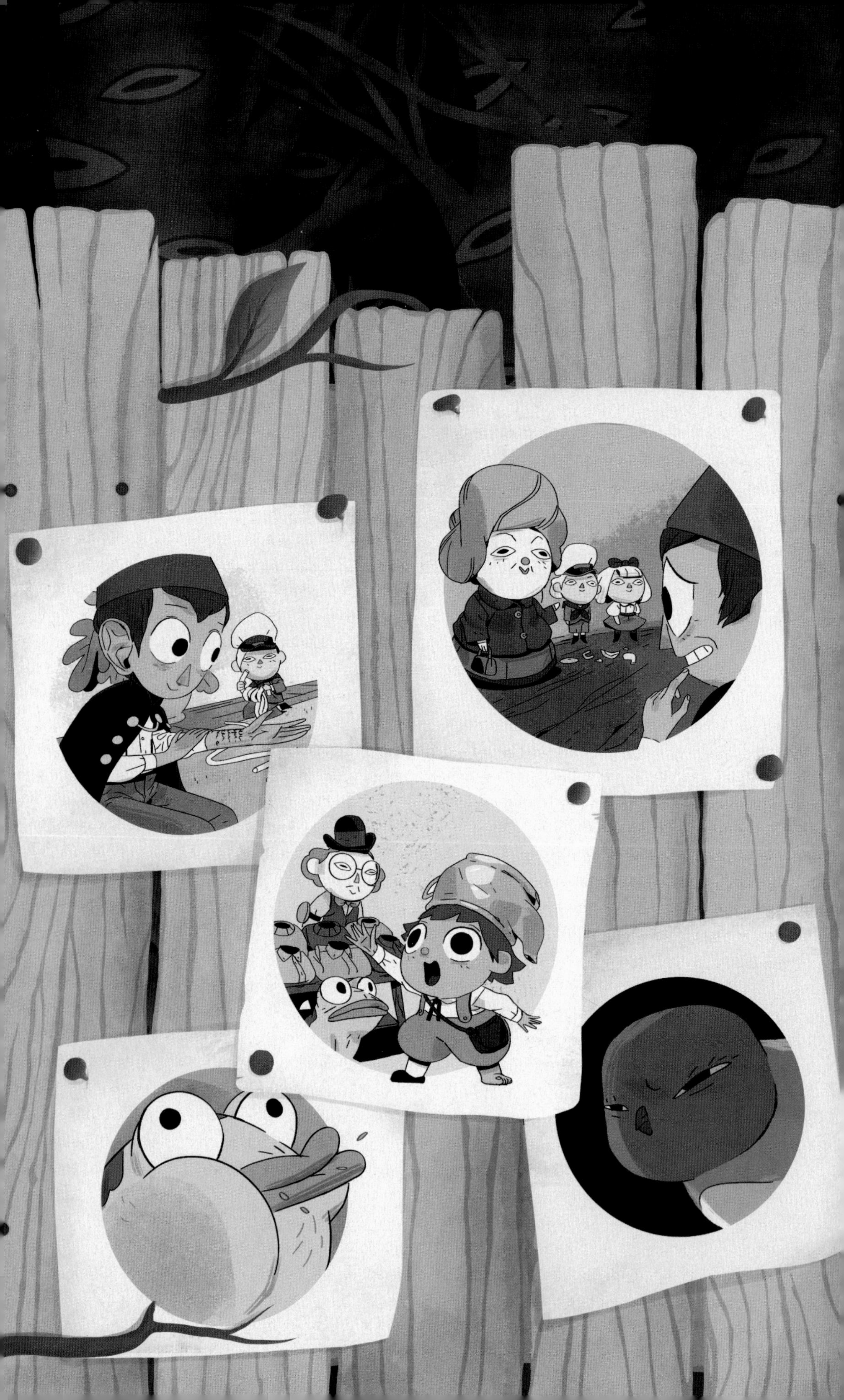

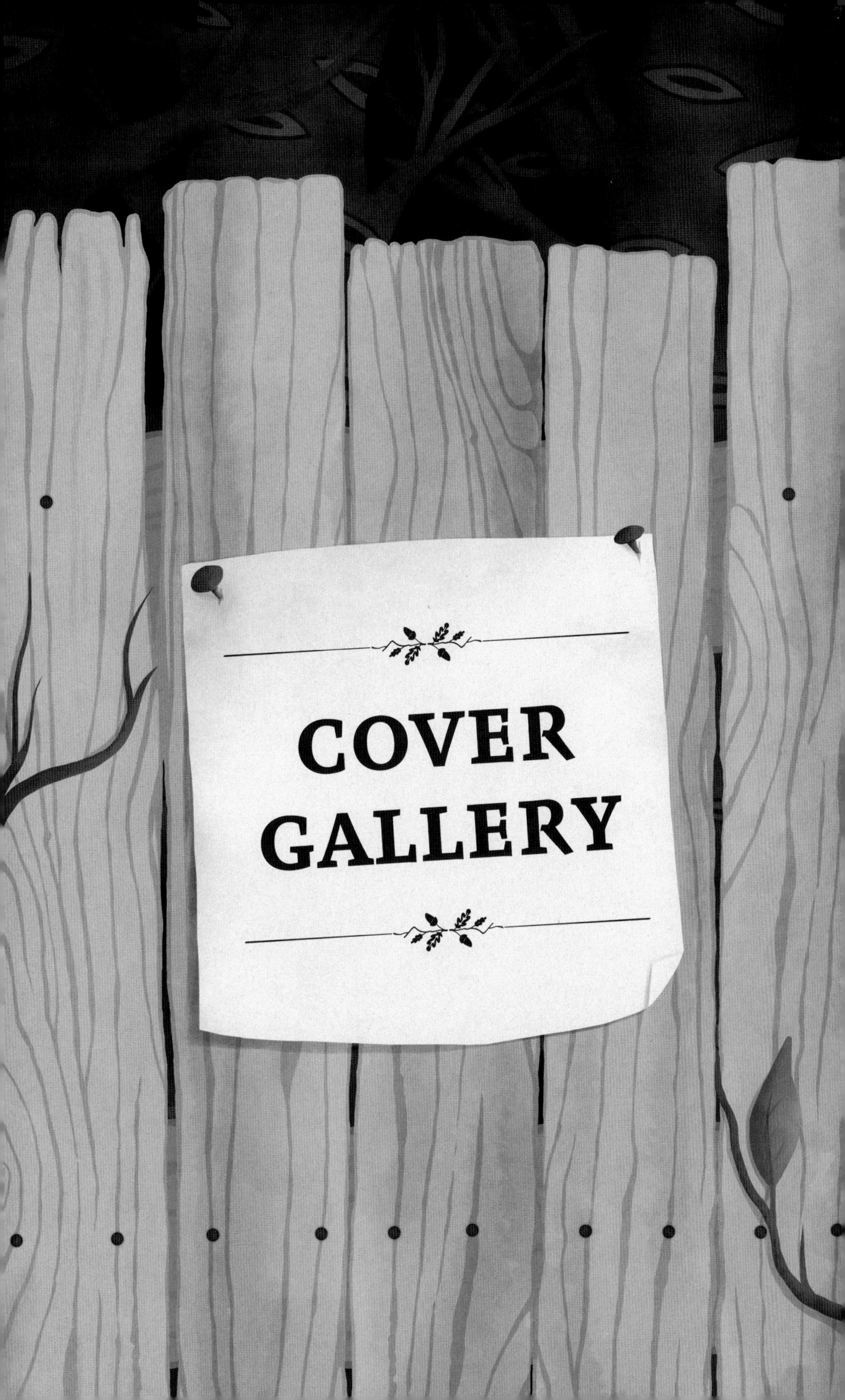
COVER
GALLERY

Issue #1 Main Cover by
Celia Lowenthal

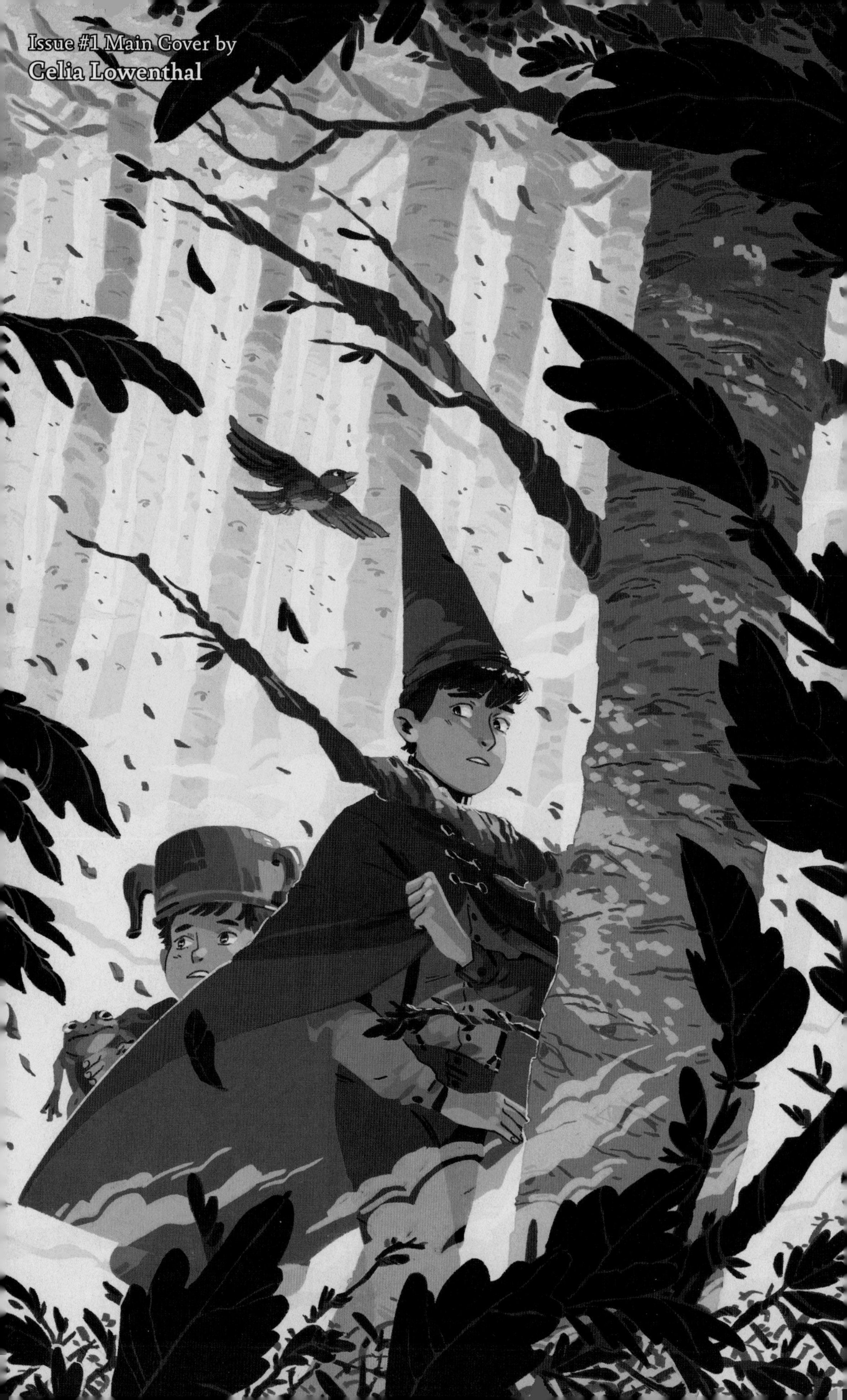

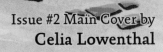
Issue #2 Main Cover by
Celia Lowenthal

Issue #3 Main Cover by
Celia Lowenthal

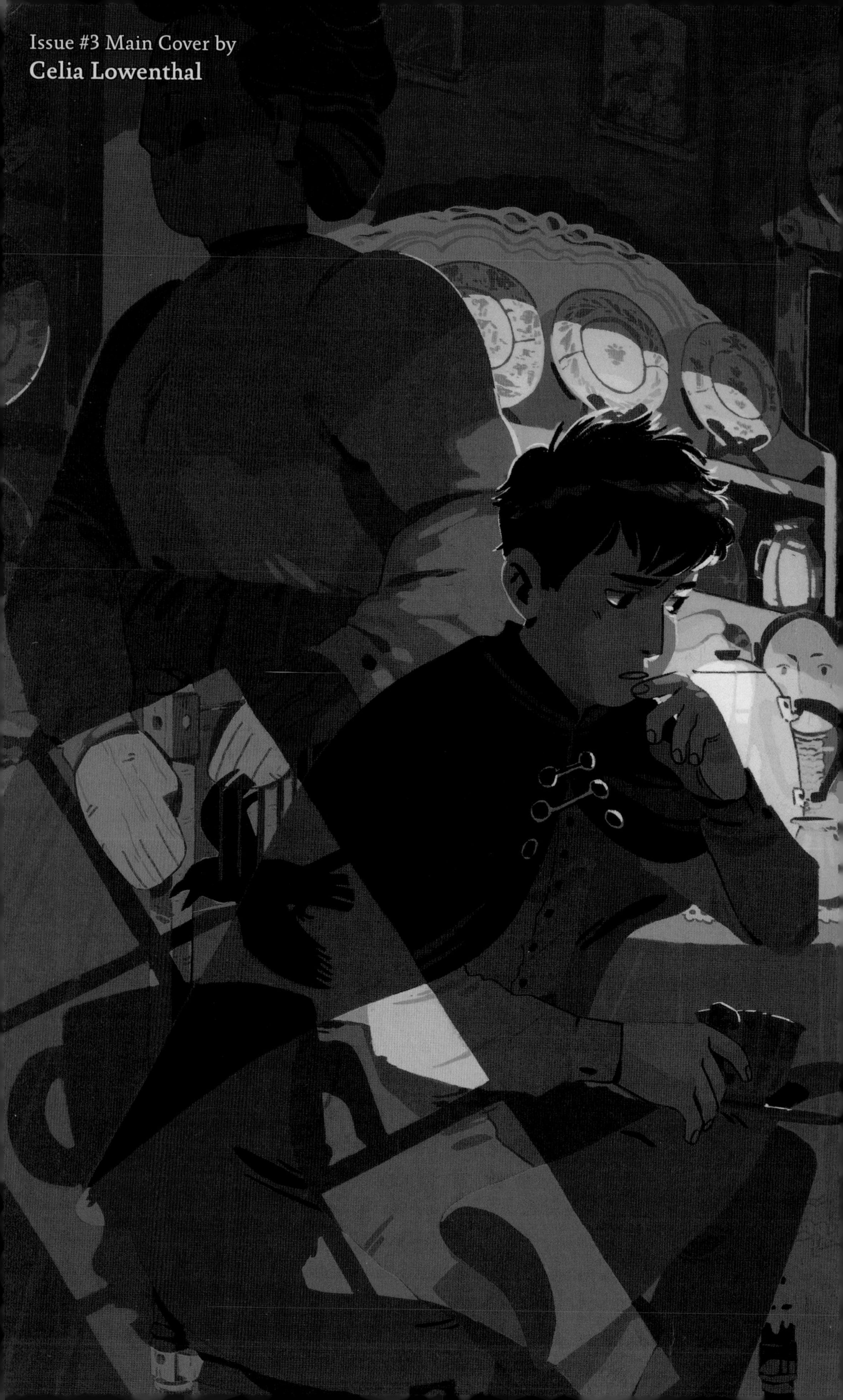

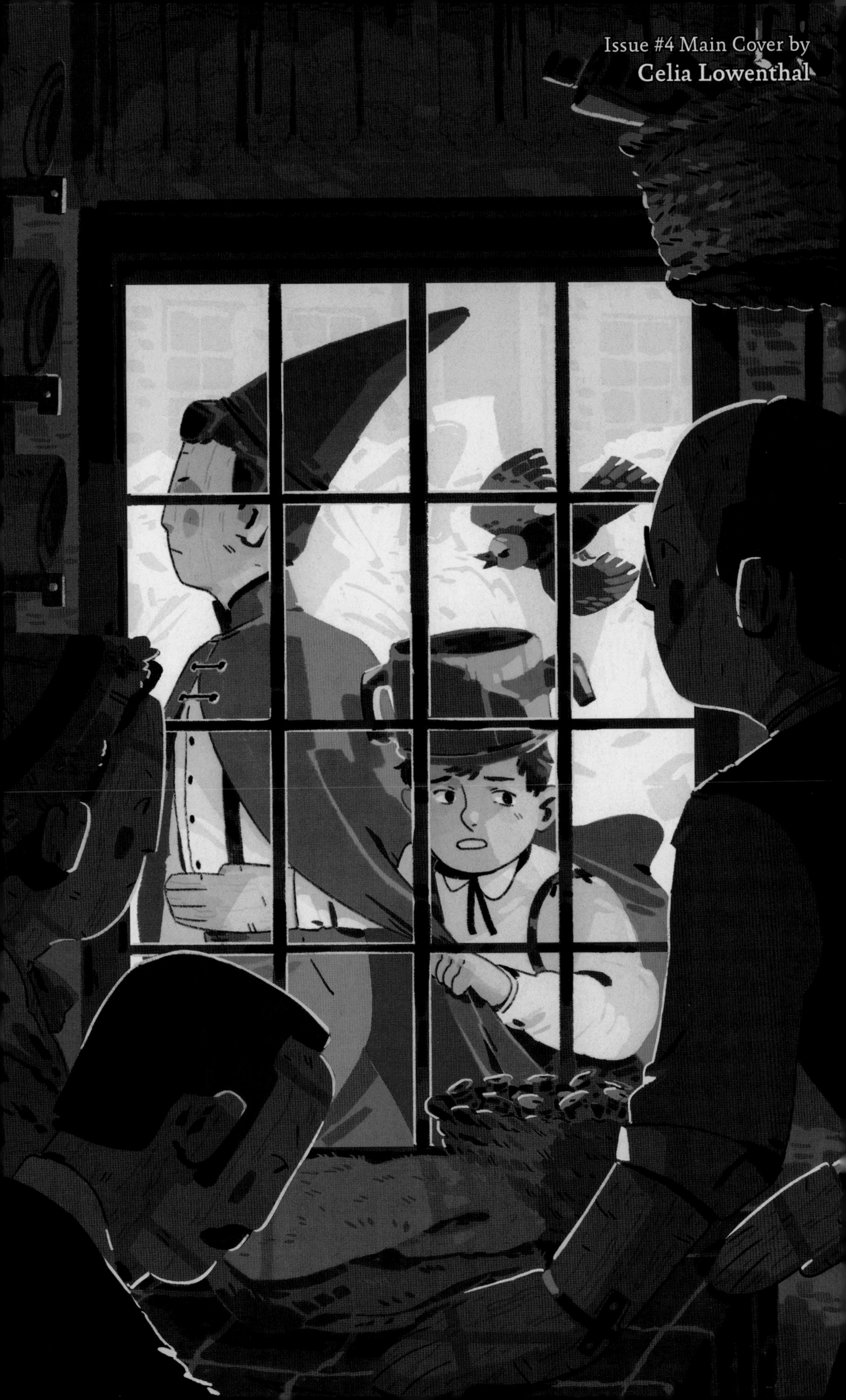

Issue #4 Main Cover by
Celia Lowenthal

Issue #5 Main Cover by
Celia Lowenthal

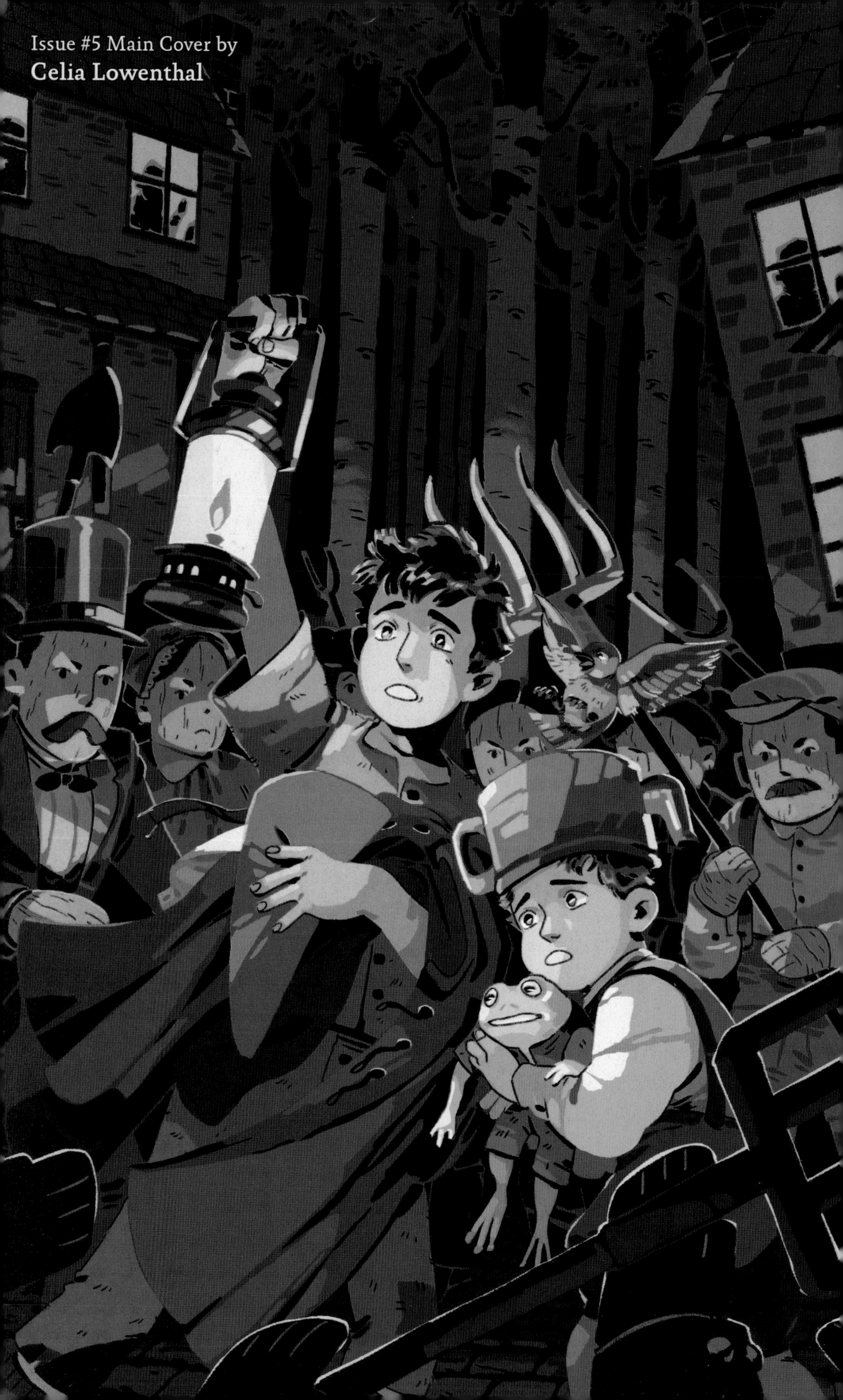

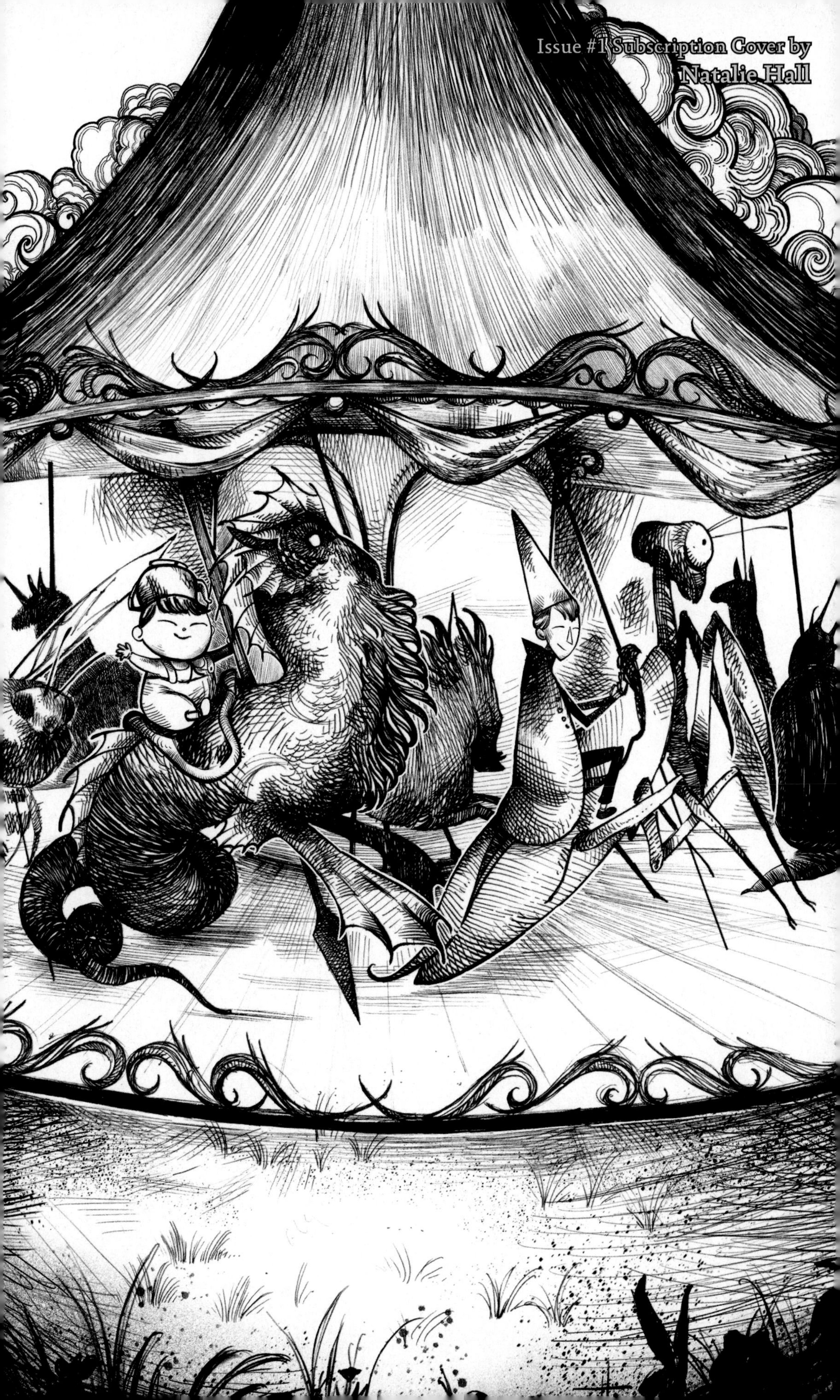

Issue #1 Subscription Cover by Natalie Hall

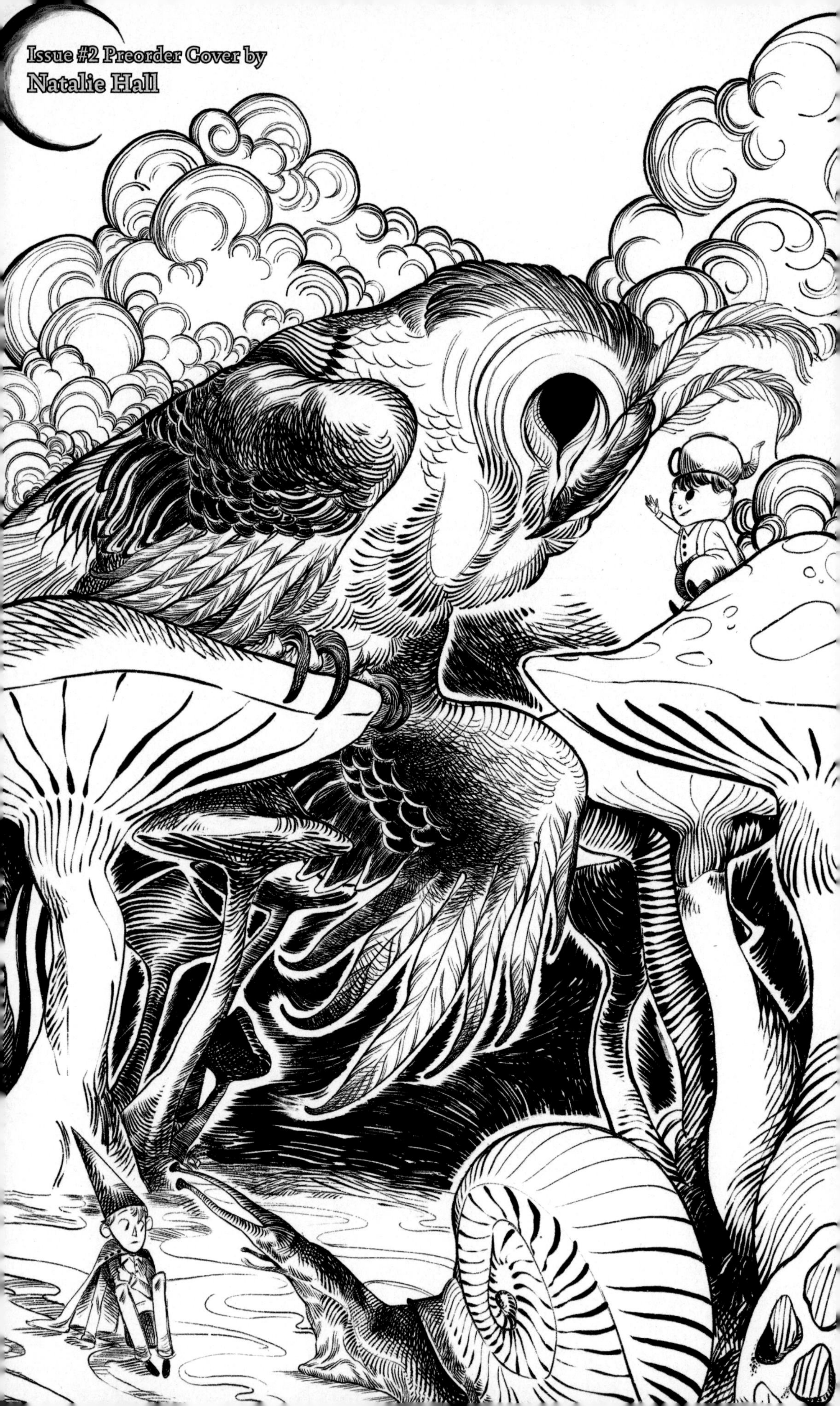

Issue #2 Preorder Cover by
Natalie Hall

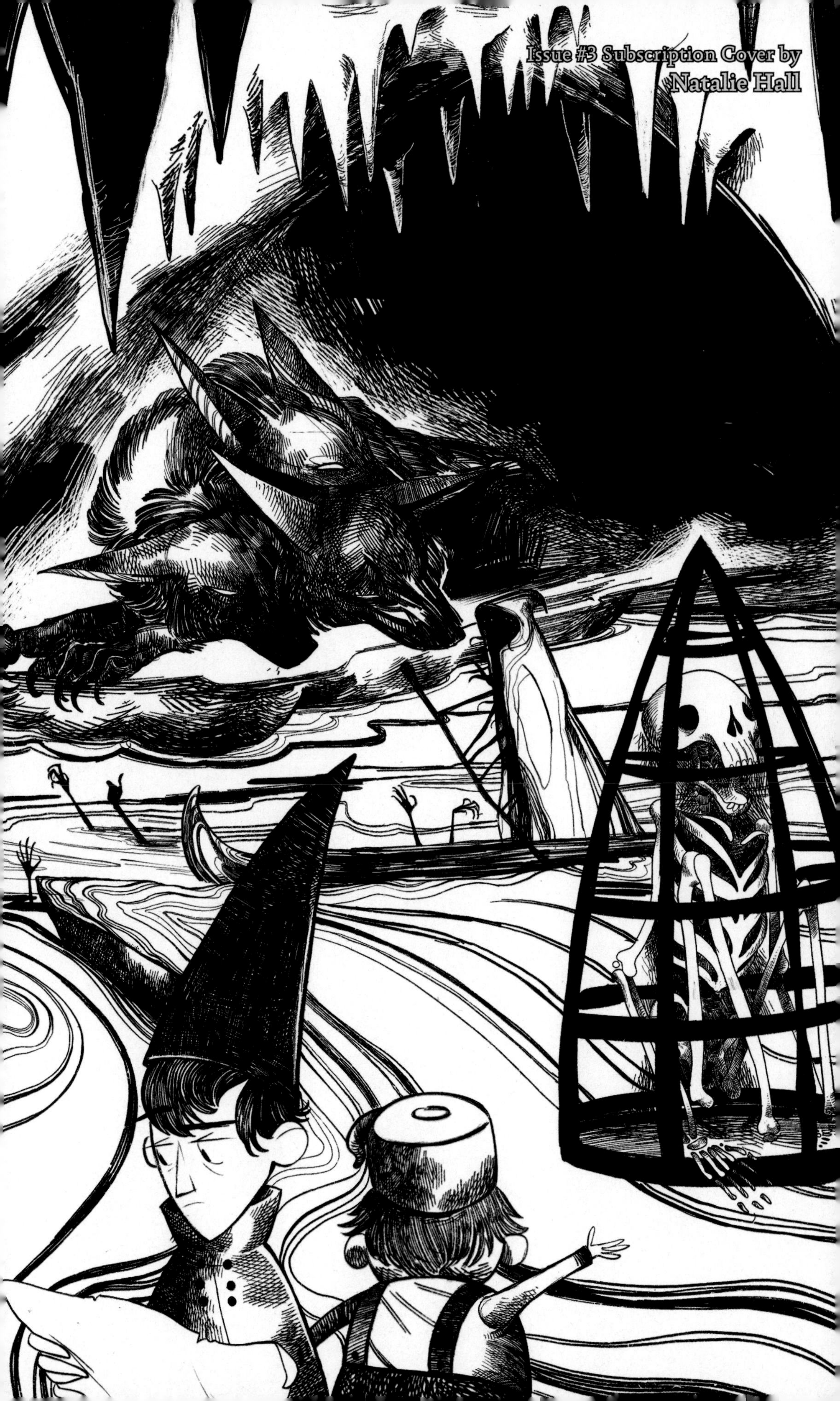

Issue #3 Subscription Cover by
Natalie Hall

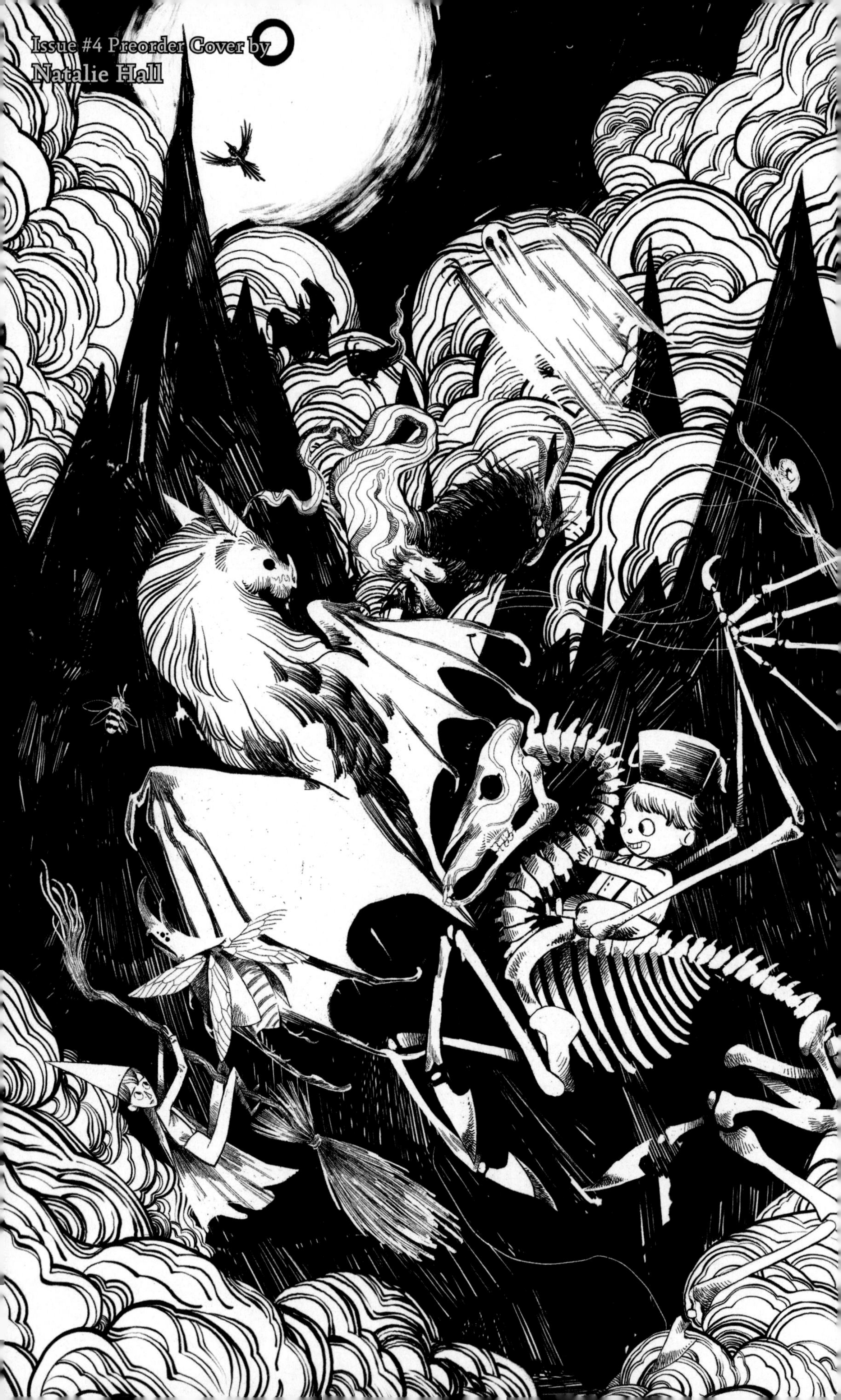

Issue #4 Preorder Cover by
Natalie Hall

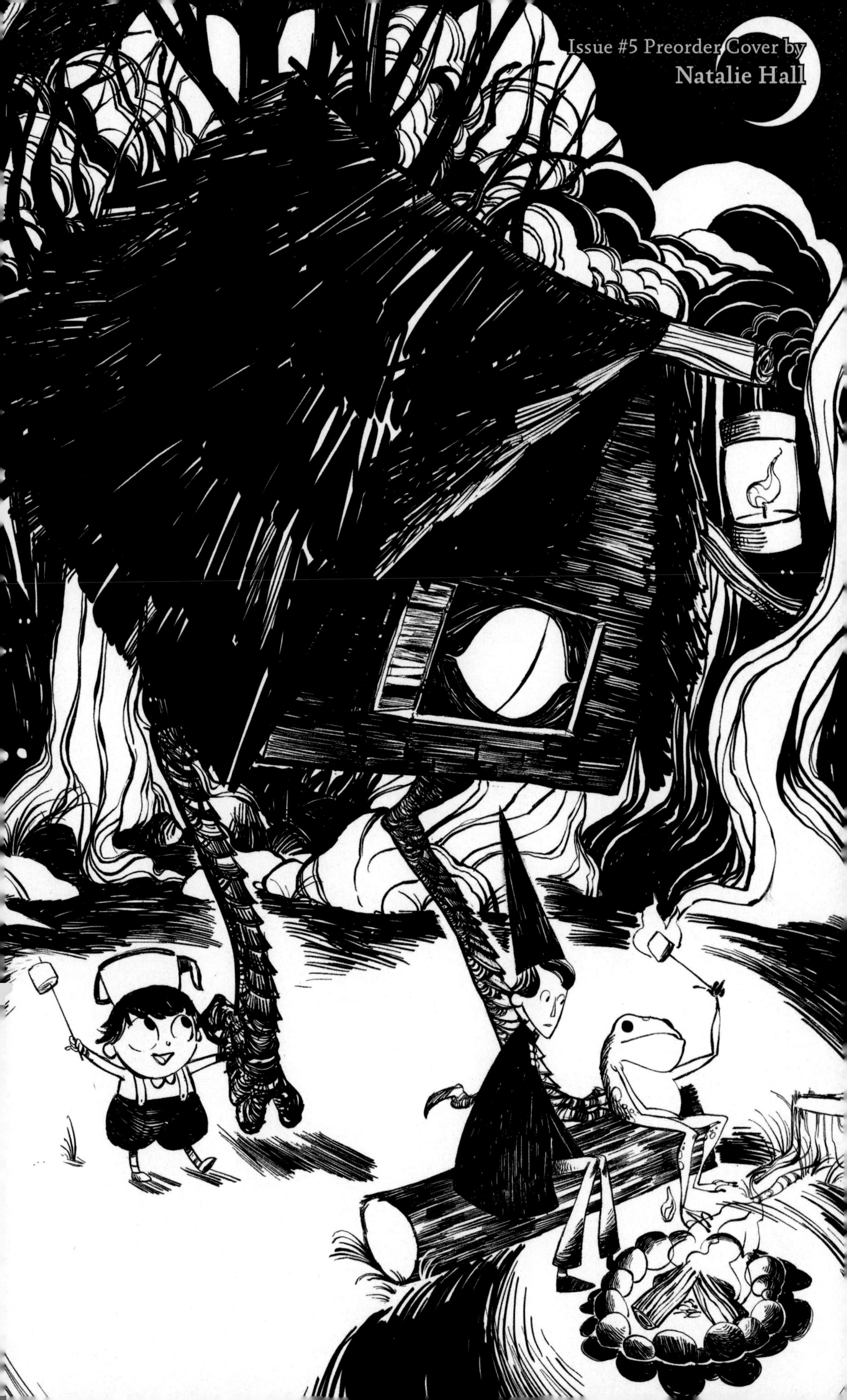
Issue #5 Preorder Cover by
Natalie Hall

Issue #1 Variant Cover by
Miguel Mercado

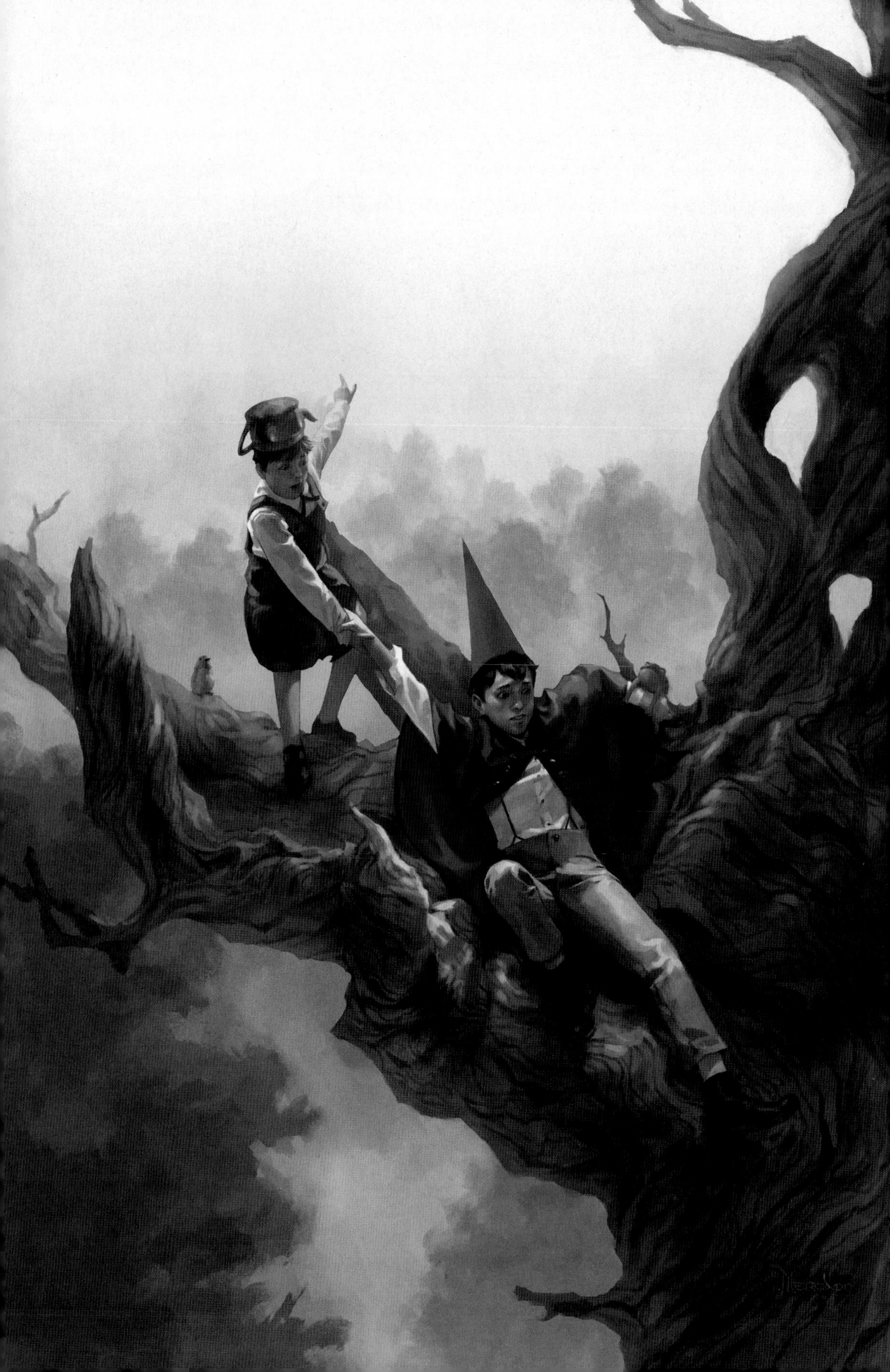

Issue #1 New York Comic Con Exclusive Cover by
Pat McHale

"IF DREAMS CAN'T COME TRUE

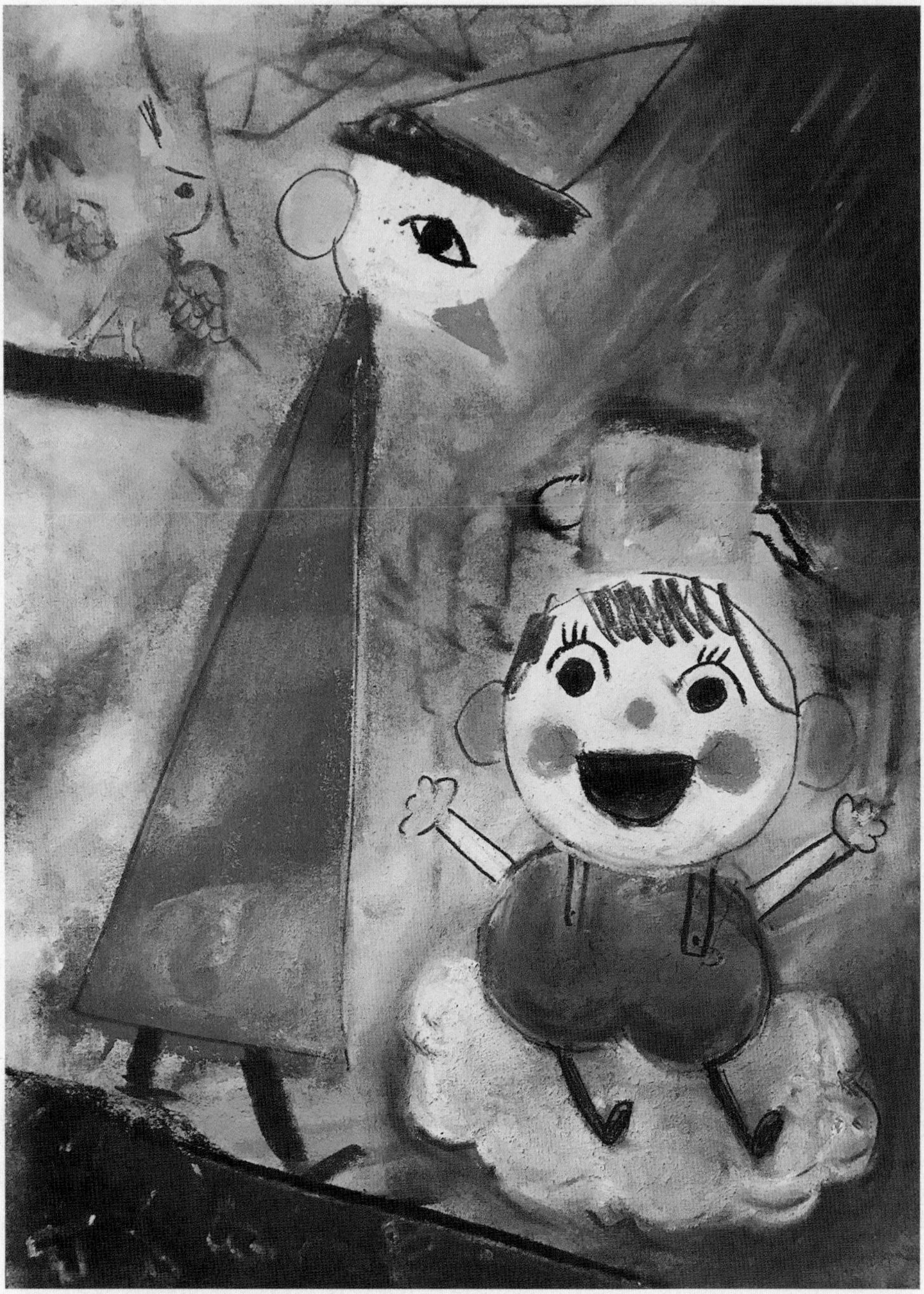

... THEN WHY NOT PRETEND?"

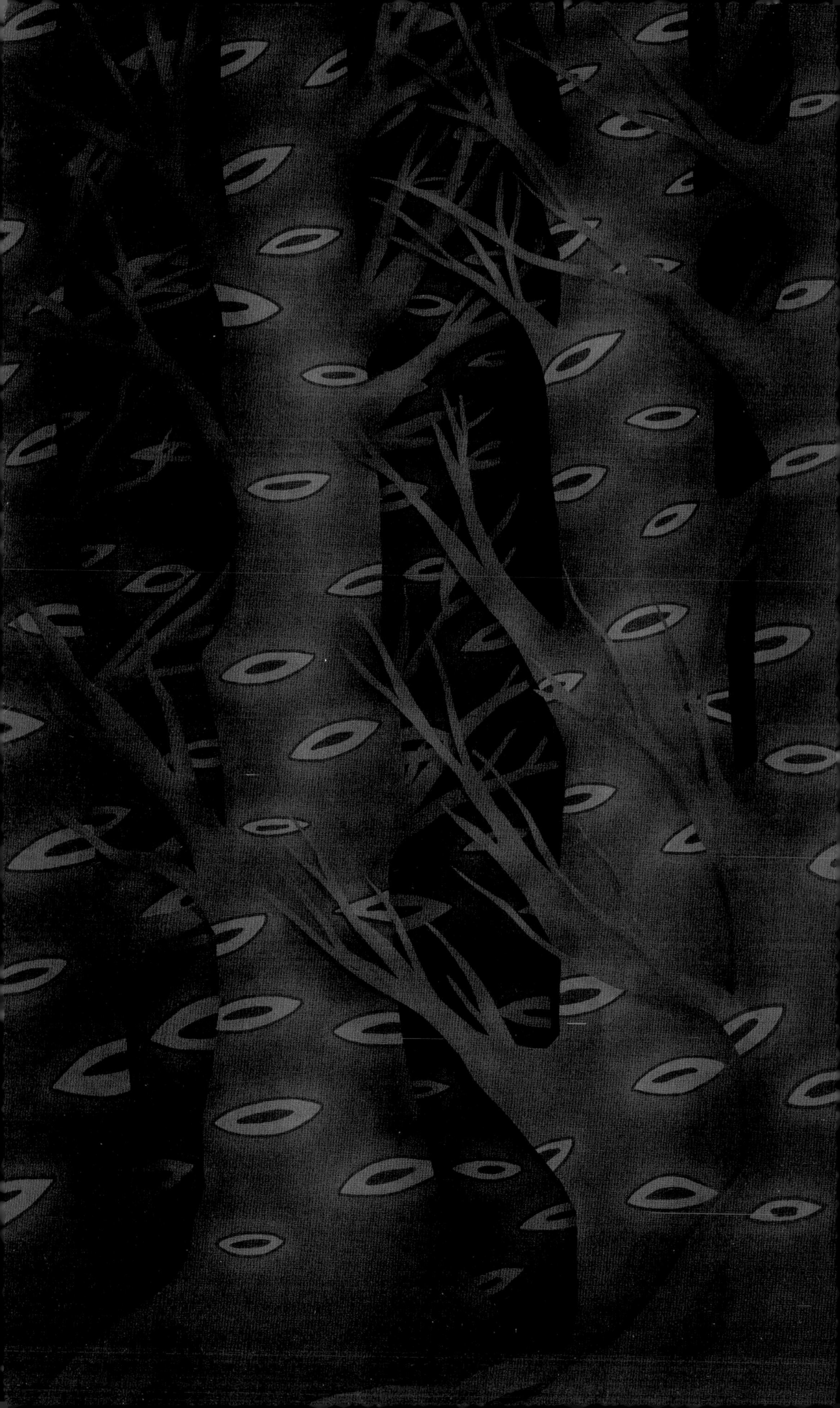

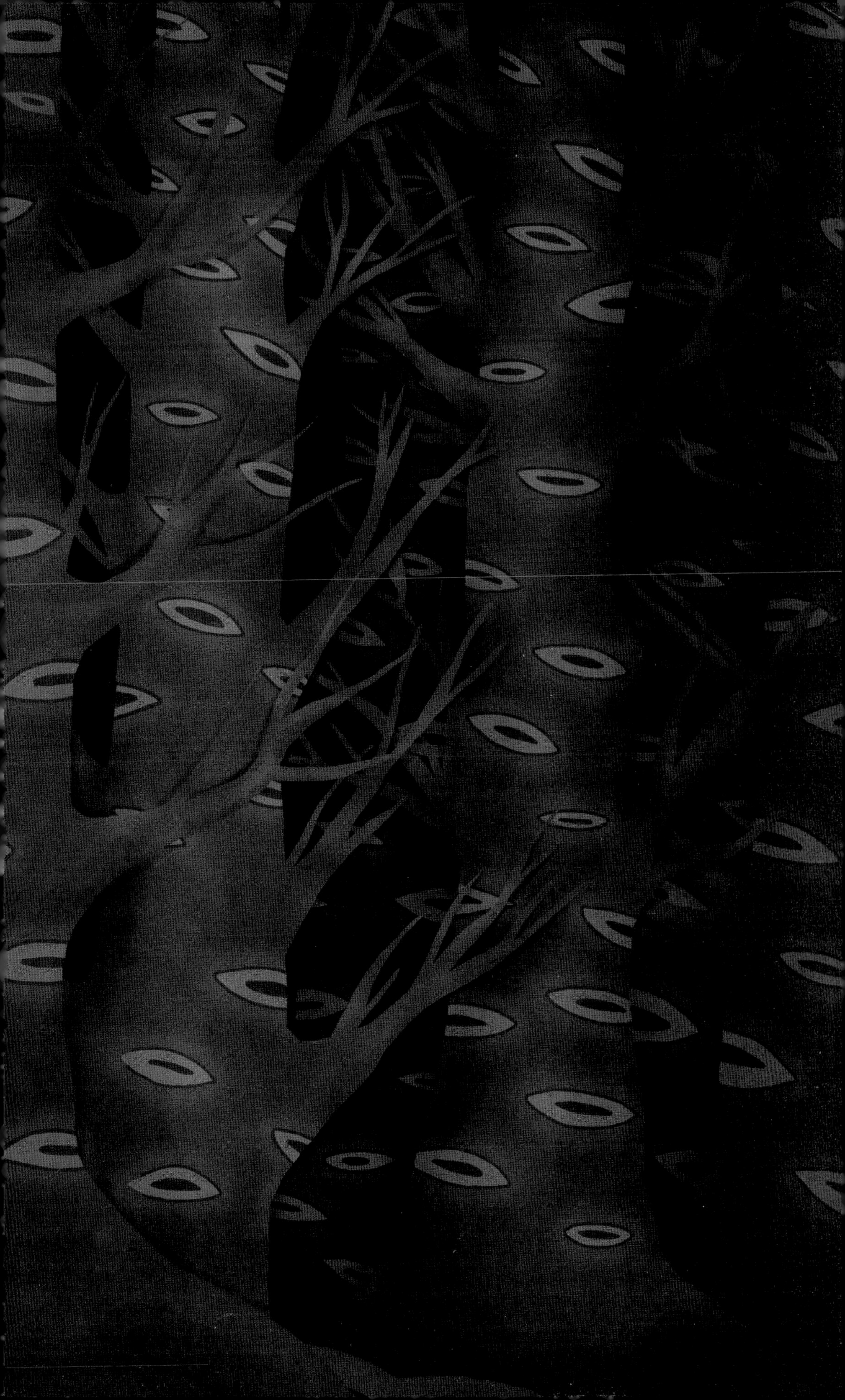

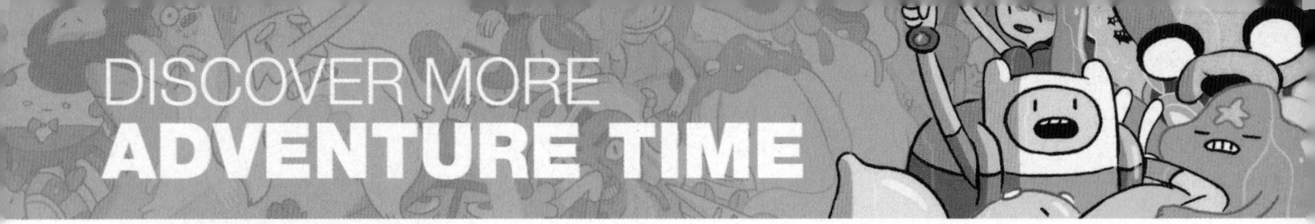
DISCOVER MORE
ADVENTURE TIME

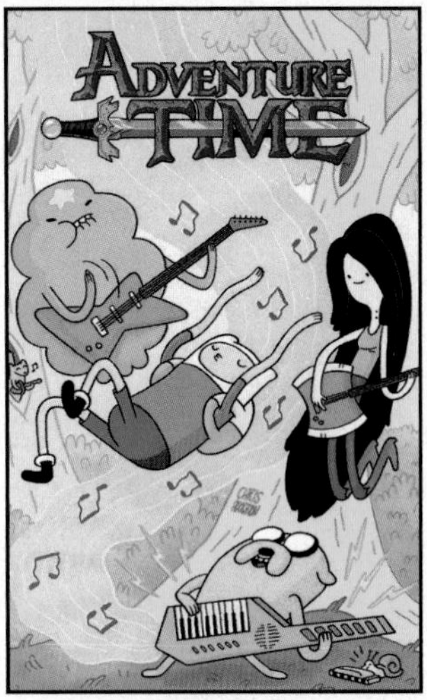
ADVENTURE TIME

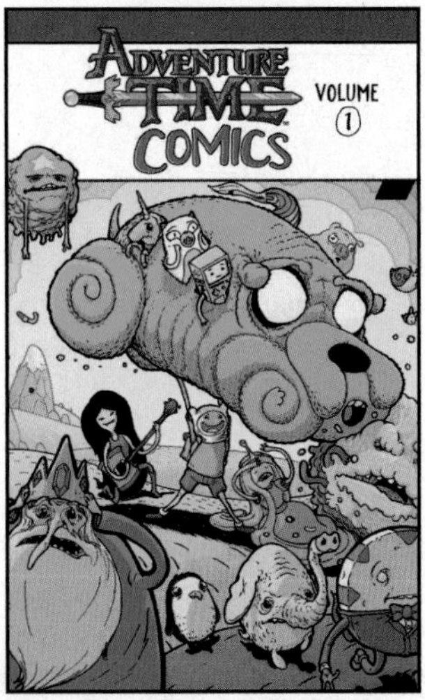
ADVENTURE TIME
COMICS
VOLUME 1

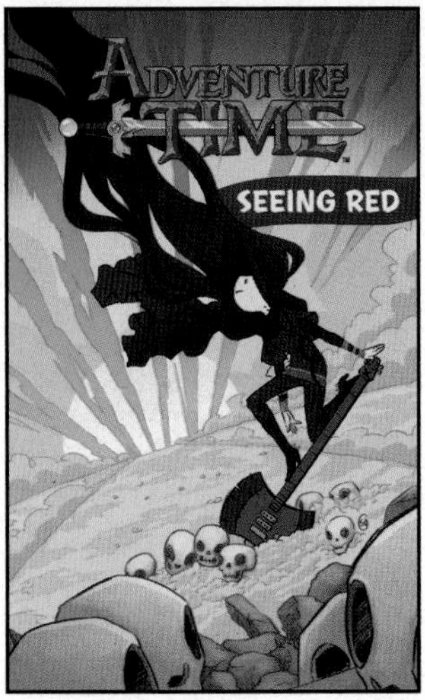
ADVENTURE TIME
SEEING RED

Adventure Time

Volume 1
ISBN: 978-1-60886-280-1 | $14.99 US

Volume 2
ISBN: 978-1-60886-323-5 | $14.99 US

Volume 3
ISBN: 978-1-60886-317-4 | $14.99

Volume 4
ISBN: 978-1-60886-351-8 | $14.99

Volume 5
ISBN: 978-1-60886-401-0 | $14.99

Volume 6
ISBN: 978-1-60886-482-9 | $14.99

Volume 7
ISBN: 978-1-60886-746-2 | $14.99

Volume 8
ISBN: 978-1-60886-795-0 | $14.99

Volume 9
ISBN: 978-1-60886-843-8 | $14.99

Volume 10
ISBN: 978-1-60886-909-1 | $14.99

Volume 11
ISBN: 978-1-60886-946-6 | $14.99

Volume 12
ISBN: 978-1-68415-005-2 | $14.99

Volume 13
ISBN: 978-1-68415-051-9 | $14.99

Volume 14
ISBN: 978-1-68415-144-8 | $14.99

Volume 15
ISBN: 978-1-68415-203-2 | $14.99

Volume 16
ISBN: 978-1-68415-272-8 | $14.99

Adventure Time Comics

Volume 1
ISBN: 978-1-60886-934-3 | $14.99

Volume 2
ISBN: 978-1-60886-984-8 | $14.99

Volume 3
ISBN: 978-1-68415-041-0 | $14.99

Volume 4
ISBN: 978-1-68415-133-2 | $14.99

Volume 5
ISBN: 978-1-68415-190-5 | $14.99

Volume 6
ISBN: 978-1-68415-258-2 | $14.99

Adventure Time Original Graphic Novels

Volume 1 Playing With Fire
ISBN: 978-1-60886-832-2 | $14.99

Volume 2 Pixel Princesses
ISBN: 978-1-60886-329-7 | $11.99

Volume 3 Seeing Red
ISBN: 978-1-60886-356-3 | $11.99

Volume 4 Bitter Sweets
ISBN: 978-1-60886-430-0 | $12.99

Volume 5 Graybles Schmaybles
ISBN: 978-1-60886-484-3 | $12.99

Volume 6 Masked Mayhem
ISBN: 978-160886-764-6 | $14.99

Volume 7 The Four Castles
ISBN: 978-160886-797-4 | $14.99

Volume 8 President Bubblegum
ISBN: 978-1-60886-846-9 | $14.99

Volume 9 The Brain Robbers
ISBN: 978-1-60886-875-9 | $14.99

Volume 10 The Orient Express
ISBN: 978-1-60886-995-4 | $14.99

Volume 11 Princess & Princess
ISBN: 978-1-68415-025-0 | $14.99

Volume 12 Thunder Road
ISBN: 978-1-68415-179-0 | $14.99

kaboom!™
A BOOM! Studios Imprint

AVAILABLE AT YOUR LOCAL COMICS SHOP AND BOOKSTORE
WWW.**BOOM-STUDIOS**.COM

CARTOON NETWORK

DISCOVER MORE
ADVENTURE TIME

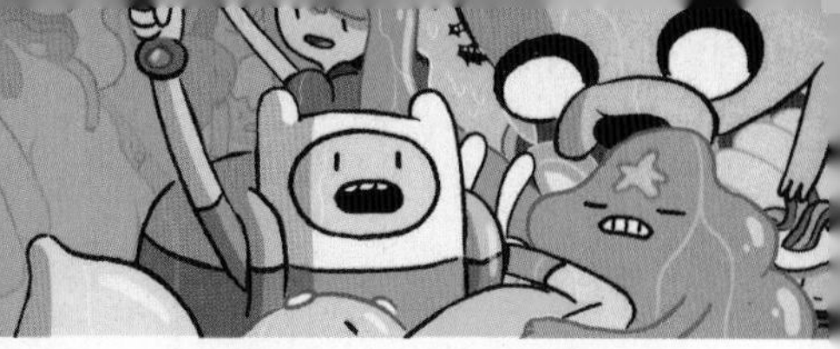

Adventure Time: Islands OGN
ISBN: 978-1-60886-972-5 | $9.99

Adventure Time Sugary Shorts

Volume 1
ISBN: 978-1-60886-361-7 | $19.99

Volume 2
ISBN: 978-1-60886-774-5 | $19.99

Volume 3
ISBN: 978-1-68415-030-4 | $19.99

Volume 4
ISBN: 978-1-68415-122-6 | $19.99

Adventure Time: Marceline & the Scream Queens
ISBN: 978-1-60886-313-6 | $19.99

Adventure Time: Fionna & Cake
ISBN: 978-1-60886-338-9 | $19.99

Adventure Time: Candy Capers
ISBN: 978-1-60886-365-5 | $19.99

Adventure Time: The Flip Side
ISBN: 978-1-60886-456-0 | $19.99

Adventure Time: Banana Guard Academy
ISBN: 978-1-60886-486-7 | $19.99

Adventure Time: Marceline Gone Adrift
ISBN: 978-1-60886-770-7 | $19.99

Adventure Time: Fionna & Cake Card Wars
ISBN: 978-1-60886-799-8 | $19.99

Adventure Time: Ice King
ISBN: 978-1-60886-920-6 | $19.99

Adventure Time/Regular Show
ISBN: 978-1-68415-166-0 | $19.99

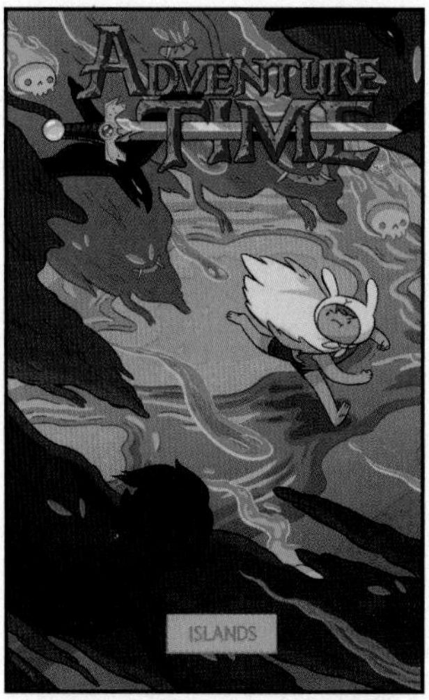
ADVENTURE TIME
ISLANDS

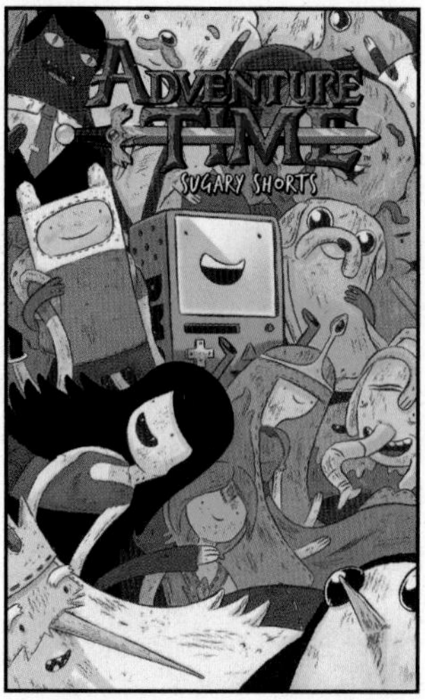
ADVENTURE TIME
SUGARY SHORTS

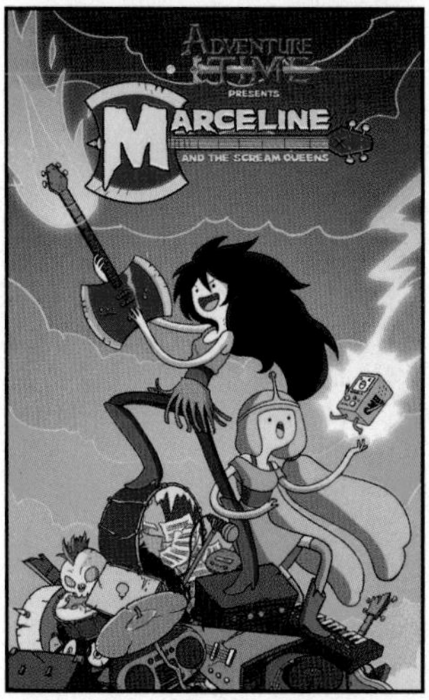
ADVENTURE TIME
PRESENTS
MARCELINE
AND THE SCREAM QUEENS

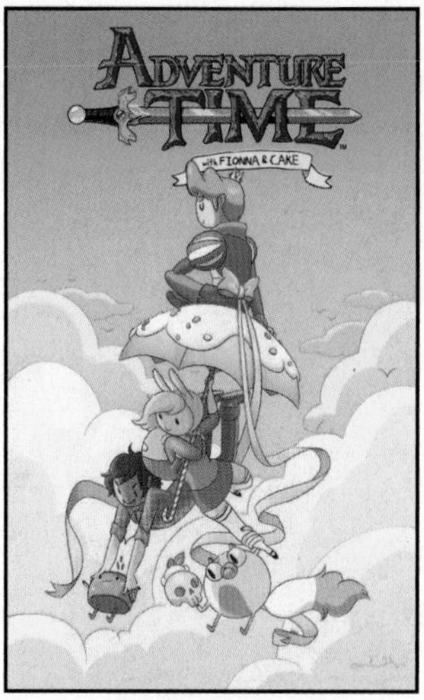
ADVENTURE TIME
FIONNA & CAKE

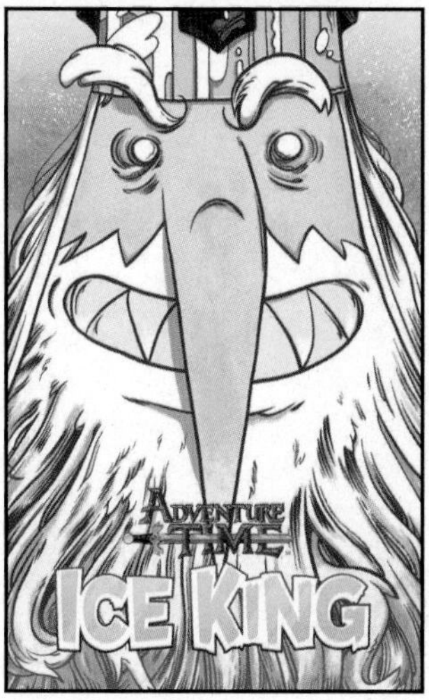
ADVENTURE TIME
ICE KING

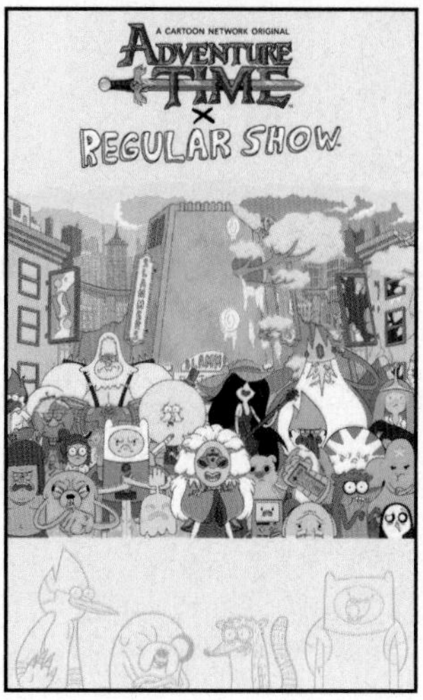
A CARTOON NETWORK ORIGINAL
ADVENTURE TIME
×
REGULAR SHOW

kaboom!™
A BOOM! Studios Imprint

AVAILABLE AT YOUR LOCAL COMICS SHOP AND BOOKSTORE

WWW.BOOM-STUDIOS.COM

CARTOON NETWORK.